Graveworld Book I
Death Magick

Ryan Z. Dawson

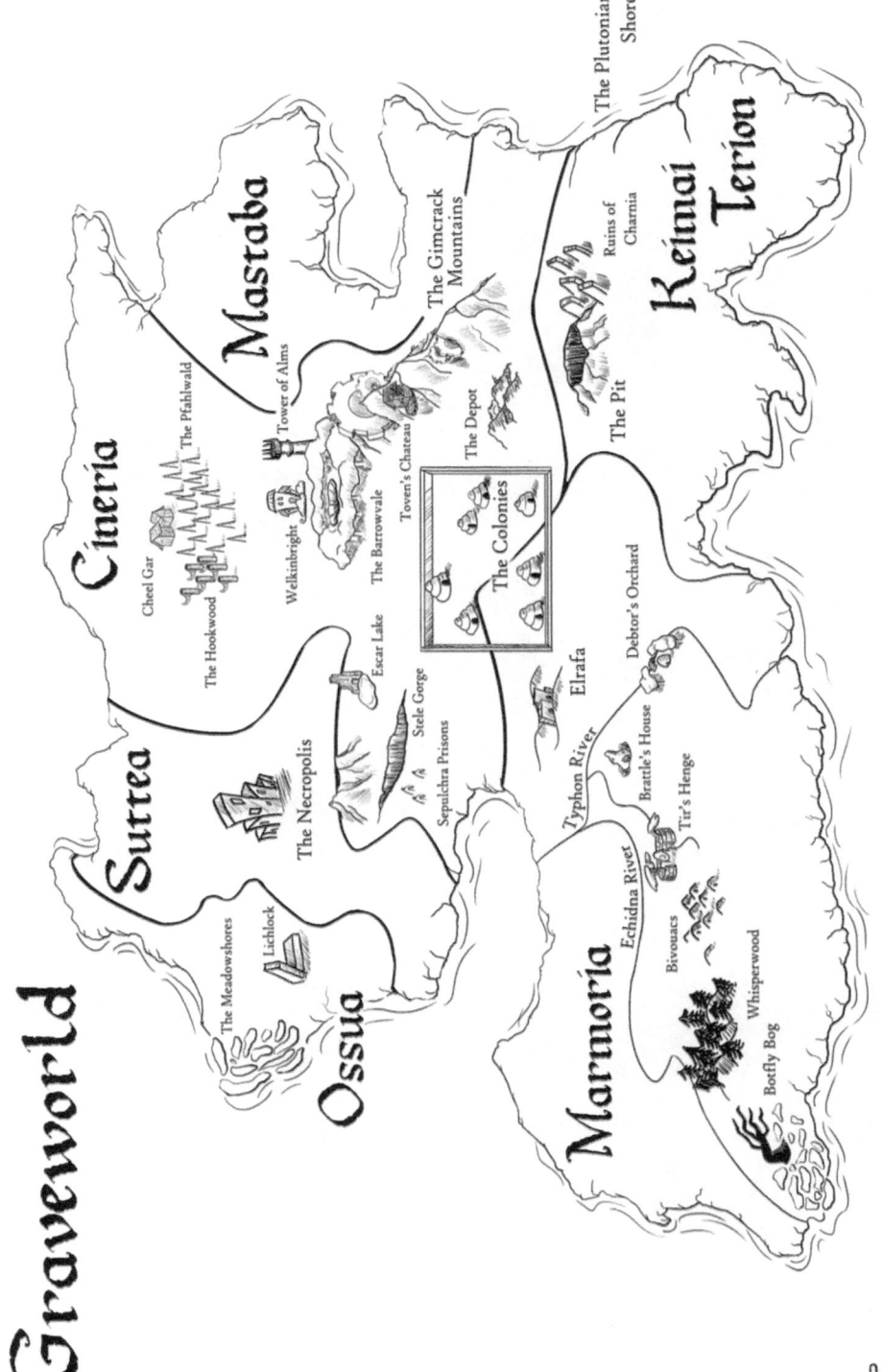

Death Magick

by
Ryan Z. Dawson

Edited by
Dara Rochlin
Buddy Wagner

Cover art by
Joshua Gilley

Inner illustration by
Elizabeth Person

First Edition: 2016

ISBN 978-0-9907920-7-9

Dire Ninja Media
Live Oak, CA 95953

www.direninja.com

For Lisa, foremost and always
For Johannes and Joe
And for Rainbow

You're all in this book.

Acknowledgements

Thanks to Dara Rochlin, Buddy Wagner, Josh Gilley, Robb Stepp, and Leonardo (Dleoblack).

Thanks to everyone at the Dragon's Rocketship, Nico Straccia, Richard Sima Jr., and all of my fellow Ccotabians: Bevlo, Salo, Marlowe, ChrisJim, Brightraven, everyone. Praise Ekmek.

Special thanks to Mom, Dad, and Ben for believing in me and for being excited about my work. And thanks to everyone who asks me, "Why didn't you write a book that *I* would like to read?"

Think nothing of it if I left you out.

"Crossing alone the nighted ferry
With the one coin for fee,
Whom, on the wharf of Lethe waiting,
Count you to find? Not me.

The brisk fond lackey to fetch and carry,
The true, sick-hearted slave,
Expect him not in the just city
And free land of the grave.

"Crossing Alone the Nighted Ferry"
-A.E. Housman (1859-1936)

One

Between the end of the lunch rush and the late start of a quiet dinner hour fades a long, winter's sunset. Alan Shade watches it over the corner of the shake machine, the soft reds blending down through thin cloud fingers, leaving the drug store on the hill in silhouette. The light is beautiful and old, a sight unfailing since the planet began to curve. It pours through the lobby windows because no one has lowered the blinds, and it wastes its glory across beam-stemmed tables and aging tile. The sight leaves Alan feeling sad; there are far better places from which to observe such beauty than the kitchens of burger joints.

As night falls, the dining room fills up. There is a sound growing in Alan's mind. It wheezes up from the depths of his frustration, rising quickly into a whistle, and becomes a screaming headache as his manager asks him to fill the shake machine. It's the howl of nothing, the empty call of all his years bearing down on him, and he can only close his eyes over the pain and wait for it to pass.

It usually helps to stand in the cooler, but that isn't the case tonight. Alan hugs his arms through shivers, and the headache pulses tirelessly away behind his forehead. Desperate, he steps through the freezer door into deeper cold, and he flips his hands against his hips at the change in pressure.

The cooler is roaring frigid. Alan puts his hands to his temples to find the clusters of pain there, but they have spread beyond his ability to massage them away. He shrinks into the roar, and it becomes his life for a few minutes. It's his loneliness and his fear, and it's all of the things he's had to bury in the last year. There is a sadness living among the leaning stacks of boxes, and Alan can feel it watching him as his fingertips start to go numb. With the freezer staring into him, Alan finally turns to leave. He carries the bag of shake mix from the cooler in his arms like an accident victim.

The headache is on a slow slide toward abating as Alan returns to the grill. He lays a run of meat and then stares down at the pink patties sizzling. He tries to be somewhere else, but he's never been good at visualizing. He imagines a beach, but it dissolves into the kitchen. The gulls squawk at each other in Spanish. Waves rush up the sand to order salads, hamburgers, and iced coffees. He tries to build a forest in the freezer when he returns there for more bacon, but the cold seizes him like death and nothing can grow. He is trapped in the here and now; stranded without his personhood in hurrying eddies of his fellow prisoners. He is alone in his mind and in his speech. Lettuce, ribs, mushrooms – his conversations languish among meat and condiments, and he is glad for the opportunity to go outside when it arises.

Snow piles up behind the parking bumpers at the far end of the lot. Trash bags stuffed in his pocket and long-handled trash masher in his hand, he walks the blacktop to check the cars on the near side of the street. It's been six months, and he still aches every night. He still feels confined. But outside, he can at least search his loneliness in peace. Sometimes he finds something of himself in it – a small thing that still has hope – but usually he simply enjoys the quiet. Today is one of those days.

The trash is devoid of aluminum cans; picked clean by scavengers. He raises the masher with both hands, imagining that he is killing his frustration as he tamps down the swell of wet food and paper waste. Pulling it out again, he gives the masher a twirl between practiced fingers. He likes its weight and balance in his hand. It would make a nice weapon. He's thought of taking it home, but that's an indulgence he can't allow himself. It isn't in Alan to give in to his impulses. He'll settle for swinging it over his head from time to time, fighting invisible enemies behind the dumpster whenever he can get a moment alone.

Alan steps off the curb, spinning the trash masher slowly. He slips, misses the catch, and the masher goes clanging into the drive-thru lane, rolling on its open, elliptical head. Without thinking, he lunges for it, smiling a little in embarrassment, and

10

then he closes his eyes against an explosion of light. A white car lurches out of the drive-thru, turning crazily into the lot with its tires squealing, and Alan finds himself diving into the beam of its headlights.

It's been six months since he started to give up. His certainty has been shaken close to ruin. And now the car hits him, and his last six months end in a roar of heat and the pained, cutting scream of bare breaks pumping. He will leave little; he realizes this in a flash that crawls out across eons before his eyes. Behind the flash, hope starves in shadow. He doesn't even believe in deliverance to Heaven.

But death is a great, green swamp. The end opens out forever, buzzing with damselflies and deep to your waist. Alan feels it wash over him, and then eternity is over. It swallows him up in its fall, inexorable, sucking him through its hot fens and cat-tailed wallows into the depths of its cavernous heart.

Two

There is a hand reaching out to him. A voice emerges from behind it, rough as a cough and chest-deep.

"Hey! Come on," the voice gargles. "Reach, stupid! Wake up!"

The wind is hot with a storm and shrieking in anger. It bangs through the cattails, throwing dust and water in blinding whirls.

Alan is dazed, and he takes the hand without thinking. He's stuck in black mud to his midsection, and it takes a lot of straining to pull him free. Eventually, he remembers to try and help, but he's so weak that he can only flail.

"Two hands, pasty!" The thing screeches at him. "I don't got this myself, and I ain't dyin' to haul a blinking sack. Look alive; we gotta get to cover!"

Alan grasps with his other hand, finding a bony wrist to pull. The skin of the arm is hairless and papery; every clinching muscle stands out beneath it.

"That's right! Now kick for your life!"

Alan struggles against the black mud. It wraps him tight, pressing his legs together, twisting him into a pipe cleaner below the waist. It hurts to fight, but the pain brings him back to his senses a bit. He tugs himself up until he is laying on his stomach in shallow bog water. At last, he wriggles free, and the owner of the sinewy arm drags him half-stumbling to the lee of a tall stone. A gust of bark shards rakes across his face, and Alan closes his eyes.

"What's going on?" Alan manages.

He brushes debris from his cheeks and looks around the rock, baffled that he should be looking around anything anymore. The sight of a black funnel whipping up the border of a reedy pit is only slightly less confounding.

"Hunch and shut up," says his rescuer, and Alan doesn't have time to look down before the funnel is howling their way.

He tucks his chin and pulls his knees toward his chest. The storm bends trees in all directions, tossing limp fronds and bark in sheets with clumps of bog mud. The sound it makes is like the squeal of stripped brake pads on spinning wheels. The swamp seems to cry out along with it, hating it. Alan can feel its fear in the seat of his bowels. As it passes the rock, the whirling darkness seems to search him. To his relief, it moves on as though it has found nothing. Alan holds the back of his head with his hands and breathes in slow ten counts until the storm-wail dissipates, and then his rescuer shakes him by the shoulders.

"Don't get much closer than that," says the gurgling voice. "Going to be a while before my tooth-skin grows back. You can uncoil now, lumpy. We made it."

Alan lifts his head and opens his eyes. The thing before him is gaunt and hunched with spindly limbs and calloused knuckles. His skin is blue-grey and plaqued with scales along his shoulders. There is a red stain around his wide mouth. He constantly nods, bulb-headed like a pedomorph with a little lima bean nose. The creature's pupilless, opalescent eyes are windows into an unsettling hunger, and Alan finds himself unable to keep from staring into them.

"What are you?" He finally says, and his voice is a creaking whisper.

"What kind of thing is that to say to someone?" snarls the creature. "Don't you think 'who' might be the word you're looking for?"

Alan's rescuer runs his hands over his towering forehead. But for the heavy knuckles, they are paddling hands – broad and wrinkled to wick away moisture. The fingers bend in at an angle, and Alan isn't surprised to see the dark little thing knuckle walking as he heads back toward the bank of the pit.

"Who, then?" Alan calls. He stands up and dusts himself off. He is still in his polo. There is black mud caked into the blue, unlikely ever to come out. "And thank you for saving me."

The creature dips his hand into the bog water, apparently ignoring Alan. He sniffs low, and then tips his chin up to test the air with his mouth open. His ears are small, drooping points, and they wag whenever he moves his head. There is a dark blanket rolled up on his back with strands of hide or gut.

"I'm curious about what you saved me *from*," Alan continues. "And where I am. What is this place?"

"It's a swamp," gurgles the creature as he sticks his finger into a bank of mud. "And my name's Brattle. I'm a ghoul– if you're really the kind of person who has to go around putting labels on everything. "

Brattle turns, a strange smile curling out toward the truncated lobes of his ears.

"Speaking of which, that's what *you* are, isn't it?" He hops toward Alan with a strangely simian grace. "A person?"

"A person, yes. A human," Alan corrects Brattle. "And it does feel a little weird to be asked what I am. I'm sorry."

Brattle interrupts with a sound that is halfway between a cough and a giggle.

"This is where the dead and dead-eaters belong," he says, "but not you. You're the outsider here." He pokes Alan with a clubbed finger. "You ain't dead."

Alan takes a deep breath as if to be sure. He puts his hand to his throat to feel his life pulsing there.

"No," he says, suddenly a bit wary of the light in Brattle's eye. "And I have you to thank."

"That was a shadowstorm," Brattle grins. "They cut across these marshes from the east, following certain flocks of crows. They tear spirits up – living and dead – and spit them out into the Old Chaos." He stops for a moment, as if waiting to see how Alan will respond. "This is the Deadlands, lumpy. Graveworld. And I'll say it again: you ain't dead."

A cawing overhead draws Brattle's eye. Alan looks up to see a murder of crows circling the forest. The sky is red-orange as the sun goes down. It looks old and worn; thin clouds hang in it precariously, as if unable to find adequate purchase. Alan watches for a long moment to see if one might fall. The crows light in the forest canopy to roost, huge and ecstatic with hacking laughter.

"Why not?" Alan asks.

Brattle doesn't respond for a long time. He watches the crows as they move among emaciated firs. Finally, he lets out a low growl punctuated by thoughtful snorts.

"The wind is changin'," he says. "I'm headed west, but the storm got me off course. It's a longer walk than I planned now, I'm lonely, and you need a guide."

"What's west?" Alan asks.

"Hopes for home and an end," Brattle replies. "Are you coming?"

Alan stands for a moment longer. The crows have vanished into the forest, but he can still hear them calling to each other. He thinks of the ladies in the kitchen back home. It's too much to process all at once, but he reasons that he's lucky to have found a friendly creature. Who knows what might have come out of that bog if Brattle hadn't been diverted by the shadowstorm? Alan shudders; he doesn't exactly know much of anything anymore. He certainly never thought he'd miss the grills and the crowds of customers.

"All right," Alan says.

Brattle claps his hands and hunkers down into a humping shuffle. "Let's get on west while we still got light. I'll fill you in, and you can do likewise. We got lots of ground to cover."

"What happens at night?" Alan asks as he starts to follow Brattle across the wet scrub toward the woods.

"We sleep," Brattle guffaws, "and we keep the high fires burning, pasty. We keep them smoking through the watches."

Three

There's always been something about the freezer where Alan works. It has always felt haunted. Low, cold, and long, with its stacks of boxes and pallets, it could go on forever from the door into a world of tombs. This is how Alan has always thought about it, especially when standing with his back to the open space while frigid air rolls from the cooling unit in a constant rumble. How long would it be before a shadow stepped out from among the meat cases at the very back to call to him?

There have been nights when he saw the shadows move. Sometimes there was a word on its frozen breath. As he follows a ghoul west across the dwindling swamps of a strange world, Alan remembers those nights and the promises from the cooling unit. "Death and mystery. Beauty in stone and sucking mud."

The Deadland marshes open for a space before the edge of the forest proper. In this otherwise naked field stand high walls of broken masonry. Tombs upon tombs stack up to ragged edges, their tops opened where time has eaten the stonework away. Alan watches the second sunset he's seen today as it streams over pillars of carven faces and humped gravestones that slant ever toward oblivion in the rising ground. Graveworld is in constant decline. Where new structures have arisen, the old ones appear to have revolted against them, infecting them with premature age. Alan shudders, feeling the cold of the freezer like grief in his throat. It's old, like everything here, and shifts about behind crumbling facades. Alan leaves it hiding; he isn't ready to face it just yet.

"Nothing stays up long out here in the country," Brattle says, knuckling along like a gorilla at a good pace. "The city's better, but not by much. It's all falling down – just always worrying away to nothing. Like time is hungrier here. So yeah, I'm sure you can see its charm."

Alan isn't sure how to reply. When he doesn't, Brattle casts a glance back over his shoulder and then continues.

"So you ain't dead, but I get the feeling that you expected to be. We don't get live humans here. It just ain't how things happen. This is one of the many spheres a human spirit might choose to come to after they leave their own. Here, they congregate on the Plutonian Shores. Why you ain't there is an int'restin' mystery, but not exactly new, strange as that sounds."

Brattle stops. They've left the fields of grave towers and entered the lean forest. The trees shake, remembering the storm from before. Many are clawed white high on their slender trunks.

"There's another living human arrived here some while ago," Brattle explains. "She's in the city, the Necropolis, where the Red Guard took her."

Brattle looks at Alan with a wicked smile, his eyes bright in the growing shadow.

"How did I get here?" Alan replies.

"That's for you to say," Brattle says. "You ain't been talking much. Not too keen to be drawn out?"

Alan has hardly been listening to Brattle since they left the swamp. Has the ghoul been naming things? Telling stories? Has he been talking about his family? Alan isn't sure. Part of him is still trying to see all of this as real.

"I think I fell and got hit by a car," Alan finally says.

"How'd you manage that?" Brattle laughs. Alan doesn't answer. For a moment, Brattle's shining eyes are headlights.

"Whatever," Brattle continues. He sits back against a stump and looks through the trees toward where the last red sliver of daylight is finally fading. "Run over. That'll usually do it, but something's got crossed, I guess. Might be my lucky day, might not. Might mean nothing. It sure don't mean good company, right?"

"I'm sorry," Alan says, and he laughs at the ridiculousness of an apology in these circumstances. "It's all a bit much. Thank you for saving me. Whatever my life is right now, I owe it to you."

"Don't bite off more than you can chew," Brattle smiles. "There's a lot to say about ghouls, true and otherwise. That we ain't kind, or that we'll leave a soul lying on the road in need of aid is one of the otherwise, just so you know. Besides, you're special – just like Winter White in her palace now."

Alan clears his throat. "Winter White?"

"The other living human in Graveworld," is Brattle's only explanation. "And what's *your* name, pasty?"

"Alan Shade."

This requires considerably more thought than it should, but saying his name seems to give Alan some strength and clarity back. He squats slowly, staring down the line of Brattle's gaze as if he might see his own life opening before him. He might see it rolling out like the night across the sky, flecked with old stars in strange constellations. He might feel home nearby, just over the horizon, but he doesn't. He only sees Graveworld.

"I've never been so lost," Alan says from the back of his throat. "Why is this happening?"

"We're each of us lost in our own little ways," Brattle replies. He turns and starts to gather white rocks to make a fire ring. "For now, make yourself useful and crush up some of this brush for the fire."

Alan decides to be satisfied with this. It's the first decision he's made in a long time that feels like it puts him in the right place.

"Where did you say they took that girl?" He asks as he crumbles brittle bark over Brattle's circle of stones.

"The Necropolis," the ghoul coughs. "The Dead Capital. There's a queen reigns there, but don't let that fool you: this place's got no real leaders. And no rules – except maybe 'watch your back'."

"Sounds like home," Alan jokes.

He drops part of a rotted log onto the pile of twigs and bark. Brattle produces a flint from the pouch over his shoulder and tries to knock a spark or two from it with dismal results. Nothing much wants to burn here, it seems. The fire curls awake only to shrink back again, as if wary.

"Yeah," Brattle laughs. "Well ashes are ashes."

Darkness brings a hush. The breeze falls still on the fields behind the trees. Alan can hear the crows fluttering in dreams on their branches, muffled caws slipping from closed beaks now and then while Brattle fans the fledgling fire. As the wood finally catches, Brattle produces a pink hunk of meat from his small satchel and begins to chew it.

"Is this really it?" Alan asks.

"Is this what?"

"The afterlife."

Brattle spits a wad of gristle into the fire. "You were expecting maybe rivers of liquor?"

There is an owl calling in the woods. It starts up with its waking hoots, searching the growing dark for wind that will take it high to hunt. Alan shudders at the strange, mewling sound of its voice.

"What about God?" He asks. "And Heaven?"

"What about them?" Brattle makes a strange, flat face. "I get the feeling you're asking me to compare two things when I only know anything about one."

"Which one is that?"

Brattle only nods in response at first. Alan can almost feel the sky dimming blue. Day dies with a fight, struggling in vain against the rise of the moon. The owl chuckles far away, an ambassador for the darkness.

"There's the Coma," Brattle replies, almost whispering. "And another place still beyond this one, if you choose to go. The options are open, you see, and there are lots of them. But I wouldn't call any of it 'afterlife'. For whatever reason, that don't quite seem to fit. "

"It's as much a mystery here as it is . . ." Alan pauses. "Well, where I come from."

"Easiest way to make a fool of yourself is to start saying you know something," Brattle says.

Alan sighs. His breath puffs out before him in a gossamer curl. The breeze is dwindling. A cold is setting in the likes of which he's never known before, and the flame is too shy to warm him.

Has it been six months? With the strange weight of a new world on his shoulders, it feels like it's only been six weeks since he got on at Ray's. Graveworld's age permeates everything here, stretching time into subtle distortion. Alan wonders what six months means among this constant decay.

"You really want to hear about me?" He asks Brattle.

Brattle smiles. "Not particularly looking forward to it," he admits. "But it has to be better than the night noises. I'm sure you've got some special kind of angle, right – some reason you ended up here alive? Start talking and maybe we can ferret it out."

Alan puts his hands up to the fire. The flame dances cold, fidgeting through the cracks in the wood. Brattle seems unaffected by the chill. He sits back into the shadow, his eyes gleaming, staring off into the middle distance. Alan looks at him for a long time and wonders what ghouls think about with their faces in the firelight.

"Think of me as your therapist," Brattle says, and Alan is repulsed by his smile.

There are eight peg teeth, each one leaning back toward the writhing tongue. Shadow sits deep in the hollows of Brattle's cheekbones, drawing him gaunt and hungry. Alan catches his breath and swallows.

"Shy?" Brattle clucks. "That's cute, ain't it? What's not to trust? Whisper to the woods, boy, if not to me. Whisper away. This place eats secrets. Sucks 'em down through the ground like blood – like rot sliming into the endless bog pit at the heart of it. Whatever you think you got to hide, trust you me that I seen and heard worse."

"I'm not hiding anything," Alan says, with difficulty.

Brattle only nods at this. Alan suddenly feels small and pink and soft. He feels exposed here, whipped raw by wind and sapling branches. He feels the bog pit at the heart of the world dragging for him, horrid, its light glowing out through Brattle's strange eyes.

He can't do it. Not yet.

"Whatever you say, pasty" Brattle finally replies. "Or whatever you won't. Wake me in an hour."

"How will I know when an hour has passed?" Alan asks.

"That's about how long we've got before the moaners start up."

Brattle unrolls his blanket and pulls it over his legs. He falls onto his side and stretches, and Alan is surprised at the length of his body. Standing erect, Brattle would probably be taller than he would, but the low hunch into which he is permanently bent normally keeps him barely at the level of Alan's waist.

"I sometimes forget my manners," Brattle says, suddenly sitting up. "I never met a living human. Alan, my friend, it's been a pleasure so far."

He extends his hand, and Alan shakes it hesitantly. Alan isn't sure what is in Brattle's eyes. It's something new – a ghoulish emotion, perhaps.

Brattle gives Alan's hand a single pump and then drops back into the dirt to rest his head on his knuckles.

"Good night," he says to Alan. "Don't get eaten."

Four

Brattle runs in his sleep like a dog. Deep in himself, fighting through a riptide of recollection, Alan watches him and manages a smile. What do ghouls dream?

Gravity returns like a wounded animal. It hesitates to settle onto Alan's shoulders, but he welcomes it there. He lets it push him into the world and finally begins to feel permanent again.

I am gone from my life, he tells himself, *but I am not dead.*

Alan finds himself flipping through his Coward List. At the seat of his mind, where his personality emerges from whatever shadows hide his subconscious, Alan keeps a record of his every social failure. Whenever he has backed away, felt awkward, or missed an opportunity to speak for himself, he has drawn a black mark on the file. For years, he has been lost in those memories, reliving embarrassments in his head in vain to engineer a better outcome. His brush with death has weakened him, but he has not been changed; the Coward List remains intact. He allows himself to sink into it now, as the cold begins to bite at his neck.

He chooses an example with which to torture himself — like a pinch to wake him from dreaming.

Iscela is a small, roundish woman with coffee-dark eyes and black hair pinched back in a bun against her neck. In Spanish, she is bright and confident, but she shrinks from English like sleeping grass. Alan approaches her as if driven to, cold with a great need for anyone to respond, but he stops in discomfiture at every encounter. He falters, dumbstruck, even when he is sure about his Spanish. It's no use learning another language if you can't believe that anyone would want to hear anything you have to say. Though she is sweet and shy and barely five feet tall, Iscela terrifies him.

Now he wishes he were sitting with her in the break room, fumbling grease-fingered through his *diccionario*, while fantasies of her ridicule pound in his head. Is Graveworld not worth a thousand similar nightmares? Alan takes a hitching breath and looks out into the forest, sick in the pit of his stomach for simpler fears.

The Coward List means nothing here, and it has held him back for most of his life. He could discard it altogether. He feels the need to be rid of it, the aching scars on his psyche from obsessing about it, but it's an anchor now. Doubt and shame are at least things to hold on to.

Alan thinks about Graveworld eating secrets. He can't allow it to devour his. In an instant, he becomes a person with something to hide, and Brattle is right after all.

There is no one back home to miss him. In a way, this is freeing. He's left himself here all at once – dumped everything he is on the Deadland soil quite against his will – and this is his home now. He tries a lie, but it won't take root: there is nothing back home for him to miss. He discards this shriveled thought right away. Alan will miss books, video games, and his soft bed. In another way – a more significant one, perhaps – this trouble is freeing. For the first time in too long, Alan has something to work toward beyond simple continuity. He has longing, and it is sweet. It sounds clichéd to him, but he finally knows exactly what he's left behind. Beyond any doubt now, Alan wants to return to the world of the living; he finally feels willing to try and live again.

The night deepens, and Alan drifts toward sleep. He is tired to the core – to whatever anchors his spirit in him. The instant he closes his eyes, a strange dream is teasing the edges of his consciousness. He searches it, curious, but he only has time to see the beginnings of a great fear before the moaners come.

They are early. The bright points of their many eyes appear just beyond the fire's weak circle, and they lift their voices to tear Alan back from the brink of his nightmare and into waking terror.

Their calls start as a chorus of needful sighs. Then they roll into dirty, wounded growls. Finally, they rise into jarring shrieks through the high boughs of the trees. The crows rise away, and the beating of larger wings drowns out their flutter.

Brattle snores through the clamor. Alan puts his hands over his ears, but that only makes the din seem worse. With the loudest sounds muffled, whispers invade his head, shattering his thoughts as he tries to cobble them together. A gust of living heat puts the fire out, and Alan waits for the moaners to close in and attack.

Their shrieks become wails. Huge wings beat, sending ash swirling from the fire. A log rolls off, splits, and then bursts apart as if torn by massive claws. The moaners crowd around the campsite, butting against each other in a hot fervor, but they do not advance any further. They hold back, and their voices become frustrated. At last, Brattle wakes, and when he feels the moaners looming so near he leaps to his feet with a shout.

"Some watch you keep!" He cries, and there is a small dagger in his hand. Alan has no idea where it emerged from. "What happened to the fire?"

"They must have blown it out," Alan tries to reply. His voice is a woody creak – like saplings bending in a storm. "I tried to wake you!"

Brattle doesn't respond. He's hopping in a little circle, dagger out, slashing at the air. The moaners snarl at him, but they maintain their distance.

"We're still alive," Brattle says, baffled. "You must be some kind of lucky charm, pasty. Why aren't they attacking?"

"How am I supposed to know?" Alan answers. "Maybe they don't eat ghoul."

"Oh, they eat ghoul right enough." Brattle backs up against Alan, his bright eyes darting. "But they must not be too fond of live human meat."

The moaners crowd in, their great wings beating against each other. The trees bend back from their mass, leaving the whole fringe of the wood squirming around them. The terrible milling sound must be the moaners gnashing their teeth.

"Or maybe it's something else," Brattle shudders. "Something keepin' em back against their hunger. I never seen nothing of that sort before."

Brattle searches the dark. The moaners begin to move away, dragging a calamitous racket into the swamp behind them. Nothing else moves for a long time after the trees have sprung back; even the crows have found another roost to haunt for the night.

Finally, Alan says, "I think they're gone."

Brattle only replies after a long series of deep breaths and gulping coughs. In the bright of his eyes, Alan can see Brattle swallowing past the knot of his prominent Adam's apple.

"You saved us," the ghoul croaks. "You saved *me*. That's one good turn for another now, highpockets, and I thank you."

Sound begins to return to the woods. Brattle collapses against a stump, his coughs slowly turning to chuckles.

"But I gotta say: you got my curiosity going, now." Brattle looks east toward where the moaners vanished. "There's a big power protecting you."

"Luck, I think," Alan says. "Though no kind I'd like ever to have again, all things considered."

"You'd rather've been ripped to strips by screaming, inter-dimensional freaks?" Brattle huffs. "You got a hell of a weird understanding of luck."

"I want to go home," Alan sighs. He falls into a crouch, and his back cramps up. He has to sit down, and then he can't keep his spine erect. The stone at his back is almost as good as a pillow if he closes his eyes and pretends as hard as he can.

"I'll do you one better then," Brattle says. He puts a heavy hand on Alan's shoulder. "There's a gate near my hut. I'll take you there tomorrow. Maybe the next day, depending." A whispery howl through the trees punctuates this last remark. The winds are picking up again. "But you got something here for you, boy. I'd not be surprised to find that portal closed. Graveworld has a will for you."

25

"It's worth trying," Alan replies. "Maybe it's you that Graveworld wants. Maybe it's your fate that matters."

"You'll lose that bet," Brattle says. "But you'd be forgiven. You're innocent. Innocence don't ever lead to nothing but corruption. *That* you'll see."

Five

It's a hot night in August. Alan has come home for the funeral, but there is a problem: his mother has woken up and is being sued for her own final expenses.

"I'll pay to bury my husband," she has said, "but I won't pay for myself. I'm not dead anymore."

Alan is supposed to be straightening things out, but the City of Chicago has gotten involved, and the case is going to court. It's the evening before the trial, and Alan is lingering on the street outside the combination courthouse and mortuary.

Rain is slanting down on the wind. Everything is happening, and Alan is nowhere. He has no time, and he can't move for the rain. He is dallying, and he doesn't know why.

"Why did you come back?" Someone asks. "You haven't done any good."

But he had to. It's the only answer; he doesn't even need to give it. Everyone just knows.

The dark sinks its claws into everything. It drops like a predator, shrieking like taxed brakes as it settles over Willis Tower. It creeps into the heart of the Loop from Roosevelt Road, hungry and hunting pushing a tide of doughty lawyers. Alan has to make a stand before they can stamp out his mother's case. If they win, she will have to be buried whether she is alive or not, and she will have to pay for the whole thing, too. He approaches the courthouse, but he doesn't remember which of the many doors opens only for sons of the deceased.

"It's not going to be your fault again," his mother says. "This time, it's going to be my fault, so don't be too hard on yourself."

The scene changes. Now it is a persistent fading, a mist of forgetting and falling away, and Alan is watching it billow out to fill an infinite space. It's like steam spilling through the open shower door; in fact, that's exactly what it is. The steam crawls out to fog the mirror, tendrils slipping over the sink and the toilet. The bathroom has become all Alan is, and he revels in this abandonment of self in the fraction of a second before he wakes in thrashing horror.

Brattle is sitting on Alan's chest. His pearly eyes are wide, his cheeks puffing out as he fights against Alan's struggling. The sight does nothing to comfort Alan, and then Brattle's hand is over his mouth.

"Relax!" The ghoul hisses. "Relax, lumpy! Come on! Chew this!"

He tries to force something wet and musty into Alan's mouth. It's a fistful of grass. Alan wrenches himself sideways, tossing Brattle like a bucking bull, and spits a few rank mouthfuls of mashed blades into the dirt.

"Dammit! Stop!" Brattle hangs on tightly, possessing the calm and poise of a lifelong scrapper.

In a flash, he is back in the mount, straddling Alan as he tries to scoop up the grass with one hand. Alan heaves himself up on his heels, his knees and thighs on fire with pulling pain. Brattle is remarkably heavy for such a skinny thing.

Finally, Alan manages to wriggle free. Brattle doesn't pursue him. He only stares as Alan pants to catch his breath, a school marm's thwarted frown on his face.

"It's dreamwort," says the ghoul. "You were having a hell of a nightmare."

Alan gets to his knees, still spitting. There is plant matter deep in his throat, sliding down to burn his gullet where it packs into a knot. Acid wells up to his collarbone, and he has no choice but to swallow the burn. Brattle straps on his little pouch and is closing the milky silver clasp. The odd hunch of his starved frame, his sagging shoulders, the ravenous light in his eyes — something breaks loose in Alan as he watches Brattle move. It is the dam of age and tired strength. It's the depths of his long frustration roaring out, spilling over Alan's teeth in the form of a primal scream.

Alan leaps at Brattle. Brattle sprawls to protect himself, silly little pouch flying back from his shoulder. They hit the dirt with

Brattle kicking and Alan aiming hammering strikes at the ghoul's near-toothless face. They roll through the remains of the campfire, crushing embers into mud. Ash swirls around them, and Alan fights through a coughing fit against Brattle's monstrous strength. He wants to go blind with rage — to be a worse kind of monster — but he doesn't find that in his depths as he disgorges his old pain. He finds himself toothless instead, no match for this cruel place, and he refuses to believe it.

Something like dawn is breaking behind them, dim and old. The morning sky tents up over the trees from the east into rotten purple. Brattle holds up his arms to protect himself, but he doesn't fight back. Alan tries to control him, but he soon tires. He sags into tears, and Brattle holds him in an awkward hug to pat his back and comfort him.

"You sure you don't want to hit me some more?" He jokes. "Is that all you got to work out?"

Dawn brings crows. They laugh at Alan, and he pushes away from Brattle with his fists in his eyes. He sucks back a sob, trying to muster more anger, but now Brattle is laughing, too. It's funny; in spite of himself, Alan can't help but smile. As he wipes wet ash from his teary cheeks, Alan allows himself a chuckle.

"I wondered how long it would be," Brattle says.

"I think that's all I have," Alan replies. "Not exactly what I hoped for."

"Wherever you are, you have to make a home," Brattle smiles. "And the first thing to making a home is to dump all your garbage and invest. If that's what you got, boy, then that's what you got, and be proud of it. Besides: you got in a couple good shots."

Brattle makes a show of rubbing his sunken chin. Alan wipes the last of his tears from the corners of his eyes with ashy fingers, leaving dark streaks across his cheeks like war paint.

"I'm still trying to wrap my head around all this," Alan says. "Alive in the land of the dead. What's happening back home? Did I just vanish, or did I somehow leave a body behind? And how am I here if that car didn't kill me? *Why* am I here?"

Brattle shakes his head. "Let it sit," he says with a knowing grin. "There's no use in speculatin'. Dust off and let's go. It's all going to unfold. Now that you're here – *really* here – the truth is going to open up."

"You still want to take me to the gate?" Alan asks, batting ash from his clothes.

"What will be will be," is all Brattle says to that. Then he winks, and dawn shadows fall across his face.

Dawn wakes fully in the gray east. It spreads a pale fire over the reaching trees as Alan kicks dirt into the ash pit of last night's campfire. With winds whipping up from behind them in the marsh and the first dim blues of a cloudless day finally growing, he and Brattle set out into the woods along a path that only the ghoul can see.

Alan watches as Brattle sniffs among the trees. Here he clings to a cloven stump, probing the dead bark; there he tastes a pinch of black moss and pulls a face. Brattle moves with the worried care of a surveyor who expects the land to change around him.

"It's not much better in the light than it was in the dark," Alan grumbles, tugging out his shirttail. His chain is still swinging at his hip. He pats to find his wallet is still in his back pocket. "I'm guessing we're not going to get to the bright and sunny part any time soon."

The trees are thickening. They shiver in a new breeze, nearly all bare and pocked on their thin boles with spots of disease. A whisper blows through them, and they arch in toward the path. They bend down in the wind – surely, it's the wind that moves them.

"No," Brattle chuckles. "Not out in the sticks. Not for a while."

Alan takes a few deep breaths. The trees are bowing ahead, revealing the path. They twist with vines, drooping at their broken tops like funeral mourners. They stir again, and Alan glances over his shoulder.

"I used to play in woods like these with my brother," he begins. "Back in Ohio."

"Not like these," Brattle replies. "I guarantee that."

He stops and mounts a fallen log. They have reached the crest of a crumbling hill. Below, the ground drops precipitously toward a shale escarpment. A belt of curved stones crosses the middle reaches of the splintering wall, their tops cut with too much care. Alan realizes they are gravestones. This part of the hill is a collapsed cemetery, and the pocks in the wall are open graves.

He's about to say, "You're probably right," but he stops at another breath of morning air.

"Play in woods like these," says the wind, slipping over his ears like velvet. "Used to play. Back in Ohio."

Another whisper rises from the gulf before them. It is the voice of the trees on the air. They are all speaking at once. A long chill coils up Alan's spine to settle fat in his throat. It falls across his shoulders like a shawl, and the fine hairs at the nape of his neck prick up. He is aware of the trees watching him.

"I used to play," hisses the forest, "in woods like these."

"Holy god," Alan swallows. "What does that mean?"

Brattle looks back at him with a smile. Alan could kick him down the hill.

"Why don't you tell me?" Brattle says. "*You* said it."

Alan puts his hands on his hips. His scalp is crawling with cold. "Come on," he says. "Don't screw with me."

"This is Whisperwood," Brattle finally explains. His smile is wild. The light in his eyes dances horribly. "Remember I told you this place eats secrets? It's the weight of your whole life – the burden you bear. The forest," he spins his finger slowly in the air, "can feel it. The longer you carry that burden, the worse it'll get."

"What's worse?" Alan asks.

Brattle doesn't answer.

There is a creaking in the woods. There is a thorny malice coming up through the leaf litter, brittle and old but still green. A heart of need beats in the breast of the hill, and its pulse is in every clawing root and branch as the trees bow toward them. Now Alan can see the faces in their trunks. He can see the fingers on their boughs, moving almost imperceptibly against the breeze.

"They need the truth," sighs the ghost of an older voice. It rushes up the bank from the mouths of the graves. "Or they take you into leaves and bark."

It has been six months, but no time has passed. The days sat down where they were and refused to move, stuck on remembering. The woods probe Alan with a green finger, impatient for sustenance. His mind is opening with blooms, and there is no use fighting. The forest doesn't want to wait, and all Alan can do is let it coax the truth from his tongue.

"I was born in Cincinnati, Ohio," he says, "between the river and Mount Airy Forest."

This is how he intends to start, but the forest adds more in its own voice. What he does not say, it draws from him like a sap. It whispers his secrets away, and Brattle wrings his hands while he listens.

He is a small thing, it says. *There has never been much to him. Always just above a murmur, skirting experience without tangling up in it. He likes his distance, this one. Death revealed itself to him at an early age, when his parents were smashed in steel on the road.*

"There's irony for you," Brattle chuckles. "Or something cosmic, if you buy into that. Road Pizza: Family Edition."

"There was no more family left after that," Alan explains, unable to muster irritation at Brattle's joke for the bristle of woody hunger in his mouth. "They put my sister in a hospital; she felt so guilty, she just stopped functioning. I went around from house to house for a while – state houses for kids that get lost in the foster system, I guess."

"No place to root," Brattle says. "And humans like a nice safe spot to stay. I seen them on the black shores, huddling and staring."

"I don't mind wandering," Alan answers. "As long as I have some place to come home to, and I didn't for a long time. When she woke up and could move around again, I went to live with her. My sister, that is. She came back with a clean bill of health, but she was haunted."

There are pockets of himself he would like to protect, but the slightest resistance to the green magic makes the skin on the back of his neck feel like mossy bark. He braves this dread for a moment, until he cannot lift his right foot off the ground. Then he sees that he will have found a permanent place to root after all if he doesn't give himself up completely.

"My sister was wild," he says, his throat full of vines. "The accident occurred while they were out looking for her, and she felt guilty. When I was old enough to get out on my own, I did, but now I'm back here."

Alan stops. That's not quite right. Here is nowhere. Here is the afterworld. Stopped stupid, he ponders this, and Whisperwood continues bleeding him.

She opened herself in the water – in the shower. Pouring red with the glass closed and steam rising around her. He found her that way, and he had to bury her, too.

Now there is a different feeling. The wood pulls away, spreading itself out in another direction, looking for something. Alan breathes a hot sigh, his lungs burning, and sinks to his knees.

"You've served its hunger for now, looks like," Brattle says. He comes to Alan with an understanding pat on the shoulder. "It's hunting for something else."

"What?" Alan struggles to say.

"We'll never know, I imagine, but we can stay and ask if you like."

"I'd rather not," Alan replies.

Brattle chuckles again, a knife in Alan's side. "I figured. Come on. Down the hill, it's less aware."

The green magic spreads west as Brattle helps Alan up. It blows out across the tops of its own trees, hunting; a weight on the wind like the threat of a storm. If it notices Brattle and Alan making their quick and careful way down the hill, it gives no sign, and Alan is glad to be free from its influence. Nonetheless, it persists to haunt him; all the way down the slope, into the field of scattered gravestones below, its seedling writhes with tendrils in his mind.

Six

"So that's it, hmm?" Brattle says.

He and Alan are standing at the foot of the fallen graveyard with twin suns beating down on them. A second moon waits low in the east, the ghost of its pale sphere partially obscured clouds.

"Is that all you got to hide?"

Alan is sitting on the knuckle of an erupted stone and drinking carefully from a phial that Brattle produced from his pouch. The purple liquid fizzes in his throat, and he coughs for a moment before answering.

"What do you mean?" He says, spitting into the sparse grass.

"Every experience is different," Brattle explains, "but I never seen one like that before. Mousey guy, dead family. It's a little boring. Don't you think? And then it turns and goes searching away." He pushes a cluck against his few teeth. "Were you resisting?"

"No," Alan lies. It's easier than explaining what he'd been through. After one quick look over each shoulder, he goes on. "Not that I had any reason to. I wasn't lying about anything; I just hadn't said any of that yet."

Alan can't tell whether Brattle is listening. He's hunching in the scrub where the cemetery gate is rotting away and looking up toward the still-swaying trees.

"You could have let me know," Alan says. "You had a secret, too. How come nothing happened to you?"

"This wood knows me," Brattle replies. "I live around here. There's nothing for me to hide anymore – no sport in torturing me. I've given it all I have to give by now. You, though – you're a new item. To be honest, I'd expected more."

Alan finds it hard to believe that there could have been anything more. He feels foul on the inside. His heart is racing to keep up with his heaving lungs, which bring up something black and ligneous once every few minutes.

"Every spirit has to undergo an unburdening when it first arrives," Brattle continues, "the Kingwatcher splits his time between different waypoints. He always knows where to be – though I haven't the faintest idea how – and he was right to come to you. I was certain he would. But you didn't unburden much before the forest turned and Minos breezed away, just like the moaners did last night."

"Mousey guy, dead family," Alan says. "Maybe the Kingwatcher thought I was boring, too."

Slowly, subtly, the whisper creeps back into the forest. It stretches along the ground like a shadow. The leaves carry it in little cradles. Alan looks up at the strange sky – at the second moon shying, almost translucent – and wonders how he ever lived with so much weight.

"Don't work that way," Brattle says. He's whispering now, too. "But nothin' works the right way lately."

"Is there anything else you'd like to tell me about before we get moving again?" Alan asks. He's breathing more easily now, but his head is pounding. He stands and hands the phial back to Brattle, who places it carefully back into his tiny pouch.

"You first," Brattle grins.

"No," Alan says, crossing his arms. "Why do you care? I'm not special. I'm nobody."

"The forest will want to know, for one," Brattle answers, clearly biting back a frown. "For two, I'm a listener is all. It's in the blood. A ghoul thing."

Alan takes a deep breath and starts to tuck his shirt back in.

"No," he says again. "There's nothing else."

"Heard and acknowledged, Mister Nobody," Brattle laughs. "We head north for a bit along the hedge to the Bivouacs. Just past there, we'll find your gate."

Brattle starts to walk past him into the forest, but Alan stops him with a hand on his wrist. There is something moving in him that has not stirred for a long time. Maybe having his mind and his memories violated jarred it loose. Whatever the case, he can't swallow his pride anymore – at least not right now.

"You knew," he says to Brattle. "You could have told me, but you didn't."

Brattle looks at him with his brows riding high up his forehead.

"I tried to get you to let it all out last night," he says.

Alan allows himself a surge of anger. It's strangely freeing, but it still scares him a little. "That's not good enough," he tries to growl.

"OK," Brattle says, pulling his arm away. "I'm sorry. For everything. Saving your life, all that. Pulling you out of the bog. I apologize. Now can we get going while we're still friends? I'd like to be home for supper."

For a moment, the two only stare at each other. Brattle rubs his wrist idly. Alan tries to find more energy to continue the confrontation, but he has tapped himself out. His newfound self-assurances limps away whimpering.

"We're friends?" He asks.

"Traveling buddies," Brattle says. "Company on the road. Right? Are we not?"

"You *have* helped me."

"Don't act so surprised."

Alan can't help but chuckle now.

"*Quid pro quo* then?" He ventures. "It's about time you told me about yourself if we're going to be traveling buddies."

"I was getting to that," Brattle replies. "I just wanted to watch you squirm a little first. You never really know a guy until you've pushed him. That's what they always say."

The two set off into the forest then, Alan lagging a bit further behind Brattle than he has been. The whisper follows, drawn to the seed of its Kingwatcher, and Alan tries not to listen as they pulse for one another. The forest is distantly aware; having sunk from age into stupor, but Alan can feel the wind of its thoughts caressing him. It still lives within itself somewhere, but it no longer cares for the truth. It wants only silence now, and the two travelers try their best to oblige.

"Best to keep quiet," Brattle says through his teeth as he stops to let Alan catch up. "Still, I gotta let you know that you're not nobody."

Alan only grunts in reply.

"You're somebody," Brattle finishes. "You gotta be. No way you got all the way here by accident."

Down they go through the tiered glens of the Whisperwood with the old trees trembling around them. The forest's heart is somewhere to the west. As they draw near it, the air is hot about their shoulders. Pollen hangs in wet clouds, practically invisible, and Alan stifles coughs in his hand as it dusts his throat. Here blow whispers of a different sort – darker and less focused – raised up on subtle breezes from deep in the forest's western pits.

Alan remembers the grill and the blasts of heat from the pie oven. Before these, there were miserable sweats in the boxy back seat of his parents' car with the A/C out in July. His mother would daub his neck in vain, and he would kill pouches of Capri Sun in single sucks. Finally, in spite of himself, he remembers the steam pouring out of the shower and his sister's dead hand pointing lazily at the mirror. The forest leans in around him, searching hard for the worst of his darkness, and he can feel through the seed in his mind that it is mad.

There are morning birds calling now. Their rolling screeches and long, ballooning honks ring across the woods from very far away, and Brattle starts talking to drown them out.

"So I'm walking the world," he begins in low tones. "Walking its circumference, that is. Watching shadows and counting my steps."

"Like Eratosthenes," Alan says after a moment. His mouth is so dry that he has to hack a hard cough first.

Brattle blows a strange expression over his shoulder like chaff. "Eric toss the knees. If that means 'shadows' where you come from, then sure." He pauses to clamber up a high bank of mud. Nimble as a cat, he has considerably more trouble helping Alan do the same. Once they are both on the shoulder of the slope upward and heading toward the open day at the edge of the woods, Brattle continues. "My brother Nettle is a keen surveyor, see? I can't get my head around the math, but I been helping him since we're young."

"Little ghoulings," Alan chuckles. "I bet those are cute."

"Don't interrupt me, smartass," Brattle spits. "You've had your say already. And yes, for your information, we were adorable.

"Anyway, he sends me out to walk due south from the old brine well near my hut and to measure out how long it took me to get to the Painted Rocks. It started out fine, but I got turned around. I didn't even make it halfway before the storms started."

The forest dwindles to a wide woodland of rust-dark mounds. Alan feels as though he is coming up for air. Anger claws at him, trying to keep him under the trees. It wants to draw him into the muttering dark at the bottom of the woods, but he finds some kind of strength to resist. He steps out into beaming sunlight and takes a deep breath of fresh air – fresher, at least, than he has had to breathe so far. Brattle simply keeps on going.

"I lost Nettle's cat and now I've turned back," says the ghoul. "It's a pain, but better to start over than do it half right. Nettle's particular about his methods."

"His cat?"

"You know, I get the feeling that living humans think their ignorance is quaint," Brattle laughs through a sneer. "But it ain't. His riding cat, yes. I forget the dumb thing's name, but it don't matter anymore. The shadowstorm took it. That's how I wound up in the swamp."

Alan's calves are tensing up. He stops briefly and puts his hand on one of the nearer piles to steady himself. It's a heap of soil, that's obvious, but it's packed as soft as a ripe pear and fuzzy with living grass tips. He sinks into it a bit, and something moves underneath it.

"Don't touch the mounds," Brattle says. "They're not stable."

"What are they?" Alan asks, brushing sandy dirt from his hands and leaving light trails on his uniform shirt.

"Bivouacs," Brattle replies. "This is the Bivouacs. They were tunnel entrances and mud huts during some old war a long time ago. Now they're cowards' graves."

Alan takes a long step back from the mound he had been leaning on.

"Cowards?"

Brattle doesn't elaborate. He is moving on. He has settled into a brisk swing forward one arm at a time, his legs and hips swiveling into effortless turns as he shifts his weight. Alan marvels at this form of locomotion: it seems simultaneously simple and impossible.

"Do you live with your brother?" He asks, hobbling to keep up on stiff arches. "Do you live in a city?"

"No and no," Brattle answers, barely even panting. He certainly isn't sweating down his back. Alan pumps his shirt at the collar, trying to get some air moving across his torso. "Ghouls don't share, but from time to time we're obliged to entertain. Nettle lives in an old fisherman's hovel. I built my digs myself. It's why everyone in my family visits me instead of him. Da's there now."

"What's the occasion?" Alan says, surprised to find himself genuinely curious.

Brattle grins. "Tomorrow's my birthday."

Birthdays! Otherwise beset in his mind with horrors, Alan jumps at the chance to remember something about his life that still seems important.

I'll be home for my next birthday, Alan says to himself. *Having survived my death to celebrate my life again.*

It is a warm thought, and he is desperately in need of them now.

"How old will you be?" He asks Brattle.

"At some point," Brattle says, "you just quit counting. I remember turning 90, and the next few birthdays just blur out after that. It don't matter, anyway. I'm just glad to be upright. I'm sure Nettle and Da don't exactly know, either."

Alan thinks, *Inasmuch as you are*, but he catches himself before he says it. He covers with "How will they know how many candles to put on your cake?"

"Candles on a cake?" Brattle says with another glance over his shoulder. "That's the stupidest thing I've ever heard."

Alan mops sweat from his brow with the blade of his hand and says, "Well happy birthday anyway."

Noon drags on. The twin suns watch the plains in searing fascination, feeding the living heat of their furnace cores into the struggling grass. The sky rolls blue forever, unblemished, stars showing faintly through it in some places. It seems burned thin. There is a beauty in its frailty that strikes Alan as sad, but it's getting far too hot to contemplate beauty for very long.

Finally, Alan has to sit down. His chest is heaving, and his eyes are stinging with sweat. His calves are numb with a tight weight, and he can't even think about lifting them anymore. He makes a noise in a weak effort to stop Brattle's tireless marching, and then he sinks onto his back with his knees up, supporting himself on his elbows.

Brattle doesn't stop. Alan waits, expecting to hear his gurgling laugh and a crack about how weak he is. It won't be long, surely. He hasn't fallen too far behind. But he can only hear the wind in the grass for a long time. When it occurs to him to be concerned, he opens his eyes.

He levers himself up to his feet with a long groan, his bad knee slipping for a painful moment. He stretches carefully and is about to call for Brattle when the ghoul's calloused hand claps over his mouth.

Alan twists in vain against Brattle's strength. Again, he is surprised by how much power is contained in that wiry little body.

He takes a knee, and then Brattle forces him backward into a full sit-down in a rocky ditch, his legs out in front of him and the back of his head against the ghoul's sunken chest.

"Get down," Brattle hisses. "Listen."

Alan nods. Still in Brattle's grasp, he strains to hear anything more than the terrified roar of his pulse in his ears. Then a high and tinny piping comes rolling up over the Bivouacs from nearby. It dances through the grass like a living thing, merry and hungry, and Brattle curses when more pipes join it.

Brattle begins to relax his grip, Alan shifts to regain control of his own mass. He peers up past the lip of the ditch and can only see grass and mounds and the wasting sky.

"Hobs," Brattle says. "They come up the river to raid graves. Can you see them?"

"No," Alan replies. "Is that them piping?"

"That's a bad sign," Brattle says. Alan wonders what a good sign might look like in this haunted place. "They could be anywhere..."

He doesn't get to finish his thought. A course of tiny voices from above them precedes the appearance of six brown-clad creatures through the grass. They are running, excited, and pointing at Brattle and Alan.

"That's not good," Brattle growls. He swears again. "You ever been in a fight?"

"A few," Alan replies, "when I was a kid."

"Well I hope you learned something good," Brattle says, "or that your weird mojo is still working, because these guys fight dirty."

In a single beat of Alan's racing heart, the creatures are upon them. The tallest of them is barely three feet from the ground at the tip of his pointed cap. He appears to be the leader of the group, and his cronies are dressed almost exactly like him: brown vests and curling shoes with dark breeches. Even their faces look alike; their clanking packs and sashes covered in pins and patches are nearly the only things that distinguish them from each other.

"Stand up," the leader shouts. Like that of the pipes at his hip, his voice is small and thin. "What's this? Live man? Turn out your pockets, both of you!"

It's immediately clear to Alan that the hobs do not intend to give him a chance to comply. The leader's orders are a little less than a formality, as the others don't pause for a second in their swarming while Alan is trying to get to his knees. There is a dry pop followed by a short whistle, and Alan's cheek is left bleeding. His eye wells up with hot tears.

"What the fuck?" Alan cannot help but exclaim.

"Wade in!" cries Brattle, and the ditch is soon running with blood.

The hobs close quickly, drawing little slingshots. Alan is hit twice high on his left thigh as he rises, but he bites back his yelps of pain. He aims a kick at the nearest hob and catches him just below his tiny rib cage, sending him sprawling with a choking case of the sobbing hiccups.

"Aggressors!" the leader wails, his hooked nose tipped up toward the cloudless blue. "See how they torment us!"

Brattle's mouth is full of hob's flesh. He pounces for the leader, and he might be saying, "Like this," but Alan can't tell. For a moment, he's distracted by the sight of a hob lying in the dirt with his life pouring from his open throat.

Then one of the hobs swings a knobbed club against his leg. Pain shoots under his knee to lodge where his kneecap jumps its groove. Alan screams, but he won't go down. Against the horrible twisting burn in his leg and with tears of fury streaming down his face, he turns and kicks in the general direction of the attack. The hob dodges away, but he has underestimated Alan. As it happens, Alan discovers that he has underestimated himself as well.

He kicks the hob in the chin. The thing goes rolling, and Alan follows him. In one stride, he is standing over the hob. It doesn't take much of a stomp for him to crush the little spine. Then he is staring down at something pitiful, his leg clenching and weak. He tries to feel cold as the hob dies, but his heart swells with sadness.

43

Emptiness eludes him, and Alan is left with hot hurt in his chest for the foolish waste. He milks it for strength as he turns to face the last enemy.

Brattle has taken three, but he's hurt. There's a bruise darkening under one of his eyes as he lays in the ditch, breathing hard. The last hob is over him, straddling the rut's shallow taper as he pulls a rock back in his slingshot's pocket. Alan takes a single step forward, his fists clenched, and the last hob looks up at him with cry of fear. In the taut space of a second, he sees that the day is lost - the hob turns and flees, leaving his slingshot behind, and Alan practically falls into the ditch to check on Brattle.

"That's right! Get out and stay out!" Brattle tries. His voice comes out in a funny wheeze. He starts to laugh at himself, and then he clutches his jaw. "Ow! Oh, that hurts. The little pinchers!" He looks up at Alan with a smile spreading crooked across his face. "Where's the last one?"

"That's the one you were just yelling at," Alan says. "He cut and run when he saw it was a rout. Are you all right? Can you stand?"

"Back off," Brattle coughs. "I took a bouncer up top and got knocked loopy is all. I ain't busted!" He shoves Alan away and makes a show of getting up all by himself. "And I don't mean the last one. I mean the first one. The one that cut your cheek and then you kicked him in the ribs. Did he hightail it, too?"

Clarity hits Alan like a rock to the face. It's no glancing blow like the one that gashed his cheek open; it's a strike right between the eyes that almost leaves him laughing at his own stupidity. He has never needed such relief so badly.

"Looks like he's not getting up," Alan says, looking across the ditch at the first hob lying motionless. He's not gasping anymore. "I guess I don't know my own strength."

"Weak hearts," Brattle explains. "Little bit like rabbits. It's a thing in some hob families – a holdover from the first clans, I think. You kicked him right into an arrest."

As Brattle climbs up the ditch, Alan closes his eyes and tries to find some calm in the dark. It's quite a hard time coming, and it doesn't last long. In the shadow of guilt, Alan's relief withers quickly. His stomach rolls, and he waits another moment to see if he's going to throw up.

"It's your first time," Brattle says as he's pawing through the dead hobs' pockets. "If you don't nut up now, it'll never get any easier."

Alan swallows. "I'm not sure how easy I ever want it to be. Honestly, I don't even like killing animals in video games."

"Just get up here and help me," Brattle says. "These things sew hidden pockets all over. They're probably carrying two of themselves each in baubles and grave treasure."

Alan gets to his feet robotically. There is something pushing through his veins that isn't quite blood. His heart is pumping hot, spreading weight to his extremities. He walks up the ditch without seeing too much, and he thinks the new plaque in his veins might be dread.

"I don't want to pat them down for spare change," he says to Brattle.

"Looks like you won't have to," Brattle replies. He hops up into a frog-legged squat and holds up a silver key. "I found it! Of course it was on the alpha. Black maid's legs! This is the key to their horde, and it's got to be nearby. These are dressed in the southern style, and these flipple pipes they have are genuine tin whistles – not the bone and ivory jobs you see in east of the Corridor. No doubt about it: these are local boys. Do you know how rare this is? These keys are supposed to be a myth."

"They didn't look like a roving band of robbers," Alan sighs, putting his hands in his pockets. "They looked like they might have been defending this spot."

"You're my good luck charm," Brattle smiles. Without waiting for a reply, he heads off through the grass with the key held out in front of him. "Don't let that weight sit on you, pasty. Come on and let's collect our parts of the inheritance."

Alan follows without a last look back. A sick knot writhes up under his belly. He feels it scarring him, and he swallows the pain. He has to nut up now, or it'll never get any easier. Nothing will get easier from here; he is suddenly as sure of this as he is of the mounting heat of the late morning.

Where am I? he finally asks himself. *And what have I gotten myself into?*

Brattle toddles ahead with both hands on the silver key, clinging as if it might fly away. He is quite clumsy when trying to walk upright, and he exaggerates his stumbling when he hears Alan laugh. Laughter is the sound of stone breaking. It's the start of the best collapse, and Alan lets it come as the images of the dead hobs fade from his mind for now.

"Hob's keys and locks are made from the same enchanted metals," Brattle says. "They seek each other. See? If you have the key, you can find their horde. At least that's what the stories say."

"Like when you catch a leprechaun," Alan adds. "And he tells you where his gold is."

Brattle staggers east toward a line of weathered larches. The ground evens out, softening into black clay and silt packed tight flecked with spare green.

"Sure. Like that," Brattle says. "The pull is getting stronger! I can't believe this is really happening."

There is a soft wind blowing. It stirs across the Bivouacs, alive and free in the grass, and Alan looks after it as it turns west, as if he might see it swirling there. Where the mound fields end, a vine-climbed wall is slowly crumbling to powder. It's far away, but Alan can make out some of the faces carved on it. They stare from stone, bald and gaping, their mouths filled with shadows. Beyond the wall's broken arch, barely visible for the trees, is a little patch of blue and violet blooms. Alan watches them swaying and realizes that they are beautiful. It runs him clean through, opening his heart to spill its sadness.

"What *are* hobs?" he asks, looking back to Brattle through a sheen of tears. "They looked just like humans."

"Yeah — only shorter. Right?" Brattle has stopped at a high bank of grassy mud with a dead trunk leaning out of it. He watches the key as it turns in his palm. "That's the thing with umans: there's always something about 'em."

"Umans?" Alan repeats.

"Yeah. Like humans, only missing something." Brattle tries to press the key into the side of the bank. Nothing happens, and he rocks on his heels a bit, looking frustrated. "Sometimes it's size, like with hobs and their ilk. Usually it's something that's harder to miss. As umans go, hobs are one of the worst kinds. But they're all bad if you ask me. Not to be trusted; and they're everywhere here. They built the Necropolis, for all the good that's done. Not sure where they came from, but I wish they'd go back."

"Hobs built the Necropolis?" Alan asks. He looks over Brattle shoulder to help him examine the key. It looks like a simple piece of metal to him. It's not even spinning anymore.

"No, no. But umans just the same. The taller kind: sylves. They look just like you — albeit a bit less pudgy most of the time." Brattle pokes Alan's gut with the key. "And probably smarter, too. I'm just guessing on that one. Now help me find this keyhole."

Alan takes the hobs' key and lets it rest in his palm, as Brattle had been doing. It is heavy for its size, and the head is crossed with a bar carved into the shape of a lightning bolt. The teeth are hooks, and each one has a single ruby chip set into it. For a long moment, it warms against Alan's skin and does nothing else. A wave of tension spreads down Alan's neck and settles into his shoulders, sending roots down into the soft place between his collarbone and his right shoulder blade. Then the key begins to turn white, and the ruby chips in its teeth start to gleam. It turns once counterclockwise, and it is suddenly so heavy that Alan has to hold it in both hands. When it pulls him, he lurches forward on one leg and jabs the muddy front of the little hill. There is a click, and then there is nothing. Alan and Brattle stand in the sunlight, staring.

"It worked," Alan finally says. "But…not very well."

47

Brattle scratches his chin. There are flecks of mud caked in his blond stubble.

"I think it worked exactly as well as it's supposed to," says the ghoul, "but we're missing something. Here."

He reaches into the mud and pulls a root-veined clod loose. Alan is surprised to see that it is dry and friable underneath the wetter surface.

He laughs to hear himself exclaim, "Aha!" and then he reaches into the mud bank himself. It isn't long before he and Brattle have uncovered a silver plate set into the dirt with a bark-plugged keyhole in the center of it.

"There it is," Brattle says, triumphant. "Let's unpack the lock and see what we've won."

With this, he plucks the key from Alan's hand and uses its hooked teeth to scrape the detritus from the keyhole. Alan looks up at the sky as he does so. There is a column of circling shapes forming above them. Vultures have come, and he supposes he shouldn't be surprised. Shouldn't they be the kings here?

"There!"

Impatient, Brattle has jammed the key home and forced it into a grinding, difficult turn. At last, the hillside opens; the wall of grass and dirt slide back into a curtained vault with a tiled floor and candles burning on the wall. Brattle tosses the key into the grass.

"Don't need it anymore anyway," he mutters as he pushes through the curtains, but Alan picks the key up and puts it in his pocket.

What can Alan do next but follow? He waits for a breath and looks back at the flowers blowing behind the ruined wall. A shaft of light is falling into the forest there, leaving the carven faces agog in richer darkness. Alan isn't sure how he wants this sight to make him feel. The remedial effects of sorrow are volatile. He doesn't necessarily turn back stronger or more assured, but his heart is still beating. After six months and so much more, he's got that. Alan follows Brattle into the hobs' cave at peace with his burden.

He has to stoop to get in. Before the shrouding red velvet is a rough antechamber. It bows out along the walls, and there are root tips probing up between the floor tiles. Through the curtain, the space has been more meticulously maintained, and it seems far wider than it appears to be from the outside even with armor, weapons, ingots, reams of paper and piles of mud spilling from the soft corners. How the torches continue to burn in the damp and stagnant air was a mystery to Alan.

"Holy bones," Brattle whistles. "Only five defendin' this? I don't much like that. There's gotta be more to have looted up such a pretty bounty."

Alan picks up a broken helmet. It falls to black dust in his hands. He doesn't know about *pretty*, exactly.

3/0.

"Then we grab and go?" he asks. "Though it doesn't look like there's too much to grab here."

"Quantity over quality," Brattle replies. He picks up a goblet that is dark with generations of tarnish. "They robbed all this from tombs, crypts, and Bivouac mounds. It's a clan's lifetime's worth of work collectin'. Look at this." He drops the goblet and holds up a figurine. Alan can't tell what it's supposed to look like. "They used to sell these off carts in Sepulchre City. That's been a long time ago, now. This ain't no single band's horde. Yeah, grab and go is best, I say. We should knuckle on out before that runaway gets back with a whole new team of slingshots."

He dusts off a cloth sack, stuffs his rolled blanket into it, and shoulders it, leaving his little pouch behind. Then he circles the room, nosing through piles like a dog.

Alan almost has to crouch to keep from bumping his head on the domed ceiling. He sifts through a few piles, finding mostly old and broken things that have lain too long in the ground. He hunts for weapons first, but he finds nothing that still looks useful.

"Quantity over quality," he jokes as he slips a rust-eaten blade pointlessly back into its scabbard. "The armor's all falling apart, too. Where I come from, we call this hoarding."

"You got hobs in the living places, too?" Brattle says, looking up from a corner with a dead rat in one hand and a sprung mousetrap in the other.

"Just very messy people," Alan replies. "People who are sick. There's nothing here we can use. Let's burn."

Brattle ignores him. He's strapped a pair of goggles around his head and is peering through them into the dark. His fingers move nimbly over tiny gears, adjusting the many smaller lenses and filters that fold down over each large eyepiece.

"So this is the land of the dead," Alan begins, swallowing hard and failing to sound nonchalant. "It's where we go when we die."

"One of them," Brattle replies without looking at him. "And sometimes. Spirits can get washed out of the energy exchange – or they can dissipate before a conduit opens. I've heard it said that –"

"OK, OK," Alan interrupts. "We come here when we die, but where do you go?"

Brattle only shrugs.

Alan tries again. "Hobs aren't from my world. Neither are ghouls. So if this is our afterlife, what's yours?"

"Did you know about this place?" Brattle finally turns, but only far enough that Alan can see one eye magnified beneath the goggles and the sunken curve of one falling cheekbone.

"No," Alan says.

Brattle shrugs again and goes back to shoveling through the piles.

"Shouldn't hang around much longer," Alan sighs.

As he says this, he sees a glint near the back of the room. There is a handle just visible under a heap of rolled up flags and mateless shoes. He reaches for it through shifting folderol.

"Wait," he says, just suppressing the wraith of a gasp. "This is mine!"

Brattle hops over sideways, his new pack stuffed full of something that is rattling and shifting against his back.

"What is it?"

Alan holds the handle up. It is solid aluminum tipped with a black grip at one end. On the other end is a prolate oval head crossed with an X of sturdy bars. He smiles at it, filled all at once with a rare kind of relief he hadn't expected to find here.

"It's a trash masher," he says. "*My* trash masher."

Brattle regards Alan's find with a prospector's doubting frown. He spins the gears on his new goggles a few times, humming, and runs a rough thumb along the shaft to trace the outline of the mashing end.

"That don't help," he huffs.

"I use it at work to push garbage down into trash cans," Alan tries to explain. He makes a downward mashing motion with his hands. "I was carrying it when I...crossed over?" He gives Brattle a questioning look, and Brattle stares back. "Well, before I woke up here. I always thought it would make a good weapon. I've practiced swinging it a bit. You know. Fighting with it."

It's actually a relief to make this last admission. With it, Alan begins to see how freeing it could be to talk to someone who knows very little about the living world.

"Then strap it on and let's crawl," Brattle says, giving Alan's trash masher a dismissive wave of his hand as he turns toward the door. "I'm as loaded up as I'm gonna get before the cavalry arrives."

"Wait!" Alan says again. He reaches further into the pile and retrieves a black hat from beneath a worm-wrecked pair of trousers. By some amazing good fortune, it isn't flattened. The golden *R* on the front still looks newly stitched — just as he remembers it. He lifts it to brush it off and sees a dark square of clean plastic beneath it. "My hat, too. And my *phone*! How lucky is that?" He pulls his work cap carefully over his head and slips his phone into his pocket. "There. Now we're ready."

Brattle laughs. "You look like a dope, but at least you're a dope who's got something to hit someone with."

The day is burning off the fields, warping the air with heat distortion for cloudless, blue miles. The scrub grass shrinks in toward cracking earth, white receding up from wet pockets as they evaporate. Here and there, bare tendrils straggle up from under prickly bushes as if tasting the sky for rain.

The Bivouacs dwindle toward a rocky slope in the north. Brattle leads Alan east along the low scarp's feet, where the forest is waging its wishful return. The trees advance along little rolling hills, and wet green prevails at last in the thickets springing up beyond the grave mounds. Just before they cross away from the fields, Alan and Brattle pause beneath an ailing tree as a troop of hobs marches past a safe distance away. They say nothing to each other as the small shapes disappear behind the mounds.

With the swelter of the Bivouacs behind them, Alan pulls his phone from his pocket and presses the single physical button on the front. The screen glows to life, but his wallpaper has been replaced with a dark field and a silver wheel of symbols.

"I can't believe this thing still works," Alan thinks aloud. "But it's acting pretty weird. I suppose that's no surprise."

"What is that?" Brattle asks. "Some kind of game?"

"It's a phone," Alan explains. "It's like a communicator. You send your voice across a distance and talk to other people."

Brattle laughs. "Human magic. So what's it doing now? It's not working?"

"Not the way it should be," Alan says. He touches the screen, and the wheel of symbols opens. He's afraid to do anything else. "Maybe I'd better not mess with it right now. I never know what to expect in this place."

"You're learnin', pasty," Brattle says, affecting surprise. "Better safe than sorry here – in the wilds at least, though Necro's not much less bad – and there's not a lotta safe goin' around."

They enter a glade under reaching elms. Gooseberries grow huge and dark around the clearing, and fat beetles buzz around them in mad, fighting clouds. The vultures are circling again – nearer this time. Alan can see them through the opening in the canopy.

"You know," Brattle says, "there ain't no such thing as luck."

He slows to a panting stop and props himself up on his new walking stick: a black horn he pried from a bleached skull in the hobs' cave.

Alan is glad for a chance to sit down. He lowers himself gingerly onto the spring carpet of leaf-mulch and grass and leans back with his legs crossed loosely. Reclining so, he suddenly finds himself unable even to think about standing back up. A week's worth of fatigue settles on him all at once, no longer held at bay by the roaring high of fear.

"You're about to tell me about fate," he says, reaching to accept a slim canteen from Brattle. The stuff it contains isn't water exactly. Alan has to swallow it hard. "I don't believe in fate."

"Why not?" Brattle asks.

"I don't know. Maybe I'm not fated to."

"Ha." Brattle sits back on his heels. "You're real funny. How do you explain all that stuff o' yours bein' in that hob hole? Smack of coincidence? Too convenient. Even if it were luck, it's a lotta luck all at once."

Alan hands the canteen back, and Brattle caps it without taking a swig. "Maybe you just suck at figuring odds. Predestination means there's someone doing the predestining. I just don't see any reason to assume that."

"Doesn't have to be a somebody," Brattle replies, suddenly somber. "It could just be that there's part of you sees a smooth groove through life and shoots for it – walks in it to a certain point that maybe others can see if they know the paths. I don't know. Maybe you make your own fate ahead of yourself. Either way."

"What's your destiny, Brattle?" Alan asks. "Have you been lucky much?"

Brattle's lips go thin and white. He tenses his jaw and stares intently at the ground in front of him.

"Ain't done nothin'," he intones. "Lived a ghoul's life: scratching around in the sticks, scrapping up after everyone else has made their marks and had their adventures. We're bottom feeders, and most of us go by with it OK without making a fuss. I don't complain. A life is a life."

Alan nods, his fires burning deep, beyond where he can control them. The light of his thoughts must shine untended for now, as he has neither the will nor the strength to guide it.

"I got a cold feelin'," Brattle says from the root of his throat. "Breathe deep for a few more, and then we go. I don't like waitin' now."

"I think I'm less tired than I am eager to get home," Alan laughs. "Though I can't promise I'm sure about that."

Brattle doesn't reply. He hunches his shoulders up around his drooping ears and sucks his teeth, the strange goggles perched ridiculously above his deep-lined brow.

Seven

The woods east of the Bivouacs are free of spirits. They roll on in struggling splendor, their living green finding ways to emerge from beneath the crush of Graveworld's assiduous wasting. The follower crows return, their calls eerily like human coughs, their wings blotched blood-red on the undersides. Alan is sure that he knows them from his first night in the swamp. They watch with familiar interest.

Brattle has been walking everywhere his whole life. Alan is soft and weak, and he misses his car. Two miles is an easy distance for an outland ghoul, but Alan has to stop every two hours for a stretch, a breath, and a swig from Brattle's flask.

"Son of the wheel," Brattle says, laughing at him. "Slave of the internal combustion engine. Ain't even any horses out here! You better toughen up fast."

"You said you had a cat," Alan pants in reply. "Don't moralize."

"Nettle's ride. And he only gave it 'cause it was part of his calculations. No cats out here either, for the most part. They're an inner lands thing. Suck a drink and let's go, knobby. Night's comin'."

They continue to the brink of nightfall. Purple light pales through the clouds where the woods thin out into a cluttered stretch of crypt-strewn badlands. Here the trees stand dead silent, only pillars now, their bark replaced by flaking rock.

"Petrified standing up," Alan says. "And look at the black patches at their bases. It's like the ground turned to glass around their roots."

"Agates I think," Brattle replies. The two are setting up camp in the lee of a massive sarcophagus. Where it is split, there is a voice nagging from within it. Alan tries to tune it out as Brattle goes on. "These're giants' graves. Old as the ground itself they say, though that don't make much sense. I'd like to move on through here fast if we can. Place gives me the crawlies."

Alan nods. His shoulders are as hard as the petrified trees. Their roots go down into glass and nickel-iron, where the impact crater of his heart is still smoldering.

"Are you feeling the cold yet, human?" Brattle asks. He's finally gotten the fire going. "It's been eating at me, and that's a rare thing. Cold crawling up my back. It's not a good sign."

"I'm still learning to be here," Alan says. "I think my emotions have been out of whack since I arrived – however that happened. More than anything, I feel catastrophically displaced."

Alan rolls this lie over in his mind for a while, hoping it'll pick up the dust of some truth. He does feel the cold now; he knows it, and he's afraid. It's deep and as sure as prophesy. His thoughts are buried in it.

He's about to admit this to Brattle when his phone vibrates in his pocket. It startles a gasp from him as he surfaces from pondering, and he slaps his hip as if his work slacks are on fire before he realizes what's happening.

It feels good to remember the sensation of his phone buzzing against his thigh. He tries to cling to that as the cold feeling continues its slow press into him.

"I'm getting a text," Alan says. He reaches into his pocket to fish for his phone. "I have absolutely no idea how that's possible."

"Ticks?" Brattle says. "In your pants? That's a pain."

Alan draws his phone out carefully and shows it to Brattle, who only frowns at it and goes back to eating rats from the traps he put into his new backpack.

"A text. It's like a written message," he explains, sliding his finger across the screen. The symbols move on the black, expanding the while into a split helix. A text box opens within the swirl. "There's no number anywhere; I don't know who it's from. It looks like... God, this is weird." He stares at the phone, his eyes bleary with fatigue. Symbols appear inside the text box, bleeding in from the helix as it collapses in a dazzling display. "It's actually *just* numbers. A string of numbers. No message. This look like anything to you?"

He holds the phone flat in his palms as he shows it to Brattle. He's not sure quite how to handle it properly anymore. The light from the display makes the whispering seed stir in his mind, and a bilious lump bobs up into his throat.

"382775 857372," Brattle reads. Then he sits and thinks a minute. His eyes move across the string of numbers in quick twitches. After two asynchronous blinks, he spreads a bright smile between the wagging lobules of his ears.

"Ya know," he nearly laughs, "I think this actually does look like something."

All at once, he is bouncing over his heels in a squat as he digs through his new pack. He lolls his tongue out to wet the corners of his mouth. The little wisps of his hair swirl in a new wind. When he turns back to Alan, he is working a tightly folded piece of paper between his fingers.

"My map," he says as he lays the quickly unfolding paper out on the grass. "Or Nettles, rather. Look: put points here and here, and those are map numbers."

He taps the phone and then goes back to unfolding the map. It has grown quite large from a yellowing square scarcely bigger than Alan's thumbnail. Alan follows faint brush lines across its deep creases. It doesn't appear to be complete.

"See this?" Brattle says, putting his finger hard in the map's center. "Nettle made me remember these two sets. It was really important, so I knew I'd forget. He gave me this to remind me. Those numbers in your tick are just like these ones here."

Alan's heart skips a beat. It's a deeply unsettling feeling. The whispering seed responds by pumping neon into the veins behind his eyelids. He blinks twice into a kaleidoscope of pulsing colors, and then he shakes his head clear again. Beneath the rough tip of Brattle's finger is a tapering circle on the map marked with sets of numbers.

"You're right," he says, breathless. "It's latitude and longitude. The first number would be north, I think, and the next one is either east or west. But it might be south. I don't remember."

"I only had to memorize these numbers," Brattle says, frustration creeping into his voice. "I don't know about north or west."

They stare in silence for another moment, Alan hunches close enough to Brattle to smell him. The cold feeling wends its way through him until it is tingling at the tips of his fingers. He realizes that it is something like power – new strength flowing through him.

"Where is it on the map?" He asks the ghoul.

"It ain't," Brattle sighs. "At least not on this one. This one was only s'posed to get me from my hut to this spot here." Suddenly limp, he touches the map. "We'll have to find a more complete map if we want to look up those coordinates."

Alan looks Brattle in the eyes. For the first time, he meets the ghoul's stare without the hair on his neck pricking up and his throat closing. Brattle returns Alan's gaze with pain banging behind his frown, but he won't let it out. He swallows, and then it is gone. Alan watches the feeling vanish from Brattle's face in a silver-lit instant.

"It's leading me somewhere," Alan says, half under his breath.

"Us," Brattle corrects him. "But I dunno about that device and what it says. I'm curious as you, but I gotta rule: I don't trust magic. Charms and such, magical artifacts. It's lies and smoke and traps. Can't nothing good come of this."

"You're very superstitious," Alan chides.

"Yeah. Says the live human with magic ticks in his pants."

Alan slips the phone back into his pocket. Brattle folds his map carefully, smoothing wrinkles along the burned edges and tracing every fold with intense precision. When it is an impossibly small wedge of paper again, he jams it down into the depths of his pack and sits with his back to the wind for a while.

"Tell me it's dangerous," Alan finally says to him. "It might be a murderer or a monster. It might be a dragon. I might die."

"It's dangerous," Brattle stews. "You might die."

"I think I'm starting to believe you."

"Good."

Alan shakes his head. "Not about that. I mean maybe I *am* here for a purpose. *Some*thing is going on here." He almost mentions the seedling in his mind, but he can't bring himself to. Thinking about it scares him too much. "You're the expert. Tell me what this is."

"I ain't the expert," Brattle replies, his eyes hooded under his furrowed brow. "But you got to be careful who and what you trust."

"All right." Alan looks up at the stars. The moon is moving across them, fat and red-gray. It wears a crown of shadow at a disgraced angle. Clouds cross its face, limned for wind-blown instants in the sad light of its longing. "Then we don't trust. We don't change the plan."

Brattle bobs a nod, and the night swallows his whispered reply in a gust of wind.

Alan dreams of his sister and of nightingales. He drowns through deep sinks of long prophecy while shapes move around him, trying to find forms that suit their wills. On dark sheets, he draws circles upon circles of insane symbols, and the new power grows in him until it is gnawing at the roots of his heart in desperation. It is a black dream – his first in Graveworld – and it is full to bursting with his loss and despair. It is bowed beneath a great weight of chaos, but at its end it is mild and harmless. It is the beginning of something, the first kicks of a new hope inside him, and he wakes from it with morning warm on his face.

Brattle is curled up like a dog. Alan stretches the lancing pain from his back and finds his phone again. He taps it to life, opens the circle, and stares at the set of coordinates while the noise in his mind builds. It starts behind his ears: a dull buzzing that ramps up slowly into a pulsing hiss like the rush of the sea. It grows into a roar behind his eyes, and his heart strains to keep time with it. It is not the voices from the split in the sarcophagus. He has managed to tune them out, much to his surprise. This is, instead, the remnant voice of the Whisperwood, and it reacts to the numbers and the helix of glyphs on his phone's touchscreen.

Brattle starts awake. He is up on his feet in an instant, strapping his pack on and yanking a rat from the board of a sprung trap to stuff the torn carcass into his mouth. The crows mutter and laugh at him while he shuffles ash and dirt over the embers of the fire.

"We'll gain the gate by late morning," Brattle says without even looking at Alan. "Then this'll either all be over, or I don't know what."

Alan stretches again and slips his phone back into his pocket. It is heavy there, and he feels comforted by that weight. Cold dread is retreating, and the new power is increasing steadily.

"I was lucky to meet you," he says to Brattle. "I just wanted to get that out there. Thanks for saving me."

Brattle turns and gives him a smile. It's strange and sharp – like the glint of a blade in the dark.

"As long as you're still here, you ain't safe," he says. "But you're welcome anyway. It's been surreal so far, and you've made my journey home a good bit more exciting than it was shaping up to be, not to mention safer. You and your weird mojo. You still think you're not meant to be here?"

"I told you I'm not sure anymore," Alan replies. "But I suppose we'll find out."

"We were always gonna find out," Brattle laughs. He leads the way down a gentle hill toward a ring of stones in the distance. "I've been fighting with it, you know. Certainty don't come easy."

"I guess not," says Alan.

The tomblands dip down into a little curving choke between two emerald hills. To the northwest, they run away as far as Alan can see. There are dark shapes moving on the ragged line of that horizon, shadows walking tall, as if on stilts. Alan watches them for a long time, and even Brattle affords them a few curious looks, but he never wonders aloud what they might be, and Alan doesn't ask.

You never know what new horror the answer may reveal, he thinks. *Best to remain uncertain about some things.*

After a surprisingly pleasant walk through open and unusually lovely country, they are near enough to the circle of stones to see that there are vultures roosting on the tallest ones and that the pedestal in the center sparkles with gems.

"My Da calls this Tir's Henge," Brattle says. "Never seen this gate used. May be illegal - not that any such things as laws rule here. Crossings are dangerous enough anyway to deter most mischief makers."

"Have you ever been through?" Alan asks, not quite sure how to phrase the question. "Not this gate, but any gate?"

"This is the only gate I ever heard of," says Brattle. "No one goes through, as far as I know. It's a bit tricky, I think – being displaced."

Alan chuckles. "I can vouch for that."

Brattle wags his head. "I think it's a bit different going the other way, but I can't swear to that. As I said, no one goes through. It just ain't done. Not anymore, at least."

The path to the gate is laid with pearly sand and humped up over the erupting knuckles of tree roots. As Alan and Brattle approach the arching entrance, one of the vultures drops from its perch to light on the ground before them. It takes one bouncing step forward, flapping piceous wings with silver shimmers running under them. Its bare head tilted, it clacks its beak at them.

"State your business, corpse-puller."

"Little lost human," Brattle says, stiffening his spine as best he can and mustering something of a bow. "Coming to gate him back if it pleases you."

"The vulture can talk," Alan laughs as the bird looks him over. "Of course it can! I don't know what I was expecting."

61

"A vulture!" the bird laughs. "Ha! A real slave to the physical. He's alive all right!"

The vulture glances back at the watching gallery of its fellows. The other birds flap on their perches, clacking out a chorus of rough chuckles amid the drum-thumps of their stardusted wings. The air quivers around them, swelling briefly around the curve of some subtle distortion, leaving Alan's head hurting.

"The Geier Venue," Brattle explains. "They guard this place. You could muster some deference, yeah?"

Alan starts to make an apologetic bow, but the Geier Venue take up a loud, rasping call atop the ring of stones. It might be more laughing, but something about it pierces him cold.

"The unclean have no need for formalities," says the lead vulture. "I am Atratus. It's something of an honor to meet a live human! Not as rare now in the Elderlands as it once was, but just as ill a sign as ever, so I say."

It fans its lozenge-shaped tail and scatters grit and soil around its feet.

"Alan," Alan offers.

"Ellen?" The vulture shakes its scaly head and corrects itself. "Alan. You don't belong here, and you want to go back. Alan, there are no promises with these gates, and if you choose to cross, we cannot aid you. Our pact is with the dead. And our power. You understand."

"Yes," Alan finds himself saying, though he's not entirely sure that he does.

Atratus draws nearer. It postures up and folds its wings back in a gesture that is powerfully suggestive of consideration. Alan finds this unnerving – this and the fire in its ember eyes.

"So it won't work?" Brattle asks. "Or will it? He's come a pretty long way for a live one."

Atratus nods and stares at Alan.

"What we mean is that you're welcome to try," it replies.

"How do I open it?" Alan asks.

62

The vulture fluffs its wings up high on its back. It shrugs until its beak is in its neck ruff, and then it wheezes at him.

"Decide."

The Geier Venue glares down at Alan and Brattle in sudden, terrible silence. Huge, they seem to blacken with impatience. Beneath their wings and along the slopes of their mottled breasts, galaxies spark against each other. It's magic, raw and pure and heavy, and this is Alan's first real taste of it. He feels giddy and swallowed in fear.

"Best of luck, boss," Brattle says. "And thanks for the travelin' company."

"What about fate?" Alan asks. "What if I'm supposed to be here? What about my destiny?"

"You have the Venue's leave to try," Atratus chirrs, "but not to tarry. Approach the dais now or turn away. Death is everyone's destiny, boy."

Alan puts his hand on his pocket to feel the hard square of his cell phone there. It's warm and stirring lightly. Something moves in him as if in reply, and he doesn't even try to make sense of it. He lets Graveworld wash over him in all its strangeness; he weathers the pull of its will, and he's proud to feel fully himself again when he finally steps forward.

The circle of standing stones surrounds a little walled garden watered by a spring that pumps up from nearby to overflow two inner rings of gutters. At its center is a slab of black stone surrounded by bluebells and honeysuckle. The seven steps that rise toward the dais are pockmarked and filigreed with ancient cracks. Red flowers bob over them, the long thorns of their tendrils dripping with golden sap.

The air is still, but a penetrating charge moves through it. In the quiet of the afternoon, Alan stands on the dais and looks up at the Geier Venue as they watch him hungrily. He looks back at Brattle, small and dark on the white sand. He starts to raise a wave, to call out his thanks for a safe trip back to where he belongs, but a power unfolding behind him turns him around on his heels.

The vultures begin to hiss. The sound pitches up to an awful, choking roar as light grows from thin air. Brattle is calling, but Alan can only hear the higher tones of his voice. The rest is lost in the new rush, the hot smack of living flame across his face as the gate opens.

For an instant, he can see the way between the worlds. It glitters like a beam, darkness falling infinitely away beneath it. He goes giddy with stomach spasms, and blinks as his head becomes lighter than air. Then heat is pouring over him, and Alan puts his hands up to shield his face.

The glittering way scatters apart, and his giddiness drops abruptly into his shoes. Alan wonders: *What am I doing?* before an explosion lifts him up and sends him flailing backward.

He falls into the garden on fire, sucking searing breaths to power a few shrieks of pain as he flails. Choking coughs and the vultures' panicked cries are the last things he knows before the gate into darkness blows closed on his mind. He goes limp with Brattle hurrying into the circle on his knuckles and the Geier Venue spreading starred wings around him.

Eight

It's early September, and the light is changing. It's streaming colder into the woods west of the Schmidt house, and the wind brings bonfire smells from across the meadow. Alan and Hannes stay out all day, trying to break the falling quiet. They play until the lightning bugs come out, and they part reluctantly for separate dinner tables with grass-cuts on their arms and sweat stinging on the backs of their necks. They can't stem the tide of autumn. With the growing shadows and the early darkness come school and schedules and distance. Alan kneels at his window, watching the first of the night creeping across the street, and feels the first real pangs of summer's sweetness dying.

Death is everyone's destiny. This thought follows Alan through the halls at school. In the restroom, he hears it trickling from behind closed stall doors. It's in the back of his social studies book, cut as if by a claw over the Van Halen "V." He carries it home, hot with it and sick to his stomach. In some strange way, in one form or another, it has always been with him. It followed him into the world from the womb, the ghost of his prenatal energies. Summer is wasting away, and he can't stop it. Hannes is two months from Maine and his father's funeral. The Schmidt house is empty tonight. It's destiny. It's fate.

Alan wakes in a fragrant embrace, petals kissing the tips of his fingers. Long curls of yellow vetch crawl over him like velvet, releasing him from their deep squeeze. Nepenthe is close, dark in heavy pitcher traps; if he could have one sip, he might return to the brink of that crucial summer – he might still find some way to stop it from ending. But the plants are receding from him and he can't strain to reach. His body is still asleep, and he can only stare into the sky.

The constellations are wrong. The moon is too close. Something heavy sinks into his stomach to pit there, pushing up bile he can't swallow. Memory expands in his skull like a balloon, stretching it apart at the sutures. When it is finally born, it glimmers like Athena in her armor, and he can't turn away.

He is the only living member of his family. The last summer of his innocence is long over. He is still in Graveworld.

"He wakes," Atratus clucks. "Alan, don't try to move. Can you understand me? Blink once for yes. Can you do that?"

Alan tries, but nothing happens. Before now, he's never thought about what it feels like to blink. Now that it's gone, the sensation is all he can focus on. He strains until pain starts to bunch along the cords in his neck, feeling no connection to any parts of his face.

"It's all right," Atratus says. "We anticipated as much."

Alan tries to remember the giddy feeling he experienced before the gate to the world of the living blew up in his face. It remains just beyond his reach, blocked by a cascade of flaming images and the preponderant memory of searing pain.

"Can you stand?" Brattle asks from somewhere nearby. Now the ghoul's face comes into view. Fear is drawn around his mouth in tight lines. It makes Alan want to laugh to see Brattle looking so worried, but he isn't sure he can do that just yet.

"I think so," he replies, and the sound of his own voice startles him. It seems to come from outside of him. His mouth doesn't seem to be moving at all. "Help me."

Brattle hops over to take Alan's arms as he presses himself up from the tangle of sweet-smelling grasses. His strength is returning quickly. He's stiff for a moment, and his legs tremble trying to support himself, but he's soon upright and looking around. He's grateful for that at least.

Alan takes a moment to pat himself down. There are ash tracks burned across the front and sides of his work shirt, fused forever with the polyester. The false pocket flap is missing from his pants, and his shoelaces are seared to the eyelets. They'll be impossible to untie now. His arms are hairless, and there are red welts running all the way up into his sleeves. These are sore to the touch, but he knows the damage could have been a lot worse.

Finally, he reaches up to touch his chin; he immediately wishes that he hadn't.

"What happened?" he asks. "Why can't I feel my face?"

Atratus approaches Alan with his bald head bobbing . "The best we can figure," he says, "the gate didn't want you. For reasons that shall remain undisclosed, it hasn't been working normally from this side for a long time. When you were able to get it open, we were all surprised. But it pushed you away quite violently in the end, and I'm afraid you've suffered some rather serious burns."

Alan puts both quivering hands on the sides of his face. What he feels there is flat, stiff, and cold. His stomach lurches, and he squats down clutching his midsection, certain that he's going to be sick.

"I wouldn't do that if you can help it," Atratus warns. "We've done our best to restore you, but it's temporary. One works with what one has. I'm sure you understand."

"You might have died," Brattle says, patting Alan on the back. "But the Venue has magic like I've never seen. I chucked up myself when I seen what that fire done to you."

"Fire?" Alan manages. Though his gut is flipping over on itself, there is no change in his voice.

Under the pain and confusion, he finds himself again. He straightens up and looks Atratus in the eye. There are waves of shining particles flowing over the vulture's head. The others wear similar crowns; when they flap, light scatters like dust from beneath their wings.

Now he finds his breath; ragged and strange as it may be, he sucks a heavy sigh through whatever it is that's passing for his nose at the moment.

"I didn't think healing was what you did," he says. With enough focus, he can muster a growl.

One of the vultures laughs, "That's gratitude for you!"

A second one chimes, "Humans!"

Atratus only flaps and bobs for a few steps, and then it straightens its spine and clacks its hooked beak smartly. Rearing so, the vulture Lord of the Geier Venue is nearly as tall as Alan.

"It took magics we haven't used in a long time to restore you as much as we did, and this place is not equipped for proper circles," Atratus explains. "But you must make no mistake: the greatest of the powers that preserved you was your own."

"Your weird mojo," Brattle adds. "It's been protecting you from the start."

"Is that why the gate rejected me?" Alan asks.

Atratus clucks, "Perhaps."

"If you want answers, I know just the place," says Brattle. "It's not far past my house. And, seein' as how it looks like we're going to have a lot more time together, I say we head there next."

"You asked about destiny," Atratus says. "The Venue knows enough to disbelieve in such, but you present a special case. It may not comfort you now, but we think it for the best that the gate turned you away."

The night sky is brightening in the east. Pink spreads out under gathering clouds. Swirling bands of color cross each other through the air, twisting together in places to spin short-lived eddies. A green cloud rises from the ground to cling at the tips of the grass blades, unstirred by the wind. It looks like fall — like the summer burning down to its last days. Alan feels Graveworld within him; the seedling of Minos has started sprouting. All around, from every foot of buried earth, he can feel a great power reaching out to him: the dreaming minds of the ancient dead.

"Not quite so much a slave to the physical anymore, hmm?" Atratus says. Alan almost thinks the vulture may be trying to smile. "Welcome to the world as it really is."

"Does this mean anything to you?" Alan asks. He fishes his phone out of his singed pocket. There is light melting damage on the screen, but it comes to life easily when he taps it to show Atratus the wheel of silver symbols.

"What is it?" the vulture says.

"I don't know," Alan laughs. To the best of his knowledge, he does so without smiling. "Destiny."

Atratus pokes at the screen with its beak. Morning shines in its obsidian eyes, lighting them up with crimson.

"These are coordinates along ley lines," he replies with a hiss of breath. "We see them where they converge. We follow them through the air in our circles. You can see them now, too, I imagine."

Alan nods. "Do you know where this is? What's there, and why is this on my phone?"

"We must keep some secrets, human," Atratus says into a new wind. Alan can't feel it ruffling his hair. He runs his hand over his head to see whether he has hair anymore.

Atratus's voice drops to a warning whisper. "You should take care who you show this to. Follow the ghoul for now, but don't trust him. Don't trust anyone here. We are a land of liars."

"Why *did* you save me?" Alan asks, looking over his shoulder. Brattle is out of sight. "What did you stand to gain?"

"We answer to a higher command," Atratus explains. Its voice becomes an airy croak. "And when there is no command, we decide what to do for ourselves."

Brattle appears near the northeast curve of the garden wall. He is wide-eyed and panting beneath his pack.

"Smoke!" He calls, pointing. "Come on, boss! I gotta bad feelin'!"

"You didn't have a bad feeling before I got blown up?" Alan tries to joke. Brattle hurries past him, his face screwed up into a snarl.

"If you're coming, then come," he says.

Alan turns to the east to see a stream of black smoke rising from the forest. The land drops into a narrow heath of straw for a space, and then it blossoms out into healthy woods in the watching shadow of a lonely mountain. As Alan begins to follow Brattle, the Geier Venue takes to the air one by one, with Atratus tarrying just long enough to offer a wave of his star-flecked wing.

"May the warm wind bear you high," Atratus squawks, "and the fields be littered with carrion."

On the white sands running down from the circle of stones, Alan overtakes Brattle. He sees his trash masher strapped to the ghoul's pack, and takes hold of it to try to slow Brattle down.

"Is it your house?" he asks. "Your hut, I mean?"

"I don't know," Brattle gripes. He slides his arms from the pack and allows Alan to shoulder it. There are little rays of greenish light disappearing above his head. "It's damn near, if it's not. I know you just been hurt, but I can't slow down. Can you keep up?

Alan stretches against the weight of the pack. There's no pain anymore; there's only the numbness above his neck.

"I can walk fine," he says. "I just hope I don't have to whistle any time soon."

Brattle manages a chuckle at that.

"Reach back in that pack," he says over his shoulder. "First pocket up from the left and then up again. There's a mirror I got from the hobs' horde."

Alan attempts to clear his throat, but he's lost his breath again. His voice echoes from the air around him, clear and hollow.

"I don't know if I'm ready for that yet. Was it...was it very bad?"

"There won't be any scars," Brattle replies. "You'd need skin for that."

Alan doesn't reach into the pack for the mirror. He runs his fingertip along his cheek, wondering what's there if it isn't skin. At his cheekbones, he can press deep enough to feel the bone – a hard ridge curving toward his orbital socket. It's cold there, where magic is holding the mask of his face together. As dawn grows across the straw and the withered sky, it only gets colder.

Nine

Alan follows Brattle across the hay and into the wall of a warm, southeasterly gale. The wind pitches hard toward the dunes just below them, carrying long ribbons of purple light. It pulls drifting bands of light in from the edges of the fields and stretches them out to coil them at its heart. There it strips them of their luster and shears them away like chaff in dull wisps. Alan's head swims as he tries to take it all in, but he pushes forward. The high laments of gulls in the east pluck at his heart. He has always loved the sound. He uses it to narrow his focus and to stave off distraction and sensory overload, and it works well for a long time.

"You seem to be handling all this pretty well," Brattle says, his eyes on the twist of smoke ahead. "Not sure whether or not I should be impressed."

"What do you mean?" Alan asks. He clings tightly to the pack straps, trying to keep the wind from pulling him off his feet.

"I mean that either you just integrate better than most, or you're burying how you really feel." Brattle's tone is cold as dagger steel. "You know that don't fly here. No secrets."

Alan thinks about the sprout of magic inside him. He can reach back and feel it if he concentrates hard enough. It moves constantly, and it produces whispers in Alan's own voice. Through these whispers, the dead creep into his mind. The boldest and strongest of them wait at the doorstep of his consciousness, darkening him, making him afraid of his own thoughts. The weaker ones simply circle, vulture-like, at the root of his animal mind. He hates this new awakening.

"No secrets," Alan replies. "You're not exactly unbiased, are you?"

Brattle shrugs, caught. "I just know that, if I were to wake up suddenly in your world, I'd have all kinds of questions. Where does the second sun set? How heavy is water? Why do you put lit candles in your food? I guess you ain't the questionin' type."

"Maybe not so much as you," Alan says. "But sure. There are things I want to know. I'm a little afraid to ask anything anymore, after what I've already seen."

"Nothing yet," Brattle laughs. "I promise. Ask away. Whadda ya got to lose?"

The hay fields are ending. They recede from the crest of a weathered knoll, and the high winds drop off with them. Beyond is a grove of enormous, stinking flowers, their violet spathes falling like skirts around the nodding horns of black spadices. Brattle breathes their rotting scent deeply, but Alan has to hold his nose as they press through the velvet curtains of their petals.

Alan turns Brattle's offer over in his head and finally decides to humor him. The truth is that he's always been good at integrating. He's even managing to work around the new lights in the sky and the cacophony of dead voices threatening to erupt in his mind. It hasn't occurred to him to ask why he hasn't felt hungry yet. But he has felt afraid, and he has felt alone, and he can see the fear in the hunch of Brattle's shoulders. The smoke is blowing away, but they are closer to it now; he can smell wood burning. Brattle needs a distraction.

Is he starting to consider Brattle a friend? He speaks to stop himself from following that question any further.

"OK," he says. "You said there were other places beyond this one. Right? The Coma and something else. Where are they? Are they physical places, like this one? Is there a god?"

Brattle sighs and knuckles a bead of sweat from the corner of his eye.

"You would ask me something I can't answer," he grumbles. "Coma's all white – blank like empty space. We call the other place the Crater, and we don't say much good about it."

"Sounds like Heaven and Hell," Alan says. "More or less. And humans go there when they die? Who else lives there?"

"You might see a wanderer from one or the other out in the wastes," Brattle replies, "though I never have. All I really have about any of that is stories, which do well enough for me, but I get the feeling you'd want something a little more solid."

Alan is about to respond when Brattle holds up a hand. The two stop behind a hedge of emaciated carrion flowers. Beyond them is a field in a round depression, sparsely treed, with a shadow falling long across it from the feet of a hill. A gnarled knuckle of rock juts up from the center of field: a meteor stuck in the heart of its crater.

Brattle whispers, "Da."

He breaks through the hedge with a wounded cry and sprints into the field. Alan drops the pack and pulls his trash masher from the catgut lashing. The weight of it in his hand is the best thing he's felt since he arrived in Graveworld. It's like he has home in his palm, solid and real and deadly.

Alan follows Brattle into the long shadow at a run, his lungs still and his pulse absent from his throat. Crows laugh in a tight murder, flying low around the smoke with their wings trailing blue sparks. They circle once and then disappear into distant trees, the watchers of the dead, perhaps, if the vultures are their guides and guardians.

A stone sinks into Alan's stomach. He can just make out that the meteor at the end of the field has windows carved into it. Every one of them is leaping with flames.

Alan's mother was afraid of fire. She didn't want her children to inherit her phobia, so she tried to hide it, but it seeped out. When the old stove would smoke and she would quietly excuse herself into the bedroom, no one was allowed in to see her gasping at the open window. When she was banging around in the basement on late night searches for phantom burning smells, Alan's father would lead him outside to teach him about the constellations. His mother's terror lived with them like a third child – or the ghost of one – and what Alan learned from it was that it was selfish to acknowledge fear.

He overtakes Brattle in the long cone of the shadow, and he thinks about the day his sister took him to the quarry to watch her burn a cardboard box. He was seven years old. He remembers the fire's wildness, its hunger as it burned fiber to smoke, and the beauty of its imitation of life. If this was the only memory of fire he had, he would have been content, but it is not to be. He is rushing headlong toward the door in the stone, which is roaring hot and billowing smoke. Brattle calls after him, trying to stop him, but he raises his masher against the ghoul's warnings.

The door splinters inward, leaving jagged points of cream-white wood that tug at his clothes as Alan pushes through it. In the burning foyer, a staircase rises up to the right toward a 90-degree elbow. The ceiling is groaning and swollen, about to give birth to a cascade of smoldering detritus. Waves of color flicker through the flames. Orbs chase each other through the living room, winking like stars in the rolling smoke. Alan heads left with fire dancing around him, oblivious to its caress, and he batters through the wreck of a collapsed bedroom to reach the open mouth of the basement.

"Da!" Alan cries. "Mister...Brattle! Hello! Is there anybody in here?"

The stone answers with a whisper of crawling flame. The basement is burning, too, but the fire here is slower. Alan leaps down a short flight of rough-cut stairs. He doesn't bother to get low as he walks through billowing veils of smoke. He's not even sure that he needs to breathe anymore.

"Hello!" he calls again. "Is anyone here? Answer me!"

The fire slinks over him, lapping at his face and hands. Pain is starting to tease him; the first stabs of heat threaten to bring him to his knees. He reaches back for the power of the bloom in his mind, seizing it where the dead are waiting in whispers. It moves something in him that pushes him forward into the purring darkness, where he finally finds the body of a ghoul lying limp on a pile of dirt.

For a second, something seems to be kneeling over Brattle's Da. The fire here is brighter, more alive, and it casts strange shadows. Alan sees a ridged back, the curve of shoulders, and the square of a chin before the flame whirls away, parting like a curtain over the ghoul's prostrate form.

Best to remain uncertain about some things, he thinks.

Da is still breathing. Alan heaves him up to stretch him across his shoulders, his masher now growing hot in his hand. On the ascent up the stairs, the fire swirls forth to block him. He surges through it, feeling his shirt catch across his back. He stops for a moment in the ruined living room, distracted by pain and the knot of fear in his throat. It's too bad he couldn't have seen this place before the fire took up residence here.

Ghouls live in rocks, he muses. *And they like to build in shadows. I guess that's not too surprising.*

Finally, he turns toward the front door, and he has to step through another ring of flame to get out into the grass beyond. Out in the cool air, he can feel his face again. It is cold and bare and hard with the wind sweeping across it. Rain begins, drowning the little flames that are spreading across his body as Brattle runs to meet him.

"Holy crap," Brattle nearly laughs. Fear is sinking around his cheekbones, drawing his features taut around his narrow skull. His stained-glass eyes seem to bulge. "Your face! Da! Is he alive?"

"We need to get him to the vultures," Alan says. He finds himself gasping. His pulse has returned to his neck, hard and racing.

Alan lays Brattle's Da on the ground. Brattle straddles his chest to pound his ribs.

"Ain't no time for that," Brattle curses. "Breathe, Da! Hey! It's Bratty-boy! You smoked tar all your life; don't tell me your lungs can't take this!"

The old ghoul's eyes move beneath tired, purple lids. He makes a sound like a cough, and then he slips away. The tension pours from his muscles like water, leaving him sagging on the grass.

Alan hears the voices of the dead in his ears now, as if they are at his shoulder all at once. There is a swelling in his chest – like the burning ceiling sagging with the weight of bookshelves and bathtubs, ready to burst. When it breaks, he finally falls to his knees, emptying power from his mouth and his hammering heart.

"Da!" Brattle cries, but then he recoils.

A charge warps the air. The voices of the dead rise horribly, straining as if competing to be the first to split Alan's head open. Alan presses his palms to his temples and feels rough bone there; the vultures' mask has burned away.

"What's that?" Brattle shouts. "Voices! Sweet pig-stealing Gwydion!"

Alan is about to ask, "You hear them, too?" before Brattle's Da starts convulsing.

The old ghoul's eyes snap open. They are black-amber and dead as pearl. A growl rolls from his throat, and he reaches for his son's neck with incredible speed.

Alan seizes control. He stems the flood inside himself, and spits it all out in a single word.

"STOP!"

At this, Brattle's Da wilts again. His grimace fades into a blissful frown. His hands fall, and he is dead.

Brattle stares, agog. For a few breaths' length, there is a black stillness hissing down with the rain. Alan tries to find some relief in it, but all his calm has burned away, too.

"What in the burning fuck was that?" Brattle asks.

Alan can only shake his head. His voice is lost for a moment. In the silence, the fire spits and screams. Rain rakes the field, slit from the bulge of an anvil cloud, and Alan can feel it running over his face and down under his collar.

Brattle gets to his feet. Alan watches him quake as everything collapses around him. The failing light of his whole life's pyre dances across his face. The clouds open up to release a deluge, and Brattle stands in it with his fists bunched, rain pouring from every angle of his face, but the fire continues to burn.

Brattle screams. The crows start from their branches, laughing after him as they head east. Alan's heart sickens and breaks, and dead murmurs trickle in to fill the split.

"I'm sorry," Alan tries. "He was all the way in the basement. I couldn't get to him soon enough."

Brattle ignores that. "Your face," he says. "You're freakin' *head*. Why'd you do that? Why'd you run in there? You're lucky it's just the magic that's gone. You got a deathwish, boy?"

Alan gets to his feet slowly, distrusting his legs. His knees strain to lift him. A cavalcade of dancing lights arrives on a low breeze, sweeping up from the roots of the grass in the shadow. They spread out into a sheet and fall over the dead ghoul's body, covering him in soft, scintillating hues. There isn't a single burn on him. But for the soft lines of age framing his mouth, Brattle's Da might be his twin. In death, he seems at peace, if a bit tired. The lights pulse over the corpse for a moment, and then there is a little airy rustle as the last traces of life rise out of him. Alan chokes on a sob as Da goes black in his new sight, and he wonders again where the next world is for ghouls.

"You've got no well, but there's water nearby," Alan tries. "I thought I heard shorebirds. We should start making trips. Do you have at least have a bucket?"

"Ain't no use," Brattle replies.

"But we have to try! The rain will help. Come on!"

Brattle shakes his head. "Water here ain't heavy enough to put out fire — at least not one this big. I've heard about your oceans and your weighty deeps, but that ain't what we got here. That fire's gonna burn, but it's got nowhere much to go through the stone. We'd best head up the hill with him."

"You want to leave?" Alan bites back a rush of anger.

"No," Brattle says. "Would you?"

But they do, Da with them on Alan's shoulders. While the fire plays through Brattle's meteor, they climb the crater wall toward a dense windbreak of black-needled trees.

At eighty-five, Alan's grandfather slipped while mowing his lawn and lost two-and-a-half toes from his right foot. Alan thinks of this now just as he had the night a police officer explained that his parents had died.

At some point, we think we've put the worst perils behind us. The fires are out and the anvil's behind us; we're as tested as we're going to be. We come to this so casually and we become so certain that we can't help but be blindsided: there's always a new horror.

"I'm sorry," Alan says as they lay the old ghoul down. "This is all my fault. You saved me, but I've only brought you this."

Brattle doesn't reply. His eyes are like stained glass. He's watching his home burn from a million miles away. In the jaws of grief, he looks small and powerless.

The dead fall silent in Alan's mind. They have what they came for.

The downpour slacks to a tender drizzle as they climb the hill behind Brattle's house. It's an easy walk with the wind behind them. At the worn crest, they lay the old ghoul on his back on a bed of thorns, crossing his bone-thin arms over his chest, and Brattle looks down into the crater for a long time.

He runs his hands over the ridges beneath his eyes where his cheeks used to be.

"Talk to me," he says. "Come on. Look at me."

Brattle turns. Alan sees himself in the pearl mirrors of his eyes; his skull is as white as bleach. His vacant smile cuts cold between his naked mandibles, seemingly pegged together by his gumless teeth.

Not so much a slave to the physical anymore, hmm?

"It's even worse than what the Venue had to heal before. Ya look like you belong here now, at least," Brattle jokes, his face dark with rage. "A regular freak."

"What do we do know?" Alan asks. His voice is still an echo from outside him. He finds he can push it now without thinking about it too much. He pitches it up a bit, allowing it to grow a hooked snarl, and is happy with the results. "Focus for me. I can see your anger rolling off you like red smoke. Can it point us in the right direction?"

Brattle frowns. "Ain't no right direction. We can ask who did this, but it's easier to ask who didn't. That's a shorter list. Folks don't like us ghouls, boss."

"You've had trouble before?"

"We always have. That's why we stick to the outlands. In the cities, they wait for us with guns and rocks. They bind us up by our wrists and lock us in labs to be pulled apart and tested on, or they take us to the gallows. Out here, it's just the occasional vandal with have to deal with."

He blinks away a tear. It falls down his gaunt face to fatten just at the line of his jaw. All of Brattle's long life is in it, beaming green rays.

Alan has to press forward against the tidal surge of sorrow.

"There must be someone who's been around recently. Your Da isn't burned; he didn't try to get out. He was in the basement – like he was waiting. I think it must have been someone he knew."

Brattle stands up and begins pacing. Where he plants his bare feet, he stirs up little flutters of fairy lights. They swing like lanterns in the wind. "It's my house," he says. "Da lives in Sepulchra. He didn't know anyone out here."

A sudden movement makes Alan spin on his heel. A shape appears in the rain, its long form sketched out in little rivulets. Brattle scowls at it, otherwise unaffected. It trickles into the grass, hands clasped before it as if in prayer, and it speaks to them in the hiss of the wind.

"Master Brattle sir, and friend," says the rain-thing. "Hear me! I offer my condolences."

Brattle bunches up like a cobra. His face lights up in anger, and Alan puts his arm up reflexively to prevent him from leaping forward. Brattle easily ducks under it and stands before the rain spirit again with his eyes flashing.

"What are you? New dead?" Brattle hisses. "This ain't the time, Shimmer. Can you see?" He swings his arm wide in a gesture toward the lump of his father. "Da's dead. He's dead, Shimmer! And the meteor's burning. Can you see that? Da's dead. Just dribble away. If you got any sense, you'll slip off now and leave us to this." Something floods his voice and he swallows, his eyes shining with tears.

Alan takes up his masher again.

"You're the thing from the basement," he says, stepping his best challenge forward. Is this thing even physical? How his shackles have slipped! He should be proud, but he's only white-knuckled with alarm. In his head, the drum of his pulse is running wild. "I saw you in the fire!"

"Step off," Brattle barks. He shoulders Alan aside to step between him and the Shimmer. "Shim didn't cause this. He's just here to hawk his white drops." And then, to the spirit, "Trespassin' me again, and at the worst possible time!"

"My business is urgent," Shimmer replies. It moves forward a space, and more of its body trickles into view. It appears to be male. Its eyes are little gems of water twinkling in the sunlight. "I can offer aid. I saw who did this."

Brattle grits his teeth in a black-gapped scowl.

"Who? Tell me, Shimmer. Tell me."

The Shimmer wavers. Like a mist, he separates for a moment. In his core, Alan sees Shimmer's heart shining like a chip of obsidian. Then he pulls himself back together around his pouring face, and puts his hand on Brattle's shoulder.

"It was Nettle," he says. "Your brother. I saw him, and he saw me, not a minute after the flames went up. I'm sorry."

Alan stands stunned. Brattle balls up tight again. The muscles along his spine clench so tightly that Alan can see the sinews straining.

"*Damn* it," Brattle whispers. "Da always trusted him — always! — but I never did. Never! I knew he was a black omen the day he broke out of that green egg!"

Alan looks at the Shimmer, who moves as if he is shrugging. His voice arises in Alan's mind.

Ghouls are born from eggs, the Shimmer says. *Healthy eggs are white. Black and green are rare.*

Alan stares. He feels dirty from the intrusion. It's yet another thing to push aside, and he realizes that the pressure is building up. For the first time, it becomes evident that Graveworld is fully capable of breaking him.

"Why would he do this?" Alan asks, but Brattle isn't listening. Instead, the ghoul breaks out in a scream to which distant dogs reply with a chorus of howls.

"I'm sorry to deliver such news," the Shimmer says. "He went east under guard. They were fairies, black-armored, on foot."

Brattle screams himself to his knees. When he is hoarse and coughing, he permits himself to stop.

"He was with umans?" Brattle wheezes. "That ain't right. Are you sure it was him?"

"I was able to get a good look."

The rain stops, and the clouds part around the golden orb of the nearest sun. The furthest peers through the parting film, stymied but determined. The Shimmer takes on the character of light, becoming nearly invisible when he stands still.

"I saw 'im," Brattle says. He spreads his hands out in front of him. "I saw 'im and his black band in the woods a day or so after I left! It was a troupe of umans — I didn't give it another thought. He's been followin' me! Probably us. Maybe since the beginning."

"We're jumping pretty far ahead here," Alan says. "Who do we call about this? How do we catch him?"

81

Brattle stands. He glares at the Shimmer as best he can, as it is merely a glint above the grass. He casts Alan's question aside and curls his fists on his thighs.

"Show me your wares, Shimmer," he says.

"What?" Now Shimmer moves. He darts on the breeze like a butterfly, barely leaving impressions where he stands. "There are better times. You said so yourself."

Brattle hacks a growl from the pit of his throat. "Now's perfect. All your tinctures. Show me."

Shimmer dims in shame. Finally, his full form appears. He is golden and clear, his proportions perfect. He has short hair and even teeth. He frowns, and the lines that pull his cheeks toward his ears are completely symmetrical.

"I cannot," he says.

Brattle approaches the Shimmer as if to push him, but the Shimmer is as empty as air. Brattle waves his hands through the fading vision, scattering particles of the spirit away from him.

"How many?" he demands.

"All of my store," Shimmer replies. "Including yours," he points to Brattle's Da, "and his."

"What's going on?" Alan asks.

"He's covering for someone," Brattle explains, "in exchange for souls. A lot of 'em, sounds like, if they bought you out. You bleeding traitor."

"Please," the Shimmer says. "I'm trying to make this right! I couldn't refuse payment. I have hungers to feed, master! But I'm no betrayer. It was Nettle, I swear it! In a battalion of fairy soldiers. They went east, and that's all I know!"

"You asked what happens here after you die," Brattle says to Alan, his eyes on Shimmer. "This is one answer. His kind eats souls, but they ain't physical. They trade white drops for the souls of ghoulish prey. We eat the bodies and they move in: the soul jackals. Spiritual carrion feeders."

"What are white drops?" Alan asks.

"Water from the Kodash Stone," Shimmer says, "prized for its restorative properties."

"Or milk with gold flakes dabbed in," Brattle laughs. "This one's been selling to me for years. I was a fool to trust him, and I won't be any longer. Tell me what's next, spirit! An ambush in the woods? How were you to get my soul from me?"

The Shimmer seems to sigh. The sound comes whistling out of him like the wind over the lip of a jar. "They are waiting at Debtors' Orchard to surprise you."

"Ah!" Brattle laughs. "Now I *know* yer lyin'! That's just where we was talking about going before. You really are a miserable liar. I can't believe I pitied you all this time!"

With this, Brattle heads for the path down the hill and motions for Alan to follow him. Alan stays for a moment, stricken dim and sluggish. He watches the Shimmer move over the body of Brattle's Da, his hands trembling at his beltline, where he holds his masher.

"Brattle is hardened against my counsel now, master," says the shining spirit, "but I hope that you will know better than he. You're quite a special little thing, aren't you? Stay away from Debtor's Orchard for a few days, Alan."

"We'll find you," Alan says, trying to sound as hard as Brattle. He can't muster the fury; he's sagging over himself, weak to whatever is left of his core. "We'll find Nettle first, and then we'll find you."

The Shimmer doesn't reply. Alan turns his back as the spirit leans down close to the old ghoul's face. He is following Brattle down the path toward the windbreak as the Shimmer teases the light of Da's spirit from his corpse and begins to consume it.

Ten

Animals are calling across the woods. Their songs are low and sad along careful pitchings; the answering changes bleed together across storm-wet distances into something familiar. It's the voice of Alan's headaches they're singing – the howl of nothing – or a close enough harmony with it. As he and Brattle descend the hill toward the trees, Alan can see the singers' long necks moving far away.

The Shimmer follows them for a while, turning through the underbrush like a little wind. He brings the hungry dead with him; Alan can hear them in his head. Where the Shimmer moves, purple runs through the air in great billows.

"You left him," Alan says to Brattle. He immediately regrets it.

Brattle pushes ahead with nothing to say for a long time. When he does speak, his voice is cold and collapsed.

"We don't eat our own," he replies.

"Eat him?" Alan frowns. "I was thinking we might bury him."

"Ah, no," Brattle explains through a sigh. "Dirt's no good here. Ground don't hold most of the time. Not unless you bury alive."

A violent shiver bashes its way up Alan's spine, leaving him gritting his teeth. His head screams with devils. The back of his tongue tastes like hot vinegar. It's been six months since his sister's funeral: Graceland Memorial Park in the fog, the trees weeping down over the tarpaulin shroud and the willow coffin.

"Tell me about the Shimmer," Alan says, trying to get Brattle's mind off his suffering. It's a doomed effort.

"Not much to tell," Brattle answers. "He's a hedge spirit, a salamander, comes around on a calendar, roughly regular, and sells to huntsmen and killers. Best indulged, not that I don't regret it now."

84

Alan spins his trash masher in his hand. His fingers are slow with pain and clumsy. He drops the masher, and Brattle scowls back at him as he scoops it up again.

"I saw him in the basement," Alan says. "He was kneeling. It was like he was made of fire. When I got close, he vanished."

Brattle says nothing to this. They are nearing the sagging carrion flowers where Alan dropped the pack. He tries in vain to avert his gaze from the smoking meteor and the fiery dancers in the highest windows.

"Do you believe him?" Alan asks. "Are we going to Debtors' Orchard?"

"*We* ain't doing anything," Brattle says as he stoops to strap the pack over his shoulders. "I'm taking you to my cousin Shal's and heading east alone."

They are standing in the crater. Evening is closing upon them like a trap, its edges hard and seething-black. Alan can feel it heavy around his heart.

"I'm sorry," he says, and he finds himself sucking back sobs.

"We been bad for each other," Brattle says. "When the levee breaks, it's gonna be worse. Yer losin' yer head – and not just the skin. You've reached your breaking point, and you need a bath, a soft bed, and a long rest before you collapse completely. You need to be somewhere safe when that happens. It's the least I can do for pushin' you to the gate when neither you nor it was ready."

"You're not going on without me," Alan asserts, though he knows that Brattle is right. The real is rushing his gates, getting tangled in the clamor. It's the shadowstorm wailing over the marsh where he awoke, the dead whispering through the Kingwatcher's bloom, the scream of brakes grinding toward him, and the empty voice of the freezer at Ray's all whirling together against his last bulwarks.

"Oh no? 'Cause you look ready to faint."

"I still owe you."

"Consider all debts abolished," Brattle scowls. "I'm taking you north to my cousin's place, and then I'm moving on, and I won't stand for any arguing."

At this a crying begins in the distance. It drowns the calls of the long-necked singers as it rises, blown up from the tomblands and drawing nearer. Brattle turns, his eyes dancing with fire; Alan has never seen anything like it. Everything he feels, every thought in his head, races backward across the screens of Brattle's eyes in a red-gold blur.

"Dammit," he says.

"Moaners?" Alan asks.

"Who knows?" Brattle replies. "Hear those drums? That's a hob march. They must have brought something with them. There's no going back that way now." He cinches the pack's straps tighter and spits a curse into the grass. "Looks like you're getting your way after all, lumpy. Come on. And try not to lose your mind before we find a safe place to hunker down for the night – or at all, if you can help it."

The carrion flowers sway a cloud of spores and a smell like rotting meat into the night air. Alan swallows, takes three long breaths, and tries to pull himself together. He's always been good at integrating, but he's never been in a situation like this before. He can't push away the intense feeling of removal, so he resolves to focus on it. As he and Brattle hurry away from the approaching mayhem, he succeeds in patching himself into clarity one more time, though he feels the press of chaos at the stitches. It won't be long before he spills out of himself, and then what will he do?

"Destiny?" he tries a joke. To his relief, Brattle gives him a smile. It's what he needed to ensure his sanity for the next few hours. "Too convenient, right? Smack of coincidence?"

"Move your ass and save the boasting," Brattle says. "You're already minus a face; self-congratulation don't look any better on you."

The stars dim out behind a spreading pall, though the sky is cloudless. The moon does not appear. Pale dusk drowns to a blind midnight, and the hobs' march continues in the northwest. Alan holds up his phone, as he used to while walking home from Ray's in the dark. It is a weak light, but he can walk by it.

"When Allison died," Alan explains, "I had to come home to put her affairs in order."

He talks to vent the pressure in his mind. Brattle offers the occasional grunt in reply, but he isn't really listening. Alan can tell. He can see the storm of Brattle's troubled thoughts swirling around his nodding head. Worries dance around him like little candles, illuminating nothing.

Alan continues. "I had little things working in Chicago, but they couldn't help me when I had to leave. I got set back to square one. Ray's was walking-distance away, and they were the only place to call me back when I applied."

They reach a bridge across a stinking river. Debtors' Orchard sits quiet on the other side, its rows of shrubs and stunted trees lit softly by lean swarms of hobby lanterns.

Through the cluttered aisles, from tree to tree and between the vine-hung trellises, a shape is moving, tall and thin as a willow sapling. It stoops as it walks, and it drags a bag behind it through the grass. Alan doesn't like the way the bag is shaped. The figure is wrapped in scar-white robes and violet sashes, and the strange angles of its raiment distort its shape as it moves among the flitting ghost lights. The point of a wide hood hangs low over its face, leaving its head in shadow. There is an emptiness about it that makes Alan heartsick. Where it goes, the orbs wink out; it snatches them from the air or from the low boughs of trees and eats them.

Alan and Brattle watch the wandering shape from a hedge along the riverbank.

"The Cuco," Brattle whispers, his eyes growing wide. "What's brought him up from the sloughs, I wonder?"

"What is it?" Alan asks.

Brattle puts his finger to his lips and says nothing more, and the Cuco heads north across the orchard, leaving darkness behind him and Alan's heart twitching in his throat. He tells himself to take comfort in that feeling.

The hobs' march is still drumming. The sound is nearer now and picking up speed. It will soon be right at their backs. Alan and Brattle creep beneath the bridge. The dark water laps at their toes, and they hug their knees with their backs against the mud bank.

The river mutters. The power of the old dead swells from underground to creak a cold wind through the orchard trees. When the hobs arrive, they start across the bridge without looking over the side, pulling a stomping fury with them to the beat of their drums. The sounds it makes are chilling, but they are not the shrieks Alan and Brattle heard earlier; these are hollow and tired, the sad fuming of a fettered beast.

Alan pushes the heels of his palms hard into the bone-rimmed pits of his eyes. A headache arrives, burning across his cranium like a comet. The lonely plaint of the shackled creature pounds into the hollows of his temples, and a tremor shoots up his spine. He arches up in a waking seizure, unable to stifle a chest-deep gnarl of pain, and knocks his head against the foot of the bridge. Brattle grabs Alan and leans on him.

"Shhhh," he rasps.

Claws drag the wood overhead. The march stops amid shouts, and a minute strains by with Alan trying to keep from bucking under Brattle's weight.

The hobs wonder to each other in a strange tongue of chirps and clicks. Alan thinks about the ladies in the kitchen at Ray's — their conversations in Spanish streaming out between them like ribbons. Hobbish speak is the same way, even with the captive monster growling under it. This is something he can sink into — something he can hide inside — while the shivers race through his muscles.

"Wak-wak," they say amongst themselves. "Tik-tik."

Leaders confer above. Scouts wade out into the reeds on the wrong side of the river. After much fruitless splashing, their snarling arguments ascend the bank again, and the bridge shakes as the march moves on, adequately reassured that their quarry remains ahead of them.

Alan's seizure leaves the wraith of pain in his shoulders when it ends. Chains clink and quirts snap as the hobs nag their monster. It isn't long before the march is across the river and gone, but it's almost an hour before Alan and Brattle feel safe enough to move.

The ghoul is the first to speak.

"Well that was exciting," he whispers.

"I'm sorry," Alan says, trying to find his breath again. It eludes him, and he continues without it. "I haven't had a seizure in a few months."

"You got excellent timing," Brattle replies. "What was that, anyway?"

Alan sits up carefully and reaches back to squeeze his shoulder. "I think I deserve a pass on this one."

Brattle unfurls slowly, like a night bloom, his great eyes burning careful light as he peers into the shadows above them. The only sound now is the mumbling of the river; the bridge is still.

"The hobs sure are persistent," he croaks. "Good thing they're also stupid."

"What was that they had with them?" Alan asks.

"Brunnmigi, maybe. Some great, black well-pisser they must've drug up from the corpse-fiords. Nobody knows much about hobs. Nobody cares much to. What they do in their secret covens is a mystery to me."

"Do you understand their language?" Alan asks. "What were they saying?"

Brattle replies with a derisive snort. "They say a lot around here that hobbish isn't real talk – just noises they hear each other make and imitate. Like I said: hobs are stupid."

Alan sags over his knees, reaching down to pull at the wet top of his sock. He must have dipped his foot in the river at some point.

"I almost got us killed," he says.

Brattle settles sleepily into a curl. "Well, the night's still young."

The wind stirs like a lover in the arms of the trees, breathing sweet nothings on the smell of dead flesh and distant fire. Alan stares up at the grey moss creeping across the boards above him and the glowing orbs that move just beneath it, coaxing patches of it down into little beards.

"Was it good work at least?" Brattle mutters, green sparks twining into the remnants of his hair.

"What?"

Alan tries to stretch without putting his feet in the river again. His back aches, and the tops of his calves are burning.

"Ray's," Brattle replies. "You were saying earlier."

"Oh," Alan says, clearing his throat. He has learned to control his strange, detached voice. When he focuses, he can make it sound as if it's coming from his mouth. "It's not bad, but it's not very rewarding. It's the same thing over and over: cooking meat and making sandwiches. Good enough for a paycheck, I guess."

Brattle nods. He finagles an awkward sprawl in the mud. The drums finally fall silent in the distance. The monster's elegiac howls give way to night noises that are only slightly less terrible.

"Cursed shades used to work these orchards a long time ago," Brattle says. "Bad souls, lonely spirits from the living world – this was one of the places where they were punished. But that stopped, and now the orchard grows wild."

"Why did it stop?" Alan asks.

"I don't know," Brattle replies. "Why does anything stop? The world moved on. "

Alan wishes for tears that don't come, and he laughs at himself.

"I'm so sorry about your Da," he says.

Brattle sighs. "Don't be, but thanks. We abolished all debts, remember? We're even. Just try and sleep if you can – if you still do. There's work for tomorrow."

Sleep proves elusive, but insomnia is at least a familiar misery. Worse than lying awake and restless is Alan's growing suspicion that he isn't fully human anymore. He listens to the inconstant murmur of his pulse and the echo of his breath in his lungs and he feels like a new creature. Light moves behind his eyelids, a persistent afterimage of the otherworldy flame that disfigured him. What other scars are there for Alan to find? He's already unable to stop running his hands over his bare skull. If he were to probe his psyche – or his spirit, whatever that might be – would he feel worse wounds there?

It's dawn when slumber takes Alan, and his anxiety follows him into the new world of his dreams. It bites at him in alleys under palls of watching shadow. It stares at him through curtains of vulture feathers, its eyes like smoke and stained glass. Sentient and hostile, it hunts him relentlessly. There is a ragged edge to his nightmares now. Alan feels the waking world bleeding upon it, fresh and open. He can't let go anymore; a savage lucidity taunts him, pins him in place with anxiety pulling at his teeth and hair. Symbols of control vanish, and symbols of fear replace them.

Alan's dreams are shallow and self-aware. When he wakes from them, the sun is high and he is not restored. Graveworld is sitting on him, holding him still, every bit as there as it has ever been. He struggles and tries to deny it, straining against a dozen new aches to get up and keep going. But he isn't in control anymore; death has taken that from him. Alan is at the mercy of outrageous circumstance, and he can't sustain the burden. He sinks back into another seizure until Brattle splashes oily water in his face.

"Wake up," the ghoul hacks, his morning coughs like dead wood splintering. "This is exactly why I wanted to leave you behind!"

Alan stares up at the bands of light streaming through the bridge boards and can't move for a long time. There is a riot in his throat; a war of sounds he cannot produce roils up from his quivering diaphragm. A knot swells in his chest, squeezes up under his heart to bang there like a trapped animal, and leaves Alan clutching his left side against terrifying pain. Coming down is like deflating; he is limp and empty afterward, even when he finds the strength to sit up.

"I'm OK," he says, the rumble in his throat dropping heavily into his stomach. "I just had a bad dream."

"Dreaming's dangerous here," Brattle replies. "You wanna avoid it if you can. We're too close to the dreaming place; things get raw, turn real. It ain't safe – 'specially since you already seem inclined to funny turns."

"I can go on," Alan asserts. He feels bold claiming such certainty. "What's in the Orchard that we're looking for?"

"Answers," Brattle says. His doubt has dripping fangs. "And maybe a little bit of relief for you, too. Can't quite say that for sure, though."

Alan gets to his feet and stoops out from under the bridge. His pants and shoes are wet and covered in mud. There are stains on the backs of his short sleeves. He can no longer tell the smears of grease from the other spots on his uniform shirt.

He digs into his pocket for his phone and draws it out slowly. His fingers brush the smooth surface of a glass vial that had not been there before. He decides to wait before bringing this up to Brattle.

"Are we going anywhere near this?" he asks, touching the screen and showing Brattle the numbers glowing there.

The ghoul leans in, sniffing through his battish nose. "I don't know where that is," he snorts. "Remember? But we might be able to find that out, too, for whatever it's worth."

Brattle leads the way up the bank and across the bridge, which is stained an ancient white and girded on both sides by dark beams with brass caps. Signs of the hobs' passing are plentiful:

the wood is gouged deep and stomped in dirty circles all the way to the opposite bank, where the mud is churned up in a westward arc.

Where grass swallows the track, the orchard opens out through a dense hedge of shrubs. The air is thick with heat and rich with the smell of giant fruits that hang blood-red in shapeless trees. Debtors' Orchard goes on into the north for acres, but Brattle's destination is a chalk dome under a black chimney at the near edge of the inner field. As they approach the structure, Brattle searches the shadowed groves with his hand on his little dagger.

He stops at the edge of a little dugout and stands looking down into it while Alan catches up.

"The last of many such ditches," he explains. "The rest were closed up long ago. Some pains stay around in the soil and won't be hid or washed out."

Alan hitches the pack up higher on his back. "You said they used to torture people here?" he asks.

"Yeah," Brattle replies. "You can still feel it a bit, but don't get caught up. Walk fast for this last space, and try not to deviate."

Alan sighs. "*Everything's* dangerous here."

The last few yards to the little hut narrow down into a corridor between towering fruit trees. Alan has never seen anything like them before. He doesn't look long at the bunched drupes rotting above them or the huge bats sleeping upside-down in the middle boughs. He tries not to think about the long thorns at the end of every low branch. When shadows move beneath the trees, he turns the other way and bites back his questions. The little wood seems long, and it watches them with familiar eyes. Alan is glad when he and Brattle emerge from under its grasping canopy.

"The Kingwatcher," he says, thinking aloud.

"Following us," Brattle answers. Then he corrects himself. "Following you."

"Why?" Alan asks.

The chalk hut has one door and no windows. Its roof is laid with tarry tiles to a copper gutter, which is choked with leaves and birds' nests in several places. It sits on a little hill, leaning a bit, the lawn rolling out gently from its porch. Standing as tall as he gets on the front step, Brattle grasps the iron knocker in both hands.

"Answers," he says, and he raps three times into moon-cold emptiness.

The whispering dead are quiet, but he can still feel them where they lie. They wave little red flags of light from the mounds behind the house. Their lights dance the roof in lazy rows.

Alan is watching himself from somewhere close by. Perhaps he is in the dark under the bat-hung trees or in the well by the little outbuilding with the props of its sweep in disrepair. He feels disturbed and ashamed of his weakness for being so, but there is a healing essence in this place.

Brattle knocks again.

"Who are we here for?" Alan asks.

"Pwysh," says Brattle, "the resident thaumaturge."

Alan crosses his arms over his chest and swallows over his hammering pulse.

"Well, I don't think he's home."

The ghoul returns to his quadruped crouch and fusses about the doorstep for a moment, digging around as if for a key.

"This ain't his home," Brattle replies. "This is his office. He don't tell no one where his home is as a matter of principle." He seems to be quoting this last bit. "But he's almost always here."

"Remember what the Shimmer said," Alan starts to say, and this only seems to make Brattle angry.

Brattle grunts, spits a curse, and drives his shoulder into the door. It crashes open, jarred sideways on its six brass hinges, and Brattle tumbles head over heels into a mess of papers, books, and broken furniture.

Alan follows just in time to catch a large amber orb as it is falling. He helps Brattle up, the orb in the crook of his arm, and then looks around the room with what might have been wide-eyed wonder had he more than empty orbits where his eyes should be. He whistles breathlessly and is briefly distracted by the strangeness of this sound.

"This ain't good," Brattle mutters as he dusts himself off. "This place has been turned over. What in the *hell* is going on here?"

There is an iron furnace in the center of the room around which the interior design must have been based, but little aesthetic remains now. Three enormous bookcases are lying atop each other like dominoes, their contents scattered across the floor. Broken glass shines from under piles of chairs, and the ringed countertops are covered in lamp oil. Loose leaves of paper are blowing out the door, flapping over each other to show line after line of tiny writing when they stick on the jamb.

"What does Pwysh *do* here?" Alan asks. "Potions and old books…and this?" He holds up the amber orb.

Brattle begins to claw through the heap toward the center of the room, where the stove lies still and appears to have been cold for some time.

"Bone-conjurer. He raises the dead," says the ghoul after some hesitation. "But I don't think he's going to be doing much of that here no more."

"Raises the dead?"

The words seem heavy. Alan struggles to get them past his lips, and once said they leave him with a shudder in his shoulders.

He picks his way along the wall, one hand trailing over the stone and the other holding the amber globe out in front of him. He steps over spilled drawers and around tipped shelves, and he lets the curious power of the place flow through him. Warmth moves over his skin, enfolds him, and sinks to his bones. The walls are bare but for a line of painted symbols that runs under the crown molding. Alan turns where he stands, following the symbols as they circle the room. He recognizes some of them as the symbols on his phone, and he is about to point them out to Brattle when a shape catches his eye.

There is a corpse in a torn cassock lying half out of the debris.

"Here," Alan says. "Oh, god. Brattle, I think I found him."

Brattle hops over sideways, a water-stained book in one hand.

"I guess I was more right than I thought," he says. "Pwysh never hurt anyone. Why do this? What the hell is Nettle's game? Help me."

Pwysh is pinned under a bookcase. Even with Brattle's strength, it takes a long time to pull him out into the open. Alan is revolted just touching the body. The skin is as dry as paper. Pwysh's weight is all in the center of his body, where his insides have settled. His cassock slides up briefly as they drag him, showing the dark spots of pooling blood in his abdomen. They lay Pwysh as near as they can to the west wall, his arms up like a referee, and Brattle crouches over him to prod his cheeks.

"Only a few days, I'd guess," Brattle sighs. "Can't never tell for sure, though. You wanna help me cut his gown open, babyface?"

Alan doesn't want to think about that question right now. He hangs on to silence as long as he can as he looks the body over. Pwysh looks mostly human. He is dark with high cheekbones and knob-knuckled fingers as long as crabs' legs. His amber eyes rolling unfettered in his head. His goateed chin sags, leaving Pwysh gaping as if in stupid shock.

Alan can't look at that dead face for too long before a retch rolls up his throat; he finally excuses himself to get some air, and then he spends several minutes doubled over with his hands on his knees.

"I'm sorry," he hears Brattle say from inside the hut. "I'm real sorry."

The little building's healing energy has gone sour. Where Alan had felt purified, he now feels sad and offended. He pumps a few careful breaths through his open mouth, trying not to fight

96

what might be coming, but the twist in Alan's gut dissipates with no upheaval. He's glad for this for all of a second before an armed band of hobs steps from the wood trees to surround him.

"There be him," chatters the nearest hob. He is huge, and he has paint on his face declaring him the leader. "Him living man what robbed from us and killed us. There he is, just as she told he'd be."

Eleven

Debtors' Orchard begins to sway. All around the little hut, the trees nod apart, and hobs of many kinds emerge from beneath them. Some are swart and thin with long hair rolling untied over broad shoulders and red armor. Others are almond-eyed and as pale as bone riding bareback on tall leopards. They close in across the grass, withered blossoms whirling up to fall around them. The bats rise from their roosts to darken the sky in a rankled, flapping cloud.

The air seems to shrink around Alan. His heart feels small in his chest. It taps only occasionally along with his thready breath. He lets the pack slide from his shoulders, but he doesn't feel any lighter. He takes up his trash masher as Brattle appears in the doorway behind him.

"I'm damned," says the ghoul, his voice like the twang of a taut band when plucked. "Shimmer set us up."

Alan was thinking just the opposite. Quickly, distractedly, he reaches into his pocket to finger the little vial there.

"What now?" he says. "I don't imagine they want to take us prisoner."

Before Brattle can answer, a mourning cry rings up through the orchard woods. Thorned branches crash aside, and the hobs' beast comes staggering into the open, a glaring of cat riders preceding it.

It is no longer chained.

"Wherever you've been all my life," Brattle says to Alan, "I'm really starting to wish you'd stayed there."

The monster waits at the edge of the wood. Its handlers mill about its feet, lashing up at its shoulders with their quirts, and it watches them with a strange light in its three eyes. Worse than its hanging jaw and white-horned head — worse than the quills bristling down its tail and the shriveled wings convulsing pitifully upon its back — is the wounded look it gives its captors. It groans as they ride around it, and the longing in its voice sinks a stone into Alan's stomach.

"Look how they torture it," he says to Brattle.

"I never seen no grave raiders organized like this," Brattle says by way of a reply. "What the hell *is* this?"

The hobs move into a formation across the lawn. Pipers in their midst blow a pinched melody, the rings in their ears swinging as they cut slow capers through the approaching lines. It's hard to tell how many hobs there are while they're moving; there is an empyreal quality to them in a certain light. They flicker from time to time, real as candles' flames and just as fickle. The brunnmigi shuffles along after them, quirted on exuberantly by its handlers, watching the hobs closely as they move through its shadow.

The trees quake apart again, and another figure emerges just above the broken line of an ancient fence. Tall and sapling-thin astride her razor-backed cat, wrapped in blue and fur collars, she commands a retinue of swart retainers that are certainly not hobs. Her hair is the color of Indian black earth. She runs a hand through it to pin it back with a silver barrette. There is so much strange power about her, and she is so gruesomely beautiful, that Alan cannot look away. He even takes a step forward, and he isn't sure that he's not going to start off across the field toward her, but Brattle brings him back to himself with a hand on his shoulder.

"Winter White," he whispers.

"Brattle Busaw," Winter calls from her bejeweled saddle. The air hums with her voice, beating like bats' wings at her will to carry her words across the Orchard. "We found your brother trying to leave a trail for you. He's dead, and you'll be his replacement."

"What?" Brattle's brows climb the curve of his forehead. He sags over the knobs of his knees and wobbles for an instant, as if struck in the back.

"Take the ghoul and kill the other one."

With this, the hobs move in concert. The generals of the gathered tribes shout to each other in their stuttering tongue.

"Tik-tik! Soc-soc! Wak-wak!"

The rest disappear beneath the rolling howls of the brunnmigi, which takes a few hesitant steps forward while its handlers busy themselves whipping it.

"Get inside," Brattle hisses. "Maybe we can finesse a way out of this before that army of anklebiters can beat the walls down."

Alan takes up his trash masher. It sits in his hands, its weight perfect, finally promising freedom. This isn't the trash corral in the parking lot at Ray's, where shame watches him from the top of every wall — where fear commands him like a god. This is the chance to take the sad stuff of his life and smash it into something better. The hobs are coming, Brattle begs him to fall back, but the bloom of Minos is opening further in Alan's mind. Graveworld's heart is beating in his chest, and he has neither the strength nor the desire to run anymore. At this moment, looking down into the flaming crater of his hopes, he has only the will to fight left in him.

The trash masher's shaft thrums in Alan's hands. White light arcs along it to spark from the crushing end. Alan feels the light leaving him and looks down, worried that he might be bleeding. He pours himself into his weapon insofar as he can, wanting to swing with it every last scintilla of anger and frustration he's ever known.

The first hobs to meet him on Pwysh's stoop feel the burden of all his wasted years. He swings in a rich frenzy, delivering hard and bloody ends in great clouts, while Brattle barricades himself in the hut. He has worked out his stance, his two-armed lift, and twirls over his head into wide strikes around him. He knows his weapon. Nonetheless, it's not like he imagined when it was just a way to kill time; the sudden stop of his masher in a hob's skull is jarring and leaves his wrists aching after less than three minutes. When Alan has tired himself out, when he has had time to think about the few lives he's left fading behind him, the hobs form a ring around him.

"Soc-soc," they laugh, sword tips bobbing in the air. "Tik-tik!"

Alan hazards a glance back to see more hobs banging at Pwysh's broken door with hammers. It won't last much longer. The white light is fading from his masher, draining away with his strength. Should he plead for his life? Should he die fighting? Nothing has prepared him for this. He pushes against monstrous fear and the chains of his old life in the land of the living. In his last moment, he will not be Alan Shade – his skull grin chipped and orbits broken wide, he will be the Grim Reaper.

The hobs hesitate. The brunnmigi is howling. Its calls shake the ground, and its keepers are scattered. It will come for him now, and it will crush him in its mouth, and there will be no last push toward heroism for Alan today.

The hobs surrounding him fall away, cowering, and the monster charges across the lawn with its arms outstretched, but when it attacks it sends its captors bleeding into the dirt. It has rebelled, and Alan marvels.

Winter White is gone with her retinue. Alan backs toward the hut, where the hobs have dropped their hammers as they fled into the forest. The brunnmigi lays waste to White's small army in a frothing fit, and it scatters the wellstones and the timbers of the sweep with a single swat. Cats howl as the generals flee; the monster leaves the animals alive and strikes their riders from their saddles to crush them underfoot. What few arrows the hobs manage to loose in its direction only seem to irritate the brunnmigi. After the archers fall, the beast combs the field to defile the dead.

Brattle hurries to let Alan in and then tips a cabinet onto the drooping door, propping it up as best he can. He pants and clutches his chest, his dappled eyes bulging wide with fright, and Alan kneels to try to calm him. It's a difficult task; fear is pounding through Alan as well, and Brattle can easily see it.

"I killed them," is the first thing Alan says. He leaves this hanging in the air for a moment while he considers it, and then he decides that he has to continue for his own sake. The bloodlust is leaving him, and it hurts wherever it recedes. "That didn't go as they'd planned. The hobs are dead or scattered. I killed them, but I had to. We're safe here, but I hope I never have to again. What a waste. What a total fucking waste."

Brattle tilts him a frown. "You got a messed up idea of safe. With that horror rampant out there?" He hunches and hugs himself through shivers. Though terrified, he is able to find it in himself to chuckle. "Well-pisser went mad, I take it? I'm failing to see the surprise."

Alan smiles, amused that a thing like Brattle would refer to something else as a horror. Then he puts his ear to the wall and listens to the brunnmigi wailing and thrashing through Pwysh's yard.

"It sounds like it's moving off," Alan says. "Winter White took off, too – probably at first sight of her monster turning the tables. What did she mean about you being a replacement?"

Brattle sinks into himself a bit. He stops his quaking, and Alan finds this more disturbing than relieving. A shadow falls across his gaunt face.

"I got no idea," he intones. "But me and that bitch got a squabble now, I'll tell you. When I find her, I'll pull Winter White apart – for Da, and for Nettle," he sucks a wet hiss and bites the inside of his cheek, "the rat-bastard. I'm never sure whether to be thankful for you or to curse the day I found you in the swamp. You got a mean luck about you, and it comes with a cost."

Pwysh's workshop shakes with Pwysh's body in it. The mess on the floor shifts, spitting up a smaller mess of drawers and crystals and big rings of keys. Outside, the dead are stirring. Alan can feel them in new parts of himself; their graves are like beacons, and all the world's a grave from a great enough distance.

Suddenly, Brattle's face lights up. From a hunching silence, he springs up and snaps his fingers.

"I might know how to find out what to do next," he says, "if nothing about what's going on around here." He dives into a pile to procure a hide-bound book that is bursting with dog-eared pages and inserts on yellowed paper. "Read this."

Alan takes the book. It is far heavier than it looks, and he has to hold it in both hands. There is an ophidian circle on the cover surrounding smaller circles and symbols, none of which Alan recognizes. He sets the book on the floor to open it, expecting more of the same arcane strangeness, but he is shocked to find that the text inside is perfectly intelligible – if a bit unusual.

"'*Grimoire of Plastromancy*,'" Alan reads, "'*Addendum to the 9th Cyprianus Mortana*, Pwysh of Marmorea, Magus.' What is this? Marmorea?"

"Marmorea is where we are now – this whole area – Marble Town," Brattle explains. He seems to be flirting with excitement, but Alan sees him holding himself back on the weights of his fresh grief. "And this is Pwysh's diary. A magician's notebook!"

Alan shrugs. The book seems to watch him from the floor. The large, dark letters glare, making him feel sick to his stomach.

"I can't read it," Brattle continues, "because I'm not a magician. But you can, Alan. Because you *are*."

The monster is howling far away. Debtors' Orchard howls with it, eager to suck down the newly-dead where they lie, greedy now that it has remembered the taste of blood. The bad souls are gone, but there is still torture here.

Alan turns the pages of Pwysh's grimoire with Brattle looking over his shoulder. He doesn't look much at the words. The Kingwatcher's gift is alive and changing in him, and he can feel it like white light coursing through his veins. Pwysh is in it, dead only in the crudest sense; the corpse whispers from its corner, reading along with Alan in something that is not quite Alan's voice.

Alan clears his throat. When the strange tang remains in his mouth, he tries swallowing.

"I don't understand," he says, feeling a bit thick. "It couldn't be plainer. You can't read this?"

"No, and that's the point," Brattle replies. "I see rows of squiggles, triangles, circles within circles. It's adept's code. You got the magic though, kid! Of course it's plain to you."

He hooks his thumbs under the thin strap of his breechcloth and struts two steps with his head swiveling. Alan doubts that Brattle would be so pleased with himself if he could hear Pwysh's worried sighing.

"I saw what you did to that club of yours," Brattle goes on. "And your mojo, your dangerous luck; I knew there was something about you. You gotta say you get it. You feel it. Right? You don't look happy."

"I'm not," Alan says from far away. Speech emerges from him while he watches, drawn to something else. The book looks deep into him. He shakes his head and makes an effort to ground himself again.

Alan drops forward onto his knees, struck. He still doesn't entirely understand. He is at once elated and terrified to be growing into his secret. Such clarity is so rare; he wants to hold onto it forever, to stay in the space between being and becoming, the king of No-Man's-Land, but there is nothing to rule in his dark places. He riffles into the deeper pages, intent on bringing the rest of this mystery to light.

"You can read this," Brattle says, settling to a crouch and putting his finger in the gutter of Pwysh's notebook, "so you're a mage, but you ain't just that. There's no such thing. Reading Pwysh's adept's code puts you right in his sphere."

"Thanoturgy," Alan nearly chokes on the word.

"Dead-raising, boss," Brattle says, a haunted kind of smile opening across his face. "I seen it, you seen it, now let's try it once and for all in a laboratory setting." He hooks his thumb in the general direction of Pwysh's shattered body. Alan trembles as deadspeak fills his mind, every bit as empty and confusing as Hobbish nonsense but nowhere near as beautiful. "Come on, bony. Time to be the reason we're here."

Alan cannot close his eyes. He cannot find a deep breath. In the aching chamber of his chest, his heart is tapping out a rhythm so slow he can barely feel it. He thinks of gone nights burning salamanders from the graveyard to sell at the bait shop with his sister, of Iscela at Ray's washing dishes in her long apron, and of sunset lights lying gold in the empty driveways of Lakewood Balmoral. In dead Pwysh's hut, with its healing power slowly returning, Alan stands.

"Yes," he says. "Let's try."

Brattle grins in his pained, hungry way. "Taking your future by the ribs," he says. "I like it. Split it open."

Pwysh is lying where Brattle left him before the hobs attacked. Loose and bent strangely, his robes piled around him in disarray, the mage is difficult to look at. Alan forces himself to meet the corpse's empty gaze.

All right, he thinks. *What are you so eager to say?*

Pwysh stares back, his gray eyes touched with creeping red. His whispers have fallen silent. Alan wonders whether or not it was Pwysh he was hearing in the first place. It occurs to him that it might be very dangerous to trust phantom whispers.

"OK," Brattle says, wringing his hands. "How do we do this?"

"I have no idea," Alan replies. "But if I'm an adept, it should come naturally. Right?"

Brattle shrugs and bites his lip. He knuckles a fleck of saliva away, smearing the red stain around his mouth.

"Best not to make assumptions like that, maybe," the ghoul says. "Not that I'm trying to talk you out of it now. Pwysh's got to have had a book on this here somewhere."

Alan crosses his arms and strokes the narrow spur of his chin.

"You knew him," Alan says. "How many times did you actually see him do anything like this – wake the dead?"

Brattle pouts. For a second, he almost looks demure. "I think he called up spirits mostly. Shades, you know. For future telling. I guess I never saw him just cold raise a corpse to life. He was really more Da's friend than mine."

Da. Alan remembers the old ghoul arching up from death in the dance of flames, his eyes changed, and clawing for his son's throat.

"You know," he says. "If we're really going to do this, we should start a little smaller." He kneels to brush Pwysh's eyes closed and then turns from the body. "Do you have any rats left in the pack?"

"Your sense of smell must be going," Brattle chuckles. "Here."

Brattle swings himself across the floor and thrusts his hands into the knapsack. It isn't long before he produces a hob's trap with a dead rat squeezed in it. He presents it with a smirk.

"Pulled as many from the hobs' store as I could scrape up," he says. They don't keep long, but this one's among the least rotten, I'd say. Still good eating."

"Drop it," Alan says. He might have stuck his tongue out if he still had one. The rat is oozing guts from a split in its side.

Brattle obeys and steps back. Alan sinks to one knee and spreads his hands out over the rat. It glowers up at him, neck broken and tarry eyes bulging. He searches himself for something, unsure of exactly what he's looking for or how he'll know when he's found it. What will a talent for thanoturgy feel like? Alan has never been particularly skilled at anything. He's prepared for frustration and embarrassment, but he's surprised to feel a power responding to his probing. It's a small matter of will to draw that power out.

The rat is full of rot. It is squirming dead, hot and almost totally lost. But there is something left within it for Alan to grasp – a thread of its tiny life that, while ragged, still clings within its broken body. Alan is disturbed by how easily he can touch that fading remnant, how quickly it responds to his coaxing, and how natural it feels to plumb death's starving reaches.

The rat hisses to life – or to something like life – and writhes in the trap to gnash its teeth at Alan and Brattle. It growls and snaps, seemingly oblivious to the utter uselessness of its body.

"Sweet grief," Brattle breathes, hissing as if to answer the rat.

106

Alan pulls the power back, pushes down toward the rat as if to suppress it with a gesture, and cuts it off with the same command that silenced Brattle's Da: "STOP!"

The rat goes stiff, pushes out a last squeak of anger, and then falls still. Alan can feel it slipping into the sleep of ages with a new gratitude. He has ended a worse pain – a greater torture – than it had known in the instant of its death. The ache in his chest worsens, and he clutches his heart as he sits back to rest.

"Well, there goes my appetite," Brattle says. He sends the rattrap clattering away with a kick. "So that's what happened with Da on the fields. If you had tried it on Pwysh, it've been just like that." His eyes look haunted. He tries to shake the sorrow from his face, to smile his pain away, but he fails. He cannot succeed now, and he clearly knows it. Brattle lets the sadness sit on him eventually, hunching a bit, ashamed of it. "Good call starting small, bony. You're an adept all right. But it looks like maybe the magic don't exactly work the way I was thinking."

"I'm sorry," Alan says, giving Brattle a pat on the shoulder that feels forced and awkward. "I think death is deep in ways we can't know from the outside. There must be something more to being alive than natural processes."

"Of course there is," Brattle snaps, shrugging Alan's hand away. "Shades, like I said. Spirits. Remember?" He sighs and suddenly appears very small. "Can't put the soul back in the body once it goes. I imagine that's the rule."

Alan tries not to look at Brattle with pity. Is he even capable of facial expressions anymore? He hopes not; he can't keep sympathy for the ghoul at bay, and Brattle would probably resent him for feeling it.

"I may not be able to do that," he says, "but at least I know I'm not powerless. There's a way to turn this to good; I know it. But we can't do much good staying here. We have to bury Pwysh, and then we have to move on. We have to follow Winter White."

"My thinking exactly," Brattle replies. "Plenty of reason to think it was she and her tomb-fiends that killed the wizard."

Alan nods. "If so, there may be something here that'll tell us why or where to go. Pwysh was mixed up in something. I think that's pretty clear."

"It's decided then," says Brattle. He stands and beats the dust and rat guts from his palms. "At least partly. If he wrote down anything about why Winter White was here – or why she wanted him dead – it'll be here, and I suspect only you will be able to read it. Start with that diary – and take it outside. We ain't gonna bury Pwysh tonight. Leave me alone to do my thing." When Alan looks ready to object, Brattle holds up his hand to stifle him. "Just go, Al. Read and make camp for a few hours. I need to do this, and it's nothing you want to see."

Twelve

Night is washing in over the mountains. The second sun retires, leaving aubergine thinning to limpid black behind a screen of mare's tails. Alan waits in the Orchard, looking out from Pwysh's stoop over the brunnmigi's desolation and the waving boughs of the green wall to the west. The bats are moving in the trees again. There is a light in the forest, sitting warm and dim where the orchard narrows to a kinked neck and a creek under a cherry bridge.

It's beautiful at the edge of collapse. Death sleeps with peace in the arms of silence. Alan is far from his last sunset in the living world – that waste of light spilling across the floor from behind the shake machine. He's even further from his parents' rainy funeral. Watching strange, starlike eyes burn in the wind above the battlefield, he feels lost and new and orphaned. The pain is a fair price for the lives he's ended, but he is growing into his secret, and that has to count for something.

He leans against the curve of the hut and looks down at the book in his hands. It isn't a diary; he's sure of that. It's something like a textbook, and it seems to be about divination with bones. He thumbs through it, distracted, and catches insight in packets from the few parts of the exceedingly technical work that he's able to comprehend. Pwysh impresses him more after every page, and he finds himself wondering what the late thanoturge was like in life. What was he involved in that had gotten someone riled up enough to kill him? The answer is not in the Grimoire of Plastromancy. Alan closes it and stuffs it into the pack, where it hums quietly for a while. Alan thinks in that hum, lets the dead reach out to him through it, and gets to work building a fire when it finally gets fully dark.

There are bones on the lawn. They are old and yellowed, and most are half-buried, but they will serve. He stacks a cone of femurs and tibias. Moved by the new power in him and the hum of insight he's picked up from Pwysh's grimoire, he strikes a spark from a big cat's pelvis with a wave of his hand, and amaranth flame shoots up the structure to crackle in a multitude of voices. Power slips from his spirit like blood when he exerts himself. What would it take to drain him completely? In the strange warmth of his bone-fire, tired as he has ever been and then some, he allows himself to rest and wonder.

Brattle emerges at last as the crumbling crown of the moon appears in the east. He is sagging over his middle, slumping forward with his shoulders rounded, and lines of worry frame his eyes. He runs a hand over the dome of his head, smoothing back the little wisps of hair that are blowing around his ears.

"Look at you," he says to Alan. He's carrying a single book. Weak as a thread, it's apparently all he could manage. "You're getting into it, eh?"

Alan nods. "I'm trying to see how much I have to learn and how much is going to come naturally."

Brattle drops the book and sits down beside him with his back to the wind. He huddles reflexively, as if trapped. He is soul-weary in a gore-fed body and Alan can see the subtle flush of satiation creeping up his neck and cheeks. Fundamental disgust wars in Alan against an abiding pity; Brattle looks much the worse for wear after having gorged on Pwysh's remains.

"You know, magic is a ruderal thing," says the ghoul. "It grows in wasted places. That's what my Da says." He gives this a second's sad thought and then spits into the grass. "Or what he did say. Inside, in the places where magic comes from, to some degree great or small, a mage is ruined. Some magics are better than others at thriving in disturbed hearts. Do you know what I mean? Do you feel it?"

Alan can only nod again and stare into the fire. There are no answers there. He is well acquainted with his own ruin. Thinking about it makes the magic move strangely in him — twists his stomach at the low end and leaves him wincing.

The fire is guttering. Without a certain amount of focus, it appears that the bones won't burn. Alan bites his lip and tries to concentrate on bringing the flame back. It dances away for a minute, dying despite his best efforts, but then it flares up in a great tongue. It licks high into the air, leaving acrid smoke curling and embers sparking up over his head.

"I couldn't do anything like this before," Alan says. "There were lots of things I couldn't do in my old life. I didn't feel like any kind of adept then. Most of the time, I felt completely powerless. Not an ounce of strength in me. Why now? I'm too far from where I was anymore to change things."

"I'm not sure what gets to me the most about that," Brattle chides, "the self pity or the question I can't answer. Magic is keeping you alive, now, you know. Plus, you're a thanoturge in *Graveworld*; I'd be surprised if location had nothing to do with it. But I ain't got explanations for you."

"I thought you said you collected secrets," Alan says.

"Ha! Yeah, I got secrets all day. Secrets an' wisdom. But I ain't a mage, Al." Brattle puts his hands up to warm them by the fire. "I got secrets about Winter White - that twisted bitch. The south is buzzing with them these days. The woods are loud with word of her."

"Like what?" Alan asks.

"Like she appeared in Cenophon at high day, where Morgan's Red Guard was billeted up in the vaults. They scooped her up right away, that's what everyone's said. But it's also told that her appearance followed the letter of some foretelling: a living human in Graveworld. She's at Necropolis now, serving the Drowned Queen herself - or I imagine she would be if she wasn't out roaming around killing ghouls. She's supposed to be some kind of redeemer of the wastes, you know? Starchild. The answer to some old prayer no one remembers praying. And now she's here." Brattle spits again. "Roaming around. Leading armies of hobs. And killing ghouls."

Night cools the clouds away, leaving the sky open on the void beyond. Alan watches the stars flashing to life in milky bands.

"A living human in Graveworld," Alan repeats. "I understood about half of what you said, but that much sounds familiar. I'm not sure how human I feel anymore, though. And I'm not sure whether or not I qualify as alive."

"Whatever you are," Brattle says, "you ain't prophesied."

"Who made this prophecy?" Alan asks.

"A King of the north," Brattle responds, "beyond the Colonies, where I never been. You find aught innat diary?"

"Oh." Alan flips back the pack's flap to show Brattle the spine of Pwysh's grimoire. "It's not really a diary. It's like a supplement to a larger work – an addendum. And no; there was nothing in it."

This isn't exactly true, of course. The grimoire is in his mind, humming away. He remembers the symbols on its pages and the way they seemed to consider him.

"I think it'll be useful though," Alan adds, "as reference, I guess."

Brattle nods and fishes his last trapped rat from the pack. By now, the pack is quite ripe with the smell of rot. Alan should find the smell revolting. Instead, he is only mildly annoyed. It stimulates him in a strange way, and this fact alone is upsetting. What is he becoming?

"I don't know if we're going to find anything that will tell us where to go next," Brattle says, pointing to the book he brought from Pwysh's hut, "but if we do, I imagine it'll be in there. I can't read the title, but it was underneath him – like he was trying to make sure someone found it. I sure ain't keen to go back in that place again and sift around, and I suggest you don't either. Pwysh deserves more respect I think. You know?" He gnaws the rat slowly, savoring it. Alan wonders how he can still think about eating after what he's just done.

"If we come empty," Brattle continues, "I've a mind for us to head north and find that prophet king. Straight to the source, you know? So to speak. It's as good a place to start as any if we want to find White – and I do."

Alan lets the whispers in his head sweep him away for a moment. The stars join in, offering dead voices of their own. All around him, death is moving like a mist – like a shadow – pulling across the ground to swirl up around his shoulders. He feels it in his fists and his bare skull. It is in the bone-fire, winking out at him from ember constellations.

"Whatever she wanted," Alan says, "Pwysh was involved. And so are you. Something ties this all together."

He picks up the book at Brattle's feet and is about to set it on his lap when a folded piece of paper falls out from between the pages. It nearly blows into the fire before Alan catches it, and in that thin light the symbols within it seem to glow. Alan peels it open carefully and blows a line of dust from the creases.

"'Rawbones,'" Alan reads, "'Eternal flame, Sepul Prisons'. What could that mean? And there's a map."

"Secrets I don't know," Brattle replies. "Though 'Sepul' is Sepulchra, I've no doubt."

Alan holds the paper up so that Brattle can inspect it. It's a map drawn in fluorescent ink. Ways wind across it in sparkling black, crossed by red letters and short series of numbers that can only be map coordinates.

"Hey," Alan says. "Do any of those numbers match this?"

He presents his phone, but Brattle doesn't look at it. He is too busy tracing a certain glistening line to a point on the map between a line of mountains and an open space marked with half circles.

"There," Brattle says. "I'm damned! He's even circled it. That's the house of the northern king, the foreteller that saw Winter White arriving in his vision. Pwysh knew about him, too. That must have been why Winter White killed him."

Alan looks at the spot that Brattle is indicating. The numbers written above it don't match the coordinates on his phone, but there is a small bit of writing there that makes his heart leap once he realizes what it says.

"This says 'Alan Shade'!" he says. "Oh my god. Brattle, you were right: this is exactly what we were looking for. He left this for us."

Brattle looks up at him. The big mirrors of his eyes seem to be reflecting a hundred different things at once. The firelight draws his smile into a messy hook across his face.

"What do you know? I was wrong. Yer prophesied after all," Brattle says. "Like I told you, there's no such thing as luck. Not in danger's teeth, and I see the mouth now chumping down. We'll away tomorrow to lands I've never seen."

"And all of this will start to make sense," Alan adds, hopefully. He looks out over the moonlit lawn, where winged shapes are bobbing over hobs' corpses. The light in the forest is pulsing like a lung, beaming into him to show his sad hope and heartsickness. "I don't think I've ever been so ready."

Sleep will not come. It circles like a fearful animal fighting curiosity. Alan reaches for it, promising a familiar embrace, but it finally shies away for good at the point of midnight. Alan stands then, fully alert and frustrated, while Brattle keeps restful oblivion for himself in greedy throatfuls of snores.

Alan looks east toward the even hills. Where they fall away toward littoral dunes, there are thin flocks of white birds circling. The dead lie away from him in two irregular channels, feet to heads, and he finds that he can extend his senses along their lines to see into the far distance. In the whispers of the trees, he can hear the nightgulls crying; on the breath of a far breeze, he can smell and taste the sting of salt. There is a power there beyond the hills, beating with the tide, tender and invisible. Sweet and old, it teases the edges of his new reach for a moment, warming him where he still feels empty.

Now he turns west and walks a little way down the knoll. The pull of the sea recedes and is replaced by something darker and deeper beneath him: The Orchard's memory is awake and moving. It bubbles up around his feet, liquid sorrow sucking at every step, as if the soil refuses to contain it. The old debtors live on in their pain, and now they have hobs' blood to strengthen them. When it finally flows away, it leaves a teary film over everything.

Alan slides three fingers over the bony ridge above his orbits. He might have quailed once from the memory of torture, but he is stronger now, for what it's worth – a Graveworlder at last, orphaned from his old life among the living.

I'm part of this place now, he thinks, and he remembers something Brattle said to him: *Wherever you are, you have to make a home.*

Alan moves on toward the woods' edge. The night is hot and wet, and the Orchard is swelling with low noise. Hobs' bodies are lumps in the dark with squat, gibbous shapes jostling over them. Lamp-eyed scavengers pull corpses into the brush amid murmuring squabbles. They are vicious among each other, but they flee from Alan as he ventures out onto the lawn.

Dead-eater. What was it that the Geier lord Atratus called Brattle? *Corpse-puller. Unclean.*

They are ghouls on the moonlit lawn, dragging the dead away to feed. They dance in strange conflict with each other though the furrows carved by the brunnmigi during its rampage. Alan can't understand their glibbers; their sounds are not speech. They're not quite Brattle's kind, but they aren't mindless either. With hooks and catgut lines and little knives glinting on their hips, they scour the orchard bare of the sad humps of hobs, and they disappear beneath the trees when there are no corpses left to pull.

How many are there? Alan wonders. *And how many different species?*

"*Follow the ghoul for now,*" Atratus said, "*but don't trust him.*"

Alan looks out over Pwysh's lawn with a splinter of ice in his throat. He is angry with himself for being so perturbed. He should be purged by now, if not healed, but part of him refuses to mend.

He decides to indulge it tonight as best he can. It's not like he's got much else to do anyway.

"A land of liars," he says to himself, and then he turns back toward the hut.

The simple ghouls took the spoils of the brunnmigi's rage, but they were deprived of the prize at the top of the hill. A greater ghoul claimed it instead. Alan puts his hands in his pockets as he heads toward Pwysh's chalk hut, feeling for his phone and the strange vial. The hut's door hangs in shadow, rolled hard on its hinges and beaten with hammer blows, but it was intact when he and Brattle arrived. Pwysh had known his murderer then – had let him in willingly.

Her, Alan corrects himself. It could only have been Winter White. He thinks of her as he steps onto the porch: small in the saddle, wrapped like a child empress, bare feet on dark cat's fur. There was an aspect of her beauty that seemed bigger than her body and a taste of her menace that haunts Alan's tongue even now, pricking down the back of his throat. She could touch him without even trying. Alan shoulders Pwysh's door open carefully and walks into the dark with his heart and his mind warring like a pair of glibbering ghouls.

Pwysh is gone. The heaps of papers and toppled furniture seem larger in the darkness. The walls curve in tighter. The ceiling could be just above Alan's head and sinking. Alan takes his phone from his pocket and touches the screen to wake it, and in the soft square of faint light it offers, he picks his way to the spot on the floor where Pwysh had been. There, he kneels for a while, waiting for his phone to darken again.

The night's heat presses over his skin like a pall. The floor is still wet with blood; the stains ooze out in fraying tendrils, as if reaching for something. They are long smudges with distorted whorls smeared in them: Brattle's fingerprints, without a doubt. Did he eat the corpse bones and all? Not even Pwysh's robe is left. Alan stands with a shudder, suddenly eager to leave, but he stops suddenly when he finds his way toward the door blocked.

Pwysh is there, faded half out of the darkness. He frowns with his eyes dead and blood drying in his hair, his face so close that Alan can smell the rot in his mouth.

"Oh, god," Alan whispers. Pwysh blinks tears of tar down his cheeks. "Stop."

Pwysh bends a smile. There is no mind behind it; there is only a flood of feelings – of memory masquerading as thought. Alan swallows over the squeeze of fear in his throat. Guilt pounds him in waves, drowning his new power and drinking his heart down into its tortured emptiness. He might have crumbled, he might have fainted before, but Alan is a stronger thing now. The Orchard has been spitting up ghosts all night, and he's endured.

"What do you want?" he asks Pwysh. "Are you testing me?"

Pwysh's ghost moves. He makes a sobbing sound as he glides across his desk. His mouth moves, but his words sound like running water. His eyes steam up like bathroom mirrors, and he presents a pale arm from behind the curtain of darkness that hides him. From the heel of his palm to the crook of his elbow, Pwysh's arm is peeled open. Triangles of carefully cut flesh hang over exposed bone and bleeding tissue. Cords twitch in the red mess when the long-nailed hand flexes. Pwysh vanishes in a swirl of steam and blood. A little wind stirs the papers on the desk, spilling quills and measuring tools and cups of sparkling stones. A globe blows over to split on the floor. Fury swells in the hut, rising slowly into a brittle shriek. It is the will to batter Alan down, to strip him apart and expose the fearful child at his core. Alan backs up a step, bolstering himself as best he can against the ghost's parting anger. He is prepared for the swirl to blow up into a storm, but it dies away suddenly, leaving papers flapping down around him. The wind whimpers out, its rage exhausted, and Alan is alone again.

A single leaf of paper remains on the desk. Dark spots of blood trail across it. Alan picks it up and examines it in the light of his phone, reading aloud the only words on the page that aren't smeared with age and stained.

"Bell, star, and spirit."

"You find something?"

Brattle's voice behind him. Alan jumps, nearly tearing the blood-stained page in half. He crumples it instead and stuffs it into his pocket as he turns toward the door.

"Jesus," he laughs.

Brattle stares, eyes shining, the light of early dawn just growing behind him.

"I saw him," Alan explains. "Pwysh was here."

"Another shimmer," Brattle replies. He takes a step forward, holding onto the doorframe as if he's afraid he might fall into the floor.

Alan shakes his head. "No. It was him. His ghost."

Brattle snorts. "Don't trust it. They can look however they want. Did it say anything to you? Show you anything?"

Alan goes rigid. A little finger of anger slips down his spine.

"No," he says, "but it made a big show over here." Alan gestures toward the mess. "It was Pwysh; I saw his face. He was practically breathing on me at one point."

"Don't trust it," Brattle says again. He casts about the room, his head tilting fast to one side on the defensive swivel of his neck. His gaze falls on one spot, and he tries hopelessly to tear it away, but he is transfixed. "I said you wouldn't want to come back in here."

"Well, you were wrong about that," Alan says, "and I'd like to be able to make decisions like that myself in the future."

His eye is drawn to the spot on the floor that Brattle is staring at. He turns to look, and whatever it is he was going to say next get stuck in his throat beneath a swell of bile: Pwysh is there, eviscerated. In the low light crawling through the doorway, he can just make out the gnawed corpse lying in the mess of its robes, the points of its ribs broken outward from the empty space where the heart had been.

"I told you," Brattle snarls. "That's what you humans get for all your curiosity. Come on."

Thirteen

Brattle packs up the camp while Alan leans against the hut with his arms crossed. It's a clear morning, and Pwysh's lawn is glowing. There is a sheet of light lying across the grass, stuck on the tip of every blade, sparking with gold and white where the ground is renewing itself. The sky opens beryl-bright behind moving shelves of clouds like continents. If he weren't too miserable to appreciate it, Alan might let the morning rejuvenate him. If he weren't lost, hurt, and haunted, he might call it beautiful.

"When the bees crowd out of their hive," Brattle recites with a sing-song rhythm, "the weather makes it good to be alive. Bees crowd into their hive again? Sign of thunder, sign of rain."

He kicks away the bones of last night's fire and throws the pack over his back with a huff. Then he sucks the tip of his finger for a second and tests the direction of the wind. It's swinging confidently in from the east, warm as promise.

"We'll have good light to walk by today," Brattle says to Alan. "Even *you* can't be glum about that."

Alan toes the ground. "Rain long foretold, long last," he counters. "Short notice, soon will pass."

Brattle gives him a gruff chuckle and starts off down the hill.

"Can't go by that one," he says. "Nope. But we'll see. The map has us going this way – to the north to cross Colony land – and that edge is as far as I've ever been. But before that is Elrafa: the last of the outland cities still standing. Ain't been there in a while, and I never had any times but bad in those ruins, but at least it's a short walk."

They head down the hill with the wind at their backs. As Alan's subtle awakening continues, he sees more and more of Graveworld's character. Under the sunshine, a bitter energy is swelling. Lights are moving behind the sky, barely visible. Worse than the little murmurs of the dead in Alan's mind – worse even than their constant pull on him from the ground, which he is surprised to find himself growing accustomed to – is the sinking feeling that there is something waiting in the wings of this world, a mirror-thing, perhaps the size of a world itself, watching him and wondering.

Alan distracts himself in the tome Brattle found. *The Book of Horns* is hundreds of pages longer than Pwysh's grimoire, but it's light as rain. Sentences switch at random between five distinct hands and voices, often partway through with changes occurring mid-word. Enormous diagrams dominate the first sections, and the text shimmers around them – often into the margins – in ink that's like ghoul's eyes in color. It's a taxing read, but Alan dives in with gusto; when meanings emerge from the chaos, they strike him with profound power.

The Desolate may be restored, he reads, *but not to any good kind of life, and not for long. The flesh will move, but it can scarcely subsist a week without the spirit.*

"What a difference one night makes," Brattle says, mostly to himself. He surveys the bare lawn, swinging his head back and forth between his undulating shoulders. "Even the gouges in the land are healing."

Alan flicks his eyes up from a passage about telekinesis.

The mind moves flesh as easily as anything else. Bone and blood respond more readily to the touch of the Ethereal Hand than to the hands of mere healers.

"I saw ghouls here last night," he says. "They dragged off all the corpses. They looked feral."

"Rustics," Brattle says. "Wild things – not refined like us." He looks back over his shoulder. Despite the fact that the pack on his back obscures half of his face, Alan can tell that Brattle is smiling. "We Busaws, I mean. Rustics live in holes, in the hills and the woods, and in swamps. Sometimes together in big nests of leaves. Glibbers and meeps, yeah? No speech?"

"No," Alan replies. "Like the hobs."

"Rustics don't talk," Brattle explains. "But they ain't dumb like hobs are. They're just wild — like animals. They're all over."

"How are they related to you?" Alan asks.

Brattle shrugs.

"It's lonely in the wastes. Some like the solitude less than others. Some got needs, you know? Greater than normal folk do — or stranger at least. Ghouls are thin in the blood as it is, and crossings with lower creatures can't but produce brutes. So we've got rustics now: part animal, and ghouls in name only. But I also heard that there was a line of us was cursed before, and fell low, and became mindless dust-eaters and scrabblers in the boneyards. None exactly know."

"And what about ghosts?" Alan begins, closing his book and pressing it in the crook of his arm. "You said there were no such things."

Brattle stops for a moment. They are at the head of the bridge where the light was shining in the woods last night. There is nothing there now but waving trees and a black brook racing over glassy stones. Tall birds wade far off down the river, jabbing knife-bills into the water.

"I never did," Brattle corrects Alan. "I said you shouldn't trust that anything is a ghost before you know for sure that it is. These are dangerous parts for greenhorns. But you're still sure, huh? What you saw was Pwysh without a doubt? And how do you know that, exactly?"

Alan covers his pocket reflexively.

"You seemed pretty sure," he replies. "If it's so hard to tell, how can you be sure that it *wasn't* Pwysh's ghost I saw? It seems to me like proof is prohibitively hard to come by here. You practically said so yourself."

"That's exactly right," Brattle growls. "The best proofs are hard-won — trust me."

"That's the point," Alan says. Frustration is stringing up his back, drawing him as tight as a bowstring, but he holds up his hands to show Brattle that he means no harm. "How do I know that I can?"

He lays his new book across his arm, opens it to point at a line of knotty pen-strokes, and continues.

"I only know from what you said that you can't read this. Maybe I'm not sure who to trust right now. I think I deserve to have my faith rewarded before I go any further."

Brattle huffs and straightens himself. He sticks out his chest, ready for anything, his body a wall against accusation. Cold tension crawls across his face, bunching furrows high up his forehead and drawing lips his so thin that they go white. Then a strange calm comes over him, and this is somehow worse than his anger.

"OK," he says, clasping his hands. "This is round two. I figured it wouldn't be long in coming. I'm just glad you burned round one's fire out on the hobs last night." He smoothes back his few wispy hairs. "I'm a ghoul, as I said, and mostly sapient. I'm a dead-eater, as I explained while I was pulling your recently so ungrateful ass out of the gunk in the swamp. I've lived here all my life. I've been a liar, yes, and I've been a killer, but this ain't my game, bony. I'm not hiding anything."

Alan pulls the blood-dotted note out of his pocket and tries to smooth it out. Then he holds it up.

"Why didn't you want me to go back into the workshop?" he asks. "This is what the ghost showed me. Did you not want me to find it? Are you working with Winter White – or someone else?"

Brattle bites back a chuckle. Alan swallows. His newfound courage is breaking high, but fear stretches out beneath him infinitely. He can feel himself faltering, but he won't allow it. This is a new world – a new life. He can choose to be a new self.

"What else did it show you?" Brattle asks. His eyes are wide. He stares at the note with intense interest, oblivious to Alan's ongoing epiphany. He may even be mocking it a little. "I can't read a word of it, but Pwysh wasn't bleeding when we found him.

Whatever killed him worked from the in, and it didn't let much of anything out. Still, there's blood. Did the spirit say anything?"

"You're avoiding the question," Alan says.

"I'm skipping it," Brattle smirks. "Indulge me."

Alan looks at the note himself now: *Bell*, *Star*, and *Spirit* beneath browning dots from an open wrist. He shifts and knocks his teeth together.

"My sister," he says, "but this is *quid pro quo*."

"And I still don't know what that means."

"Allison Lane," Alan continues. "She died. It was something she took into her own hands. I had to come back home to put her affairs in order, because there's just nobody left anymore."

Brattle nods. He drives one palm over the other: *splat*. Family style.

Alan pushes ahead. "I was staying in her place. I saw her there, in the bathtub, bleeding. It was terrible. Pwysh didn't say anything last night, but he showed me that to let me know that he meant this message for me. He pulled it right out of my head and showed me."

"You saw her ghost," Brattle says.

"I think so," Alan replies. "But I don't know."

"Spirits are dangerous. They get in your mind and trick you. We'll keep that note handy, but I still think suspicion is the best policy."

Alan nods. "Atratus told me I shouldn't trust you," he says.

"Did he now?" Brattle chuckles. "I imagine that's to be expected. No honor among scavengers."

Brattle is silent for a moment. A light moves across his face like the light in the woods last night. When he finally speaks again, his expression is flat and shadowless.

"I'm slowly starting to see why you belong here," he says. "Death has been following you around for a while. It's in the bones for some, they say — so to speak. And I can say that; we share a sense, you know? The deadcall. I know you hear it, too. It's in every ghoul from our first cries. Being so close with death —

being a part of it and feeling its wheels turning all around you everywhere you go – can easily get to you. It gets to other folks, too; they don't want you around if you've got that blackness about you.

"What I wanted to keep you from seeing was the mess I'd made of old Pwysh in that workshop. We ghouls eat the dead. It's what we do. It's how we honor them, but shame comes with it – shame, shame. And hatred – hate so huge and so wild that nobody and nothing can fight it. It throws you down into the blood-dark with the dogs, and you see how something beautiful can become a desecration. No one is above it, not even the Geier Venue. I didn't want you to see what I had done and hate me. Da is dead, and Nettle's gone, and I can't keep going alone."

With this Brattle hoists the pack up a bit toward his shoulders and hooks a thumb in the direction of the bridge and the deepening forest beyond it.

"You honor the dead by eating them," Alan says, "but you don't eat your own?"

"We ain't rustics. My kind don't need transforming," Brattle replies, effortlessly. "We're already transformed. Now I hope you're pro quo is quid enough for one day. If we're out of this lame round two, I'd like to move right into building up so more weirdness between us. I'm determined to make round three a real barn burner."

They walk on into the warming woods. The trees thin to leafless spikes; the sky sags from point to point across them like cured hide. Dust blows up in angry columns where the ground is bare, swirling dark as tanning acid. They arrive at the gate of Elrafa in the early heat of the afternoon, and Brattle wraps a pall from their pack around his head to cover his mouth.

"Urbem Pulveris," says the ghoul, clutching the mortcloth to his sunken chin, "Elrafa. This was a capital of something once. Umans actually used to live out here; there were whole nations. But not anymore. Something bad happened, and it hasn't stopped happening. A wasting curse was cast, and it spread out from somewhere far away. This was one of the last cities to die."

Alan isn't bothered by the wind. He has nothing for it to irritate – nothing to close or cover against it. He can barely feel the grit whipping across his face. It's strange how much he misses the wind moving his hair around. He looks up at the black arch and the towering statues on either side of it. They are all that's left of the outer wall save the broad furrow in the dirt where it stood and the guts of a smashed bastion spilling down its crumbling glacis slope.

"What's the quickest way through?" he asks.

"Never been through," Brattle replies. "But let's start with straight."

"Sounds like a plan," Alan says. He pulls his trash masher from the strapping on the pack. It warms in his hand, as if remembering him. He feels a slight pull deep within himself as the masher draws some of his power into itself. He is a little afraid of its enthusiasm. "What can we expect to find in there?"

Brattle replies with a shudder. "Keeners have moved in recently, and they're bad enough, but what we really gotta keep a look out for is Dela in the Flames."

"Something tells me I know her when I see her," Alan laughs.

"Indeed you will. And I'd be surprised if we didn't see her. She likes the south corners, I've found. When she pokes her head out, we'll be running. Hopefully, you have enough sense in your head not to wait for me to say 'go'."

"Why don't you drop the coy act and tell me what we're walking into?" Alan asks. "Tell me a secret."

There are shapes moving above them. Above the scouring wind and the whirling dust, black shapes are circling in a column: vultures.

"All right," Brattle says, feigning disappointment. "This is a place where the world runs thin. There's a wearing here between the world; certain kinds of mass death create them. Forms come shinin' through the odic force and get trapped, and they anchor here in bodies like cages. You follow? Dela is something like that, they say. An astral fire lost from her place among the spirits and stuck forever here as a young drake – or something like. A salamander. She's big, she's mad, and she'll kill you. So run when you see her. How's that?"

"That's good," Alan says. "I think I got enough of that to know to run when I see a giant monster."

"How much more do you really need, then?" Brattle grins. "Come on. The sooner we move, the sooner we're out and on our way."

Elrafa must have been beautiful once. Cambered roads run under the high and falling bones of obsidian arches, still patched with ivory in places. The wind hisses hard in weary doorways. Its living voice calls in gusts down stairwells where they stand in heaps of floors and ashlar stones. Statues watch from the square in shambles. They are humanoid, but there is an aspect of their faces that turns Alan's stomach. He's glad to hurry by them.

Above the square, Brattle stops to get his bearings. Someone has put up walls of plywood to form a corridor. A white horn lantern swings beneath a crude tripod above the remains of a fire.

"Who's been here?" Alan wonders aloud. Brattle stops his pacing long enough to kick at the pile of ashes.

"Don't know," he replies. "Don't really care. Lots of treasure hunters and such in the wilds. Whoever it was will be back for his gear, but we'll be gone by then. Too bad we don't have any oil, or we might take this light. He's lucky in that regard."

Alan stands looking into the wind.

"I can feel this place fraying," he says. "It's eroding around us. It's subtle until you notice it, and then it's big and harsh –like the air is going to burst open. What happens when the boundary breaks? The wall between the worlds, I mean. Is that possible?"

"Worlds don't work that way, as I understand," Brattle replies. "It's not like banging down a wall. Probably a good thing, too."

Alan holds up his hand. He can feel the world warping against his palm. There is something huge behind the distortion; Alan can sense it watching him through the weakening screen.

"I don't like it here," he says. "I've felt this before in the freezer at work: this sort of tickle up my spine like I'm in danger. Like I shouldn't stay here for too long."

"You got some fucked up freezers," Brattle laughs. "But you're right. We gotta get on. It won't take a full-on rip in the real to fling us into the shit here. I think I can suss out the way from here. Just follow me and keep your head down."

At this, a wild cry rings out from above them. Alan and Brattle turn in unison.

"That's no animal," Alan says. "It almost sounds like a word."

"Sounded like 'get out' to me," Brattle answers. His eyes have gone nearly white. "It's keeners, and they're right in our way."

The cry comes again, louder this time. It is ragged with desperation. Urgency has thinned it out into a warble, but it is unmistakably speech

"Help me! Please!"

"Don't listen," Brattle says, pressing his palm against Alan's chest. "That's how they get you. Just follow me and try to tune it out."

They flee up the corridor toward the high districts. The city opens up, and the roads disappear. Buildings stand as if dropped in place randomly. Most of them are collapsing, exenterated husks. Brattle wends his way through the ruins like a shadow, and Alan follows him as best he can. The calls plead on, never getting any closer. Ignoring them causes Alan more and more pain; his heart begins to race in his chest, stirring his slumberous blood to a hot roar, and his head starts to ache so much that he has to stop for fear that he might pass out. When he drops to a knee, Brattle does a hesitant little dance before he decides to come to Alan's side.

"It's a trick," he urges, pulling on Alan's arm and shoulder. "It affects everybody this way. Come on, or they'll overtake us!"

"Wait!" Alan demands. "It's just one voice, and it's not even moving. I think this is real, Brattle. Someone really needs help, and you know what will happen to them if we don't do something."

Brattle takes a step back and frowns. The mortcloth snaps behind him in the stiff wind. He is sweating, tense as a spring, and fear is bunched in lines around his eyes, but his voice is calm when he speaks.

"No," he says. "No way. I've seen this before, and you ain't. You don't help anyone in the outlands, Alan. Now come on!"

"I helped you," Alan says. "And you helped me."

This hits Brattle hard. He stands back and puts his hands on his hips. He is awkward upright, and the wind nearly blows him over.

"I do not approve of this," he gurgles. "This is a stupid idea, and I'm not going to die humoring you. Let's hurry, and you keep in mind that I'm going to bolt if anything looks bad. And I'm humoring you when I say that I hope you have the good sense to do the same in that case. Dammit! I've gone soft since I met you!"

The wind is racing into a shriek as Alan and Brattle make their way south again. They follow the cries into a blocked common whipping with shredded awnings. Dust pours through the square over shattered roofs and blocks the midday sun behind shifting screens. Brattle hunkers down against the outburst, struggling as the wind threatens to pull him off his feet. Alan takes his hand, worried that it's only the weight of the pack on his back that keeps him grounded.

"Is it always this bad?" he asks. He doesn't have to shout; it seems his voice comes from somewhere outside the pull of the wind.

Brattle tries to yell a reply into the cloth around his mouth, but Alan can't make out what he's saying. He forges ahead instead, making for a dark mass spreading out from behind the ruins of a fountain, with the ghoul scrabbling tight as a wire behind him.

For a moment, the dust clouds blow apart. The wind arcs back, turned howling on some invisible corner, and Alan can see more clearly through the falling veil. The shape is a great cat, piebald black and violet, with a mane feathering down its back and throat to spill around it like a patch of oil. It is long and sleek and hyperventilating, its right front paw bleeding in the teeth of a trap, and Alan can hear it sobbing as he nears it.

"My paw is broken," it says. Its voice rolls deep in the barrel of its chest, strong as the dawn even in defeat. "Please don't let me die here."

The cat looks up, and Alan is struck by the sight of its malachite eyes. They could be Allison's twin headlight eyes rushing toward him out of the perfect, flocculent darkness. He kneels before it, his hands out and shaken.

"It's all right," he promises. "We're here to help. Brattle, how do I get this trap open?"

The big cat sighs. Its breath is sweet and spring-warm. The animal seems ready to sink into the dust, but it looks up again despite its weakness.

"There's a pin," the cat explains. "Pull it from the center."

"A talking saddlecat," Brattle marvels, letting the cloth fall away from his mouth for a moment. "I've only heard stories. Hold still. I know how these work."

Brattle settles over the trap carefully, crouching to straddle it as he fishes between the gleaming teeth to find the pin beneath the cat's paw. He probes with deft hands, willow-fingers moving through the mechanism fearlessly.

The cat falls silent. Its breathing slows so dramatically, that Alan worries that it's stopped completely. Brattle, disengages the trap and it falls open, but the cat stays in the dirt and doesn't move. Alan draws a hesitant stroke up its velvet side, fingers knuckle-deep in that luxurious fur. There is a faint thrum beneath the cat's ribs; Alan can feel the cat's life the way he can feel rain coming when a storm is on the air.

"He's still alive," Alan says. "Can you hear me, saddlecat? Can you move?"

The wind is howling its fury nearby. Brattle stands up tall and tastes the air with his tongue. His small ears waggle as he paces a circle in the dust.

"I think we're about a slice of a second distant from wearing out our welcome," he says. "Can you get up, big guy? Bony ain't gonna leave you here, and I sure don't want to either, but I'm feeling a little bit uncomfortable sticking around."

The cat stirs at last. He writhes, kicking scrapes in the dirt beneath his back legs. He beats his bobbed tail, and his chest quivers through a moan as he tries to stand. Alan and Brattle try to help him, but it doesn't look good. His paw is shattered open. The ground is soaked with blood beneath the trap.

"A saddlecat is bred," says the cat through strained groans. "I was *caught*. I am a basteta – free as the day I was born despite the saddle I'm made to wear."

"You don't have a saddle," Alan says. The cat starts to reply, but he collapses as he tries to put weight on his paw. His answer is lost in a yelp and a thunderous growl.

"My rider was *removed* with his saddle," he struggles to say as he recovers, "by that tomb-wailer. And you are the ghoul and the spirit; I know you from the orchard. I'd have killed you there, but now I can only beg: do you have anything with which to bind my foot? Will you? I too fear what may become of me if we stay much longer."

"I can help," Alan says, claiming complete certainty in spite of himself. "Just lie where you are."

Alan is pleasantly surprised when Brattle speaks up to bolster his confidence.

"Al here's a sorcerer-in-training," he says, crouching in his froglike way to put his face as close to the cat's as he can. "I ain't seen him do much yet, but I get the feeling he's a fast learner."

130

The cat's great mouth droops at the corners, where black whiskers sag flecked with blood. He tilts his tufted ears back and twitches his char-black rhinarium.

"I'll take a sorcerer's apprentice over a ghoul," he says.

Before Brattle can respond, Alan tells him, "Leave it." The big cat's sorrow is palpable. It flows into him as he carefully searches the wound, hoping for his new facility to activate on its own.

The pain is something to focus on. The wind returns, madder than before, and Alan forces himself to concentrate. The bone is splintered, but it is still alive. With the right thought, he can make it respond, but the magic eludes him for a long moment. Brattle stares, mouth hanging open, and the cat sighs its sorrow on the ground, but Alan cannot find the power to move the bones. It only emerges when he accepts the cat's pain and weakness into himself; then, the magic grows, and he knows it all at once and subtly, the way he knows how to dream – as distant now as that memory feels.

Wracked with pain, his stomach rolling, Alan brings the bones together again. He whispers to them *knit, knit*, and he wills the flesh to close up safely around them as the cat's paw heals. If thanoturgy is an art of death, then it must be, on some side of it, an art of life. In no greater time than it takes the wind to turn again, the cat's paw is whole, and he is standing up on all four legs, flexing it. Alan sits down on the ground, deeply tired, and wonders how far his facility goes. If he can heal with a thought, can he kill with one?

"Spirit," the cat is purring, "you have done me a great kindness. I'd not have done the same for you – I admit it. I am in your debt."

Alan stands slowly. His knees ache. He feels a tremor coming on, but he fights it away. It will return later, stranger and more intense, but he hasn't got time to fall to pieces now. The air has changed in an ominous way.

"Sure," he says. "No need for any debts. You needed help, and I had the means. I'm just glad it worked. And you can call me Alan."

"Brattle," Brattle says, pressing his thumb against his chest. "Judged right, yes, and still wrong. I'd have waited a bit before I had my way with you, you know? And, if I can say so, it's an honor to be eaten by a ghoul. If Al's saved you, he's also deprived you of that. No hard feelings, of course."

"I am Stag's Blood," the cat announces. He still seems terribly sad, but his strength is coming back. Alan can see it in his posture. "My father was Fearsome, and my mother was in servitude in the north. We are well met," he sneers a little at Brattle, "for what it's worth. And I take life debts seriously. Wherever you need to ride, I will carry you, Alan. It's the very least I can do."

"You're a basteta," Alan says, "free as the day you were born. Right? You won't have to carry me anywhere, Stag's Blood. I don't think you should have to carry anyone ever again."

Stag's Blood smiles. It's an odd expression for a cat's face. Again, Alan sees his sister's green eyes there, staring from beneath the cat's plumose brows.

"I hope you can keep up, then," Stag's Blood says. He tries a laugh and coughs a bit, lifting his healed paw reflexively. "I don't like the smells on the wind."

Brattle opens his mouth to chime in, but the wind itself stops him. It rips open, clapping up a funnel of dust as it splits, and a roar of singing voices emerges from the collapsing rift. Long shapes become visible in the air, dark and rendered all in strange angles. Faces emerge, and then flowing hair, and then swords shining in ring-laden fists. Three figures in all materialize from the thunder, and they sing along with the wind in rage as they approach the ruined fountain.

"Keeners," Alan says. His masher is in his hand before he knows it. It leaps like a child, excited by his stress, practically swinging itself until he squeezes it still.

"No," Stag's Blood says, sinking into a defensive crouch. His hackles go up, giving his glower a galvanic, flowing intensity as the wind tugs his mane.

"Those ain't no keeners," Brattle concurs. "Those are worse."

Fourteen

The creatures hang in the air. They are lean and built strangely; the fraying rags and bands with which they've wrapped themselves barely fit over the angles of their bodies. Their skin blows behind them like slaked lime powder, never fully disintegrating. Time strains, bogged down trying to contain them. The dust parts away from them in great breaking curls. Light gloats over them, clinging like a battered lover, all its hopes to shine for eternity pinned to their malice and savage beauty. They drop like slow lightning, their song rolling out from behind faceless masks, grieving the dust and the dead city with glory.

"Good lord," Alan says.

Brattle stares, his hands limp at his sides. He droops over himself as if the work of existing in such creatures' presence requires all his energy.

"Watchers," he says. "High Coma rollers."

"What do they want?" Alan asks."

Brattle can't muster the strength to reply again.

"We have no chance to run," says Stag's Blood. "And they are not known for their mercy."

Alan fights through a sickening lightness. The Watchers are moving their hands, pointing, and readying their weapons. They push a terrible gravity before them: an irresistible weight of peril that threatens to crush Alan into his fear. If he doesn't fight now, they will kill him. They are bringing death, promising it beyond any doubt, and there is no choice but to kill them first.

Alan lifts his trash masher and grips the handle in both hands. He spreads his legs a bit, steadying himself, and turns to tell Brattle and Stag's Blood to stand behind him.

The Watchers bring death, but it's already here. Alan feels it inside him, stirring, whispering. He reaches back to the heart of Kingwatcher's bloom to find the ultimate seat of his new power.

"There's no trial like a trial by fire," he tries to say.

134

The ghoul and the cat cower together in silence. Brattle pushes his face into Stag's Blood's flowing mane.

Alan turns to face the Watchers. They have stopped a few feet from the ground and are spreading out. They sing back and forth, and their voices are impossible to distinguish from one another. One of them appears to be the leader. Alan calls to him, pushing his voice as loud as he can.

"Stop!" he cries. "I'm warning you! Get back!"

The Watchers share a look. Then they start to shake and toss their heads, and their song bounces out into rolling, falling tones. They are laughing. They point at him, singing derision, and then they raise their silver swords again.

Nothing sparks hate like perfect beauty. In this instant, all of a sudden, Alan has never hated anything more in his whole life. The dead are shouting within him. They are darkness, they are in darkness forever, and he is kin to them now. He is the brother of shadow. The bloom is blowing open, revealing impossible depths. The power there is a universe all its own. Alan would draw it all out at once, but he's shaking. He draws as much as he can, bringing himself to the brink of collapse, and forces the power out through the head of his trash masher.

The day darkens. At Alan's command, shadows slide from their corners. They curl from the wrecks of homes, and they rise from the fountain like dust on the whipping wind. The Watchers' song falters as a shadowstorm opens around them.

Alan empties everything into the storm. It swells and spins as shadows slip from cracks in the earth. The darkness pulses in, and all other noise is lost beneath a pounding roar. At the heart of the black is a memory of home. Ray's in the starlight, its roof beams blazing. Lakewood Balmoral with summer shimmering above the street, burning the last of wet spring away. And true home, his birthplace, where he left so much pain and struggle: the grave of his youth and innocence. He has grown without thinking; oblivious to the forces changing him, and now he is so far from home that he hardly knows it anymore. Sick with power and hurting deep in his body, he stretches out to strike the Coma's Watchers dead.

In an effort that blinds him with pain, Alan wrenches the darkness closed. It falls in on the Watchers, consuming them. They burst into powder beneath it, leaving only shrieks in their stead. Alan feels their deaths in his stomach and wretches. His head exploding with pain, Alan collapses, and the shadowstorm whirls apart. The roar of the darkness wilts into the wind.

Shadows bleed back into their places. The dust kicks up into a whirl again, and Elrafa goes back to being wind-swept and dead. The terrible light is gone, but Alan feels broken from strain. Brattle and Stag's Blood rush to his side, and he rolls onto his back to look up at them. He is only conscious long enough to realize they are trying to lift him up, and then he slips into the crush of darkness himself.

It is a long, cold sleep. Alan dreams of his breaths, and the rhythm is maddening. His heartbeats fall into the void and are lost, and he can't go after them. The void isn't for him yet; it won't let him in. His breath is too loud, and his heart is too strong. Death turns him away. When he finally wakes in his flesh again, the stars are out and he's supine on onyx-marble stones.

Alan pushes himself up into a sitting position. Every joint aches. His spine is a rod of fire. He looks around, his hand on the back of his creaking neck as pain spreads up the back of his head.

He is on a sunken floor in a roofless ring of columns. Some gold capping still remains on the top of the wall. The stones are dark with years of old stains. This might have been a pool once, but there's no drain at the center. The wind plays around the columns, and there is no dust in it. Beyond the high edge of the deck, a hillside falls away into darkness and treetops. Brattle is near him, sprawled as if he's fainted, and Alan is about to test his legs and go to him when Stag's Blood approaches from the shadow of an entablature.

"Shh," says the cat. "He's only just fallen asleep."

Alan wobbles and his bad knee feels frighteningly out of place, but his legs hold. He stands into a penetrating headache and a wave of pain that rushes down his shoulders, clenching every muscle there along the way.

"Is he all right?" he asks.

Stag's Blood pads silently to his side. The moonlight plays over his impressive coat, illuminating twin lines that run down his back to join at the bob of his tail.

"You should lie back down," the cat insists. "You shouldn't be up. You still look sick."

"I've seen worse," Alan says. He believes this until a few seconds after he says it, when his guts flop over themselves inside him.

"Well the ghoul's exhausted," Stag's Blood explains. His whisper has teeth. It gnarls in his throat like hunger. "He's been walking for days with barely anything to eat or drink, sleeping on the ground. By his own admission, he's had a rough go of it for a while. Like you, he needs to rest and he hasn't been. He's quite stubborn."

Alan considers this in silence. It's still hard to find his voice sometimes. He's embarrassed to find that he hadn't been able to see the hurt beneath Brattle's veneer. He'd been too caught up in himself.

"How are *you*?" Alan finally says. "You seem to be walking fine."

"Kitten-fit and ready to hunt," Stag's Blood replies, smiling. "Thanks to you. If you won't lie down again, then come."

Stag's Blood stands again and motions with his head for Alan to follow him. They mount four steps to a gap where a pillar is missing and look down over the nighted forest.

"Where are we?" Alan asks.

Stag's Blood answers in a warm purr. He looks down the hill, his green eyes bright and his brows low.

"This is a resting place. I carried you here on my back from the City of Dust. We feared you dead, but you are resilient."

"It looks like you saved my life," Alan says. "And I saved yours. So now we're even, I guess."

"Oh, is that the way it goes?" Stag's Blood hums. "You save me, I save you, then, good deeds done, we go our separate ways?"

Alan casts a painful look back at Brattle.

"I guess not," he says. "I don't know."

"I've never seen that kind of magic before. Not even among my own kind," Stag's Blood says, ignoring Alan's answer. "What was it? What sorcerer are you apprenticed to?"

Alan leans back against the stump of a column, trying to stretch the pain from his ribs.

"We haven't actually met, exactly," he says. "He's dead. He was a thanoturge."

"The dead arts. Dangerous magic," Stag's Blood replies. "And you overreached yourself."

"Some apprentice I am, huh?" Alan says with half a smile.

"But it worked. You have talent, Alan. You might thank it before me for saving you. I get the feeling that you are still learning, but there are experienced mages who might have been far worse off than you are after what you did. Your natural ability protected you."

Alan kicks at the stones. He's not quite sure about that. If he could have stayed in the shadow of death, he can't say for certain that he wouldn't have. For the time being, his fleshly body offends him. It is weak and hurt. He feels trapped in it – and hungry. He fed the darkness, and now it grumbles in him, wanting more.

"He lost someone recently," Stag's Blood continues. He shakes his head toward Brattle, his mane billowing. It loves the wind; even the slightest breeze tosses it up into a heroic flutter. "I was there when they killed his brother, but I needn't have been to know. Grief is on his neck like a yoke. I can see that. It's my gift. But you," he gives Alan a hunter's smile, "I doubt there are many like you in the world, are there? A living human – and then some?"

Alan couldn't smile back if he wanted to.

"I don't know," he says again. Then, pushing through his reticence and distraction, he expands. "You know, to be honest, I'm not really sure *what* I am anymore. I stopped being impressed with myself a long time ago. I just feel lost."

The cat clucks his disapproval. "Tch! Here is your first new lesson, apprentice – and you might not understand this for a while: *no one* can ever make you less than what you are, no matter how much they make you suffer. You can only be greater. You can only be more." Stag's Blood lies down and crosses his paws in front of him. "What's human, then? Is it how you look?"

Alan shakes his head.

"Must be something else," the cat goes on. "Where are you from, Alan?"

Alan replies with some difficulty. His stomach is still turning. The whispers are returning to his head.

"Chicago by way of Cicero. I spent some time in Lakewood Balmoral, too, and I guess I'd call that home. Illinois through and through."

"Well that's a *where*," Stag's Blood says, "but maybe I should rephrase: *what* did you come from? Peace? Fear? Joy?"

After a long thought, Alan says, "Death."

"Ah," Stag's Blood says, his voice rolling like stones in his chest. Without the note of sorrow it carried before, it is a predator's voice, cruel and politic. It's beautiful, snarling music. "What death? Whose?"

Alan tries to send the pain in his body flying out over the hillside in a big balloon. He bundles up all his negative thoughts, blows them into a black beach ball, and tries to push it away from himself, but he's only left feeling silly. He's never been good with visualization.

"My sister was a problem child," he begins. "Running around, keeping company with bad crowds, getting in trouble, very rebellious."

Stag's Blood nods again. "I know the type," he says. "Believe me."

"One night, she didn't get home before dark. Mom and dad took me and went out looking for her. It was late, it was a bad part of town, and there was an accident. My parents didn't survive."

"And she was to blame."

"No, but she *took* the blame."

"What a burden to bear!" Stag's Blood thrashes his tail and looks concerned. His eyes burn in the moonlight, cold and beautiful, just like Allison's. "I don't know humans, but I imagine she must have been devastated."

Alan thinks about this for a long time. It actually hadn't ever occurred to him. Even now, as he is laying himself bare, he can't remember Allison grieving. He can only remember how wasteful she had been – how thoroughly she had destroyed herself. But of course it was because of pain. Of course she had been devastated. He'd been too focused on himself then, also. Alan feels a weight shift from him. It is immediately replaced by a greater one.

"She was old enough to take care of me," he says, "but I ended up taking care of her. And then I moved away, I started trying to build something, and she just gave up."

"She gave up?"

"She just kept falling more and more apart. I couldn't believe how much of her there was to just wreck, but she always found more. Then took her own life. Killed herself. And I had to come back home to put her to rest. She hadn't made any preparations."

"And you were relieved?" Stag's Blood asks, matter-of-factly.

Alan is stunned. He straightens up and bunches his fists, but he isn't sure what he wants to do beyond that. There is a part of wherein the cat is right. His deep shame skewered, his guilt dragged out at last, he has to temper the anger in his voice as he responds.

"No. Not in any way at all. I'm the last person left in my family; I was," he searches for a big enough word, but Stag's Blood interrupts him.

"Devastated," he purrs.

"Yes," Alan says. His fury is burning itself out. He lets it happen; he doesn't have the energy to sustain it. "I was devastated."

"Certainly," smiles the cat. He gives his whiskers a little press, smoothing them back along his angular cheekbones and the sleek curve of his violet chops. "What a burden to bear."

Alan puts his hands on his hips. "What is this?" he sighs. "Are you looking into *me* now?"

"Oh, there's no need to look into you, Alan," Stag's Blood replies. "You give yourself completely away. It's all right there on your face."

Alan laughs. The wind whistles the last of the brief tension away. He slides down, his back against the broken pillar, and sits on the stones with his hands on the cold curve of his skull. The headache screams in his empty temples.

"All right," he says. "Your turn now. I've never met a talking cat before. Where are you from? Or *what*, if that works better."

Stag's Blood settles onto his side. A stretch begins at the base of his skull and he dips his head. His legs stiffen, his toes spreading to reveal glittering, ruby claws. He yawns and curls his tongue away from his dagger teeth. Where his harness was, there is a thin patch on his underbelly. Beneath it, his skin is eggplant black.

"I owe you that, I guess," he says. "It's late, and I'll try to be brief.

"My mother was born in the mountains of Mastaba – into captivity. I remember that she was beautiful and I remember that she was sad, but I never truly knew her. The stables called her Pearly, because her coat was white, but my father called her Gatebreaker. It was a name that he gave her when she escaped the kennels with him.

"As he told it, he first saw her when she was out on exercise, bearing a rider, and came back to the pens that night to find her alone. They spoke every following evening through the bars of her cage, and he must have wooed her thoroughly; when the opportunity to escape arose, she took it, unconcerned for the repercussions.

"They hunted her down, of course. And they killed her, because she was only a misbehaving animal to them. But she had lived long enough to give birth to me, so her death was not in vain."

"Didn't they know she could talk?" Alan asks. "That she was different?"

"A basteta," Stag's Blood says. "And I don't know. I suspect that she kept that fact hidden from the captors. Sometimes, being different is a curse. They wouldn't have cared; they can only hear themselves anymore. Their ears are closed to the larger world.

"When they learned I'd been born, they came for me. They were short a cat after all. And Fearsome was already faded and gone by that time. He quit the world, sick of it. He couldn't go on. I was alone when they found me. I've grown up in their castles, walking their white halls with barefoot fairy ladies. I've been north and west and back again, and now I am free. I'm afraid that's the whole of it, now; I'm young, and there is more of my story to be written."

"Who were your captors?" Alan asks. "You must hate them now. What will you do?"

"Hate feels like a terrible waste of my freedom, don't you think? I have none, and I have no plans. It is better that way. You've laid the whole world out before me."

"That's not all of it," Alan says. "That's not even close. You said you would have killed us in the orchard. Why? You talk like you hated captivity as much as your mother did. And what do you mean your father quit the world?"

"What have you done to shield yourself, human?" Stag's Blood growls. His eyes are smiling, but there is a fire of anger behind them. The hate is there; Alan sees it. He doesn't have to be gifted to recognize it. "I have bided my time, I have obeyed as much as I could, because they neither punish nor suspect the compliant ones."

"You were planning your escape?"

"I was earning it. In that way, I am not like my mother and father. But in a deeper way, I am every bit the basteta they were. I have the fire inside me, as you have doubtlessly seen. I am wild in the blood in spite of myself. I am young, but we bastethai are old – the last vestiges of an old guard for an old world. We are not long for this place anymore; we are leaving. I will, too, and I may see my father wherever he's gone, if we all go to the same place when we fade." He looks at Alan and winks. His ears swivel as the wind tugs at them. Dawn is coming.

"But no one knows whether we do or not."

Alan laces his fingers in his lap. "Are you talking about dying?"

"Your next new lesson, apprentice," Stag's Blood says. "Death is not the only way a life can end."

A bird begins to call in the woods. Smoke rises from far away, spiraling up to mar the perfect sky. The trees tremble in a moving line, their whipping tops scattering winged seeds into the wind. Alan thinks of the world he left and finds, for the first time, that he can hold it still and consider it without wondering whether he can ever go back.

"If you really have no plans," he says, "you're welcome to travel with us. I have a feeling that we're going to need all the help we can get. You certainly took better care of Brattle than I have so far. I kind of feel like I've cursed him."

Stag's Blood considers this with a light, laughing purr. Alan wonders what he's thinking that he might find so funny.

"Where are you going?" asks the cat.

"I'm not sure. North to find a prophet king. We're following a map. It should be in our pack." He looks around, remembering the old satchel Brattle dug out of the hobs' hoard. It's nowhere to be seen, and he starts to get up, but Stag's Blood stops him with a breathy trill.

"We brought it," says the cat. "The ghoul was insistent. Even as we fled the ruins for our lives, he was checking to make sure he still had it. We also brought your wand, you'll be glad to hear. Are you going to Gimcrack?"

Alan can see the map in his mind. It's there with all the other things he's absorbed from Pwysh's books, buzzing like a wasps' nests, hot and bright. He remembers it down to the smallest detail; there is no such name on it.

"I don't know. Maybe. What's Gimcrack?"

"A mountain," says Stag's Blood. "And a machine – with a machine for its king. It's where I was caught. There are no other kings in the north to the best of my knowledge. As for prophets: I don't know."

New enthusiasm swells in Alan. He is surprised at how good it feels to be excited about something again. "Maybe there's a reason we ran into you, Stags," he offers. "Certain things seem to be falling in a line recently, if you know what I mean. If you come, it might start to get clearer, but I don't want to walk you into danger."

"Interesting," Stag's Blood replies. "I do know a way through the Colonies. How *very* interesting."

Dawn is still hours away. Stag's Blood rises with midnight at its deepest pouring down his back like a liquid. The starlight shivers around his shoulders. He shakes himself lazily, and the moon is caught in his mane for a moment.

"Maybe I will join you, Alan," Stag's Blood says, puffing out his chest. It could be good for the both of us, now that I think about it. And I *do* owe you. At the very least, it may prove exciting."

Alan starts to speak, but Stag's Blood cuts him off again.

"Say no more," he commands. "Go back and lie down. Lean on me if you need to."

"I'm pretty sure I don't need to sleep anymore," Alan says.

"Sleep will take you."

Stag's Blood is sure, but he's wrong. Alan gets to his feet, propping himself up on the cat's high, furry shoulder. He returns to the pool with Stag's Blood practically dragging him. He feels spilled empty, and it hurts to move, but sleep just isn't in his repertoire anymore. It's beyond him, and it stays there, ignoring him. He is divorced from it. At dawn, he hears moaners down in the woods. They are moving east along the rocky drops to the coast. As noon comes on and Brattle begins to stir, Alan is slumped on the deck with his legs out in front of him, staring straight at the climbing sun from the fog of a stupor.

Fifteen

Descending the hill is a trick. The ground is spongy and gives easily; it is only with great care and trouble that they are able to manage the slope. Alan's strength returns slowly, and healing is torture. Frequent cold flashes leave him shivering. Magic moves through him in little rioting clusters, and he turns his stomach up a few times along the trail. There's nothing in it but black phlegm and knuckle-shaped chunks that feel like melted rubber. By the time they reach the bottom of the hill and decide to stop for a rest, Alan is almost walking and talking normally again, but there is something in him that feels like it might always be wrong. Part of him stays begging at death's door, and he hates it as much as he fears being without it. To his horror, he realizes he's developed an appetite for the magic that nearly killed him.

Brattle worries over Alan like a nursemaid. There's not much he can do – Alan no longer feels the need to eat or drink anything, and hot packs can't help soul-deep chills – so he's left toiling fruitlessly. His overbearing concern quickly becomes obnoxious, but Alan doesn't have it in himself to push the sad ghoul aside. He can't see the dangerous, hungry Brattle anymore; he can only see the limp thing sprawled on moonlit tile, hurt and tired of hiding it. Unsettlingly, Brattle doesn't seem to mind the pity.

The three stop in a shaded clearing and wait for noon to pass. Stag's Blood sits at the edge and stares north into the thinning scrub, regal even in repose. Then he circles the clearing twice at a slink. When he is satisfied that they are reasonably safe, he lies down at the center of the glade to pull burrs from his paw pads with his teeth.

There is a waiting heaviness over everything: an expectation of gravity. There is a storm of work and worry growing, and Alan feels trapped in its path. He holds his head, covering the gaps of his orbits with the heels of his palms. Darkness makes nothing better.

"Tell us about Winter, cat," Brattle says into the taut silence, his mouth full of one of the black rabbits Stag's Blood helped him catch. "I'm further from home than I've ever been, and I didn't come this far for nothing."

"She is cold," Stag's Blood replies.

Brattle affects a laugh.

The basteta continues. "She moves in terror, and she is filled with despair. There is a gloom about her, and her servants carry it with them. She has been robbing graves. I know that she wants to move an army of more than just hobs, and that she is frustrated searching for something, but I don't know why or what she wants. May it not surprise you that she and her servants rarely engaged in conversation with their livestock. The hobs love her though, and that is unsettling."

"How big is her operation?" asks Brattle.

"She is searching everywhere. I don't know where her boundaries are, but they are far apart."

Alan looks up. "That won't help us find her, but it at least gives us some idea of what we're facing."

"Yeah," Brattle laughs. "Insurmountable odds."

"And what are *your* goals, the two of you?" Stag's Blood asks. "How are you involved with Winter White?"

"We ain't," Brattle replies. "Yet."

"We got pulled into this," says Alan. "We're not sure why or where it's taking us, but it keeps getting bigger all the time."

Brattle adds, "We got three dead behind us already."

Stag's Blood looks at Alan and Brattle with a gleam of pity in his eyes. Brattle may be fine with that now, but Alan definitely isn't. He puts his head down again and is quiet for a while, resenting it.

"I know she has made inroads west from the Necropolis," Stag's Blood says. "She has an outpost in Gimcrack, and there's a good chance the prophet king you're looking for will be able to help you find it. Take that as good news, at least. And I'll help, too, for a while. We'll get to the heart of this."

147

"At this point, I'm rolling along out of curiosity more than anything," Brattle says. "I've paid just about everything into it now, and I can't but stick it out. You know? I gotta see where it's leadin', and may it nor surprise you that I hope there's a good neck to wring at the end of it."

Stag's Blood nods. The wind tugs his mane, scattering ribbons of Elrafa dust.

"The Colonies are just ahead of us," he says. "We'll head east for a bit and then turn north again. That will put us right at the dradtails' front gate. From there, I know the fastest way over the plains. It'll be easy on all of us."

Brattle opens the map on his lap. He takes a swig of water from his canteen, swishes it around in his mouth, and then swallows hugely.

"I don't trust hymies," he growls. "I say we sneak in from further up. My cousin got in and out that way once. The wall's just mud and paper, you know. "

"It's best to announce ourselves," the cat replies. "If we're caught sneaking, there'll be no getting through the Colonies at all."

"What are dradtails?" Alan asks. "I get the feeling that they're hostile."

Stag's Blood tilts his head from side to side, considering this description.

"Territorial, yes," he says. "And distrustful of southerners, definitely, but I'd hesitate to call them hostile. They must be dealt with tactfully; the same could be said of anyone. "

"Hymies are tall and thin, and they sting," Brattle says, hooking his fingers and making a stinging motion. "Paralyze you, take you back to their cathedrals, and fill your chest with little hymies. Talk about nightmares! Tact or no, they're on their own side. Just keep your beater stick handy, Al."

"I don't want to kill anymore," Alan says. It's a good thing. He feels lighter for admitting it. "If tact fails and we can't get across the Colonies diplomatically, can we buy our way through? Or go around?"

Stag's Blood scoffs. "If we went around to the northwest, we'd be walking for months."

Brattle adds, "And to the east are the Pit and the ruins of Charnea." Even Stag's Blood shudders at the mention of these places. "The hymies bought their real estate smart. Won it, actually, in many long wars. There's no way but through, I'm afraid."

Alan crosses his arms. "Let's just decide," he says. "The gate is the best option. As hesitant as I am to count on strangers' mercy, it's probably better than drawing their ire – I'd rather lay all our cards out than be caught sneaking in. Stags, you're probably the most diplomatic of us. You try and talk us in, and, if that gets us nowhere, we'll play it by ear."

Brattle sucks his cheek and says no more. Alan is at once glad and sorry that grief has made him so pliable.

Stag's Blood stands and stretches, saying, "Then we go."

The suns are slipping west. Clouds move in to blanket the sky in anvil gray. Alan, Brattle, and Stag's Blood pack up and march on into the dwindling woods. Their discussion continues in lowering whispers as they near the mud walls. The trees shrink away, white and dying where someone has trimmed them back. Dark bloom appears on the scrubby bushes, their petals flexing open to reveal storm-black hearts in swarms of wasps and winged ants. Alan can feel the bloom in his mind; it is fully matured, and it stays open now. He feeds it his fear and the pain from his magic-sickness. It pours out its response in dead praise. There are graves along the foot of the wall; their occupants are wrapped in paper and burst open from the inside. Alan can feel them pointing the way, and he follows. He has no choice but to learn to trust them. When the three reach the great south gates of the Colonies, day is cooling into a pre-storm evening, and sunset is burning the feet of the thunderheads pink.

The woods dry out to the east. Cracks form in the ground as it heaves up with the last straggles of grass flattening against it. Huge tombs lean along the path, erupting through great tears and bulges in the rock like ghouls' teeth, their webbed arches open on blowing darkness. Some of the larger ones have split open, spilling their penetralia in heaps at their feet. Columbaria sprawl, exploded, in plumes of ashes. There are cart tracks through the debris; Alan shudders wondering what business anyone could have in that wasted pile of graves.

Finally, the forest falls away and the land rises. The ruins spread out to the base of the wall. Funeral baubles watch the road from the red dust, winking. Evening blue bleeds into the east over the needle-tops of granite pillars, and the Colonies' south gate stands beneath them.

It is a wall of mud, bark, and paper with a wood arch over it. The arch has huge racks of antlers nailed and pasted to it. New patches of white pulp cover holes and worn spots near the top. There are symbols carved in the wall's face; Stag's Blood reads them out as a litany of curses against intruders.

"That we will pull ourselves apart with our stings in you," he says, "and drag you down into the martyr-cells with us to be drowned in poison."

"They aren't kidding around," says Alan, propped up on his trash masher in another spell of weakness. "If this is the gate, where are the guards?"

"I was just wondering that myself," Stag's Blood replies. "I can smell them. They left here recently. I can't imagine why."

"So much for knocking on the front door, then," Brattle says. "Now what?"

Stag's Blood paces, his nose in the air. He takes three deep sniffs every few feet, and he scratches at the red ground with his paws. Finally, he returns to the gate and sits on his haunches, looking frustrated.

"Maybe they're just waiting inside," Brattle says. "They left the door open, after all."

He points to the bottom of the wall. There is a hole there just large enough for Stag's Blood to fit through with some discomfort. The thick plug of pulp that was blocking it is laid on its side against a boulder.

"We could camp out here," Alan offers.

Stag's Blood shakes his head. "Night is coming," he says. "Worse things than moaners are moving in the woods; there's no choice but to try the hole."

The tunnel goes in for a way and then tilts up. The wall is thick, and there is very little air moving inside it. There are white dots moving over the walls, small as fingernails and bright in the dark. They glide about on brushing legs, oblivious to the intrusion. Brattle enters feet first, helping Alan along as he can. Even backwards, he shows considerable skill at crawling through tight spaces. Alan isn't surprised. Stag's Blood struggles at the rear; he can hardly keep from tearing the paper as he inches his way up the passage.

Near the end the pulp begins to sag, and some delicate buttressing work has been done to support it. This leaves it firmer for a space, and with less give to the mud it becomes even more difficult to traverse the tunnel. Alan starts to feel sick, and his arms nearly give out on him; their strength bleeds away suddenly, and Brattle has to squeeze his wrists hard to keep him from slipping. Stag's Blood lunged forward, pushing him from behind with Alan's heels on the big cat's forehead. The buttresses can't handle the strain; with a creak and loud, wet sound of slipping, the end of the tunnel gives way. The three come tumbling out of the wall, and Alan is the only one who doesn't land on his feet.

It's a short fall into a pile of wet clay. Alan manages to get to his side before Brattle comes to help him up, but he can't do much more than that on his own. The sickness is pitching up inside him. It storms in his gut, a knot the size of a fist moving though his intestines toward his heart. He can only get to his knees as Brattle tugs on him, and then he has to double over to keep from passing out.

"They must be in the process of sealing that tunnel," Stag's Blood says, shaking himself mostly clean. "We could have managed that better. Are you all right, Alan?"

Brattle answers when he sees that Alan is too dizzy to speak.

"We gotta get him somewhere," he says. "He's magick sick bad. Get in my pack if you can and see if there's anything in Pwysh's magic books about throwin' up and passin' out. A diagram or something – anything we can make out without having to read it."

Before Stag's Blood can give Brattle an angry look – before he can spend his aggravation on a hot remark – a dradtail guard approaches them with a lantern. Alan looks up, sensing her strangeness. Her life is spread out over miles. She carries the dead ends of lives inside her, the branching scars of chemical divorce shared by the multitudinous consciousness she serves.

"I see you," the dradtail shouts between angry beats of her narrow wings. "Don't move, separates! South gate closed now. What you doing on this side?"

From the toes of her hard-soled moccasins to the waggling tips of her antennae, the dradtail is seven feet tall. She wears a beaded breastplate and a headdress of quills that falls to her bowing, willow-switch waist. Her bulbous thorax swings behind her, banded and tipped with a barbed sting. The pale light of her lantern swings across a parti-colored simian face, drawing the lines of her pout and her fighter's nose in tight shadow. Her prominent brow and cheekbones frame eyes that sink to black through pinkish depths. Long pedipalps quiver at her jawline as she starts to speak again.

"You break the wall." Her voice is high and strong. She substitutes wing beats for the missing words in her speech. "Now I have to rebuild. Take all day tomorrow! You trespassers!"

"We mean no harm," Stag's Blood says. "We're sorry about your wall. I am Stag's Blood, a former servant of Winter White, and this is Alan and Brattle. We are only trying to get to the Depot and out of your lands as soon as we can. Tell us what you want to let us pass, and we'll give it."

"Friend of White no good here anymore," says the dradtail. "Former friend better, but not much. Whatever you are, you not go anywhere with him like that." She indicates Alan, who has slumped down again and is fighting back an attack of gags. "Bad sick. Tend to him first or he'll die, looks like. Come here."

The dradtail hangs her lantern and approaches Alan. Alan is on his hands and knees coughing. A dam has burst, and the darkness won't respond to him anymore. It moves in him, changing things, stealing his strength. It's like Winter White inside him, insane with prophecy and looting his graves. The wasp runs her six fingers over the curve of his skull. She plucks at his shirt, slipping a hand under his collar to poke at Alan's chest. Her touch is hot with a strange charge.

"Poison bite?" she buzzes. "Can you hear, one-mind? What happen?"

Alan doesn't have the muscle to shake his head.

"He hurt himself protecting us," Brattle snarls, hands on his hips, "and talkin' ain't making him any better. Help us or don't, but we're in a rush."

"Busy yourselves to lift him, then," the dradtail says. Two more appear in the air, coming cautiously over the rise ahead with their wings blurred in speed behind them. The dradtail sniffs along Alan's cheekbone. Then she stands and levels a dark look at Brattle and Stag's Blood.

Alan feels the dradtail reaching out to her mothermind. She speaks with it in smells he can't detect, but he sees them curling through the air in bands of gold when he's able to lift his head again.

"Follow to red rocks and wait," says the dradtail. Or is it one of the other two speaking now? It's difficult to tell; Alan is too foggy. "Lashaseph do what we can for him, and then we see to you."

Alan is only dimly aware of going north. The moon looks down into him from a theater of stars. The Colonylands bump by above him to the beat of Stag's Blood's hurried step. Painted spires fling themselves skyward, their crags snow-capped where they are visible beneath the clouds. Every shelf hides a cluster of organ-pipe nests. Dradtails crawl from them in droves to see the trespassers, and Alan can feel their hivemind buzzing. His vision falters, incense burns his throat, and then he is gone. He sinks away from everything, leaving flesh and weakness behind.

Alan wakes to the sound of a drum beating nearby. He is prostrate at the mouth of a dradtail cathedral with mud and paint smeared on his chest. His head aches. Graveworld welcomes him back with a cool breeze and a starry dawn. Brattle is looking down at him with worried eyes; his hope is hanging on the lip of a spout, doming out and ready to burst. Stag's Blood is in an impatient crouch behind a row of armed wasp-guards.

"Sick pull back for now," says an elaborately dressed dradtail with a rattle in one hand and a censer in another. "He awake, but need to move on to Gimcrack soon. Find help there we can't give. Can you stand?"

Alan is relieved to find that he can. He gets to his feet amid strange laughs and buzzing. The knot in his stomach is all but gone.

"Thank you," is the first thing he can think to say. Unable to help himself, he follows it up with, "I'm sorry."

"Lashaseph help," says the old dradtail. His voice is weak as a whisper, but there is a threat of power roaring beneath it. It sends chills up Alan's spine. "We're not cruel. What you bring back?"

"What do you mean?" Alan asks.

"Always something to bring back from the brink of death. Open your hands. Show your gift."

Alan opens his hands. They are scratched and red. His knuckles ache when he flexes his fingers. One of his nails is splitting down the middle.

"Nothing," he says. "I guess death didn't have anything for me. Nothing but a headache, maybe."

The dradtail shakes his rattle lightly. "A spirit gift," he says, and the other dradtails whisper the same in response.

"We'll see about that," Alan says, suddenly feeling a bit sheepish. "What happened?"

"Too many magic all at once," the dradtail replies. "You should be more careful."

"Yeah. I think I'm getting that," Alan says.

He looks around at the sea of wings and chitinous faces. Red eyes watch him, mystified. Brilliant orbs dart over the swarm, playing through curtains of colored light and sparks. Even Brattle is wearing a rainbow above his head. Only Stag's Blood remains unaffected, sitting in his own shadow, pawing his whiskers clean. There is a spirit here unlike anything Alan has seen in either world, and he can't help but feel humbled by it.

"Still in danger," says the wasp-shaman. "And we are in danger, too – the Lashaseph here in the south." He looks to the intruders, his mouth a hard line in horn beneath his nose ring. "Lashaseph not cruel. Won't send you away to die, but don't trust outsiders. This a time of trouble. Black winds in the far northwest draw our attention, stir the forest outside. We watch for bad warnings. Separates have to leave."

Alan can't decide whether or not to bow, so he just hangs his head.

"We won't waste any more of your time or resources, but we have to keep going," he says. "We just want to pass through here. This is the only way." He looks to Brattle. "What is it we're looking for?"

"The Depot," says the ghoul. "Point us there, and we'll scram. You don't got anything more to worry about from us."

The wasp-shaman's frown is implacable. His eyes flick back and forth, hating everything about these outsiders. The whole group sits silent, sharing the hostility, and Alan feels scrutinized. He shifts his weight and crosses his hands behind his back.

The old dradtail stands. Backlit before the rising sun, the white stripe of paint on his face stands out like an exclamation point. "Separates can't find Depot with just pointing," he growls. "Everything in the canyon want you dead. Winter White leave the south in pain when she turn. We ask more for her passage, and she kill our children at the South gate. Lashaseph done lead separates, now. No agreements with anyone anymore."

This is the grief that Alan has felt running through the hive-mind. Where there were once living nodes, active extensions of Lashaseph's collective consciousness, there is now only aching emptiness. This whole part of the colony is in mourning.

"We're not Winter White," Brattle insists. "We're trying to find her! She did us just as wrong. You want us gone, you hate Winter White. We want to leave, and we ain't friends of hers either! You got nothing to lose here."

Alan reaches into his pocket as the shaman is preparing a reply. His pockets are filled with sand, mud, and pulp, but all his things are still there. He fingers his phone and the vial the Shimmer left him, and then he finds what he's looking for. He pulls it out and presents it to the shaman on his open palm.

"Winter White denied you this," he says, "but I'm offering it. This is a hob's key. You can use it to find their horde."

The old dradtail puts down his censer and takes the key between two scopulated fingers. Alan is surprised to see him blink as he inspects the key.

"Cricket whispers," he snorts. "Stories of the dawn spiders hear for centuries. Myths, yes. But a smell on this one. I can feel the pull – the little spell spin onto it. Do you see, one-mind?"

He holds the key up to the crowd, which stands to circle him in a jerking shuffle. Alan finds the dradtails' nervous movements as unnerving as their shared life is beautiful.

Brattle chimes in with a quick smile for Alan. "It worked for us. It's the real deal, paddle wheel. I guarantee."

156

"Ghouls' word is no good," the shaman-wasp says, "most of the time. But I can see for myself that key is real. Has the smell of filthy hobs on it, and the spell there on it, too."

With this another dradtail steps out of the crowd to stand beside the shaman.

"We show you to the Depot," the shaman continues, "and get you out of the Colonylands by tomorrow. Maybe death's gift was for Lashaseph as much for you. We'll need all we can raid for what's to come."

The dradtail puts his hand on Alan's shoulder.

"Peace to you," Alan says. He immediately feels ridiculous for it. "And thank you again. It's been an honor."

The wasp-shaman finally smiles. His kernel teeth seem to float in his mouth. The dradtail beside him imitates him.

"Stay with Lashaseph tonight," he says with a flit of his glassy wings. "The cat, too. Rest to regain your strength. Shadows left inside you yet, thanoturge."

Sixteen

"Why don't ride?" asks a dradtail. "You still weak, and ride what cat is for."

Alan looks back at Stag's Blood. He is moving as quickly as he can at the spearpoints of his dradtail guards.

"Stags isn't a saddlecat," Alan replies. "He's a free animal with a mind and a will of his own."

"Mind and will are overrate," the dradtail laughs in response, "and not much use when strength is spend."

"You're lucky he hasn't seen fit to throw your 'hospitality' back in your faces," Brattle says. "I would've long ago even if you hadn't saved Al. I told you he's no danger."

The dradtail only snorts. His name is Saylekali, and he is leading them northwest through windy passages toward a permanent hunters' camp. They will stay there until the young hunters return in the evening, and then they will be taken back to the cathedral in the red rocks. This was the tribal council's decision on how best to keep the strangers out of the way. They wouldn't explain it any further.

Alan goes to the back of the line without saying anything to Saylekali. He steps between the guards to walk beside Stag's Blood, and the big cat greets him with a purr.

"Why are they treating you like this?" Alan asks Stag's Blood. "And why aren't you doing anything about it?"

"They're afraid," says Stag's Blood. "They remembered me, in their swarm's mind, as a mount in Winter White's service. I don't stop it because I don't want to give them further reason to distrust me. I want to prove that I can be trusted by acquiescence. This is something you learn when you live your formative years in slavery."

Alan only nods. It makes sense, but the unfairness of the dradtail's singling Stag's Blood out still makes his guts boil. The last thing he needs is more of that right now; the shaman's magic helped, but the darkness is still upon him, churning in his stomach. It's in his skull like an alarm clock's hammer.

"Winter won't be coming back this way soon, I guess," he says.

Stag's Blood shakes his head. "What are you going to do when you find her?" he asks. "What are you looking for?"

"A little vengeance" Alan says, "at least in Brattle's case. And, for whatever good it'll do him, he deserves it. As for me: I want to know what we're caught up in. Brattle will have to extract the former from Winter herself. I'm hoping we can get the latter from this prophet king. Here. Look."

He fishes his phone out of his pocket. After all he's been through, it looks none the worse for wear. In fact, he's never seen it so clean. Once, there were fingerprint whorls and smears of grease from Ray's on its face. Now it looks factory-new. He taps the screen to bring it to life and then holds it out to show Stag's Blood.

"Do you know what these numbers mean?" he asks.

Stag's Blood squints at the phone. His whiskers dance up into little curls against his cheeks.

"No," he says. "What is that thing?"

"It's my phone," Alan sighs. He keeps forgetting that he has to explain this. "You use it to communicate with people that are far away. I found it and it was like this: changed, with these weird symbols on it. It showed me this string of numbers. I think it's something I'm supposed to understand or someplace I'm supposed to go; Brattle says they're coordinates, but he doesn't recognize them either."

"Endless unfolding wonders," says the cat. He stops for a moment to lick his paw wet and slick his mane back between his shoulders. The dradtail guard following him makes as if to poke Stag's Blood with the butt of his spear, but a broad-knuckled hand seizes the shaft before he can deliver the blow – Brattle has dropped back from the head of the column to eavesdrop.

"We're movin'," he snarls at the warrior wasp.

Stag's Blood gives Brattle a gracious tip of his head and continues.

"It certainly seems you're meant for something, though I can't imagine who might be doing the meaning, so to speak. You've piqued my curiosity, too, Alan. I hope the king you seek will have an answer."

"My guess would be Pwysh – the thanoturge that..." Alan stops himself. He assumes that Stag's Blood knows full well what happened at Pwysh's workshop. "Well, the thanoturge. We've got some notes he wrote, too. And our map has my name on it."

Stag's Blood interrupts. "Speaking of curiosity – have you tried to contact anyone with that device? You say that's what it's for, yes?"

Alan looks at his phone and feels stupid. How has he not thought of this before?

"I wouldn't know how," he tries to explain. "The interface is totally different – the buttons and controls are gone, and these symbols are there instead." The symbols swirl, and he can feel their movement in his mind.

"Perhaps you should try and speak to it," Stag's Blood says. "Certainly stranger things have worked."

Alan looks around him at the spear-wasps. They are glancing over their shoulders at him one at a time, taking turns giving him angry frowns.

"It's worth a shot," Brattle says to him. "We ain't got anything to lose by trying – though I suppose that stranger things have harmed, too. Just try not to bring out anymore Watchers."

Alan holds the phone up at the level of his mouth, touches the screen again, and waits. He listens for the dead whispers and searches the corners of his mind for the Kingwatcher. Nothing comes to him. For the moment, his sickness has driven the magic so deep that he can't access it. He's not sure whether that's a good thing or a bad thing as he begins to speak.

"Call Ray's," he says.

The phone does nothing. The dradtails look back at him, perplexed. When the screen goes black again, Alan puts the phone back into his pocket.

"Another option crossed off our list, then," Stag's Blood says. A smile flashes across his face like a shooting star. "Our hopes remain pinned where they were. But, as you said, Brattle, it was worth a shot."

"Seek and you shall find," Brattle says, "a reason to keep hold on those low expectations."

Alan feels a twist in his chest. Pain shoots up his spine to spread across the top of his skull like warm pinpricks.

"What if there's nothing?" Stag's Blood asks with his eyes on the brightening sky. The breeze is dead, and noon is blooming its hot pomp over the canyons. "No answers? No vengeance?"

Alan says, "There's always the journey."

"That's the way to look at it," Stag's Blood says with a smile. "That's why I'm not fighting, if you get me. I'm letting life happen to me. That's another thing you learn as a slave."

Alan considers this for a moment.

"A pretty good philosophy," he says. "Within reason, of course."

"Of course," says Stag's Blood. "Within reason."

The hunters' camp is situated at the base of a high crag and the slope of scree that falls from its shoulders. There is nothing to do at the camp once they reach it. Alan and Brattle sit between mud huts and watch the suns wane over the horn. Their chaperones hang their spears on a rack and gather on the talus to share honeyed blossoms. Stag's Blood pads through the camp unattended, a shadow on its eastern edge. There is a fire pit with embers burning in it, but there are no tools in the camp for cooking anything. The huts shield paper sleeping cones from the elements, and there is little else in the way of furnishings inside them.

Alan spends a long time staring directly at the nearest sun. He doesn't need to look away anymore. He lives in the intensity for a while and tries to be aware of himself. It's strange to be so still inside. He hadn't realized how much effort breathing regularly had been. As daylight dims along the horizon, he tells Brattle about Chicago. He talks to keep the sickness at bay; it moves in him all the time, spreading through him, draining him slowly. He feels polluted, but sharing with Brattle restores him a little, even when the ghoul starts to get angry talking about Nettle and his Da. A hurt friend is still company, and Alan is grateful. He admits this to himself with no small amount of surprise.

"I don't think I've ever talked to anyone as much as I've talked to you," he tells Brattle. "How is it that I'm more comfortable around a ghoul than I ever was around people?"

"It's my charm," Brattle says. "I'm handsome, I've got a heart of gold, and I don't go around ruining perfectly good rants with sobby, pansy crap."

"You might actually be right about some of that," Alan laughs.

"You'd think you'd know by now," Brattle coughs, crossing his arms over his chest. He is so strangely proportioned that he could reach around and scratch his back that way if he wanted. "I'm *always* right."

The dradtail hunters return to their camp with strange prey in tow. They come strutting in from the east, too green yet for their solemn pride. One of them is moulting. They glower at the strangers, wearing their scorn emptily, like the paint on their faces, in imitation of their fathers. Alan searches them as Saylekali rallies the chaperones, and he's surprised to find how small they are as individuals. The hivemind still dominates them, despite their affectations; they are almost a single organism. They string up trophy grubs as Saylekali leads the party away from the camp; Alan tries not to think about what they might be planning on doing with them.

Innocence doesn't last, he thinks. *But they have its fall plotted out. Maybe they've hunted it since they were grubs themselves, dreaming of first blood, worshipping death in fevers like men.*

Alan remembers the little boys at his elementary school and their destructive games. A terrified animal was a badge of honor among them. He never understood the impulse to dominate, and he still doesn't. It's never been in him, as far as he knows.

The band takes a different path back to the red rocks. The guards following Stag's Blood barely notice him anymore. Brattle knuckles along quietly beside Alan, his spirit half gone. He stares down at ruddy sand and sees nothing. Alan feels too sick to try and reach out to him. They stop once to watch a meteor shower begin, and Saylekali tells a story about the first wars of the daubers and the dawn spiders. Then they move on, and when they reach the cathedrals Brattle and Stag's Blood curl up to sleep in pits the council dug for them.

Alan sits up and reads. There is nothing in either of Pwysh's books about his condition. He sinks into the mage's argot in search of the resonance and power he felt there before, hoping it will heal him. When their new dradtail guide comes to find him the next morning, he has scratched spell circles all around his sleeping pit and is sitting among them in a cold sweat with his trash masher in one hand.

"Time to go," she says, and Alan recognizes her as the guard at the South gate. "Are you well, one-mind?"

"Not getting any better," Alan replies. He stands, using his trash masher to prop himself up. "Let's burn."

The near sun is an ember on the horizon. A hush is on the canyon, thick as rain. The wind is still sleeping. The dradtail woman brings a few bindles from the council. Stag's Blood uncoils from his pit without so much as a yawn and is ready to go, but Brattle needs some shaking. He groans and drags his feet, and he puts his complicated goggles on to shield his eyes from the light of morning. While Alan helps him load their new provisions into the pack, Stag's Blood addresses the dradtail guard.

"We're grateful for all your help," he says, "and we're glad to meet you again."

"I see you in," she buzzes in reply, "and I see you out. Nobody go to the Depot from here anymore but me, so no thanks necessary."

She looks west, her face storming with worry.

"What may we call you?" asks Stag's Blood.

The wasp-woman waits a long time to reply. Alan straps the bulging pack onto his back. There's barely enough room in it for Pwysh's books now. The wrapped parcels of honeyed bread look delicious, but Alan has no desire to eat them.

"Neshushuni," the dradtail finally says. "Shuni maybe. Fifteen mile walk for the wingless. How fast you go?"

"We don't know, Shuni," Alan replies. He has finally gotten Brattle up and running, though the ghoul is swaying on his feet and staring blankly. "Just go easy on us. It's been a long time since we had this much rest."

"You not rest at all, gone-face," Shuni says. "But no time now. Come on."

They head north toward the humps of stony foothills. In the pre-dawn gloom, with pink light stopped breathlessly in the east, they file through sleeping purlieus following the swing of Shuni's lantern. Basalt shelves hide vast complexes of pulp nests in the wider spaces.

Walls rise around them. Alan runs his fingers over the rock, feeling the networks of petroglyph scars.

Shuni pauses to look at the symbols. "Others live here before," she says. "Many rocks tell the stories now, but nothing else. They are forgotten."

"I seen marks like this in swamp caves," Brattle says.

The carvings flow together. Time is pressed into them. Alan thinks about the lives and the history they represent and the sickness twists within him. He hasn't the strength to be a hunter; he sees no symbols of power in the sky. He's never lived anything fit to chisel. Confronted with such passion, he feels soft and simple.

Alan is particularly interested in the figure of a man with a feathered head.

"Coco Man," Shuni explains when she sees him staring at the carving. "Hide his face like you, one-mind. Very old, and see here now and again. He pass through, but have no dealings with us. Bad to have dealings with the Coco Man. Everybody know."

"What does he want when he passes through?" Alan asks, tracing the engraving with his thumb.

"Same Winter White want, I gather," Shuni replies. "Finder of gone things."

Stag's Blood is unimpressed by the petroglyphs. He sits at the head of the path and surveys the area, his ears twitching.

"And what did Winter White want?" he asks.

"Don't know," Shuni says. "To bring danger everywhere. Like the Coco Man."

They continue into a maze of diverging paths. Twists and branches complicate the way until Alan is thoroughly confused; he instinctively tries to remember the carvings as they go, but he finds that they shimmer and vanish as he looks back at them. The cliffs are barren – or else dotted with abandoned pipe-hives. Wolf shapes walk the overhangs, watching the group with eyes like cinders. They howl to each other across the canyons. Even as the sky begins to brighten and Alan loses sight of them, he can still hear their windy screams.

"Shrieker hounds," Shuni says. "Only keep their distance because they know me."

"I've seen them in the northern woods," Stag's Blood explains, "hunting poltergeists."

Shuni hisses disdain. "Thieves and destroyers. Dangerous, but they are learn to fear us. Maybe the only things they fear."

Daybreak walks up the sky with shadows, cold and somber, calming the last stars one by one. The way drops into a dusty gulch. Shuni puts out her lantern and hangs it on a stick along the path, and the group stops to rest.

"You climb all right?" Shuni asks the others.

"It doesn't look very steep," Alan lies. "I think we'll be OK. Don't stop on our account." He wonders if Shuni can see through him. It must be obvious that the soul-sickness is draining him of the will to continue. She must be able to see how exhausted he is, but she says nothing.

They proceed down a gentle slope. The ground is solid rock with red sand grinding over it. The wind has awoken capricious, and it pulls hard around their shoulders at its most enthusiastic. Shuni beats her wings and shrugs it off, but Alan occasionally finds himself clinging to Stag's Blood for balance. Brattle makes his way down in jerking, reptilian bursts.

Finally, the path evens out a little and the gulch opens to their right. Here clusters of wooden longhouses sit on tiered ledges. They are ten to twelve feet high and sixty feet long with stone caps for roofs and honeycomb cornices. Each has a single round entrance that is matted over with chewed pulp. There are thick vines and enormous, bell-shaped flowers growing all over them – golden-spotted petals peeling back in complex whorls from dark centers bunched with bobbing anthers. They nod strangely as the travelers approach, and pollen drifts down from them like snow on the coltish breeze. Alan catches what remains of his breath.

"What is this?" he asks, awed and distracted. "It's unbelievable."

"Nectaries," Shuni says. Her tone is reverent, but Alan can tell that she's holding back. "Many like this, and most larger. There is fields of these great wayflowers a long time ago, but not anymore."

Brattle is fully awake now. He sniffs the air, closes his eyes, and smiles. As they step down into the riot of vines, he raises a hand to paw at a silken petal. It shrinks from his touch, and the head of the bloom tilts away on its woody stem.

"How do you keep these growing?" he asks. "I never seen anything so beautiful last for more than a month, but these roots have got to run deep. This," he swings his arm out in front of him to indicate the whole vast complex, "took time."

Shuni doesn't stop to admire the flowers. She pushes on through the nectaries at a purposeful clip. The blossoms don't recoil from her. When she walks through them, they reach down to caress her face. She buzzes for them, but keeps moving. Pollen collects on her wings and thorax like dusted gold.

"Wasting everywhere," she says. "Even here. Dark spots, cut root, and rot. You can see it, but not like outside among the one-minds. Wasting is deathless death, but Lashaseph is life. We are more, and more is stronger, and when wasting come it not touch us as deeply. Not rot our hearts like those of the one-minds. So flowers grow and don't waste too much."

"What happened," Alan asks, "that caused the wasting?"

Stag's Blood answers before Shuni can speak. "There's no one left to remember," he says.

"That don't stop anybody from telling stories," Brattle adds. He's about to continue when Shuni raises a hand to shush him.

"Be still," she says. "Wayflowers very sensitive. No more talk for now, one-minds. Please. Walk and look only."

They continue through the nectaries in silence. The blooms rustle in protest, but they don't have far to go to escape the invaders' touch. Alan can see Brattle fighting to contain his urge to lunge at them and press his face between their petals. Many of the wayflowers trail runners with wiry plantlets on their ends. He thinks about the potted spider plant on his porch and wonders who is going to care for it now. The longhouses groan in the grip of the vines, and moving things are visible inside them where the wood is splitting. These might be engines, but they are whisper-quiet. Alan imagines that they are made of living plant parts.

After a long walk, they scale a wall, and then the path drops into a great pit of blowing sand and pulverized stone. The field is littered with corpses that lie half-excavated, their copper pipes and furnaces spilling from the split, steel cages of their ribs. Broken masts with bellied sails emerge from seas of wheels and winking rivets. This is the Depot, a graveyard for ships and machines, and it expands for dry miles to meet the horizon.

Shuni has a rod strapped to her back. She unstraps it, plants it in the ground, and lights the bulb on top of it with a flint spark. The bulb burns a blinding green for a moment and then dies down, leaving smoke pouring out that only Alan can see. Green curls waft from it, twining through stronger billows of red and barley-gold. Stag's Blood sniffs hard and sneezes, and Brattle holds his nose. The smell is strong enough that even Alan gets a whiff of it.

"Mahaduchet," Shuni says. "The Depot. Where fairy hubris come to die. Most Lashaseph not come here anymore. What you want for these wrecks, I don't understand, but you are here now."

"What's that you've got burning?" Brattle asks as he moves downwind. "What an awful stench!"

"You should know from that, dead eater," Shuni smiles, folding her arms over her chest. "Pheromone torch. Let Lashaseph know my task is done."

"Are you coming with us, then?" Stag's Blood says, hopefully. "You're not going back to the hives right away?"

Shuni frowns across the sands of Mahaduchet in disgust.

"Not go in there," she replies. "Nowhere left to guide you now. I go to the wall, where Lashaseph need me. More important things to do." She turns to regard her three charges. "Tulabek want you gone. Doesn't trust you. But I do. Winter White want the wayflowers for her own. You see them, walk among them, and have no greed for them. Torch will tell that, too. Say a good thing for you. So go well and safe in the sand graves, and find what you want, and get where you're go. Goodbye."

"Wait," Alan says. Then a cramp seizes him and he has strain against it for a moment with his hands on his knees. He continues, trembling. "Wait. You mean taking us through the nectaries was a test?"

"Something like," says Shuni.

Stag's Blood twitches his lip into a snarl. His whiskers fan out, and there are flecks of dust caught in them. "What if we had failed?"

Shuni replies, "Kshonshok." Then she beats her wings into a loud blur and rises into the air to waggle her thorax at them between her legs. Her stinger is long and wet with poison. "But you do well. Even you, saddlecat, who we remember. Prove Lashaseph wrong, and you go with your lives. Go the right way. Goodbye again, separates. Peace to you! Short flights to free blossoms."

With this, Shuni turns and rises away. For a second, she is a dark speck with her limbs hanging beneath her. Then she vanishes.

"As good a send off as we're like to get," Brattle says. "And more than I expected."

"The dradtails do not indulge in long goodbyes," Stag's Blood explains, "and that was an exception, from what I've seen. Take it as an honor."

Brattle snorts. "We got lucky. If Al hadn't been so sick, they'd have pitched us out."

They start down the hill away from the pheromone torch. Its scent trails up into the sky for miles, blowing south on wind that Alan can't feel.

"It had to have helped that we had nothing to hide," Alan says. "What would Winter want with the nectaries?"

"Can't imagine," Brattle says, "but we can ask her when we find her."

Alan nods. The dead are rolling in his brain. The hunger is back, huge and demanding. He spits, feeling polluted.

"Lead on, Stags," he says. "The sooner we get to Gimcrack the better."

Seventeen

Alan follows Stag's Blood down toward the Depot. Brattle is close behind, wrapping his pall around his head again. The ground shifts constantly beneath them, making it difficult to find a walking rhythm. The wind is pleasant and steady. It croons around the rusted hulks that dominate the crater, bending sighs over hulls and broken angles. Its caresses fall down around them in sheets of fine, black sand.

The going is slow, and the suns pour out a killing heat. The three take refuge as they need to in the wrecks' colossal shadows. Stag's Blood sniffs around every shell and frame. He paws carefully through piles of metal and rotted wood as the day drains away. Alan tries to enjoy the tour of these spectacular ruins, but sickness and impatience are wearing on him. He turns to collecting bones; there are pits everywhere filled with them. Evening comes early, the wind turns its chill edge, and they have nothing to show for all their searching but distance. The rim of the crater is far away now. They make a little camp at the foot of a loess hill, but Alan can't bring fire from the bones he's gathered. He is growing weak, but his magic is stronger than ever, and he's afraid of what might happen if he uses it.

Brattle coaxes a licking flame from a decaying plank and feeds it with dried witchgrass panicles. When it is healthy and crackling, he squats beside it, peels the mortcloth from his head, and opens the pack to find the food Shuni brought them. Stag's Blood settles beside him, huge and sandy, and begins to pull at a shard of glass that's stuck in his paw. He makes no sound as he extracts it. Alan lies on his back and looks up at the stars as night grows. The sky is choked with them. They wink down in death, bathing the crater in light that has long outlasted them. It makes Alan's heart ache to think about it.

"All right," Brattle says. He has unrolled a bun from its paper wrapping and is considering eating it with a frown on his face.

"What are we lookin' for, Stags? You gonna tell us, or will we just know when we find it?"

Stag's Blood licks his bleeding paw. Alan watches him thinking; colors dance over his head like little flames.

"A myth," Stags says at last. "A fairy story. The Mercy Gale."

He looks at Brattle and Alan in turn. Brattle rolls his eyes, but when neither of them interrupts, Stag's Blood continues with a smile in his voice and his eyes flashing.

"When I first passed through the Colonies," he says, "Winter White's guards told stories about a ship that sailed over dry land. They were wild tales – ghost stories mostly – but there was a common thread through their histrionics. The Mercy Gale was the jewel of the north in living memory, but now she's lost. If she's anywhere, the guards agreed that she must be here. It was all they could talk about for a while, and they convinced me thoroughly."

"Landship," Brattle snorts, but Alan can tell he's not ready to dismiss the story out of hand. "Assumin' all's crazy and you're right, what makes you think she ain't all busted up like the rest of these heaps? You know the way things fall apart here. This place is already a scrap yard."

"I cannot claim to be certain of that," Stag's Blood replies, "but it's worth our time to look. The guards claimed that a powerful mage built her for his wife. They said it could only be powered by magic. Perhaps magic has protected her all these years. We know that diligent spellwork can keep the wasting at bay."

Brattle shakes his head. "I don't know nothing of the sort."

"It's all the certainty we're likely to get at the moment," Alan says. "I'll take it. We're already going north. We might as well look for the Mercy Gale on the way."

"Yeah," Brattle says. "We might as well look for the great screamin' squash lord, too."

With this, Alan sits up and hugs his knees to his chest. He looks into the fire without seeing it. Smoke threads up to encircle his head, and he slides his hand over the dome of his skull. His jaw aches terribly. Gripping his chin, he can move his lower mandible a bit in its place. Where connective tissue should be, there are only smooth grooves at the edges of his cheekbones. It's magic holding his head together; maybe there's a ship in this giants' boneyard being preserved by the same forces.

"Speakin' of which," Brattle says, clearing his throat, "how you doin', Al? You look better than you did when we broke through that wall, but you're startin' to get pale again. Just how urgent a situation are we looking at right now? Are you gonna be OK sifting through sand and rubble all day tomorrow?"

"Pale?" Alan wonders aloud.

"Yeah," Brattle smiles. "Right around the temples."

Stag's Blood chuckles.

"Ha ha," Alan says, grateful that he doesn't have to move his mouth to speak.

"Whatever the dradtails did is wearing off, slowly but surely. I think I can manage a few more days, but I'm just not sure about anything." He shifts and wrings his wrist before he goes on. "You and I can both hear the deadcall, right?"

Brattle nods.

"Well I feel like there's a little more to it with me, if that makes sense. I can hear them from more than just the ground. It's like I can hear them from everywhere. Like I'm taking them with me."

"That's a new one," Brattle says, scratching his head. "What do you mean?"

Alan struggles to put his thoughts into words. His pounding headache doesn't help.

"Shuni kept calling us 'one-mind,'" he says, "but I don't know that I'm only one mind anymore. Let's say you have a cupboard, and you want to think about what's in it. You can kind of look through it in your head – take a kind of mental inventory – without actually opening the door and looking inside. Right? That's what it's like, only more so. It's like they're *physically* there in my mind. I hear them muttering almost all the time – like a million other thoughts intruding in my head, all of them talking over each other. Many minds inside my own. I'm conscious of it the way you know what's in your cupboard."

"When did this start?" Stag's Blood asks.

Brattle adds, "After the accident?"

Alan centers himself. The floodgates are opening, but he has to stem the tide. He thinks about the dead hobs in Debtors' Orchard and what it felt like to lose control.

"Yes," he replies. "But then no. It actually started with the Whisperwood."

"Tell me everything," Stag's Blood insists. "Begin at the beginning."

Alan goes on to tell them about the seed of the Kingwatcher and the lights he can see – the new beauty of the world that emerged after the incident at the gate. At Stag's Blood's continued prodding, and with Brattle interrupting to add color, he tries to relate the whole story. He feels clumsy, but the release is sublime. He stumbles over parts, but it's surprisingly easy to push the tale through his natural bashfulness. He realizes he had been dreading this admission. He hadn't wanted to speak it solid, to give it power by naming it as his experience. Keeping it inside had hurt, and pain had reminded him that he was still real. He had been clinging to it, but now he is letting go. The last tatters of his life among the living swirl away on the sighing breeze. At last, and to his great relief, Alan is making himself a home.

Stag's Blood listens intently the whole time, nodding and swishing his tail through the dirt. When Alan is done, he says, "you aren't the most confident storyteller, are you?"

"It actually feels good to let this out," Alan replies. "But I've never been comfortable being the center of attention."

Brattle turns a cough into a chuckle. "Al ain't quite ready to go native yet."

Stag's Blood softens. He settles into the soil like a rooting tree, sagging around the blade of his smile. Sickle teeth glint behind that grin.

"Effort is, in itself, a victory," says the cat.

"You don't know how long I wanted to just leave," Alan says. "I had this fantasy: there would be a catastrophe. Right? A cataclysm. Cities razed to the ground. Dust clouds choking the sky. Subterranean fires burning oil forever. Everything I love incinerated with everything I fear; it would have been worth it. And I would survive. I'd live like a rat in the ruins of society. It would be hard, and I would struggle. There would be days when I would bleed and hurt and want to give up. But every night, I could look at everything I had and know that I'd fought for it and won. It would be struggle with a purpose. Where I'm from, it's just struggle – just work – and it's never over. You can't stop it no matter what you do. The crush keeps you powerless because power doesn't mean anything. Fighting doesn't mean anything. People don't mean anything. I wanted to feel effective. I wanted – for so long – for all my anger and frustration to collapse into something I could hold in my hand. To know that I had poured out my life for a *reason*."

Brattle is looking at Alan with a sick, hilarious pity. Alan hates him for it.

"Look at what you been through," Brattle says, "and tell me you ain't worked for everything you have."

"The ghoul is right," Stag's Blood adds. "And those are four words I never thought I'd say. The world does not give reasons. You have to make your own."

Alan wants the warmth in his chest to last forever. The sickness peels away for a starlit moment. When it returns, it is diminished. He wants to let himself be glad, but he can't. It is voracious. Still, he feels like he's bought himself some time.

He's about to speak, but Brattle beats him to the punch.

"This wasp shit is not going to cut it," Brattle announces. "I need nourishment."

He stands and dusts himself off. Stag's Blood looks up at him. Reaching into the bag past Pwysh's books and more paper-wrapped honey rolls, he finds the goggles he stole from the hobs' horde.

"Where are you going?" Stag's Blood asks.

"You can hear it, right?" Brattle says to Alan by way of an answer. "This ain't just a graveyard for fairy tale landships. I'm off for a bit of a dig. Watch the bag and don't pass out."

Stag's Blood frowns. "Perhaps, as a courtesy to those of us who are sick, you could try and eat one of the honeyed biscuits Shuni brought us instead."

"I gave it a fair shake," Brattle replies, feigning indignation. "I took one bite of it and couldn't go on. Effort is, in itself, a victory."

"Be careful, then," Stag's Blood says. "There are shrieker hounds about. I can smell them. Don't stray too far."

Brattle chuckles and his whole skinny frame shakes. There is a hollowness to his laugh that makes Alan feel sorry for him. He turns away and knuckles off into the dark toward the wreck of an enormous, iron clad tank.

"Don't worry about me," he calls as he disappears. "Maybe I'll find your ghost ship while I'm at it!"

Alan lies down again. The pain lessens when he curls into the fetal position, but the stain on his spirit continues to spread unabated.

Stag's Blood watches the fire in distracted silence for a long time. Alan envies the fact that he doesn't have to mask his savagery; he wears it in his stillness like a gem, content with it as inextricable from who he is. There is power even in Stag's Blood's absence.

"I can't stop thinking about them," Alan finds himself saying. "I know they would have killed us, but I don't know why. I destroyed them – I crushed them – and I hated it. I think I hate myself for it. Killing isn't what I do. I think doing it is part of what's made me sick."

"You're talking about the Watchers in Elrafa," Stag's Blood purrs. "Yes, they would have killed us. That was what they were there to do. The Coma is hostile."

"Hobs, too." Alan feels a seizure coiling in his stomach. "The guilt is the worst thing I've ever had to endure. Like I said: I can't stop thinking about it. Killing seems like an unforgivable waste. I've never liked wasting things or breaking things. I want things to be together. I want things to continue."

"Shall I absolve you?" asks the cat. "I don't think I have the authority. Be unabsolved. Be guilty, and let that power you. Work with what you have and don't torture yourself about what you don't. That has always worked for me."

Alan tries to make himself still. It doesn't work, so he tries to immerse himself in being perturbed. He tenses against the seizure and stops it in its tracks.

"Have you ever seen the Plutonian Shores?" he asks.

"You can't find people there, Alan."

"Why not?"

Stag's Blood stares into the fire and seems to draw his answer from within it.

"People stop being people when they die. Humans are gestalt – irreducible complexity. Do you see? If you take one part away, they aren't human anymore. Without a spirit, a body can't truly live. And without a body, a spirit is little more than a sentient dream."

Alan sighs. It's a strange and empty sound – like blowing through a conch.

"I dreamed about my parents every night for a month after they died," he says.

Stag's Blood smiles. "Dreams are like deaths. The two are deeply related."

"I don't dream anymore." Alan tries on Stag's Blood knowing calm. It fits just well enough. "And I won't kill anymore, either. I'm not a violent person."

"Don't sell yourself short," Stag's Blood says. "I'm sure you'll find a way to surprise yourself." With this, he puts his chin on his paw and closes his eyes.

Brattle comes swinging back to camp at sunrise with blood on his face and hands. The wisps of his hair are standing up behind his goggles where he's pushed them up onto his forehead. His face is drawn tight over his skull to deepen the hollows of his cheekbones.

Alan puts Pwysh's book down and stands to greet him.

"Where were you?" he asks.

"Morning," Brattle replies. Then he falls spread-eagled at the base of the hill and sleeps motionless for four hours.

At the early end of noon, he rolls into a huge stretch and then stands, groaning. Stag's Blood has been up since the first tendrils of dawn touched the sand. He regards Brattle suspiciously from near the ash of the fire.

"Let's try this again," Alan says to Brattle. "Where were you last night?"

A band of creases goes up Brattle's brow. He stares back as if shocked.

"Scouting, boss," he replies. "Eating first, you know, but then just wandering, trying to create a perimeter. Stags said he smelled shrieker dogs, but I didn't see nothing for a mile around here: no birds, no little lizards, not even a hungry dog. That ain't good."

"They must have been here recently," Stag's Blood says. "I still smell them now. But we didn't hear any last night, did we? Hmm. That *is* odd."

Alan looks north across the crater. The land ahead flattens out into an erg bounded by shifting dunes. Sand flows over the high curves of their shoulders, caught by the wind to billow like banners. There is nothing in the slacks but lost machines. The dead hum in that emptiness. There are strange bodies here with alien voices, but there is nothing alive – nothing that Alan can see, anyway. A chill slips up his spine.

"We'll be careful," he says, taking up his trash masher. It feels like lightning in his hand. He squeezes it tight to suppress it, and it tugs on him inside. It is hungry; he has put some of his soul sickness into it. "Are you good to go, Brattle? I'd like to get some ground behind us."

A storm gathers above the Depot. It threatens the crater like a waiting hand, and the three set out into the erg in its shadow. Stag's Blood finds a strong acid scent in the sand and follows it for a long time. As the silence deepens around them, Alan remembers his first hours in Graveworld and the hush that fell the night he beat the moaners back. He grips his trash masher and tries to squeeze all his mounting fear into it.

Down the slip side of a crescent dune, there is so much metal debris scattered across the sand that they can barely move without kicking a piece. They pick their way through, headed for shelter on the less side of a tower of wreckage, and but they stop suddenly as a shadow passes over them.

"That was no cloud shadow," Stag's Blood says.

Brattle growls. "What have you led us into, cat?"

"Stay calm," Alan hisses, hunkering down instinctively. "Apparently, there's something alive here after all. That's a good sign. Right?"

"Let's keep moving," Stag's Blood says.

Alan and Brattle follow him to the tower of ruin. It is a heap of disparate parts that sags west under its own weight. There, the three press back against the crumbling east side and look up. There's nothing to see in the sky but swelling storm anvils. They wait for several minutes, taut as bowstrings. Nothing falls from the cloud wall. The sky goes on forever, hot and wet and pregnant. Finally, Stag's Blood speaks.

"One more wreck ahead. That's where the acid smell is coming from — I'm sure of it. We can head there and take a real rest; I'm all bunched up from this tension, and my mouth is dry. Do you think it's safe to venture out?"

"We ain't heard nothing," Brattle replies. "It's worth a shot for a drink, but I don't see why we can't just take our rest here."

"One more pile," Stag's Blood says. "Indulge me. It's not far."

Alan continues to search the sky. The dead have nothing to say. Even the sickness has drawn back a bit. The quiet is like a fist in his throat. He swallows and looks toward the wreck.

"The smell's coming from there?" he asks.

Stag's Blood nods.

"Let's check it out," Alan continues. "That looks like the curve of the back there. The keel? And maybe that's a mast."

"No shortage of those here," Brattle grumps. "And every one of these heaps reeks lampblack and train oil. I don't see how you can sort one odor from the rest." He takes a longer look at the black shape of the wreck in the distance. His eyes swirl with troubled colors. "Hmm. I guess it just might be something. It's supposed to be a ship, right – something like a boat – that we're looking for?"

"That's what the stories say," Stag's Blood says, clearly getting more excited now. His nostrils twitch and he tilts his whole head up with each sniff, as if trying to inhale as much of the scent as possible. "And it does look something like one, doesn't it? The longer I look, the clearer it becomes. This has to be right! I'm ready to be out from under these shadows, now. Follow me!"

Stag's Blood breaks across the sand in a lope, his mane flying behind him. As it blows back from his face, Alan can see the narrow outline of his skull. Brattle follows after, knuckling faster than it looks as if he should be able to. He is all lean meat and wires. He swings his legs in front of him to spring forward in huge strides, his goggles bouncing on his forehead. It is all Alan can do to keep up with them, and it isn't long before his best isn't sufficient. Even pushed by fear, he isn't fast enough. He hobbles into a jog when his legs begin to burn, and he slows to a walk as Brattle and Stag's Blood reach the halfway point.

It is further to the wreck than it looked. Heat shimmers warp distance, making refuge seem closer than it really is. Brattle and

Stag's Blood vanish behind a dune. By the time Alan begins to scale it, the blood is screaming in his veins. His chest is heavy, but his lungs are barely moving. He counts this as a blessing; if he'd had to pump air the way he used to, he might have passed out by now.

Stag's Blood is crouched on the other side of the dune with Brattle nearby on his hands and knees. They are staring straight ahead as if riveted to that one spot. Alan slides down the sand face sideways, using his trash masher to prop himself up. At the base of the dune, he kneels beside the others and looks out at their destination.

"Is that it?" he asks. And then he sees what they see. "Wait. Oh my god. *What?*"

The Mercy Gale is less than a mile away. She is half buried in sand, but she's upright and mostly intact. Her prow is narrow, and there are three decks tiered atop one another at her richly decorated aft. There are windowed boxes on either side cf her, mounted high beneath the quarterdeck. Dark flags snap from her single mast. A bronze figurehead stares from beneath her tapered bowsprit, its great wings angling back and up to press valiantly toward the forecastle. She's beautiful, but there's something wrong about her. There is a black mass at the top of her mast, spoiling her profile.

"It's her," Brattle says. His voice is a quavering whisper. Alan can barely hear him over the squeaking of the sand beneath them. "The myth is real. The myth is real burnin' real."

Stag's Blood has been struck dumb. He can only stare at the shape curled around the mast.

The huge head is bent over the crow's nest. The body is a perfect coil gleaming with iridescent scales. It wraps its thick tail around the prow with enough length left at the end to twitch against the deck. The wings open as it situates itself. It flaps once, clawing at the wood, and heaves a huge breath as it sags back to trembling sleep.

"Oh my god," Alan repeats. It's all he can say for the moment.

There's a dragon on the Mercy Gale.

Eighteen

"A serpent," Stag's Blood whispers. "But I've never seen one like that before. Is it one of the westers? What's it doing here?"

"Ain't a serpent," Brattle says. "No dragon that small would wander alone, especially not here. It's something else wearing a serpent's skin." He narrows his eyes. Between the great bags beneath them and deep creases above them, they almost disappear. "It's a Crater-thing come up from Avernus. This is bad."

"What do you mean?" Alan asks. His own whisper gives him chills. "It's like a demon in disguise?"

"No more than you are, bony. The Crater's deep, and not wholly part of the physical plane. Shades come up from low down inside have to abide by the laws of things that are, if you get me. They have form forced upon 'em, and this has got a nasty one."

"Crossing from their non-physical world to a physical one like ours," Stag's Blood explains, "daemons become physical. It's the only way they can manifest. "

"Too bad this one didn't end up as a squirrel," Alan moans.

Brattle snorts, covers his face with his mortcloth, and tries to sneeze quietly. "Probably wouldn't have seen it if it had," he says.

The dragon stretches its wings again. It shifts, trying to find a more comfortable perch. When it yawns, the air around its mouth freezes. It searches the sand around the ship for a moment, sweeping the sand with subtle beams from its moon-gray eyes. The sand turns black and hard in its gaze. It cranes its neck to stare into the nearby wrecks, and they wither.

"Jesus," Alan says. "What do we do?"

"I know it might be pointless to ask," Brattle answers, "but what's the magic situation like right now?"

Alan hangs his head. The hunger he awoke to destroy the watchers is storming back in the presence of this new threat. It covers his heart to squeeze, bulges up his throat in a knot, and holds the base of his skull in the jaws of a piercing headache. It wants out; he can feel it stoking his magic, but he can't give in.

Not now, at any rate. Though he swells to burst with his new power, he centers himself and tries to contain it.

"Not good," he says. "I've barely got control. If I give it an inch, I'm pretty sure it'll start taking yards."

"I have some of my own," Stag's Blood says. "It may do us some good here."

"Anything is welcome, I think," Brattle growls. "If you've got something we can use, now is the time to tell us."

Stag's Blood bristles, and he looks ready to deliver a chiding response, but he bites it back. "Tricks I learned from my father. Some sound throwing, some lights – diversions, really. My range is bad, but maybe we could draw it away."

Alan sits down and turns his back to the Mercy Gale. The sand is hot under his shirt. It grinds at him, rattling over his skull, and he shields the sockets of his eyes meaninglessly from the blowing grains. "Before we try anything," he begins. "How badly *do* we need this ship? Can we go around? There must be some other heap in this desert that works at least as well."

Stag's Blood replies with a sigh. "Gimcrack is seventy miles away, and we don't know how well you're doing. If you pass out again, you might die for all we know. This looks like our best chance."

Alan shakes his head. The pain has brought frustration. He can't sit around wondering anymore – fearing – while the sickness breaks him down inside. He can hear his father's voice in his head telling him to pick a road and walk it. It tears from the dead noise with disastrous clarity, dragging a new weight of grief behind it. But a cool breeze kicks up, and Alan finds something like strength in it.

"There may be a weapon on the ship," he says. "We'll sneak on, nail him with it, and hope we can hit him hard enough to give us time to get that crate going. Stags?"

Stag's Blood sits up. The wind plucks at his mane. "We have to get close first," he says, "but I should be able to start off a big noise a little way away once we do. I'll do whatever I can to help."

Alan gives him a pat on the back. Stag's Blood's muscles are taut. They stretch over his shoulders in hard bands, ready to propel him forward.

"You don't have to go on with us from here, you know," Alan says. "You've taken us as far as you said you would."

"I've decided to extend the terms of my involvement in your adventure," the cat replies. "Your adventure *needs* me."

"Let's hook out west toward the bigger wrecks," Brattle offers. "Try an' get around its back if we can, quick and quiet. And should we wait 'til nightfall?"

Alan turns to look at the dragon again. It's crowned with orbs and ribbon shimmers. It's a legend made real, and he tries to will it to be beautiful, but he can't. He can only see the daemon in its open mouth. Every inch of its coil is hostile.

"It's got eyes like headlights," Alan says. "And it's not here for the view. Why did it choose this spot? It's precisely where it wants to be, and I have a pretty strong feeling it's looking for us."

"Or standing guard over the ship for another," Stag's Blood adds. "I'm not the only one who loved the legends of that ship. If the serpent is roosting now, it might be more active around nightfall. I'd rather go now and have it perched and searching than try to keep track of it circling overhead. It's easier to dodge if it's stationary."

"If it's waiting for someone, they might be coming up quick before us," Brattle says, nodding. "I can't imagine what we could've done to make such enemies: this and the watchers before." He sighs, and deep creases fall across his face. He droops until he looks desiccated, like a peat mummy pulled from a bog somewhere and trotted around in a traveling circus. "You're bad luck, Al. I wish I was back in my swamp with naught but a dead Da facing me tomorrow."

There are five wrecks standing in colossal columns before the Mercy Gale. Three of them are to the left abaft her beam, and the rest are on her starboard side. The dragon stares mainly down the

184

space between the rows, where the wind beats little whirls up from big bellies of sand. Now and again, it turns to look north. When it does, Alan, Brattle, and Stag's Blood dash for the nearest decaying pillar, heading left toward the longer line. The first wreck is a low heap of what might have been printing presses once, and it has gaps in its base that are wide enough for all three to hide in while still watching the dragon. From his cranny, Alan can see that the other two wrecks are standing on the blocks of huge motors and offer no such shelter.

"You said this dragon looks young?" he whispers to Brattle, his eyes on the beast as it slithers over the Mercy Gale's copper and crystal studded hull. The ship must still be quite sturdy if it can handle all that weight and clawing. "It's 100 yards long easily! Are you saying you've seen larger?"

Brattle is nearby in the crook of an L pipe, bent up like an insect with his knees on his shoulders. Alan can just see him.

"The biggest lay across mountains in the west," the ghouls replies. "I seen one once when I was very small. They slow and quit breathing — become like stone in their old age. This one had snow all down its back and tree-line stubble on its chin. Thought it was part of the cliff before it turned its head."

"Thank goodness for small favors," Stag's Blood jokes from somewhere in the mess. He sounds close, but Alan can't find him.

Feeling exposed all of a sudden, Alan tries to wriggle deeper into the wreck's guts. From behind a screen of tangled wires and wood that has shrunk black from its gaze, he watches the dragon paw an itch behind its head. Its claws are huge. Chaos moves in its every sinew, practically screaming from it. The dead cry out around the dragon, rebelling against it, averse to its Avernal nature, and their shrieks stir Alan's sickness until he is swaying on his knees. Darkness claws at his peripheral vision, and he fights it for a long time. The wreck creaks above him, promising collapse, but the high wails of creaking metal are better than big desert silence.

Just before Alan is sure that he's going to pass out, the dragon looks north again. Stag's Blood erupts from his hiding place to make a break for the next column. Brattle shoots out after him. Alan marvels that, as tired as he is, Brattle can still muster such speed. Alan is far worse off; he stumbles onto the sand, leaning on his trash masher, and has to push himself against a rolling stomach to keep up with his companions.

For a long moment, he languishes in the open. His legs are going weak, and he is stuck in a nightmare run through the shifting sand. The dragon turns to climb the mast again. It beats its wings as if to fly away, but it doesn't look in Alan's direction until he is already behind the next wreck. Then it levels its gaze and blackens the sand where he was struggling. It's a stroke of luck he should be grateful for, but Alan is too busy biting back coughs to enjoy any relief.

"Can you do this?" Brattle asks him. "What's it like right now? How bad are you?"

"I don't know," Alan replies in between stifled moans. "Stags, what have you got for us?"

Stag's Blood frowns.

"It'd be nice to get closer," he says, "but I'll see if I can conjure something that will get its attention. Sit astride me, Alan. I know how you feel about it, but I'm volunteering. We're going to have to hurry soon, and you need help."

Alan doesn't want to admit it, but he has no choice but to acquiesce. He lets Brattle help him onto Stag's Blood's back and tries not to feel guilty.

"Only this once," he tells the cat. "And only because you insist. Let's get phase two rolling."

Stag's Blood's coat is deep, soft, and warm. The skin beneath it is like purple satin stretched taut moving hydraulic struts and pistons. His mane is so fine that Alan's fingers slide through almost as if it isn't even there. It reminds him of his mother's cherished vicuña scarf, permanently saturated with her light, soapy smell – the eternal symbol of her goodness in Alan's mind.

"You can put your arms around my neck," Stag's Blood says. "And try to lock your feet around my waist. Don't worry about hurting me. I can handle you."

Alan does as Stag's Blood says. The cat slinks into place just at the corner of the column. When he feels secure, he presses his face into Stag's Blood's mane and tries to inhale. With his nasal aperture against Stag's Blood's skin, he can just detect the scent of ylang-ylang.

"Here we go," Stag's Blood says.

He closes his eyes and his body tenses up. His shoulders quiver for just a second, and then there is a loud pop from behind the left row of columns. A series of flashes accompany the sound – bright, dying bursts like light bulbs exploding. Alan looks up to see the dragon twist taut around the mast. It stiffens its neck like a pointer dog, its eyes and their wasting beams glaring hard toward the source of the sound. Stag's Blood starts to move, but the dragon's distraction does not last long. In a flash, it swings its head around to look directly at Stag's Blood. Brattle is further out in the open, frozen in a quadrupedal hunch. The light of the dragon's stare falls around them, and Alan feels his skin beginning to burn.

"Maid save us," Brattle cries.

Stag's Blood leaps into a sprint, heading for the Mercy Gale with Alan on his back. Brattle swings himself forward to catch up as the ground around them blackens. The dragon blows a foghorn roar, and then it spreads its wings into a ferocious flap that rocks the ship where she rests in the sand. With this, it powers itself upward into the cloud bellies and vanishes.

"It traced my magic," Stag's Blood says. His voice is steady, unaffected by his pounding the sand at a lope. "I was a fool to think I could trick it."

"No time for blame now," Alan replies. "We've got to improvise."

They are almost at the ship. Alan tries to muster up what remains of his strength. He draws all he can from wells that are

187

achingly dry, swallowing the burn of the sickness as it rises in his throat. The dragon circles from the cloud bank at a controlled plummet, black as death and huge above the landship's mast. Ice pours from its open mouth in a fog, crystals shimmering as they vaporize in the wind.

Stag's Blood doesn't look back, and he doesn't slow down until the Mercy Gale looms above them.

"There's a ladder on the port side," he says. He's panting now, and Alan can feel his pulse banging in his throat. Brattle and I will circle around to draw it off. Go!"

"No! What?" is all Alan manages to say before Stag's Blood hitches his shoulders and tosses him into the dirt.

He tries to get to his feet from a roll, but his sinews are made of lead. He falls to one knee and forces himself up through bolts of pain. Stag's Blood is gone before he can stand and raise his hand in protest. Light shimmers strangely around him as as he races away, and Alan can just hear him calling to Brattle.

Alan puts his hand on the Mercy Gale's hull where the sand and loam are rising in a slow attempt to swallow her. Her rivets are still gleaming. Her name on the keel plate looks freshly painted. She's in remarkably good shape, but there is still quite a bit of wear and damage on her iron cladding. Alan sees the rope ladder hanging down from the main deck, just visible under the forecastle's port gunwale, the barrel of some kind of cannon. He rushes for the ladder as fast as he can, ignoring the painful slip of his knee and the giddy twist of fear and sickness in his stomach.

"OK," he tells himself over the stymied dragon's screams. "Improvise."

The ladder barely holds his weight. The rungs are heavy and edged with gold. The strange rope is frayed around the knots where it passes through them. It's unlike any rope Alan has ever seen, with fibers shine with red and silver flecks and seem to split infinitely at the ends. He climbs, swaying in the breeze from the dragon's wings, and when he finally falls in over the board, his arms are aching. His hands are stained with crystalline powder, and he wipes them on his skull, leaving black stripes down his temporal bones.

There is no time to admire the jeweled panes of warping glass along the gunwales or the bleached horn of the bowsprit. Alan gets to his feet with a long groan and pushes himself across the deck toward the cannon assembly. Below him, Stag's Blood rounds the base of the nearest column and hauls back toward the ship at breakneck speed. He is a brushstroke across the sand, a flowing streak with the dragon circling to track him, and Brattle is on his back. They are drawing the dragon in, and Alan doesn't have long to act.

Alan heaves up the stairs toward the forecastle. The cannon is mounted on rails and can be pushed athwart the beam. It isn't a gunpowder cannon at all; Alan isn't sure what it's supposed to fire, but the barrel is too narrow for any kind of shot he's ever seen. He frets over it in the kicking breeze, his clothes beating against him as the dragon comes around for a pass at the ship. He can't find the gun's firing mechanism; it sits cold, mocking him, a tapering tube with no way to wake it anymore after so many years in oblivion. Alan stands, fists balled at his sides, strung so tight that he feels like crying. He looks around and realizes that the whole ship looks dead. There is a fog around her, hovering just above the boards, swirling faintly even in the mad blast from beneath the dragon's wings. It dims the ship – silences her – like a curse. The Mercy Gale is a corpse, no more fit to bear them out of danger than any other monolithic ruin. Alan swears to himself, and the darkness in his blood seems to heat up. He sags over his middle, and fear almost paralyzes him, but then he remembers something.

Powered by magic, Stag's Blood had said.

After a moment more of silent hesitation, Alan leaps back down the stairs and sprints astern. He hopes there's something on the quarterdeck that will pull this ship back from the mist. She's got to have a heart; Alan hopes it isn't down on the orlop somewhere. The dragon roars, much too close now. Ice blows hard across the ship, rocking her in the sand, scattering the weather decks with glittering patches of black and smoking crystal. Alan isn't sure what will happen if he lets his magic loose; he shudders to think of the hunger having free reign within him, but there's no choice anymore. The Mercy Gale will be his first resurrection.

On the quarterdeck, there is a short pedestal with an enormous black orb mounted on it. This is set into the deck a bit in a coped depression that might once have held water. Alan remembers the empty pool at the resting place and tries to see himself there again, before the sickness took hold. The stone orb has been rubbed smooth on top by years of palms. Alan steps into the square, puts his hands on the orb, and nothing happens. The dragon is coming around the stern of the ship, bearing down shrieking fury, but Alan tries to block it out. Its wings are pounding around him, and still nothing happens. Stag's Blood and Brattle are nowhere to be seen. Alan feels the dragon's frigid breath covering his back and shoulders with frost. The wind from beneath its wings buffets him, making him feel as if he is wearing a storm. He stands still, if not calm, and he tries to pour himself into the orb, but still nothing happens.

Maybe this isn't the heart of the ship, Alan thinks. *Maybe her heart is as dead as the rest of her.*

Alan steps back, empty and furious. The black orb stares up at him like the eye of a god – blind and stupid. The dragon starts to climb up the stern of the Mercy Gale, and Alan raises his trash masher over his head.

It's been so long. Maybe she just needs a little CPR.

He brings the masher down on the black orb, driving the prolate head down to ring against the orb's glassy surface, and he grits his teeth as shivers run up the handle to rattle in his skull. Then he hits it again, and again, counting to himself as he hefts the masher. White lightning dances over the masher's shaft, crackling brilliantly each time Alan strikes the orb. At last, after a blow that sends spider web cracks spreading out over its surface, and as the dragon plants its claws in the poop deck's boards and opens its jaws around Alan, the black orb burns to violet life. The ship begins to thrum and shake with creaking motions of old engines. Alan is suddenly weak with joy.

With the Mercy Gale reanimated, the dragon beats an uncertain retreat. It wings back to hang in the air, staring at the living ship with a look of shock that makes Alan laugh. With every muscle aching and the poison in his body now roaring up from his gut as if to consume him, he races back toward the bow, slides across a patch of ice without thinking, and mounts the gem-spangled steps to the forecastle with two great hops.

He drops his trash masher on the deck and mans the cannon as the dragon banks skyward to prepare for a dive. He pulls it back from the bulwark on its rails and yanks it up with the last of strength. It squeals, un-oiled for decades, but it yields to him. It warms under his hands, and white light crackles over its surface as it has around the handle of his trash masher since the magic inside him awoke. Alan feeds himself into the cannon, holding nothing back, and it is frighteningly easy to let go. His walls were close to crumbling anyway. Doubled over the back of the gun, Alan watches the dragon as it drops from the cloud wall. It arcs up, flaps once, and reaches a zenith near enough to the Mercy Gale that Alan can see the veins in its wings pulsing. He holds back as it pauses, waiting for it, saving the height of his power in the cannon's barrel. Before the dragon can drop, he commands the gun to fire.

He doesn't need to worry about what to do: the cannon is made to respond to him. It accepts his will readily, as much an extension of him now as his trash masher is. Alan is its firing mechanism. It focuses his power into a lancing blast that opens the dragon's chest like a head of lettuce. The dragon screams, falls back, and beats its wings in a pathetic effort to stay aloft. It almost manages to climb again; it finds the strength to begin to recover even as it stains the ship's deck with its dark blood, but then the cannon fires again. There is more within him than Alan realized. The hunger swells satiated beautifully. He is sick to feel its glee.

The dragon falls, dead and blown apart, and the daemon fire dies away from it. Avernus bleeds out across the sand beneath the carcass, and the ground goes black. Alan slumps to the deck, enervated but giddy with relief. The machines inside the Mercy Gale bang in triumph, though he thinks he can hear a voice chastising him in that sound.

I can't rest, he thinks. *Nothing's done yet.*

With a herculean effort, Alan levers himself to his feet. He staggers to the edge of the deck and drapes himself over the gunwale. Below, the dead serpent is disintegrating. The Crater is taking it piecemeal, swallowing the corpse in ash. Alan wonders where daemons go when they die.

"Brattle!" he calls. His voice is as strong as ever. He's glad that it seems to come from outside his debilitated body. "Stags! Where are you?"

After a tense and windy silence, Stag's Blood emerges from behind one of the wreck towers. He walks swiftly, thankfully uninjured, and avoids the dragon's blood.

"We're here." Stag's Blood calls up in answer, and Alan can barely hear him. "By the stone, you did it! I knew you could do it. The ship is ours, and not a moment too soon. Hurry and find a way to lower the gangplank."

As he draws nearer, Alan realizes that Brattle is draped over his back.

"Lower the gangplank," Stag's Blood repeats. "The ghoul is wounded."

Nineteen

Stag's Blood rolls Brattle gently onto the main deck of the Mercy Gale while Alan pulls in the gangplank. The ghoul is curled into a ball, covered in blue-white frost, and shivering uncontrollably. He can only speak to curse.

Alan puts the plank back on its rails and rushes to Brattle's side. Stag's Blood lies down beside him and drapes his body over Brattle's.

"He's not hurt," he explains to Alan. "It could have been far worse, but this is deep cold. You got about as much of it as he did; I can't imagine how you're still standing."

"I guess I'm lucky," Alan says as he digs through the pack to find Brattle's blanket. Thank goodness Stag's Blood had the presence of mind to retrieve it. "I can barely feel the cold. I guess I'm not as susceptible anymore." He remembers the night he spent in the grip of a bone-deep chill — his first night in Graveworld. He remembers the freezer at Ray's, and he can almost hear it roaring along with the dead voices in his head. "What do we do? How do we make him warmer?"

Alan whips off the hide ties and rolls the blanket around Brattle's quivering form. It doesn't seem to help much.

"Let's look below," Stag's Blood says. "Maybe this ship has a furnace."

Brattle sucks a trembling breath and exhales with his lips pulled tight over his bluing gums.

"Anything is worth trying," he chatters. "I ain't the picky type, bones."

Alan helps Brattle onto Stag's Blood's back, where he holds fast to two fistfuls of pelt and mane. Then they take the aft staircase from the quarterdeck into the ship's belly.

Time is heavy in the dark. Alan runs his hands along the boards of the inner hull, recalling something Brattle told him soon after he arrived in Graveworld.

Time is hungrier here.

The Mercy Gale has been asleep for a long time, but now something is awake inside her. It breathes through the huge screens of cobwebs, a whisper of anxiety. It watches them from the upper crooks of load-bearing members; its many eyes are swimming lights only Alan can see.

"We're here as friends," Alan tells it in the mold-dank gloom of the middle deck. "Don't worry. We're not going to hurt you."

"What's that about?" Stag's Blood whispers.

The weather decks creak above them as if in response. A breeze stirs decades of dust across the floor.

"She's watching us," Alan says. "It's been a long time. She needs to be sure we mean well."

They make their way down to the orlop from decks that are stacked with rotting provisions. At the bottom of the ship, casks under the stairwell are leaking vinegar. There is nothing like a furnace anywhere. There is no bilge either. There is a large cylinder in the middle of the deck with an orb in its center.

"This must be the engine," Alan says. "There's a stone like that up top. It looks like it's partially active, but I don't think it's going to give out any heat."

Stag's Blood sinks to the floor in a careful arch, his forepaws out in front of him, and Alan helps Brattle to the deck. Then Stag's Blood stalks off toward a bank of shelves and skids. While Alan pulls the blanket tighter around Brattle, the cat calls out from behind tilting chair not far away.

"Here," he says. "I know how to warm him up."

He returns to Brattle's side with something in his mouth. Alan takes it from him and examines it: it is a sleek oval of polished copper with a wooden grip on the bottom and a bundle of small pipes and wires spilling off the butt end. On the top is a double row of metal teeth.

"From a pack full of barber's supplies," Stag's Blood explains. "Powered shears. This was probably the only place the ship's barber could use them. Plug them into the core here, and I'll bet they'll still work."

"Wait. You want me to shave you?" Alan asks. He flips the little switch on the device's handle, and nothing happens. He thinks of never having to shave or cut his hair again. "And then what? I don't know if we have time to knit anything, Stags."

Stag's Blood frowns and gestures toward the core cylinder with a toss of his bristling mane.

"There will be no need to knit," he says. "I am a basteta; my coat is thick as carpet, and will pull away in one piece if you're careful enough. Plug it in now. See if it works. Anything is worth trying. Remember?"

Alan finds the end of the bundle of wires attached to the shears. It is a square hunk of rubber with four prongs coming out of it, and it fits perfectly in one of the slots on the base of the core cylinder.

"I've never heard of anything like that," he says, "but I'm not exactly an expert on fur. I'm trusting you here."

"Good," Stag's Blood purrs.

Alan stands with his toes against the core cylinder's base. He tries to listen to the power coursing through it. There is light in the orb, but it's dim. The power there is thrumming like a weak pulse; it responds when Alan puts his hand on the orb.

"Do you have enough left to wake the whole ship?" Stag's Blood asks.

"We're about to see," Alan replies.

The sickness is suddenly red hot inside him. The Mercy Gale responds with a terrible surge of fear. Alan staggers back and drops the clippers to the deck, but he keeps his hand on the orb. His magic is like an organ; he isn't sure how he makes it work, but it hardly takes any effort. He has plenty of strength left, but the sickness is attached to every last scintilla. As magic flows from Alan, the sickness siphons it to power itself. It squeezes his stomach and he retches, but Alan can't back down now. Luckily, it doesn't take much to stoke the flame. The orb in the core beings

195

to blaze, and the ship groans. A thunderous racket begins inside her – a chorus of rhythmic clanks that shake the hull so hard that Alan loses his balance and falls to one knee. He grabs the shears as he fumbles to catch himself.

"She purrs like a kitten," Stag's Blood laughs. "Who'd have thought? It's wonderful!"

"You did," Brattle says through clenched teeth. "That's what got us on this deathtrap in the first place! Can we hurry things along at all, now?"

Alan needs a moment to steady himself. The ship rocks as if trying to wrench itself from the sand, as his guts turn over themselves in time with her shaking. Each flex of his magic muscle leaves the sickness stronger; now it is in his bones, making him feel as heavy as lead. It's all he can do to get himself standing again.

"How careful do I have to be to do this right?" Alan asks Stag's Blood. "I think I've given just about everything at this point, and this rocking isn't helping."

"The best you can do will be enough, my friend," Stag's Blood says. There is a calming light in his eyes. Alan stares at it, trying to absorb it. It's something to cling to here, at the bleeding edge of his vigor. "Relax."

"All right," Alan says. He flips the switch on the clippers and they wheeze to life with a series of dusty puffs and hisses. The little mechanisms inside them squeak and whir; Alan can see them moving through the gaps beneath the marching teeth. "Here we go."

Stag's Blood turns just as Alan starts to cut.

"Just the pelt, if you please," he says. "Leave the mane."

Alan puts the clippers to Stag's Blood's piebald coat just below the points of his shoulders. It is crimped broadly underneath, and it grows in a single huge staple from the base of his main to the bob of bristles on his tail. Alan peels it away in long, careful sweeps and piles it on the floor as it goes, amazed at how easily it comes away.

"It's more like wool than fur," he says. "Though not as rough, I guess. On the one hand, your fur reminds me of cashmere; but then I've never really felt anything like it. There aren't even any snarls in it."

"We pride ourselves on cleanliness," Stag's Blood replies. "You won't find grease or burs in a basteta pelt!" He rolls over to let Alan do his belly just as the ship finally stops shaking.

"Well there is *some* dirt," Alan says. "I just can't believe it comes away all in one piece like this." He looks around for a moment. The Mercy Gale is groaning like a birthing woman. A mighty heave accompanies each labored squeal; Alan can feel her tugging herself upward, but the deck remains level. "She's stabilizing. Thank god for that – or somebody."

Brattle rolls on the floor, moaning along with the ship, his lips just purple lines pressed tight over the shivering slit of his mouth. He hugs his shoulders, pressing his nails rosy around their big lunulae. Alan knows he needs to hurry, but he's no gun shearer. Stag's Blood's fleecy coat yields easily, and he knows he could rush without too much risk, but he works with an abundance of caution. He pulls the clippers slowly over Stag's Blood's sternum, leaving a layer of stubble, making sure to stay as far away from bare skin as he can and still get a good cut. The fur here should be wispy, but it's just as thick it is on his back.

At Stag's Blood's ninth's rib, Alan stops.

"What's this scar?" he asks.

Stag's Blood replies quietly. Alan can't read him. "My brand," he says. "I'd almost forgotten."

The scar is rumpled pink beneath a newer layer of fuzz, but there are no scabs. It's years old, but still angry. Alan stops himself from touching it.

"You didn't cry out or anything," Alan says, "even when they burned you? You didn't scream for them to stop?"

"There is a pain beyond screaming," Stag's Blood replies. "There is a hurt you can only swallow, because giving it a voice would kill you. It's beyond the reach of hope, dead to love, and immune to mercy. It's anger in the highest and the blackest, worse and more than any pain you have ever endured, but the only way to be any better for it is to endure it, and the only way to endure it is silently. Nothing hurts forever."

"I'd have been shrieking like a little girl," Alan says. He pushes on past the scar, nearly done with the shearing. "You're a better cat than me."

Stag's Blood chuckles and says, "I do have an advantage."

With each inch of fur he shears away, his right shoulder tightens. By the time he's got a big enough heap of honey-soft basteta fur beside him – and Stag's Blood is shorn rump to shoulder to the filmy nap of his undercoat – Alan's whole arm is aching with tension.

"You see now why we are killed for our pelts," Stag's Blood says. He's shivering a little himself now. "Cover him up quickly. Pull it tight around his chest. He's looking worse by the moment."

This pressure doesn't help Alan's shoulder. The ship seems to be settling on the sand; she sings a free song in creaks and clacks that run all the way from her bow to her stern under the orlop. She's out of the sand; there's no doubt about it. It's obvious that she's sitting higher and straighter, and there's no more hiss of dirt and grit falling through the pressure separations in her hull. Alan rolls Stag's Blood's coat around Brattle and folds it over itself at the prominent ring of his collarbone and tries to imagine that the Mercy Gale's descending whines of relief are the sound of his shoulder untwisting itself.

"Hold that tight around you," Alan tells Brattle. "How does it feel?"

He puts his hand on Brattle's arm. The bones there are as light as a bird's. The skin is taut and dry and creased by purpling veins. Alan feels Brattle's pain seeping into him; there is a touch of death in it, but he is greatly relieved to sense that it is weakening. He looks into the pools of Brattle's eyes and the tension slips away from his shoulder at last. The sickness pulls back, revolted. Alan realizes it is allergic to love.

"Talk to us," he says. "Any warmer?"

Brattle blinks up at him. He smiles ghoulishly, and his jaw quavers.

"We all gotta give something up," is all Brattle says.

Half an hour goes by. The sounds in the ship become low, dragging whispers. Rhythmic thumps move across the ceiling, as if someone is moving around on the upper decks. Shadows deepen in near corners, and Alan finds himself looking over his shoulder. Healthy color creeps beack across Brattle's gaunt face, and his shivers dwindle to nothing. Twenty minutes later, he is up and hobbling. Stag's Blood and Alan follow him around the deck to support him as he tests his stride. The Mercy Gale warms herself slowly with Alan's magic. She turns ancient engines in her lowest depths, and her lights finally flicker on. Up on the weather decks, there is an ordered commotion. Loud bangs resound from behind the walls, startling gasps from everyone. The orlop begins to feel uncomfortably small. Brattle sways on fragile stems and looks around the orlop with Stag's Blood's pelt pulled over his head like a hood.

"What's the hell's that racket?" he asks.

"I think it's the ship waking up," says Alan.

Brattle takes a deep breath and nods. "We did it," he says. "By Nettle and my old Da, we actually did it. Thanks, Stags. Bonehead. You're a better barber than a thanoturge, I think. Color me surprised."

"It beats ice-blue," Stag's Blood replies.

"I *did* get the ship running," Alan says. "But now we get to see if I can pull off being a captain, too. Do you think you can tackle the stairs?"

Brattle sniffs a dismissive laugh and staggers toward the aft staircase, his new piebald blanket dragging dust across the floor behind him.

The Mercy Gale is buzzing with shadows. They flutter through the new light on every deck, moving blurs too big for moths to be

199

casting them. Some move with a sound, and some of their sounds are like voices. A cold pressure pursues them up the companionway — an empty, basement pawing that makes Alan feel small and vulnerable in spite of himself. He used to know it was just his mind playing tricks on him because that's what his dad had said when he was young. Now he can feel the dead moving within him, and he isn't so sure anymore.

"Ship wakin' up," Brattle says as they climb toward the main deck. "That's what you said, but there's something on this ship ain't been sleeping: some grave-lost watcher. You feel it?"

"I feel something," Alan replies.

"This is how they move. They tingle in the air a bit, you know. And they call you softly in your own voice — the waking dead. Sometimes you can see them like gray shapes standing in your periphery. That shit gives me the creeps."

"Are they dangerous?" Stag's Blood asks.

"Always."

The mouth of the companionway is golden bright. Day is straining through the clouds, failing to dusk through pink storm skirts. A cool breeze stirs the sand where there is no dead dragon; even the ash of its remains has blown away. Alan looks over the bulwark to see that the Mercy Gale has pulled herself from the sand on four huge legs.

"Unbelievable," Stag's Blood says.

Brattle points toward the bow from beneath his wrap. "You ain't seen nothing."

Shadows lie long across the main deck. There is movement there and on the forecastle: misty shapes swirl around the gun and the base of the mast. For a brief moment, they aren't real at all; they're a trick of the last light until the ship groans and flexes her legs to test her stabilizers, and then they begin to bustle. Alan, Brattle, and Stag's Blood stand under the hood of the quarterdeck and watch as dim figures appear on the gangways. The longer Alan looks the more wisps he can see. They are in one place, and then they are everywhere. They rise from the ship as if they are parts of it. Eyes glisten in them like constellations. Alan remembers them from Debtors' Orchard.

"By the stone," Stag's Blood says. "Wraiths. Are we in danger?"

"No," Alan answers. "Look. Look what they're doing."

The wraiths hover over the rigging. A group of them moves the cannon back to its original position on the port side and locks it to the gunwale. They crawl over the ship's legs like smoke, cleaning the joints of sand and rust. Astern, more wraiths swirl around the orb on the quarterdeck. They call to each other, and Alan can hear their susurrus voices if he strains.

"The ship ain't haunted," Brattle says as he realizes what he's seeing.

"No," Alan says again. "This is our crew."

Twenty

A shade approaches, roughly man-shaped. It flickers like a flame, only minimally affected by gravity. There is a shape above its head like a starry crown; its clusters of eyes burn beneath it, shifting from silver-white, through Kelly green, to cornflower on the way to brand-scar red. The night breeze pulls at it, drawing the filmy stuff of its body out into a fading smudge, but it won't blow away. It only ripples, stoked by something stronger than the wind.

"Captain," it says. Its voice is a genderless wheeze, and it comes from the same non-space as Alan's. Alan isn't sure whether the light in its eyes is intelligence or something worse. "Where are we headed?"

Stag's Blood steps forward. "Are you the chief mate?" he asks.

The wraith shivers. A disturbance swells along its red edges, so subtle that Alan nearly misses it. "Captain," it rasps again. "Our heading?"

It hurts Alan's head to read the wraith. Looking too long at it from a certain angle leaves a taste like dirt in his mouth. There is a shimmer in its darkness like the gate that burned his face, but this one is frigid and airless. Alan marshals his wits and asks, "What is your name?"

The shade moves again. It seems to tilt itself. The billowing bulb of its head bends down and outward, turning its eyes to the mast for a moment.

"Alan," says the wraith. "Shall we turn her home, captain?"

Alan looks at Brattle and Stag's Blood. Brattle tugs his new pelt tighter around him, pinching it at his neck. It has a little bit of blood on it, and there are faint stains on his shoulders. His eyes are shadowed beneath the droop of the pelt over his head, and his jaw is quivering again. Stag's Blood only nods.

"Gimcrack," Alan says.

The wraith hisses satisfaction. "Home, then," it says. "Take the quarterdeck, captain. We're soon underway."

With this, the wraiths begin to drift together on the deck. As the sky darkens, they become almost invisible; only their collective mass gives them away as they work.

The Mercy Gale heaves against the pull of the sand. Her huge legs moan, puffing steam from their joints. With a cacophony of creaks and a steady whine building in her depths, the ship lifts herself into her first limping step. The deck stays level but for a gentle rocking. As the landship picks up speed, heading north into the storm winds, Alan mounts the bridge with Brattle and Stag's Blood close behind him.

"These ain't rustic wraiths," Brattle says. "They're boundlings – slave spirits tied to the ship's running. We're lucky for that, I think, but it's still damn creepy. I never been around so many hinkypunk spirits at once. Don't know how much sleep I'm going to get tonight."

"You did all this?" Stag's Blood asks Alan. "Impressive. You must not have been as weak as you let on."

Alan puts his hands on the globe and looks out across the main deck. The wraiths are just blots in the dark. With the Kingwatcher's bloom open, he can feel a part of himself in every spirit. The Mercy Gale herself is rolling with his power – moving through it like a sailing ship on a real ocean. "I think the core was designed to amplify magical charges," he says. "But I'm not even sure that makes any sense."

"Yer something special, bones," Brattle declares. "Don't go doubting now. You're kind of holding this whole gig together."

"No pressure, right?" Alan laughs. The pressure is real. It pours over him like dragon's ice. He can actually taste it. "What is this all about? How did I get so far from home?"

Stag's Blood shakes his voluminous mane. He should look silly with so much of his coat shorn down, but he doesn't. With the broad slabs of his muscles visible under his skin, he manages to look even more striking.

"Hopefully," purrs the cat, "you're soon to find out."

The Depot goes on for leagues. The Mercy Gale follows the worn curve of the crater's eastern wall. Her old flag snapping, she steps over piles and rusted hulks, impossibly light on her feet; when she finds her stride, nothing can slow her down.

"Topped out at nine knots, captain," the chief mate announces, "and the storm is swelling."

When the clouds finally burst, rain comes hot and is spent in a hundred drops. After a few tries of toothless thunder, the storm moves on and leaves the sky open. Alan looks up from the quarterdeck into starshine.

Brattle is balled up on the poop, and Stag's Blood is curled warm around him. The rumpled scar of a galactic arm splits the sky from north to south. Stars clot around it, winking white fire. From there, they pitch outward like sea foam. The sky is beautiful, but Alan looks away with a headache. He misses the darkness of the city, where light bleeds into the night until it is flat and black – the non-sky. He wishes he could close his eyes and feel the headache crawling over his brow, pushing at the backs of his eyeballs. But there is no dark anymore – no refuge – not really. There is no void. The starry spray mocks him and the oblivion of pain that has been taken away.

Daemons, dragons, watchers, and wraiths.

Alan stares through the night, all his focus wound around a desperate stillness. Sleep is lost to him now; he's forgotten the way across its borders, but he isn't suffering physically for it. He takes rest from other sources – like an earthworm breathing through its skin – but his mind still needs to dream. It isn't hard here: he can't enter sleep's misty country, but there is a way over it. Or perhaps he's like a worm digging under it, through the ground that will no longer have him, until he reaches its dreaming core.

He has a waking nightmare while bent over the bulwark of the Mercy Gale. He sees the curtains of steam billow away from his sister's tub. Allison is in there, her eyes silver. She's cut her wrists. Her throat is open too; she wears a bib of blood over her bare chest. Her toes wiggle as she suffocates. The vision won't go away. It fights to be seen, plying its horror sweetly, like a con artist, but Alan can't give in. He resists, and lucidity helps.

I've seen it all before, Alan says. *I don't need it. It's useless.*

Night bleeds away in blue fires. Dawn is peach-pink over the desert, and there are no clouds. A veil of color waves across whole sky as far as Alan can see. The new light sparkles through it like water. Alan's heart swells in his throat. He's seeing things differently these days. Maybe it's time to give his old nightmare another chance.

"How long has it been?" Stag's Blood says.

He's up and yawning behind Alan, his eyes rheumy. Alan starts at the sound of his voice, and stammers an answer.

"Six months," he says. Stag's Blood smiles at him.

"I mean since you've slept," says the cat, and Alan sniffs a laugh.

"Since this?" he replies. He moves his hand in front of his face. "Or do you mean *well*?"

"Whichever you care to calculate," Stag's Blood says. "But maybe there's something else on your mind."

Alan looks up at the mast. The veil of light is split on the full rays of morning. He watched the entire night slip by and hardly noticed.

"Nothing new," he says. "Same old, same old. Displaced from my plane of existence, sleepless, faceless, poisoned by magic. You know. All that."

Stag's Blood's smile is dripping with condescension. He starts to reply, but something cuts him off before he can begin to speak.

There is an anguished wail coming up from ahead of them. It's a few loud voices raised in funereal song. The singers come into view as the Mercy Gale comes down across the shoulder of a dune: a troupe of blood-dark robes walking in step through the sand. Darkness hides their faces beneath their sagging hoods. They wear large packs on their backs, and the leader swings a black censer. Smoke pours around them, and silver orbs dance over their heads.

Their singing wakes Brattle. He gets to his feet, grumbling, and shuffles over to look out at the procession from beneath the gunwale.

"Beanies," he says, his voice deep and rattling in phlegm. He's been snoring all night. Alan remembers that, at least. "Mourners."

"What are they?" Alan asks.

"Human spirits get lost sometimes," Brattle replies in between coughs and deep-lung hocks to spit over the side. "When the gates don't work right. Or maybe they stray from the black shores. Mourners ain't come to grips with their deaths yet. Prob'ly never will. They move through the wastes, crying, mostly mindless.

"The passage here will drive a reluctant soul insane," Stag's Blood adds. "There've been more and more in the northeast lately."

"More wastes to wander these days," says Brattle. "And maybe more gates spitting souls out burned mad. This whole damn place is going springy." He knocks his chest with his fist for a second and then seems to straighten, finding himself fully again as the haze of sleep wears off. Alan misses that feeling.

Brattle continues. "Let's hope our crew knows well enough to keep a wide berth."

The mourners leave red flowers blooming behind them. They wear petals on their brows like crowns. Two of them are carrying red gonfalons shaped like poppy blossoms. Their song is wordless and empty. There is no melody and no meter. It's barely like music at all. It flows from them like dawn light – like smoke from the flattened ember mess of a warning fire. It is sorrow made manifest. The whole procession advances as if pressing into a stiff wind, and their clothes and flags flap back hard behind them, though the only breeze Alan feels is calm and coming from the opposite direction. He realizes they are straining against the force of their own elegy. Alan can't listen for long before the sickness kicks up along his spine and leaves his legs too weak to support him. He sinks back against the bulwark and tips his chin up to look at the sky.

"Human spirits," he says. "Most of my life, I didn't believe in them."

Stag's Blood watches the mourners as long as he can before the ship turns away from them. He and Brattle are unaffected by their keening.

"Not everything has got one," Brattle explains. "It's too big a burden to bear — takes a certain kind of something to bear it. Spirits are taxing."

"I wonder who they were before they died," Alan says, casting a careful glance back toward the red procession. "I bet they had no idea what was on the other side of death."

The mourners are tall specks at the foot of a shrinking dune. Their song is on the real breeze, preceding them, following the Mercy Gale like a seabird circling a garbage scow. Alan tries to put his hands on the sides of his head where his ears used to be, but this doesn't affect his hearing.

"Few do," Stag's Blood replies.

"What are they?" Alan asks. He points at the wraiths working on the deck.

Brattle explains without looking at him. He's too busy wrapping Stag's Blood's coat around himself. He looks absurd in it: a dark thing lost in plush folds. His eyes shine out from beneath it like twin mirrors of oil. "Opposite of mourners," he says. "More or less. Unborn things. Fetches of people and things that ain't lived yet."

Alan nods. His heart feels like a lump of lead.

"Life begins here, too," he says, feeling the weight of that idea in his mind.

"Yeah," snorts Brattle. "Guess you could say that."

The Mercy Gale crawls on through the morning, and the crater flattens out. Alan and Brattle move to the forecastle, and Stag's Blood goes below to sleep in the thrumming dark. The air grows cooler, and patches of cautious flora appear among the ruins. Scrubby trees twist frost-white from pads of alabaster grass. Soon they are moving through white fields, and the high desert is behind them.

There are no towering machine remnants here. The white goes on forever down a loving slope, spoiled only by the rare sight of hard packed black soil. There are butterflies in abundance. Deserted dradtail nests cling here and there beneath white willows – darker bulges like tumors on bark that is fine as marble. The wraiths drive the Mercy Gale along a wagon track that cuts along the hillside through occasional sprouts of bamboo, and Alan hates to see the crushed wake she leaves behind her.

"The Empties," Brattle says. "Da used to talk about them. Always wanted to get up here."

Alan watches red birds bobbing in a copse of pearly larches. "There's no rot," he says. "This place isn't wasting like the south."

Brattle shrugs the fur up over his shoulders. He is still cold, but he is fighting it. Alan can see it on his face. This journey has taken a heavy toll.

Brattle pulls his hands into the fur to hide his shivering. "Every place rots in its own way."

Alan thinks of the dradtails and their hidden nectaries. How have they been rotting that the wasps can't see? The question haunts him for the rest of the morning.

Not long after midday, the Empties thin and roll up into shining foothills at the base of the Gimcrack Mountains. The white grass tapers toward a shriveling heath, and a path cuts through it toward a copper-roofed castle with a single spire. The heath is dotted with dolmens —portal graves made of huge standing stones. They lean across the field like tables. Most of them wear mud and white foliage, but some are weathered bare. Alan looks out at them, feeling small and far away. There are dead things in and around them; voices breathe toward him, whispering in languages he doesn't know. The Mercy Gale begins to slow, and he returns to the forecastle to consult the chief mate.

"Home is in sight," the wraith says. It looks away from Alan, transfixed by the looming dolmens and the shadows swirling under their ragged roofs. "We have been long in returning, and we are diminished. It will be good to rest."

"What are we going to find?" Alan asks. There is smoke rising from the castle's little chimneys. Alan looks hard at the mountains behind it. Are they just a little bit different than they were just a minute ago?

"Whatever you seek," the wraith replies. Then it sinks into the deck, leaving Alan to cross his arms, annoyed.

After a long round of metallic shrieks, the Mercy Gale begins to slow. She crosses the heath at a crawl, and a thumping begins deep inside of her, in her aft section. The deck rocks as the landship tilts, and Alan grips the gunwale for purchase. Stag's Blood emerges from his nap, his claws out, clinging to the boards with his mane flying.

The ship rights herself after a long effort. Her legs strain to continue functioning. Age and the Wasting are finally catching up to her. Alan starts to feel dizzy, and her strength wanes; his sickness is in her, too. She finally comes to a stop at the north edge of the heath, her hull blown thick with white blossoms, and she groans mightily for long minutes as the wraiths lower her to her beam.

Alan's head is swimming. He feels contaminated. His blood is stopped in his veins, stagnant, hard as glass. He can taste kerosene, and he tries to move his tongue, but there is nothing on the floor of his mouth. Standing is a struggle, but he can manage it. He's fought through so much thus far. Brattle helps Alan down the gangplank, but he can stand on his own at the bottom.

There is a cambered road running from the castle to an empty spot in the heath. It is old and cracking; it reminds Alan of

Elrafa. Torches stand crossed along it, lit even now in the light of day. A small group of armored guards is coming down the road toward the Mercy Gale. Alan and Brattle watch them while Stag's Blood descends the gangplank. They measure their steps meticulously, as if unsure about the strength of gravity. Butterflies dance around their legs, drawn to them by an ambrosial smell that Brattle describes to Alan in detail as they draw nearer.

"Scented soldiers," he marvels. "And here comes someone important. Prop yourself up the best you can, Al. Are you going to be able to do this?"

"It's bad, but I can do it," Alan replies. "I've weathered worse."

"That remains to be seen," Stag's Blood chirrs.

A humanoid figure approaches through the guards' ranks – a fairy, certainly, as Alan has come to know them. He is tall, and he is wearing a broad cloak with a white-ruffed collar. Color surrounds him like a nebula, giving birth to red-gold orbs and ribbon flashes above his head. A shifting, gray mass follows right on his heels; Alan can see through it to the cobbles. Shapes rise out of it, linger as if stalking, and then recede to make way for different forms. Alan can hear the mass thinking. Like the wraith-crew of the Mercy Gale, it is hungry, mad, and subservient. The important fairy is dragging death in a semi-sentient cloud behind him.

"A thanoturge," Alan whispers.

The soldiers muster under the Gale's bowsprit. The cloaked fairy walks the length of the landship's beam with his hands on his hips. Butterflies light on his shoulders as he stands admiring her, a light of love on his face. He whirs a bit when he moves, and he wears copper plates over his knees and elbows. There's a pair of goggles on his head like the ones Brattle dug out of the hobs' cave.

"You found her!" the fairy exclaims. "My Mercy Gale! Oh, my loving stars."

The fairy takes a big step toward Alan. His hair swings at his jawline in careful angles. It is soot-black with orange seething in it like the heart of an ember. His eyes are stone gray and sit at slightly different heights.

Alan wonders how they must look: a shorn basteta, an emaciated ghoul draped in its fur, and a spell-sick junior mage with no face.

As if reading Alan's mind, the fairy says, "I've never seen anyone looking so bedraggled. You've clearly come far and seen much, but why? And where have you come from?"

This isn't a question, and he doesn't wait for an answer. Instead, he folds his arms and addresses Alan with his index finger on the dimple in his slightly ptotic chin.

"You're the captain of the Mercy Gale?" he asks.

"Yes. I'm Alan," Alan replies. He dips a wobbly little bow, clinging to Stag's Blood for support. "Alan Shade. Thanoturge."

"Toven," says the fairy, "King of the North. I assume you have no idea what you've returned to me today, but I'm in your debt."

"I hope you don't expect us to wait long to cash in," Alan tries. "We need your help."

Toven only nods and turns to Brattle.

"Are you a Busaw?" he asks.

Brattle clears his throat and sways just a bit on his heels, clearly taken aback.

"You've an uncanny eye," he replies. "Most can't tell one ghoul from the other. Did you know my Da?"

"You must be Pick's youngest," the prince continues. "*Did I know him?* I'm sorry to hear that his tense has past. I met him several times."

Before Brattle can reply, Toven moves on, chasing something. He smiles his curiosity. His expressions are deep and alien in their intensity. He seems to have facial muscles that no human possesses; emotions unfold across his face in complex patterns, wheeling around his fulcrum smile like branching ice.

211

"One of Winter White's saddlecats," he muses, looking at the brand on Stag's Blood's side. "You must be looking for her, then." He looks at Brattle, waiting.

"Are you the prophet?" Stag's Blood asks.

Something washes through the gathered troops. It might be surprise. They all emote at once, quietly. Toven stares at Stag's Blood with his mouth open. His teeth are unsettlingly perfect. Alan wonders if he might be having a seizure; his face is smooth and tight, as if under constant strain. He looks oddly familiar.

"A basteta," Toven says. He bows and holds his hand out to Stag's Blood. "I'm honored. I thought the last of your kind had lit out for brighter shores."

Stag's Blood's paw dwarfs Toven's hand.

"Not yet," he replies.

Toven removes his crown and turns it over in his hands. Alan notices that his fingernails are black. The guards move past him as if responding to a silent command; they mount the gangplank and begin to search the Mercy Gale. The wraiths are gone; there is no one to stop them. They turn through barrels and pry crates open with bars, their armor clanking. Their eyes are like panes of glass. They stare constantly, as if awed to silence in the presence of something sacred. There is something bad fulminating behind their wanton expressions. When they disappear into the hold, Alan can hear them bumping around on the orlop while Toven smiles down at him. He feels a sting of jealousy.

"She's in remarkably good shape," Toven says. "Where did you find her, captain?"

Alan takes a step toward Toven, but magic rises in him suddenly, and he nearly falls over. The fairy king has to catch Alan before he can plant his face in the dirt.

There is a flash. It leaps up from Toven's touch, and Alan hears Toven gasp. In an instant, he sees Toven's power. It is cleft and stunted, but it puts his own to shame. Toven's magic lives in a single, horrible moment. It has become trapped there, but it is still stronger than Alan's. When Toven stands Alan back up and pulls

212

his hands away, he break the connection, and Alan is left stupefied for a second.

"Corruption," Toven says, aghast. "You're riddled with it! My stars, where are your charms? You need purifying, Alan Shade."

Alan suddenly feels every speck of dirt and sweat on his skin. The muck of the swamp is sucking at his feet, and Elrafa's dust is burning in his throat. A hot pain is digging its claws into his lower back and sinking its teeth into his shoulder.

Toven looks him directly in the face. Alan sees his depths roiling. Something is banging in Toven's brain, screaming to be free. It looks out from behind his eyes, a beautiful thing, made terrible in the grip of emptiness. Toven is fighting hard against something at the level of his deepest nature. Alan watches in horror as he appears to lose, but then his smile returns. It creeps back to his face, small and careful – a little victory.

"Come quickly to rest," Toven says. "And when all are well again, you can tell me how you've earned it."

Twenty-One

There's no doubt anymore. Alan can see it clearly now that they have reached the gate of the castle: the Gimcrack Mountains are moving.

It's most noticeable on the peaks. They wave like fronds in a kelp forest; the rock is actually undulating. The mountains' conical caps rotate, shaking powdered rock and flecks of lead-dark shale down the sheer slopes. A shiver runs down the whole range, east to west, huge and slow. Ridges flow in shallow patterns. Only Toven's castle is still. How could the moving cliffs be passable? What must the ground look like beneath them? Alan imagines deep, black soil churned up around great axles and pouring from between the giant teeth of impossible gears. The mountains are a wounding machine perpetually gouging a scar across the face of Graveworld.

Toven's castle is a three-story château with a keep on the east wall. Crouched on the fallen remains of a motte flecked with white grass, it is compact by necessity, but it loses none of its grandeur for being small. The roof is wrought iron with brass eaves and shingles of silvered copper. Its columns are delicately filigreed, and marble daemons glare down from the archways. The glazed windows bulge like fish eyes in spacious boxes, their frames veined with cultivated ivy.

Entering the lawn through the silver gate, Alan immediately feels his sickness retreating. He'd almost forgotten what relief was like. Now he puffs his chest up and stretches, light beneath his heels, seizing this reprieve for all it's worth. Once he's through the doors, his footsteps ringing off mirrored tile and vaulted ceilings, nausea and weakness are a fading memory.

Toven stops in the foyer. His soldiers drift away along practiced routes. Only a few stay to watch the newcomers, standing so still that they nearly vanish.

"You should be feeling better," Toven says to Alan. "The entryway is pure ivory over meteor steel. I have the best resonator on this side of the Colonies. Do you feel it?"

Alan walks a slow circle and looks up at the terraced ceiling. He traces its beams down toward the top of the wall, where sinuous glyphs dance along bone-white ogee curves to frame the doors. Shadows convene in every corner, plotting against each other in beetling voices. The dead are loud here, but the foyer is made to bend their voices away. Magic facilitates the formation of a psychic barrier. The dead claw at Alan across a new divide, but they can't reach him. They have no hope. Alan's mind is his alone; he is amazed at how freeing this is — how long has he suffered with his psyche exposed? — but he keeps turning back to watch the darkness.

"I don't trust silence," Toven says after a moment.

"Neither do I," Alan replies.

Stag's Blood prowls the entryway, mirroring Alan's motions. Brattle leans against the front door with his arms crossed. The Gimcrack Mountains grouse like thunder. Alan can feel their turning through the floor.

"I feel it," Alan continues. "but I'm not sure what it is. The sickness is receding, but it's not gone. It's watching me from the outside. It'll be back."

Toven puts his finger on his chin again. He is stingy with his expressions. For a minute, Alan thinks Toven is smiling, but this turns out to be a trick of the hard light.

"You're new to this. What you have is not a sickness," he explains, "it's an invasion. I take it that you don't know anything about purification."

Alan shakes his head. Then he crosses the room to his pack and yanks it open. He takes out Pwysh's books and shows them to Toven.

"Everything I know is in here," he says.

Toven can't hide his surprise, no matter how hard he tries to keep it blocked behind his practiced frown.

"My cousin's books," Toven gasps. "Have you seen him? He gave these to you?"

Of course, Alan thinks. Toven has his cousin's cheekbones, but there is no blood pooling in his cheeks. His eyes are the same shape as Pwysh's were. His nose hooks down lower and looks a bit heavier, but the resemblance is there.

"You might say that," Brattle grunts. "He's dead. We found him murdered." He steps forward a bit, dragging the fur behind him, looking wizened and small. He adds, "By Winter White."

Toven's face contorts as Alan studies it. He looks at Brattle, then at the books, and then at his own hands. His eyes flit twice back and forth, and then he stills them. He works his jaw as if grinding cud behind his back teeth, but he doesn't say anything. Instead, Toven walks over to Alan and takes the grimoire and *The Book of Horns* in shaking hands.

"There's more," Alan says.

Toven interrupts. "And I would hear it, but you are a guest in my house, and you're in need." He nods to Brattle. "You, too. I want the story, but the story can wait. Brattle, Mawn will take you to the apothecary. Alan Shade, come with me. Telling me everything will be part of your cleansing ritual. And perhaps it will be part of mine tonight as well."

Mawn steps forward, a blank-faced uman with nothing to contribute to the conversation but his size and obeisance. His bronze right arm ends in a turning hook. Something in his chest is clicking.

"And me?" Stag's Blood asks.

"The kitchen is in the east wing," Toven says. "Eat your fill; your ribs are showing. But don't go into the cellar, please. There is dangerous machinery there."

Alan wonders if Toven can see Stag's Blood's mischievous smile for what it is. If he does, he gives no sign. He only nods to the room and sweeps a beckoning gesture toward Alan. Then he turns down the hall, his cloak bellying out behind him like a sail, and Alan follows.

Lamps burning blue gems like flames light the hall along its carven arches, casting shadows in soft lines. Eyeless statues with star-like faces stand guard at every door. Alan wants to stop and inspect every painting and carving, every vase of gaping violets, but Toven is a fast walker. Two guards follow Alan and Toven down the passage at a careful distance, spears raised. There's no choice but to try and keep up. It isn't long before Alan's calves are tight and burning with the effort to match Toven's stride.

"Thanoturgy is a dark art," Toven says, still looking straight ahead. "All magic is bound to life, but thanoturgy draws on the user's life to wield the power of death. Put simply, overusing thanoturgic magic causes corruption of the spirit. This is why the most powerful wielders are spiritless — Bleeding monsters — agents of chaos. Do you understand?"

"Mostly," Alan replies. "But a little more information wouldn't hurt. I'm new to all this. I've only just arrived in Graveworld."

"*Graveworld*?" Toven laughs. "A ghoulish name — and not exactly accurate. You must have been traveling with Brattle too long. You're new to Midion, Alan Shade — the sphere between form and formlessness. That is its proper name. But where did you come from? I've never encountered a spirit like you before."

Alan rolls the name through his head for a moment. *Midion.* It's light and as smooth as water. It doesn't sit well in his mind. He wonders if there's any such thing as a proper name.

"The living world," Alan replies. "And I'm not a spirit. I'm human."

Toven stops for a moment and looks him over. There is a new light in his strange eyes; it's as if he's seeing Alan for the first time again. The guards behind them shuffle to a halt, quiet as oblivion.

"A living human?" Toven asks, raising an eyebrow. He leans in toward Alan, suddenly piqued and doing a poor job of hiding it. "These are strange times. I wouldn't have guessed." He steeples his fingers, and Alan realizes that his nails are purple. "You gave your flesh in the passing then? Did Minos offer you a choice, or did he take your sacrifice against your will?"

Alan prepares to tell his story, but Toven doesn't stop long enough for him to answer. He just starts walking again with a hum on his lips and his finger on his chin. He steps into huge strides, and Alan rushes to catch up.

"Your sphere is called Animus," Toven continues. "It is the sphere of form. War split the formless sphere into Avernus and the Coma, and Midion is in between with aspects of both. The Bleeding surrounds us – the remnants of an aeon that failed. It is old and dark, and it seeps into everything. Chaos lives there. The Bleeding is where thanoturgy was born. "

They stop at a door, and Toven opens it with a rectangular key. Beyond it is a lavish washroom. Stars wink from the porcelain. Pink light pours from a gem on the sink.

"First you must bathe," Toven says. He sweeps his arm out, inviting Alan into the room. "Then we'll talk more. There's a lot to learn if you'll stay at Gimcrack a while. Take your time, and knock on the door when you're ready."

Once he's alone in the washroom, Alan piles his clothes on the squared bowl of what can only be a toilet and spends a long time looking at himself in the mirror. He is pale and thinning, and there are bruises all over his body. They cross each other in deep purples and blacks, and some of them are yellow around their edges. His neck is a dry mess that he can't look at for long. He runs his hands over his face, following the small ridge of his brow with fingertips from which his nails are receding, trying to find himself somewhere in the bone. There are chips and burns on his skull. One tooth is loose, but he can't wiggle it out even though it can't have any root holding it in place. He stares into the pits of his own eyes, seeing them from somewhere else.

The windows to the soul, he thinks, but you can't see in to me, and I can't see out.

He lets loneliness hit him, and he tries to hold on to it. He chokes on a sob that won't come and feels more present for it – more real. For all he's lost, he still has pain.

The tub is full of something that isn't quite water. Alan slips into it carefully. It's hot, and it reacts to his touch by stiffening a bit against his skin. After a moment, it begins to whisper. Alan lies back to stare at the mirrored ceiling, his arms on the sides of the tub, and he listens to the strange bath fluid speak to him in a language he's never heard. The sound gives him warm shivers. It's been so much longer than six months. It's been his whole life, but now he can let himself relax. He can't resist, so he stops trying. He lets the whispering liquid soothe him and drifts easily to the borderland of sleep.

Memories are waiting for him there. They stand gray-robed and quiet, looking down. Their hands are folded together in their sleeves. Alan approaches them one by one, aching to see what they have to show him.

The first is rural Ohio in autumn: trees lambent against browning grass, bright as torches, losing their leaves slowly to cool winds that smell like fire. Cardinals pip through the bushes, chasing each other. The sun sets into the lake, drawing Gildersleeve Mountain in vivid shadow.

The next figure is his mother. She is crying. Alan is choking on guilt. This is his first emotional memory.

The line goes on for a long time. Alan lets his memories flow over and through him. He loves them all, and he misses his old life; after so long, he can admit that to himself. The whispers urge him to open himself completely, and he obeys. He allows himself to indulge in a deep and cleansing sadness, and his magic sickness retreats from it.

The last figure is Allison, but he doesn't linger there. She wants to draw him down into her bloodbath, into the wasted heat of her desperate life, but he resists. She lords over him, suddenly terrible, and hisses her anger in jets of steam, but he doesn't want that memory anymore. He leaves her and stands at the border, looking out into sleep as an exile. It waves silver grass at him; it blows bonfire air in his face, but it doesn't want him back. He doesn't mind. He has to leave, anyway.

Alan climbs out of the tub as the liquid starts to cool. He drapes a towel around himself, but there's no need; the liquid dries away almost instantly. When he knocks on the door, a servant opens it, carrying some clothes on hangers.

"How do you feel?" she asks. Her face isn't blank. Her eyes move over him, really seeing him, and a living blush spreads across her cheeks. She clears her throat before continuing. "Put these on. They're for you."

Alan buttons a sturdy shirt over his sunken chest and pulls a pair of incredibly comfortable slipper socks up to his knees. Plus-fours complete the outfit, leaving him feeling a little bit like an Ivy League golfer. He tucks his wallet into his back pocket and buttons the loop of its chain under a thin, red belt. The act of dressing feels almost like a ceremony, though he realizes that its Toven's way of asserting his authority, and he tries to enjoy it as long as possible. How long can he go on feeling clean and renewed? The dead voices are growing again. The sickness is returning. Graveworld is moving in him, giving him dreamlets through the seed of the Kingwatcher. A final look in the mirror fails to tell him who he is, and he decides to be all right with that for now.

He folds up his work shirt and slacks and tucks them under his arm as the servant girl leads him down the hall. He leaves only the new hide monk-straps behind, preferring his non-slip work shoes. Thus, he retains some authority over himself, and the ceremony is complete. He goes to meet Toven feeling strong and ready.

The King of the North is waiting in a wide chamber at the end of the hall. A globe like the ones on the Mercy Gale stands free in the center of the space, its heart light flickering. There is a large portrait on the east wall: a woman sits in a high-backed chair, her white collar ruffling up around her thin face. Her gloved hand is on her breast, reaching for the green jewel on her choker.

"Who's she?" Alan asks as he enters the alcove where Toven is reading.

Toven closes his book and looks up at Alan with a measured smile. "The Lady Nightjar," he says, a note of pain in his voice. "Annun, my wife. She sat for that painting ten years to the day before she vanished. I search for her still, hoping."

"I'm sorry," Alan says. The painting looks ancient. Lady Nightjar's features are hard to make out, but there is a sad light to her face. Shadows gather behind her, giving the painting a slightly threatening aspect.

"We weep for ourselves," Toven replies. "How was your bath? Do you feel restored?"

Alan crosses his arms over his chest. "What's going on with my friends?" he asks.

"Brattle was nearly frozen to death," Toven says, "but your quick action saved him. He is recuperating now in the garden, and I imagine that the cat is with him."

"Stag's Blood," Alan insists.

"Another barbarous name, but I suppose there's no getting around that one."

"What about the Mercy Gale?"

Toven nods. "Home at last and in for repairs. I owe you my gratitude for finding her. I've been searching for years. You've made me very happy."

Alan looks up at Lady Nightjar again, half expecting to see her scowling in anger. "She was seventy miles south in the Depot," he says.

"I assure you," Toven chuckles, "she has not always been there."

Alan takes a moment to look around the room. The walls bow outward, and there are no windows. Faces watch from the rafters, stitched blue or gold onto banners of dark silk brocade. Rows of S-shaped bookshelves cross the chamber, almost bisecting it, arranged to follow an intricate pattern on the floor. Each tile is burned with Toven's mark, and each shelf is topped with funeral artifacts in glass display cases. Barring a few design discrepancies, this room is essentially a larger version of Pwysh's workshop. Alan's sickness responds to the power of the space by shrinking even further.

"Tell me what more there is," Toven says, standing. "Do you have something else of Pwysh's? You mentioned as much earlier."

Alan takes his phone, the light-lined map, and Pwysh's note out of his hip pocket. He looks at them for a second, feeling their weight in his hand.

"He was my blood," Toven urges. He steps forward and holds out his hand. "And I haven't seen him in three months. "

"Do you know where to find Winter White?" Alan asks.

"*Quid pro quo*, then," Toven sighs. "It's as good a place to start as any, I suppose." He crosses to the globe and motions for Alan to join him. Alan does so cautiously. "I'll play along, but I'm afraid I have nothing of equal value to trade. I haven't spoken to her either. In fact, she and Pwysh left here together the last time I saw either of them."

"Left to do what?"

Toven holds out his hand again and says, "As per your terms, Alan. Don't set up shop if you have nothing for sale."

Alan hands Toven the note and the map first. "This was in his big book, *The Book of Horns*," he explains. "There are two lists of three things. I'm not sure what they mean, but the map has my name on it."

Toven sits motionless for a full minute, staring down at the papers. Then he nods.

"And this castle circled," he says. "So that's why you've come here."

"Brattle seems to think that you're some kind of prophet," Alan says. "We're looking for answers. Might as well go to the circled spot on the secret map, right?"

Toven continues nodding. He returns to his chair and leans backward into it, barely looking up. "Well," he begins, "I don't know about prophecy, but I can tell you what these lists are."

"Did you foretell Winter White's coming?" Alan asks.

Toven looks up with his eyes swimming in tears. He doesn't speak until he's blinked the sheen away.

"I had a dream," he says, "but it wasn't about Winter White. It was a long time ago. When she appeared, folks started to remember it, calling it a prophecy. It was very complex, and almost none of it has come true. If it's a prophet you seek, I can't help. I'm only Pwysh's cousin, and I can only offer insight as such, I'm afraid. Sit down, and I'll show you."

Alan sits next to Toven in a high-backed chair and puts his heels to the ground as best he can to keep it from rocking. His stomach is turning strangely. The sickness is rebelling against this chamber. Alan relishes its fear.

"Rawbones, eternal flame, and Sepulchra prisons," Toven says. "These are tests: Pwysh's way of mentoring you, it seems. Posthumously. All adept students must endure trials to reach their full potential. Pwysh clearly had a crash course in mind for you, though. Trials by fire. I wonder why."

"What about bell, star, and spirit?" Alan asks.

"I think those would be the ways to pass the tests," Toven's practiced expression slips into a frown. "But I'm guessing. Pwysh must not have had a lot of time to leave more information."

"His workshop was destroyed," Alan explains. "We don't know how much more he left. If there was more, White might have taken it."

"Bring me my quill and an inkwell," Toven says. Alan does as he's asked, and Toven starts drawing circles on the map. "Rawbones is a brunnmigi – the terror of Cheel Ghar, in Kidhia. It has been haunting the Pfahlwald for longer than I can remember. The Sepulchra prisons are here, in Stele Gorge. They are filled with the Dead in Disgrace. The Eternal Flame is in Welkinbright, the Empyrean City. You won't find it on this map –it floats in the sky above Cineria – but the Barrowvale is probably the best place to start looking."

"But what did he want me to do in these places?" Alan asks. He takes the newly marked map back and looks down at it.

"That may be what bell, star and spirit are about," Toven replies. "I can't think of what else they might signify."

He is silent a very long time. His eyes move across the floor, as if searching for an answer there. He barely blinks. Alan blows on the map carefully trying to dry the ink before he folds it up again. He doesn't like the look on Toven's face.

"Well, Rawbones is the plainest," Toven finally says. "Kill him. Many have tried, but Pwysh clearly expected you to be something special. The dead in Sepulchra are cursed; I imagine that you might lift the curse somehow. As for the eternal flame, I'm not sure what there is to do with it besides put it out. I know nothing of Welkinbright. They are a secretive people, but Pwysh collected secrets. I don't know how he found them – probably the same way he found you. He saw something in you." Toven squints at Alan and purses his lips. "He saw something I do not. What secrets was Pwysh keeping from me? I can't think about it now. It's too upsetting."

Toven stands and begins to pace. Alan feels small and stupid for remaining seated, but he doesn't know what else to do.

"I can't do these things," Alan says, slowly. "I don't have any idea how Pwysh knew me or why he would set out these tasks for me, but I can't do them. I'm nobody. I barely survived this long."

"Pwysh led you to me," Toven replies, "and that means that he meant for me to be part of your fledging. I'm honored, then, and I can't let him down by abetting your reluctance. You'll do what he wanted, you'll become who he expected you to be, and then we might see his plan for what it is. I trust Pwysh. He knew what he was doing. I just wish that I did."

Alan stands and sets the map and the note in his chair. He holds his phone out to Toven like a bouquet of funeral flowers.

"There's this, too," he says. "Do you know what this means?"

Toven takes the phone and spends a few moments tapping at the screen, trying to understand it. Alan watches, hoping to see him frown again or make a frustrated face, but it doesn't happen. The King of the North remains implacable this time.

"What is this device?" Toven asks.

"It's like a long range communicator," Alan explains. "It doesn't work the way it did in my world. Now all it will do is show these symbols and these numbers. Brattle says they're coordinates. Do you recognize them?"

Toven breathes a tight sigh through his nose. He slits his eyes, and his cheeks bunch up like wrapping paper. The colors over his head change subtly; the shift makes Alan feel uneasy.

"This is something different," Toven says, thinking aloud in a conspiratorial whisper. "Ley lines! Yes. These are coordinates along a map of ley lines. Give me that map again."

Alan complies, and Toven takes up his quill and draws wavy lines over certain points, shaking his head the whole time, as if unhappy with what he's doing. Alan tries and fails to read his face. There is something huge and heavy there, but Toven hides it.

I don't trust silence, Alan remembers. In Toven's case, he doesn't trust a lack of it any less.

"There are veins of force passing through all spheres," Toven says. "These coordinates are a juncture of three of them, but I can't find them here. They're ancient and dead; I need an older map. Do you mind if I keep this object for a while to study it?"

Alan hesitates, almost agrees, and then stops himself. He steps forward to take the phone out of Toven's tense, mauling grip. For a second, he isn't sure that Toven is going to let go. Then Toven's hand goes slack, and the light returns to his face.

"If you find an older map," he says, "you can bring it to me. I'd like to hold on to that for now."

Toven nods. His demeanor has changed. Walls have gone up around him. "Your purpose is rolling out in front of you, Alan," he says. "It's rolling out in front of me, too. Follow these clues. *They* are the real reason you're here."

Alan slips the phone back into his pocket. He circles Toven, taking him in, trying to penetrate his new barriers. He watches the

225

orbs moving above his head, hoping to find the meaning in their dancing. There's a secret to it; he's certain. Perhaps it's looking out from behind Toven's eyes. Perhaps it's in his sanctimonious lean – the way he cants to the left with one foot slightly up on its ball. Whatever it is, it sits in Alan's stomach like a hot coal. He can't suffer it.

"With all due respect," Alan says, "I can decide that for myself. I don't think you've told me everything. What does Winter White want?" He almost laughs at the alliteration. "How does she fit into this?"

"Why do you care about her?" Toven asks. "Forget about Winter White. She's meaningless to you."

"She killed Pwysh," Alan answers. "She convinced Brattle's brother, Nettle, to kill their father. And, when she caught him betraying her, she killed him, too. She's in this. She's right in the middle. Whatever Pwysh wanted for me, I think she wants it for herself. That's why we're here."

Toven gathers himself together. Alan watches him rebuilding. He sticks out his chin as he musters his superiority again. Alan has the sudden, sinking feeling that he's spoiled things.

"I don't know," Toven says, measuring each word with care.

He starts for the door, his shadow growing long behind him, like a threat. Alan pities him. He can't have lived so long in this wounding machine without ending up wounded himself.

"And I'm sorry, Alan, but I have work to do. This dome is a purifier, and the eyestone here is its power source. You touched chaos, and you have to purify. You'll die if you don't. Look into the eye; sit down if you want. Think about the sphere you left – or, better yet, the trials you'll have to face in this one. Stay as long as you need, and then stay longer. I'll send your companions in later to check on you."

Toven stops in the doorway and looks back at Alan over his shoulder. He is dimmed and small under the doorframe. His smile cuts cold across his face, illuminating nothing.

"Thank you for showing me Pwysh's papers," he says. And then he is gone into the hall, and Alan can hear his footsteps tapping crisply away.

Twenty-Two

Toven's catharsium becomes Alan's home for a week. Ice storms pound Gimcrack, and the days creep by, cold and maimed. Nights when the winds are at their worst, the castle lies in a kind of torpor. The lights go out, and the halls shrink in stillness. Some deep parts of the basement flood. Alan learns to find comfort in the sound of water filling the foundations.

Alan spends the first hours of every morning and the last ones of every evening staring into the eyestone and meditating. Brattle and Stag's Blood sit with him through every session. Their stories and their presence calm him, expediting a process that might otherwise have taken a month.

The sickness is alive. Alan only begins to feel its mind as it leaves him, clawing for purchase. It hates his focus, and it screams against him, but it can't stand before the light. It finally dwindles away, and, on several occasions, Alan sees the Bleeding in its death throes.

"It's not a place like Graveworld is a place," Alan explains. It's not long after midday, and he is sitting with Brattle and Stag's Blood in a pillared gallery overlooking one of Toven's frost-wet gardens. "It's more like a state – as in a state of being, like ruin or confusion. If you could stand inside those states, or be lost in them, then that would be like being in the Bleeding, I think. Basically, it's not a good feeling."

"The derelict universe," Brattle says. "We felt it when you crushed those Watchers. Hard to believe you could contain all that power, bony. And a little scary, too."

"I wonder why Toven bothers to teach you," Stag's Blood purrs. The wind sings over the windowsills to ruffle his growing coat. His fur is coming back in more quickly than Alan had expected. "He hardly seems interested in us anymore. I imagine he's afraid of what might happen if you lose control."

"Or if *he* does," Brattle says.

"I don't blame him, then," Alan replies. "But I don't trust him either."

Toven has barely been around. He stays locked in his room, or he wanders the heather for hours, refusing to be disturbed. Servants and armed guards follow him everywhere, apparently lead by the ticking, mindless Mawn.

Unlike his master, Toven's giant is a constant presence in the halls of Gimcrack Castle. Mawn walks the grounds every night, silent and tireless, on a circuitous survey. Alan begins spending a lot of time in the sheltered yard where the Mercy Gale is under repairs, and he occasionally sees Mawn there supervising things. He moves as if crushed under the weight of some terrible duty; Alan can't decide whether to fear him or pity him.

When Toven does meet with Alan, he refuses to speak about Winter White. Instead, they discuss his burgeoning power, and the king seems more and more afraid after every encounter. Suspicious that Toven might be trying to mold him into something dangerous, Alan is careful about what he really learns. There is a science to the basics that can't be overlooked, and he tries to cling to that. He brings every lesson to the eyestone and pores over it, trying to wring the essentials out.

Stag's Blood and Brattle are quartered in the château proper, but Alan's apartments are in the keep. It's cold, and the furnishings are sparse, but he has little need for niceties anyway. He only uses the bed when he's reading.

There are several grimoires on a black rowan shelf near the dresser, and they are all Alan really needs to pass his time. When he's not walking the halls of the castle with Brattle and Stag's Blood or searching the dolmens by torchlight on dry nights, he busies himself studying volumes on driromancy and shadow manipulation. All are written in Toven's neat hand and marked on their covers by his simple triskelion seal. Alan wonders whether Toven might have placed them there deliberately.

In the first dark hours of the next week, Toven and two of his guards climb the turret keep to Alan's room. Alan is sitting in a chalk circle drawing shadows across the floor. The magic is like a muscle in his mind; he can move it without understanding the process. The dark responds to his every whispered command. For the first time in his life, he is getting good at being what he is. When Toven knocks, Alan opens the door from where he sits. The king enters with a smile, staring down at the congress of shades. His escorts glower into the room from beyond the threshold like terracotta warriors.

"I'd hoped to find you practicing," he says. "Come with me."

Alan relaxes and the shadows return to their corners. He follows Toven through haunted halls to the apothecary. Black shapes amass behind them, cluttering his peripheral vision with flickering motion. Alan has had little success learning to ignore the château's many ghosts. This morning, one of them is weeping. The sound is thread-thin and barely audible, rolling along the vaguest edges of perception. Alan feels it more than he hears it; sympathetic sorrow wells in his throat, and he coughs. Horror creeps down his back like a cape of insects. It helps a little when Toven starts speaking, but Alan continues to look back over his shoulder.

"Most magi carry trinkets," Toven explains. His voice is raw, he is out of breath, and he constantly clears his throat. Has he been screaming? "Even the light arts draw life from the artist, as you know. But beads and worry stones can be lost. Your power is unusual, Alan. It's strong, and in strange ways. You need something more permanent to purify you."

"What did you have in mind?" Alan asks.

They have reached the apothecary's office. Mawn is out in the hall, standing straight as a rail, his face bent around a ponderous frown. Alan nods to him. The door is open, and the apothecary is waiting inside, his small form swimming in his long habit. Alan catches glimpses of his lutrine face under the brown shadows of his hood.

"Please come in, Mr. Shade," he grumbles. His voice has retired from him. He can barely command it anymore. It only says what he wants out of pity.

Alan enters the office. It is cluttered and small, and there is green smoke rising from a smudge stick in the fireplace. The walls lean in, giving the whole room an unsettling curve.

"What is this?" Alan asks, nervous.

Toven steps in from the hall and pulls the door closed. The apothecary pulls up a bucket of water, lights another smudge stick on a burning ball of wax, and then hands Toven a long-handled instrument. For an instant, before he realizes what it is, Alan thinks it might be his trash masher.

"A trial by fire," Toven says. He's holding a branding iron. The head is burning orange and black, like Toven's hair. Smoke is rolling off of it in twisting ribbons. "Focus now, Alan. I'm not entirely sure whether this is going to hurt or not."

With this, Toven pushes the iron against Alan's forehead with all his strength. Alan writhes, and Toven steadies him with a hand on the back of his skull. He flails, and Toven weathers the storm. The force is tremendous, and the sound of his bone burning is terrible, but there isn't actually any pain. His skull is mostly numb; the only sensation is a swell of intense prickles washing back from his brow to the base of his neck.

Alan calms wave after wave of panic almost without thinking; his new power seems to move on its own, healing him, protecting him, lifting him up from the depths of fear. Practice has made him buoyant. With great effort, he manages to remain standing. He can't close his eyes, but he's learned how to look inward; he concentrates on the darkness there, willing all his remaining fear into it. Finally, he goes still and lets his arms hang at his sides. When Toven is finished, he pulls the brand away and drops it in its bucket to smoke and spit. The apothecary steps forward at once to rub a poultice of wax and honey onto Alan's head.

"There," Toven says. "That wasn't as bad as I'd feared. Are you all right?"

The apothecary hands Alan a cold towel. He squeezes it over his forehead, causing a faint hiss of steam. Then he lays it over his new brand. There is no cooling sensation. There is only wet, sliding weight.

"Far more all right than I'd have been if I'd felt that the way I should have," Alan says. "You could have warned me!"

Toven turns to look for something for a minute. "You've been doing good work in the catharsium, but no purge is thorough enough to cure magic sickness completely. An apotropaic ritual is necessary, and they must be fast. I apologize." He produces a mirror from the stacks of books and papers on the apothecary's desk and hands it to Alan, who takes it carefully while still trying to keep the cloth on his brow. "A sigil fit to contain your power: the Seal of Aiwass. This iron was not easily forged, and it won't take any natural kind of heat. I've never used it before; you're the first to bear this sigil in an eon. I envy you."

Alan removes the cloth and uncovers the sigil. It is a round mass of points and complex intersections with words and symbols encircling it. It is charred black in counter-relief between his empty orbits and above the ridge of his brow. As he watches, it fills up with amber light until it is beaming.

"Typhon," Alan says, trying to read the sigil in the mirror, "Gnosis, Egregore." The words have a profound weight to them. He says them again, feeling them in his ethereal voice, warmed by their power. There is no twist in his stomach. The dead cry freedom in his mind, praising him. The Kingwatcher whispers strength into his body that he has forgotten he ever had. At long last, the sickness is gone.

"Purifying meditation is one thing, but nothing can stand against this seal," Toven explains. "The sickness knew everything you knew. If you had known what was going to happen, it might have sacrificed itself: it might have killed you in your sleep. But it should be silent now. How do you feel?"

Alan sets the mirror face down on the apothecary's chair. He takes a few steps around the room, testing himself. He can feel

232

the sigil on his head. It's an odd sensation: like wearing a crooked crown. He runs his hands over it, unable to resist touching it. The light in the brand burns inward, too; its intensity leaves him fascinated for a moment.

"I feel like myself again," he finally says. "And then some."

The feeling doesn't last. Alan stops by Brattle's room, but the ghoul is fast asleep in his four-poster bed. The sheets are streaked black where he's rolled on them, and his pillow is nearly flat. He's put on quite a bit of mass, but Alan never asks where he's been eating. Stag's Blood is pooled beside the bed like a liquid, looking equally well-fed. His barrel chest rises and falls with long, dreaming purrs, and the tip of his tail flicks back and forth as if it has a mind of its own. Alan doesn't want to wake them, so he returns to his room in the keep. There, he looks into the mirror at his new brand, but he can't do that without confronting the horror of his face.

His skull stares back at him from the silvered glass. He thinks about how his eyes had always seemed half closed and how he had always hated his tall forehead. He had never been confident about his crooked smile, but all that's left of that is a lipless, funeral grin. Unfettered by gums, his teeth look enormous. He'd had nice eyes – everyone had told him that – but now he has only chasmal, thirty-millimeter orbital pits. Looking closely, he can just make out the grooves in the bone where his optic nerves used to be; the irony of visually inspecting his sightless eye sockets almost makes him laugh. Where is he seeing from? He thinks about what Brattle said: *Magic is keeping you alive now, you know*. He wonders if magic has replaced his humanity. It's never occurred to him to wonder what it might be like not to be human anymore.

Alan straightens his spine. He swallows hard to stifle a sob, refusing to be reduced to self pity again. At the very least, he can pretend to refuse. He returns to the catharsium, though he's not sure he really needs it anymore; the Seal of Aiwass shines from his forehead, banishing stairwell shadows, asserting itself relentlessly.

233

There is no trace of his magic sickness anymore, but he sees no reason to stop meditating.

It's almost light when he arrives at the chamber door. He stops his hand inches above the knob: there is a small voice coming from inside. It tinkles like falling tin, and it's so high that he can barely make out what it's saying. He opens the door slowly and peeks in to see if he's interrupting anything, and the high voice screams in fear at the sight of his face.

"Oh my slivers!" chimes a crystal fairy. "Who are you?"

Alan steps all the way into the room with his hand up to show that he means no harm.

"I'm sorry," he says. "I'm a guest here. I didn't mean to disturb you. My name is Alan."

He holds out his hand to the fairy, and she lands on it. She hardly weighs more than an apple. She is vaguely humanoid, her every line and surface smooth and featureless, and there's nothing to her shape that's anything like clothing. Her wings beat so rapidly that they ring. Light scatters through them, leaving her surrounded by a rainbow haze. Her hair is a sculpted wave that falls down her back in delicate curls, as translucent as the rest of her. Looking hard, Alan can barely see her tiny face. He can see himself reflected there: a hundred little skulls in perfect, miniscule angles.

"Shines, Alan Shade," she says, her voice like a rain of pins. "Yes, there's word spreading about you: the Lashaseph's spirit. I wondered if I would see you here!" She gives a half curtsey. Her limbs articulate oddly. The crystal sings when she moves, warping and throwing rainbows. "My name is Sophia. I am a guest here, too, on a pilgrimage from Leadlight. My first pilgrimage! And I am pleased to make your acquaintance. You are not anything like the rumors say."

"Rumors about me?" Alan asks, suddenly wary. "What are they?"

Sophia takes flight and hovers in front of Alan's face for an instant. She seems to be inspecting his skull. He shrinks from her, embarrassed.

"The Mothers discourage gossip," she says, "and I always abide by their rules. I am one of the good ones. Do not trouble yourself about it. The stories are not true anyway."

Sophia hums over to the eyestone and begins flying slow circles around it. Now and then, she runs her hand over its surface, making a little pinging sound. A light grows within her like the light in the stone, something that's more than just a reflection. She's in communion with the eyestone somehow — or with the pulsing glow inside it. She starts to sing a mantra that Alan doesn't understand.

"Maybe you can tell me where the rumors started then," Alan tries. "Who is spreading them?"

Sophia continues to circle the stone as she answers. Her song continues, too. She can divide her voice. Her speaking voice finds a new, slightly lower register.

"Everyone," she replies. "Sometimes I think I am the only good one at Saint M's — besides the Mothers, of course. But that is pride, I know. The rumors are on everyone's lips, but they first arose in the woods. The Mothers heard them there in whispers."

"I guess that makes sense." Alan nods and steps toward the eyestone as well. Careful not to disturb Sophia's flight pattern, he puts his hand flat against it, feeling the life inside it pushing under his palm. The eyestone can still calm him. He listens to Sophia's high song for a while before continuing. "What are you doing? Where is your pilgrimage to?"

"Wherever I have to go," Sophia says. "I am a Sister at Saint M's — a servant of the world. We go where we are needed when we are needed. My task is to find out what's happened to the Necropolis."

"And what's happened to it?" Alan asks. "Do you know? I imagine you've heard of Winter White if you've heard of me."

"I am still trying to find out," Sophia explains, "so no and yes. There are rumors about her, too, but I have never met her. I am going north to west via the south, following the Framer Gems to ask them for insight. Or maybe even prophecy. I have not been traveling long, though. All I know so far is what I started with: the Necropolis has been moved."

"How do you know that?" Alan asks. "The whole city? Are you sure that's not more gossip?"

"I have seen it," Sophia says. She stops singing and lights on top of the eyestone to sit cross-legged. "There is an empty space where it used to be. It is just a pit, a great hole, full of stone and dust where they left the broken parts of the city behind. Something big is happening. I'm a little scared of it, but I'll find out what it is. The Framer Gems have never let us down. We are the last ones that still serve them earnestly."

"I think we might be on the same pilgrimage," Alan says, "though I came from a lot farther away."

The door groans open and Brattle enters the catharsium. He is wearing a smart brown suit, but his feet are bare.

"There you are, Al," he says. "Look, I'm gettin' tired of waiting for Toven to say somethin' helpful. Now that it's light, Stags and I are going to go and try to make him. Come help me look out in the fields." He sees Sophia and smiles, tipping an invisible hat. "Morning, Sister. Didn't know Toven was hosting pilgrims here. I'm sorry to interrupt, but Al and me got business."

Before Alan can reply, Sophia comes buzzing down from the top of the eyestone to fly a little circle around Brattle.

"Good morning, Conservator," she chimes. "I am Sister Sophia. You are not interrupting. I would like to come with you, if I may! I need to speak with King Toven as well, and I have never met a Conservator before."

Brattle sags in his clothes. He's still tired. His eyes are barely open. He makes an assenting sound and turns back toward the door to shuffle through it, his brown pants rustling on a form they were clearly not made to contain.

"Your call, Soph," he says. "I ain't got no say in what you do. We're going out to the dolmens."

Sophia flits down onto Alan's shoulder. She's panting a little from exertion; he imagines that it must be hard to move such a rigid frame the way she does. He looks into her briefly, trying to see her lungs through her body.

Alan follows Brattle out into the hall and pulls the door to the catharsium closed. As the three head down the ghost-watched corridor toward the east exit, he laughs and tugs on Brattle's lapel.

"Whether we find Toven or not," he says to Brattle, "I think this is going to be an informative morning."

"What's that on your forehead?" Brattle asks, yawning.

"The Seal of Aiwass," Alan replies. "A ward against magic sickness. I just got it today. Toven did it. It's a brand."

"Feel different?"

"I do. It's amazing." Alan thinks about this for a moment, idly running his fingers over the brand. "But I'm not sure about it. It feels a little bit like a proof of purchase – like Toven thinks he owns me. At least the sickness is gone."

"Completely gone, huh?" Brattle snorts. "You look it."

"I look completely gone?" Alan asks. He laughs, but Brattle doesn't.

"Something funny about this place," Brattle explains. "It makes everything look rotten."

Alan looks around. They are on the other side of the main hall. The passage is broad and open, but the air isn't moving. Nothing follows them toward the east door; it's too quiet even for ghosts this morning. Where does all the sickness go? Maybe it bleeds down into the foundations and comes up again through unwatched walls, a wasting curse disguised as heat and dead-still air. It has to go somewhere. Alan finally admits to himself that Brattle is right.

"Rotten? Not you," he says. "You look downright dapper! What's the story?"

Brattle plucks at his clothes, disgusted. "Toven was supposed to meet me before dawn. He said he was going to tell me everything I wanted to know, and his servant left these cumb ropes for me. You should see Stags, though! Anyway, Toven ditched, and I'm pissed."

"Maybe he was busy with me," Alan offers.

"He ain't ever doin' what he's maybe doin'," Brattle replies. "He's been stringing us along. I'm spent for patience."

"Stringing you along to where, Conservator?" Sophia asks. "What are you looking for?"

"Nowhere," Brattle replies with a growl. He looks toward Sophia and Alan is struck by the anger in his eyes.

All at once, Alan is spent for patience, too. He realizes that his vulnerability has made him a prisoner, and the last vestige of esteem for Gimcrack and its king fades from him like a bad dream.

Brattle corrects himself: "Whatever direction leads us away from Winter White."

They reach the west door and open it. The moon is still out. It burns small, like a talon poised to eviscerate the storm. The morning is cold under cloud shadows. Stag's Blood is waiting just beyond the portico, brown heads of heather bobbing around his sternum. His mane is crimped and pinned back with a silver barrette. There are lines of white dye on his flanks, and his claws are capped.

"Good morning," he says. His voice is huge and booming. He wears his new strength proudly, and it makes him even more beautiful. He rises and bows to Sophia. "Fair Sister! Hello. Good morning to all. Toven was not in his quarters, and the kitchen hadn't seen him, but there is someone out in the field. Look."

Alan and Brattle peer out across the field. Rain is in the air, cold and heavy. The breeze tastes like copper. A figure is kneeling near one of the furthest dolmens. The distance shimmers; it's hard to make out how large the shape is.

238

"I'm Stag's Blood," the cat says to Sophia while Alan and Brattle are watching the figure. "It's a pleasure to meet you. I wasn't aware the pilgrimages ran so late into the year, but you're the first Sister of M I've ever met. I have a lot to learn."

"As do we all, it seems," Sophia replies from Alan's shoulder. "Happy meetings, Stag's Blood. We travel year-round. Change is coming. We feel it in the air. We see it in the sky. We hear it whispered in the woods: rumors of some approaching darkness. Avernus and the Coma at war again. We are discouraged from sowing fear, you should know, but, this is a special case. I have come to find Toven because he seems to be at the center of it."

"I've feared as much," Stag's Blood answers. "But I distrust forest whispers. I'd rather see the darkness approaching for myself."

"Might be him," Brattle says, oblivious to the conversation.

Alan starts off across the heather, and the others follow. Sophia darts from his shoulder to the crown of his skull in the song of her wings. Something of him is returning. He is back on the ground in clean boots. It's a good feeling, and he tries not to think about it for fear of losing it.

It isn't Toven at the far end of the field. As Alan approaches with Brattle and Stag's Blood in tow, the figure stands and turns to meet them.

"Mawn," Alan says.

"The puppet," Brattle hisses. "Reckon we can just follow the strings from here back to the pupeteer?"

"What is he doing?" Sophia chimes.

Alan shouts to Mawn, asking him. Mawn stands still except for his prosthetic arm, which turns its clawed hand incessantly, opening and closing it like a mute and longing mouth.

"Toven," Stag's Blood says as they stop before Mawn. "He sent for us, but we can't find him. Do you know where he is?"

Everything Mawn has to say is right on his face. Nothing comes out of his mouth. It's not a stupid silence. Alan is actually a little frightened by it. Mawn lifts his claw hand and then lets it fall again. He aborts this gesture twice more before anyone says anything.

"Look here," Sophia says. She's on top of the dolmen. Alan barely felt her leave.

Sophia is standing on what is almost the last of the portal graves. It is bare and skeletal, canted into the belly of a hill, with a long pit under its slab roof. On a mound at the pit's deeper side is a pile of polished stones, beads, withering blossoms, and heath brush. Incense cones smolder nearby, not smoking anymore. Their scent blows up from them like ribbons drawn over hard curves, as if tracing the lines of a body. Alan watches the black curls for a minute, his heart a cold weight in his throat.

Mawn isn't looking at the grave anymore. He's looking over Alan's shoulder instead. Alan turns to see Toven coming across the field at a strut, four guards flanking him.

"There you are!" Toven cries. "What are you all doing out here? Brattle, Stag's Blood, I asked you to meet me in the main chamber. I'm sorry I was late. I was detained! But it's well that you're all here now. I have news."

Either Toven hasn't noticed Sophia yet, or he's decided not to acknowledge her. Whatever the case, she doesn't seem to be in a hurry to change the situation. She sits down on the slab, crosses her legs, and flicks her wings behind her, listening.

"We were done waiting," Brattle snarls. "And I ain't too interested in news at the moment. I want to know about Winter White, and I ain't gonnna let you off for dodging me, either."

"Please," Stag's Blood interrupts. "You've helped us, but you've kept your secrets. We want Winter White. Tell us where she is, and you won't have to house us anymore. We're grateful, and we're eager to be out of your hair."

"That is my news precisely," Toven smiles. "I've received word from Winter White. She's coming here. She's on her way."

He swings his arms out, opening himself to them. Alan doesn't buy it. Mawn makes a noise behind him: a low grunt that rattles through his sinuses. It doesn't put Alan any more at ease.

"Pardon my doubtin'," Brattle says, "but you been no action and hardly any talk since we got here, Your Highness. How do we know this is really happening?"

"Wait a day or two and you'll see for sure," Toven replies. "I know I've been aloof, and I apologize. I am a king without a kingdom, and I face singular challenges. Matters have been pressing on me, and it looks as if they shall continue to do so, but I wanted to make myself available at least long enough to tell you this. This is what you wanted."

"And now, you shall make yourself available to me," says Sophia. She flutters from the rock and circles toward Toven. Her feelings flash inside her like lightning.

"Fair Sister," Toven says, bowing. "Yes, my servants said you'd arrived. Please come back to the castle, all of you. There's a storm coming, and we need to prepare. Sister, we can speak in my apartments. I assure you that all your questions will be answered."

Stag's Blood looks at Alan. Brattle spits between them. His sleeves are soiled from walking across the heather on his knuckles.

"This ain't satisfaction, Your Highness," he says. "You dunno what's at stake."

Toven turns around and heads back toward the château, his guards fast on his heels. Sophia looks back over her shoulder, colors burning out of her. Alan isn't sure how to read her yet.

"He knows the stakes," Stag's Blood says to Brattle. "He's played them perfectly this whole time. What I don't see is why."

"Because she's controlling him," Alan says, "and he's trying to make sure that she has all the power so we can't trace the puppet strings back to her from here."

They watch Toven marching away. He doesn't turn back to see if they're following. Two of his guards approach to escort Alan, Brattle, and Stag's Blood back to the castle. Mawn stays still behind them, staring after his master. His silence sits on the rest of the group for a few moments, and then Brattle finds his tongue again.

"She'll have the advantage," says the ghoul as the guards begin to prod them forward. "She'll come prepared, and we'd die in a showdown. We can't meet her here. We gotta leave."

Twenty-Three

King Toven stays in his chambers with Sophia for the rest of the day. After another visit to the Mercy Gale's sheltered yard, Alan, Brattle, and Stag's Blood meet to plan in the highest room of the keep, where balistariae look out over the château grounds from each of the cardinal directions. The storm rumples up around the castle, wrapping the writhing peaks of the mountains in keening wind and early spells of hail. There is nothing beyond its reach; the cloud wall stretches as far as Alan can see in every direction

Stag's Blood is curled on the floor, with Brattle helping him pick his claw sheaths off.

"There's no question," he begins, "we have to leave."

"The questions are when," Alan adds, turning away from the east-facing arrowslit to pace, "and how."

Stag's Blood trills a laugh. "Our departure has been too long in coming, in my opinion," he says. "Winter White wants you dead, and we have to assume that Toven knows."

"Soon as possible, then," Brattle says. "Tonight's my vote. We're good as we're gonna be to bug out now, and by the west door, I think."

"No," Alan says. "I want the Mercy Gale."

Brattle cocks his head. Thunder comes rolling over the castle, following a distant flash of cloud-caught lightning.

"Why?" Brattle asks.

"If we leave her, Toven could use her to catch up to us," Alan says. "Besides: I've put a little part of myself in her. It kind of feels like she's partly mine now."

Claw sheaths piled in the dust at last, Stag's Blood stands and shakes the clips from his mane. His full, glossy glory blows free in the wind whistling in through the loop holes. It may have been nearly too long for safety, but the stay here has certainly improved his health. He is bursting with cool power.

"I think that's a good enough justification for theft," he says. "Three hours after nightfall, and then we'll sneak down to her yard. The storm should be in full swing; I doubt anyone will stop us."

Alan and Brattle nod, and the matter is decided. A sense of purpose hangs in the room for a minute, heavy as the storm-wet air. Then it bursts apart and begins to dissipate, undone by its own gravity – its own deep seriousness. Alan looks out the window again, watching the lights of the storm dance circles around the moving mountains.

"Just once in my life," he says into the silence, "I'd like to find a welcoming place. I feel like I've been travelling my whole life."

Brattle coughs a laugh. "Well, Al, I think you looked in the wrong rat hole for that."

Gimcrack Castle settles into a huge, empty tension as darkness falls. The mountains grind and moan, shaking the whole château in long fits. The servants vanish, and Mawn leads the guards into their barracks. When the storm unreels at last, laying its rage on the whole of the north all at once, Stag's Blood and Brattle return to their chambers. Alan stays in the attic for a while, trying to find a piece of that exploded purpose left over. Alone in the attic with dead voices crying in his head to beat the gale, he remembers promising his parents on the night of their funeral that he would never be a child again. He tried to sell his innocence for immunity to pain, but the universe didn't keep up its end of the deal. He was left with a pain that wouldn't stop, no matter how much of himself he swore away. Graveworld had him long before the accident that brought him here physically. Maybe that's the real reason he's here.

With no more purpose left and nothing to do but wait, Alan tries to return to his room. He turns the knob, but the door into the stairwell doesn't open. It's locked, and no amount of pushing will make it budge.

For a moment, Alan panics. Then he remembers his new strength and puts both hands on the knob. He has a new muscle now; he sends his will into the keyhole and feels the lock's simple parts through his living bond with the Bleeding. Magic streams through him calmly, responsive as water, and he swirls his thoughts through it to move the tumblers. They are fragile pins, and they move easily. There is a ward on the lock that feels proud and sure of its strength; reaching through it is like reaching through a curtain of red mist. Its confidence shatters after a few minutes, and Alan casts it aside. In complete control, he turns the cam, and the lock opens with a satisfying click. Alan finishes with a flourish, turning the knob with his hands behind his back. As the door swings open, he allows himself a chuckle. Toven has underestimated him.

There are shadows on the stairs to his room. At his door, he finds a gray figure waiting, attended by eye-like orbs. It is tall and thin, and he can't see its face. It won't move for him, and it won't look up from the sag of its hood. It will only whisper horribly when Alan gets close. There's no choice but to push through it, turning inward away from the poisonous issue of secrets as best he can. Alan ducks his head, gathers his magic around him like a cloak, and rushes through the door of his room to find it ransacked.

Very little is missing, but every piece of furniture has been turned over. His work pants and shirt are hung balled up in the elbows of the rafters. His knapsack is in Brattle's room, so he knows his books are safe, but his phone is nowhere in the mess. Alan searches through the small piles for half an hour, but he doesn't go near the bed. Books spill across the floor, forming a circle around it. The covers are turned down, and a clean pillow awaits his head. The magic on the bed is huge and terrible; if his phone has been kicked under it, Alan will never know. The bed is a trap. Toven probably has the phone anyway.

Alan takes his clothes and turns to leave. There is more to do, and the new, wild spirits in the halls will make it difficult to get around. The gray figure is now inside Alan's room, still blocking the door, its gold and silver lights circling it in tight spirals. Its hood is thrown back, revealing an eyeless, star-like face on a head that is little more than a mass of thorns. Alan holds up his hand,

245

fingers straight and palm facing the spirit, his thumb tucked in an apotropaic gesture.

"Guardian," he says, "stand aside."

The spirit on the doorsill takes a single step forward. There is nothing beneath its robes to move it over the ground; it mists toward Alan like a storm, blown toward its eventual rupture by imperceptible winds. It tilts its head as if amused.

"Beyond me is the dark," it says, pouring out its voice like honey. "And the dark is mine."

Alan's anger swells. All his life, he has been afraid of it. Fear has made it seem huge, but now he has it in his hand. He can move it, use it, change it into a force of his will. He sweeps his hand to the right in a violent motion, pushing all his anger with it, and the guardian of the threshold scatters apart like sand. The door opens as it blows away. Its orbs wink out and Alan waves through a cloud of their vanishing embers as he heads into the stairwell.

Outside, the storm is bawling. Caught in the tower's eaves, the wind sounds like a weeping woman. The machines under the mountains shriek along with it, and the whole château begins to shake with their sudden vigor. Alan can feel them pounding beneath the floor of the east wing. They have never been so active.

The new sounds have stirred up mobs of angry ghosts in the château proper. Alan struggles shoulder-first through screaming clouds to get to the main hall. Much to his frustration, tiny hands snatch Alan's bundled clothes from under his arm and disappear with them. Shades flutter around his mouth and paw at his shoulders, pulling long tears in his shirt and ripping his belt loops. They flee before magic in great clots, but there are always more to swarm into the void. The throng only thins out in the entryway, where it turns in revulsion from the faint curtains of moonlight falling through the high windows.

Here, Alan rests and collects himself. He feels weighed down with psychic energy. In the foyer's purifying circle, hate, despair, and violence peel away from him like an old skin. He's left feeling hot and dirty with sweat and remembering long nights over the grill at Ray's. Before his emotional defenses recover, grief for those long-gone nights nearly overwhelms him.

As he leans against the huge front window, movement outside draws his attention. He looks up through the races of silver droplets down the glass to see a shape standing in the rain. Alan recognizes the Cuco from its scar-white robes and the black bag of bony lumps at its feet. It is far from Debtors' Orchard. The Cuco's hand is out; it hooks a beckoning finger back and forth, and the front doors whine open on their own. After a long, quiet moment, Alan steps out onto the porch.

It's dead black outside, but Alan can see by the lights dancing through the storm. The Cuco is drawn sharply beneath them; shadows cut across its body, changing its shape. Its face is like an owl's; its orange eyes burn from the center of a huge, feathered disc. Its beak is a just a black slash – like a nail pushed into a snowbank. Alan hates the Cuco. He wishes he didn't have to look at it. Being so close to it makes him want to retch. The bag before it might be moving slightly, or the Cuco might be dragging it towards itself as if to protect it from him.

"What do you want?" Alan asks.

The Cuco says nothing. It doesn't even begin to reply. It isn't alive the way he is. It's a hunger caught in an empty body; Alan can see the real Cuco, burning hateful and small, in the fires of its eyes.

"Something's moving you," he says to it. "That's why you've come up from your sloughs. Come on. Show me. Where are we going?"

The wind tugs Alan's clothes into wet rags around his lanky frame. The Cuco starts across the yard, untouched by the rain; water pours around it, stopped on some invisible field. It stops some yards away and turns to motion toward him again, and Alan finally steps off the porch to follow.

There is an art to most storms. They rhyme with themselves, internally perfect. The forces that move them are like will and reason, and they seem to destroy in anger, but they are spiritless. They have no hearts and no life.

This storm is different. It roars with life and spirit. It is a mover, a god-tempest; it gives birth to smaller storms that go wheeling away toward the scorpion tail of the Gimcrack Mountains. It is wild, artless, and as cruel as only a living thing can be.

Alan walks the yard against the wind, taking slow, heavy steps to keep from being swept off his feet. He follows the Cuco through the driving rain, and he wonders if the storm might be an extension of whatever power is controlling it.

The walk drags on. The moon looks shattered in the sky, and there are no stars to shine through the gloom. Over the clockwork mountain wall, cloud tendrils coiling fat through the high passes, the storm sprawls like a feeding beast. It scours the slopes of Gimcrack, beats the roofs of the château bare, and rips dolmens down across the heather. In its frenzy, it scours even time thin, and there is a flash and a tinny crack as Graveworld twists apart around the wound. Terrified, Alan wants to turn away, but he follows the Cuco into the wave of distortion anyway. There's a pull in it that he feels more with his spirit than his body. It is a hot, wrenching tug, and it seems to last forever as time struggles to heal. Alan cries out in pain, but thunder swallows his voice. He feels the seal burning on his forehead and its protective power working throughout his body. He tells himself that soul-agony is proof that he still has a soul to harm, and he tries to focus on that as he advances across the yard.

There is a knoll at the edge of the heath. It is low and round, hardly more than a rumple in the heather, and thick mats of blue sod fall down its shoulders like a stole. The only sign that it's more than it appears to be is the burgundy door in its south face, and this is barely visible through the raking sheets of rain. Alan has never seen this knoll before; it has been hidden under subtle magics, a dot on his periphery not worth his attention until now.

The Cuco weaves toward the knoll with its head down, and Alan lags behind it at a careful distance. It stops on the patch of worn ground before the door and turns to look at Alan, eyes dimming in anger. Does it feel the same pain in its shadow? Is there a soul inside it to torture? The storm settles in to focus all of its madness, and the strange tear in the world disappears as if it had never been there. The Cuco vanishes with it, leaving no marks across the yard where it had walked, and Alan approaches the door so light with relief that he barely touches the ground himself.

"The cellar, of course," Alan says as he tugs on the iron door pull. "OK, Toven. Let's see what you've got down here to beat that."

The door into the cellar is a solid slab of painted ivory. It pushes easily into the dark throat of the stairwell, and isn't locked. There is no way to wedge it open, so Alan tries to close it slowly, hoping that the ancient hinges will hold it back from the jamb. Despite his care, it slips shut tight against Alan's back. Alan tries to relax against it, his palms flat against the cool surface, but a sudden rattle of heavy blows on the opposite side startles him. The banging continues for a good minute, and Alan cowers in the corner near the hinges until it stops. After a tense moment waiting for more knocking, he tries to open it again, but he finds it impossible to pull. The ivory wicks his magic away; he is trapped at this end, but the cellar must come up in the castle somewhere. Alan stands and looks down the staircase, fear roaring in his head, and tries to remove himself from the situation. He looks inward, past the mounting tension and the cold crawl of dread along his spine, to find a distraction.

I was born on November first in Paloma, Illinois, he thinks. He imagines James Lipton interviewing him. *What was your father's name? Ronald. And your mother's? Virginia. If Heaven exists, what would you like to hear God say when you arrive at the Pearly Gates?*

Reaching out for his Earthly past feels wasteful, and it hurts. The parts of Alan that belonged among the living are empty now. What he had been before is dead, and the recently deceased

249

resist him. Still the question wants an answer. It smokes in his mind, a sudden advocate for the last, angry embers of his old life.

"It was all a dream," Alan says aloud. "Time to wake up."

Seconds creep by in the dark, and Alan's fear doesn't diminish. It's worse than it's ever been; there is something in the cellar that amplifies it – or feeds on it. Having no choice now but to go on in spite of it, he starts down the stairs on laggard legs.

"Come on, bony," he says, trying Brattle's voice, "Get your shit together and go."

The stairs fall down from the door at an extreme angle, and there are no handrails or lights until they reach the distant cellar floor. Ages of wear have rounded the limestone steps in places. A strange, luminous moss is slowly swallowing the lower quarter; the last few feet of the staircase would be impassable if not for a rough plank laid over the mat of green tendrils.

Alan descends sideways, putting two feet firmly on each step before advancing. The urge to run is huge in his head. He imagines hands reaching for his ankles from under the stairs. Tingles bloom across his back, and he can't keep from glancing over his shoulder at the door. Something is behind him, watching and advancing, stalking him down into the darkness. He feels it; it is as real as the wet walls under his hands and weight of the fields above him.

Alan curses himself and the human weakness inside him that just won't die. Not even the bleeding ghost of his sister could kill it. He has always raised it from the dead somehow; no strength has ever lasted. He's been a thanoturge all his life, resurrecting his self-doubt after every victory. Alan weakens and the fear almost wins, and then he remembers that his life is over and that this is something else. He remembers at last that he has real power in this world, and he pushes himself through the storm of fear until the last step is behind him.

The room at the bottom of the stairs opens to the left of the stairwell. Alan turns into it and leans back against the wall, trying to relax. He doesn't remember sliding down the plank. The last stretch of the stairs is a moss-bright blur. He's never knocked through so much fear before; he should be celebrating, but his heart is a cinder. Pride eludes him, leaving him weary in his skin. Alan sags into a corner and rests for as long as he can. When he stands again, there is no victory. Triumph can't live in this place; he'll only see it again when he's out of this cellar and on his way to forgetting it forever,

"I did it," Alan says. "And now I have to do it again. Come on."

The antechamber at the foot of the stairs is low and coffin-shaped. Gem lamps cast the room in fairy blue, set into stellate recesses along the ceiling. Deep shadows gather in the corners, sulking. Alan can feel them watching him. He can hear their voices in the rattling hum that shakes this place; he's sick to death of Graveworld's whispers.

Every threat has a voice, he thinks. *Every secret slithers out from somewhere.*

There's no way back to the long hush of his first night here. For a moment, he feels too far from everything. He is lonely in the worst parts of his mind, in the corners sulking deep with shadows. He can only move on, trusting time to dull the pain.

The cellar stretches out to the east through a series of octagonal passageways into larger and larger chambers. From the first room, Alan can see through six chambers to a tangle of moving shadow at the mouth of the seventh. Messy bundles of pipes and bare cables run along the walls, connecting long banks of consoles and panels. The machines look primitive. They tick and hiss, pumping steam through spliced hoses and coils turned over burnished gears. Their lights blink in humming vacuum tubes. This is scrap science, but there is a strong magical element to it as well. A strange power holds it all together, stretching itself through every copper rivet; Alan can feel it crawling over his skin, pricking the hairs on his arms straight up like the threat of lightning. Every console bears Toven's triskelion seal.

"Nothing stays up long out here." Alan can hear Brattle's voice on the night of his arrival. "It's all falling down."

251

But Gimcrack is perfect. The château is host to decades' spans of restless dead. The peaks behind them curve into unbroken points, but there should be slips and calves of rust and stone wearing away from them all the time. Alan realizes what Toven has been doing: he is in the business of preservation. His skillful marriage of junk science to funeral magic has kept Gimcrack from wasting away for a long time, but what purpose is it serving now?

At the heart of each knot of cable is a large pod in a copper frame with sparks and steam cascading around it. There are at least one hundred of these in every chamber by Alan's most conservative estimate, and each looks large enough to hold at least five adult humans. He walks a catwalk through the middle of the first chamber and counts them, trying to keep himself too busy to be afraid and not having much success. It's hard to see what's in the pods, but there is clearly movement going on in many of them. Beneath frosted domes of bottle-green glass, there are often dark things squirming against each other. Whatever they are, looking at them makes Alan feel sick with terror.

The dead are loud here, and they aren't resting. Through the curving floors of solid rock, they scream up into Alan as if to tear him apart with their voices alone. Their pain is horrible, and their pleas are clear: they howl for annihilation, mad with the need for it. Alan enters the second pod chamber, unsure that he'll be able to go on to the third without being overwhelmed by their grief.

Dangerous machinery, Alan thinks, *that's what Toven said was down here. He wasn't exactly lying.*

Through his new facility, Alan can feel the pods' thanoturgic taint. He weaves rudimentary searching spells into them with his hands on their hyaline halves and is aghast at what he finds: there are fairies trapped inside that have been abandoned just beyond the brink of death. In his mind's eye, he sees a black gulf. A ribbon of light crosses it, extending infinitely, and the fairies are on the far side of it. Their souls are screaming to die, but the machines won't let them. They exist in the physical only as vessels for Bleeding consciousnesses and other horrors. What's happening here is profane, and Alan is grateful that he doesn't fully understand it.

Halfway through the second chamber, he decides he's seen enough. He has no strength left to endure the screams in his head anymore. The door into the château must be far away from where he is, and some of the pods in the next chamber have started to rock. Taxed, the Seal of Aiwass on his forehead begins to beam, throwing dancing shadows across the walls whenever Alan moves. It's holding, but this is no place to push his luck. He is about to turn back, but something catches his eye and he stops to stare.

The third chamber is gone — lost in creeping emptiness. The moving shadow had been several chambers away, but now it is near enough to Alan that he can feel its breath. It reaches out from nowhere, pulling everything it touches down into sentient emptiness. Pods and catwalks vanish soundlessly before it. The walls themselves disappear, and nothing replaces them. The cavern starts to shake, and, where the shadow eats the soil thin, the voice of Gimcrack's wounding machine emerges as a grinding roar.

Alan scrambles away, knees flying against his chest. The ivory door at the top of the stairs will just have to give. It can't stand in his way now. He'll throw everything he has at it when he gets there. The second chamber winks out behind him as he bolts through the passage toward the first. His feet bang the catwalk, oblivious to the pain of the impacts. His calves spasm painfully as Alan tries to squeeze every last ounce of strength out of them. He is almost at the coffin room when three pods rock open beside him, spilling their pale and shrieking abominations around his ankles. He steps high, trying to avoid clutching hands. Mouths filled with green-glass teeth gnash up from the floor, mindless and hungry. Two wobble to their feet, and Alan rams into them with desperate force. Their eyes are like lightning wounds in heads that are held onto their necks by brass trusses. Their spines are stuck straight on gruesome prosthetics. Only one goes down; the other catches Alan's torn shirt in its jaws and bites down as hard as it can, ripping the rags from Alan's chest. It claws at him with copper-cuffed fingers, gears wheezing beneath its skin. Alan spins and almost topples, but the dead thing hasn't found its balance yet. It falls in a fury, snarling and beating the floor with flailing fists, and Alan pivots back into a sprint toward the stairs. The rest of the pod-things are too weak to walk yet, and they can only writhe helplessly as Alan flees. The shadow consumes them as well.

At the base of the stairs, Alan is forced onto all fours. He scales the plank and starts sinking into the glowing moss, which produces brilliant, golden blooms as it twists over his bare skin. Alan tugs, tearing tendrils up by their roots, and the moss wheezes in pain all around him. The golden blooms explode, dusting Alan with burning pollen. The shadow slows, stretched thin. Heat streams off it, flooding the stairwell. Bright flashes branch across it like lightning. There is a voice crackling inside it, driving it forward in desperate fury. It's Toven, sounding far away in the black. The shadow is an extension of him, and he is weakening. Straining now, the living dark pulls the last of the stairs and the lambent moss into itself.

Alan clambers toward the door. He musters all his magical strength and is surprised by how much he has. He prepares to empty himself completely against the side of the hill. If he can, he'll blow it open and leave the ivory door standing.

He freezes near the top of the stairs. The crawling dark has been losing speed, but it is still coming. He can feel it pulling at the billows of his pant legs. The painted ivory door remains shut tight, and, before it, owl-eyes gleaming from beneath the hood of its habit and its awful bag over one shoulder, is the Cuco.

Twenty-Four

There is a summer of reckless hope and a golden age of faith. We learn passion peering into haunted basements or watching mirrors in the dark for dead faces. For months, the walls of the real become thin, and we can press our cheeks against them to feel the warmth of the strange on the other side. We can let phantoms out into the world through the palms of our hands. Then, in one breath of autumn wind, we are too old for that special fear. The strange becomes familiar, and we give up on it. We move on. We can grow through our faith, but only if we let faith die.

Alan remembers shaking on darkened stairwells, sure that he could feel that other world pushing against him. His faith died easily when his family exploded and there was neither any great evil to blame nor anything like an ultimate good to petition. There was only oppressive grief and the fire of his sister's self-destruction. The walls of the real closed in on him, and he shrank. It was the end of his love for the world, and he'd thought that it was the end of his wonder as well, but he was wrong. The golden age of his faith never ended; it only turned black.

The dark tide rolls back, and Alan steps toward the door. The Cuco might still want to help. It brought him here, after all. It showed him Toven's secret. But there's nothing left of the good light that was in it before. Its eyes roll empty now, open on the abyss of its hunger. This is not a helper any longer. This is the horror that children see darkly, pursue rashly, and kill wisely in the twilight of their credulity: a faith that has lived too long, grown wild, and become a monster.

He marshals all his power at last, ready to defend himself. It quivers in him, a living thing, and he's intimidated by it. The Cuco advances, its beak opening, unafraid of anything Alan can do.

"Stand aside," Alan says, but the Cuco doesn't falter.

The bag twitches. The Cuco lets it slip open between its fingers and Alan sees shapes moving inside it. Suddenly, the banging on the door begins again, louder and faster this time. The Cuco seems to turn, and then the door crashes in on bursting hinges. The owl-thing vanishes in a breath, leaving a mist of dim gold and powdered stone. Brattle stands on the threshold, Alan's trash masher in both hands.

Alan twitches back and almost steps off the half-gone staircase. Brattle reaches out, and Alan takes his hand.

"Morning, lumpy," Brattle shouts over the storm. "Grab your ass and let's haul. The escape's going down."

The three stand at the mouth of the cellar for a moment. Brattle produces a heavy roll of fur from his knapsack and hands it to Alan. It is Stag's Blood's pelt. The servants at Gimcrack Castle have worked it into a magnificent robe.

"They weren't sure what to do with it when they took it," Stag's Blood explains, "so they did this. It's fine work, but then they *were* working with the finest material. I wouldn't have expected any less."

Alan rolls it out and runs his hands into it; it still feels warm and alive, even when soaked with rain. He slips his arms into the silk-lined sleeves and finds pockets inside them to warm his hands. The collar is impossibly light; it goes up around his neck like a lover's breath. The front falls marvelously over him, sending tingles across his whole torso. There is calm in the crown of the plush hood; he pulls it up against the storm and feels pleasantly dark and powerful.

"That hole was the cellar," Alan says. "It was huge; it went on and on under the fields. There were machines there keeping umans suspended in some kind of spiritual twilight zone between life and death. I could see it like it was a real thing – a white line in darkness. They were just beyond it, close enough to life to have some kind of semblance of it but trapped on the other side. The dead side. I've never felt so much evil. I never believed in it, to be honest."

"The draug," Brattle says. "The state between life and death – the curtain hiding our lives from whatever comes after. I never seen it, but I know it. All corpse-eaters do. You say these umans were stuck there? How? And why?"

"Maybe it's an army," Stag's Blood adds. His eyes are coals in the dark. They burn through the rain, inextinguishable. "For Winter White – or against her."

"They were wearing metal prosthetics," Alan says. "It's science serving magic, somehow. Whatever that place is for, he's taking it all away now; he's hiding it or something. I felt him reaching out through darkness. The Cuco showed me how to find the door. If it hadn't, I probably wouldn't have seen all that before it was totally gone. But who led you?"

Brattle nearly spits. "The Cuco? You followed that shimmer-thing?"

Stag's Blood shakes his head. "You're lucky to be alive, Alan," he says. "The Cuco is a luring flame. He could only have wanted you dead; that's all he does."

"Call it luck if you want," Alan replies. "I saw what I saw, and now we know more than we did."

"It won't avail us much if we can't get away," Stag's Blood says.

"Toven locked us in our rooms," Brattle explains. "But we got out and went to look for him."

"How did you get out?" Alan asks.

"I was out almost as soon as they turned the key," Stag's Blood brags. "I'm Gatebreaker's son, after all! But there was no one in the hall when I emerged. Only Brattle and Mawn."

"Mawn?"

"Mawn opened my door," Brattle says. "And he showed us to Toven's chambers, but it was gone – the whole thing! No Toven, no nothing."

"That's what's happening: he's taking it all away," Alan says, looking up at the château. It is huge before the mountains and fully in the teeth of shadow. Shadows reach from its windows to swallow the rain. The tower is slowly disappearing into them. The whole compound is wrapped in Toven's darkness; there is even a mist of it drifting across the heath to fade the grass. He thinks of Sophia and a little pain rises in his throat. It was her first pilgrimage. He could have spoken up; he might have stopped her from going to Toven's chambers. "He's moving the whole castle. It's sciomancy."

"Can you stop it?" Stag's Blood asks.

Alan feels Gimcrack Castle looking back at him. Fed by the storm's rising fury, Toven's spell is colossal. It makes Alan shake just to sense it.

"No," he says. "I couldn't even start. It's too big. I'm not strong enough yet."

Brattle continues. "It was Mawn sent us out to the cellar to look for you. Dunno how he knew you were there."

"Who knows what Mawn has seen?" Stag's Blood asks. "His waters run deep – deeper even than Toven's, I suspect. I pity him his slavery, but he has made his own shackles, and slaves can become masters."

"However strong Toven is," Alan says, "there are limits to his reach. How long did you look for me?"

"Something like two hours, thank you very much," Brattle replies. "And I'm thinkin' time's up. We gotta get the Gale out past his limits now, so it's time to be as strong as you can be."

Stag's Blood musters a chuckle. "We chase the lady again," he says, "and we will win her once and for all. At least there's no dragon this time."

The three set off into the wind, half a mile between them and the mooring yard. The Mercy Gale is there with her legs pulled tight against her hull. A tarp with weighted corners blows from her forecastle. Her repairs are complete; even in the dark and through the sheeting rain, she is gorgeous. Alan is glad to put any amount of distance between himself and Toven's cellar. It helps his relief to see his ship just ahead, waiting for him – to hear her loving call over the roar of thunder. But there are tall shapes moving steadily toward her from the vanishing château. They will reach her first – relief will have to wait.

The mooring yard is a large, open-walled structure built around an iron track in a rutted berth roughly ninety feet long. It sits facing south in the east corner of the castle grounds, standards flapping from the gutters of its tin roofs. A copper-barred scaffold climbs its northwestern pillar to the plank decks of a dry dock from which a gangway extends onto the Mercy Gale amidships. Her beam is in the iron track, and her legs are holding her aright with help from ten taut ropes on ten massive, anvil cleats.

Stag's Blood is the first to meet Toven's men at the base of the scaffold. There are eight of them in full armor, their spears at the ready. A blue gem-light under the dock casts rocking shadows over them. Stag's Blood approaches them carefully, circling in with his side turned to them.

"We are taking this ship," he says when he is near enough to speak with them. "We do not require your permission, but we would appreciate your standing aside. You know we don't need to fight for this."

The soldiers move before Stag's Blood is finished. They fall toward him without a sound, wearing eight identical scowls. Stag's Blood dodges away and retaliates with terrible speed, leaving one soldier dead and another on his knees in pain. As the others regroup, Alan arrives in the yard with a cry.

"Don't kill them!" he says. "No more killing!"

He turns toward Brattle and can barely see him knuckling across the field. He is low to the ground and faster in the dark. He doesn't even stop to wipe the rain from his face. There is no promise of mercy in his eyes.

Alan rushes the scaffold, ready to fight, but there is a great fear waiting there, and it stops him in his tracks. To his horror, he finds himself cringing, frozen, before the points of two soldier's spears. His muscles won't move; the veil of his courage slips, and he shrinks from the sight of his weakness beneath it. Then the spear tips strike him, and he cries out in pain, but there is no blood. The soldiers stop, astonished, and the ticking in their chests falters as they process their failure: their spears stopped on Alan's new robe. Alan forces himself to respond while he has the chance. He must burn like a gem to pierce the shadow of fear. His limbs like lead, he must be stronger than ever as he tugs his masher back to strike.

He swings his trash masher for the enemies' knees, and he fells them with magic when they stumble. He reaches out with his mind to push them past the edge of the draug, stranding them in the death-sleep he learned of in Toven's cellar. They are empty things, and their minds wither quickly on that brink, but their paralyzed bodies survive. He can't offer much more clemency than that, and he isn't sure he cares to. Anger is the only thing keeping him fighting. He allows them to live for his own moral satisfaction, but he makes no bones about wanting them dead.

Stag's Blood is less precise, but he is utterly fearless and he has more control. Alan is amazed watching him move. He glides from leaps to crouches, his whole body like one perfect muscle. He seems to see Alan's injunction as a challenge. The wounds he leaves will not heal in any short amount of time, but they are not fatal. In two bright bursts of lightning, Stag's Blood leaves four of Toven's soldiers crippled on the scaffold stairs.

The last foes fall before Brattle. He beats them to death with aplomb, untroubled by conscience. Rage pours out of him to encircle his head like a crown of fire. He bites sparks from his teeth and breathes long, rolling breaths of smoke. When the battle is over, his bloodlust dies slowly; it remains in the light of his stained-glass eyes as he piles his kills and climbs up to crouch on their backs.

"No wonder King Toven needs an army of draug-lost umans," he pants, cheeks stippled with flecks of blood-mist. "These pet soldiers tear like paper. Up that stair, now. More on the way."

"Hang on," Alan says. "I said no killing! What's wrong with you?" He points his fury down the length of his finger. Brattle brushes his hand away.

"Say it all you want. That's your rule, Al," he replies. "It ain't mine. You come at me – you die. Cause n' effect. That's my rule."

Stag's Blood interjects. "One fight at a time, allies," he says. He springs up the scaffold, and Brattle follows him.

Alan takes a moment to kneel and search the dead faces. They are terrible to look at. Close inspection reveals that they aren't as identical as he'd thought. Some of them have deep scars on their jawlines. Others are losing their hair. They aren't like men, especially not up close, but Alan wonders how different their concerns were from his. Had they loved? Had they hoped and planned? Had they feared death? Nothing in Midion is theirs anymore – nothing in Graveworld. They are gone somewhere else – through the Bleeding. At least they are no longer Toven's slaves. When he can, Alan closes the corpses' eyes.

"I'm sorry," he says to them. And then he hurries up the stairs after the others.

Papers, tools, and blown-over furniture litter the dock. A huge blackboard lies cracked across the edge of a tipped table, its frame is nowhere to be seen. A pouch of chalk has fallen from it to burst on the planks, leaving white powder strewn around the table. There are footprints in it moving away from the Mercy Gale. The servants working here must have stayed with her until the last possible minute.

"She's in good shape, looks like," Brattle says. "Get her started. Me 'n Stags'll work on the ropes."

Alan nods, but before he can act, he sees several bright flashes from nearby and hears a salvo of echoing clangs. The sound is strangely clear beneath the storm; even a simultaneous peal of thunder can't obscure it. White puffs rise from the yard to the north, and the broken blackboard disintegrates. Chalk and slate blows up into the air in thin clouds, and small masses slash through it at whining speed. Several of them strike Alan and send him tilting on his heels. They are stones with nails and shards of glass embedded in them. He ducks and lefts his arm over his head, and a rock hits the shaft of his trash masher, causing it to ring and shiver.

"Rock guns," Stag's Blood says.

His next few sentences disappear beneath the pop and the scream of the next volley. Alan sees the shooters in their muzzle flashes: more clockwork soldiers, and these are wearing sighting goggles. Toven's shadow moves behind them, huge and expanding as they advance. It has almost consumed the château completely.

Alan crosses the dock in leaping strides, his arms out to make his robe as wide as possible. Stonefire that might otherwise have knocked Stag's Blood and Brattle to shreds falls harmlessly from his back. The impacts aren't heavy enough to bruise, but they sting badly and rock him forward. He keeps his head down, unsure what will happen if one of the soldiers scores a hit on the back of his hood.

"Your coat!" Stag's Blood says as he moves with Alan toward the gangplank.

Alan corrects him. "*Your* coat," he says. "Get below decks. We'll just pull the ropes free on our way out."

"Someone's looking out for you, bony!" Brattle laughs. Nearing the rail, he leaps the short distance onto the Mercy Gale's main deck. From there, he scampers toward the hold, and Stag's Blood follows close behind.

Alan groans as a particularly large rock thumps high into his armpit. He tucks onto one knee, grasping his side against the excruciating pain. Lights dance before him for a moment, and he shakes his head to get his focus back. The rock is at his feet, its surface covered with screw tips and long slivers of fire-blacked iron. He wraps his fingers around it and can barely lift it.

Someone's looking out for me, he thinks. *What will I owe them when this is all over? Who will my stone kill when I pull the trigger?*

Stag's Blood and Brattle call to him from beneath the bridge, out of any rock's reach. Alan stands carefully, waiting for another hit, but no more come. The pinging of the guns has stopped; the soldiers must have reached the stairs. He turns and doesn't see them on the stone-strewn dock. Then there is a cry from the fields below, and Alan risks a peek over the near rail to look down on a scene of torchlit chaos.

Mawn is on the heather. A polearm on his back burns a swinging bindle of oil-soaked rags. He swings a flat-headed maul with one hand and a short mace with the other, and he smashes through the ranks of the rock gunners to beat them back toward the encroaching shadow.

Brattle and Stag's Blood climb astern to watch over the poop's gunwale. The ghoul gapes in shock. No one says anything about what's happening. Alan crosses the gangplank and mounts the bridge, where the Mercy Gale's eyestone is waiting, asleep. He slips his hood back and gathers himself, but the orb comes to life before he can put his hands on it.

A shimmer moves across the eyestone's surface. It begins to bulge on one side, its colors racing away from the swell. A point of perfect crystal emerges from the orb, and then a leg, and then a hunched back with two wings buzzing against it. Sophia steps from the eyestone into thin air, and when she sees Alan watching her, she lets out a jingling scream and almost falls. Alan reaches out to catch her, and she hits the palm of his hand like a puff of air.

"Alan Shade!" she exclaims. "Twice-blessed stars, I am happy to see you safe! King Toven is turning his hand at last. How did you escape?"

"Likewise, Sophia," Alan says. He is warmed as she hugs his thumb. "But we haven't escaped yet. Toven's still reaching for us, and we have to get this ship moving. Can you pass through these stones? Can you wake them up?"

Sophia nods. The light of Mawn's fire finds its way into her. It whirls there for a moment, at war with itself, and then it dies away.

"We are the same," she explains, "and I know exactly what you need. Stay here. I will wake the other Framer Gem."

With this, she passes back into the eyestone and is gone in a small pulse of rosy light. Alan slides his hands over the curves of the orb, reaching out for it through the voices of the dead in his mind and the quivering bloom of the Kingwatcher. It responds with waves of color, remembering him, and the Mercy Gale stirs with a long groan. The wraith mist arises, and the wraiths rise with it as the ship flexes her legs. They swarm over the deck, preparing the Mercy Gale for her departure. They cut the guide ropes from the anvil cleats with flashing, formless swords, and the ship takes her first step on her new stabilizers.

"Let's get!" Brattle cries from the poop. "No better time than now, Al! No better time!"

The Mercy Gale hauls free of the mooring structures. She heaves up to crash through the docking platforms on either side of her, tossing wood and copper beams to the storm. The chief mate builds itself from the vapor and stalks once around the main deck before approaching Alan on the bridge.

"Welcome back, captain," it says in its well-deep voice. "Our heading?"

"West away from here," Alan replies. "As fast as we can go to outpace the shadow tide behind us. And don't stop until it's far behind us."

"Aye," the chief mate says, and then it slips back into the swirl again, lost in the mist and the beating of the storm as the Mercy Gale steps out from beneath the tin roofs of the mooring structure.

Alan makes his way up to the poop deck as the ship is picking up speed. He stands against the gunwale between Brattle and Stag's Blood and looks down at the shrinking shape of Mawn under his torch. There are bodies at his feet. He stands among them, triumphant, and watches the Mercy Gale pulling away. Toven's shadow laps up around him. It curls up his legs, snakes over his shoulders, and pulls at his bloodied hands. It pitches high to break around him like a wave. For a second, Alan thinks he is trying to take a step away from it, but then he falls still and lets the darkness wash over him. The emptiness rolls across the heather, covering the remains of the mooring yard, and Mawn is nowhere within it. Gimcrack Castle disappears at last, pulled away through Toven's shadow, leaving only bare rock and earth in gaping pits. The mountains stand quiet, sadly and strangely motionless.

"Beyond me is the dark," Alan whispers, "and the dark is mine."

Twenty-Five

Sophia returns to the upper decks through the eyestone. Alan is there to meet her, his hood up, standing on the head of his trash masher to keep it upright. He offers her his hands as she arrives to protect from the whipping headwind. She is warm and bright – a star in the cup of his palms. He turns and puts his back against the eyestone's pedestal, rain pouring over his shoulders.

"It is done," Sophia says. "Should we not be down below where it is dry? Why are you still standing in the rain?"

"I don't have a good answer for that," Alan replies with a little laugh. He presses Sophia to his chest, where she clings to the bristling trim of his broad hood. "Come on."

Brattle and Stag's Blood follow him down from the stern decks and onto the middle deck. The lights are burning strong, and the cobwebs have been cleared away. The floor has been sealed with urethane and polished to a vitreous shine. There are new tables set against the hull on either side of the deck, and pleasant heat is coming in from somewhere, but the watching otherness about the Mercy Gale remains where it always was. Alan feels the ship considering him as he crosses to sit on a new-cut bench, and he is grateful that, at least, she isn't angry and careful anymore. He sets Sophia down on the table behind him, and she rings her wings together as she walks the boards.

Stag's Blood shakes, flinging the rain from his fur. Brattle takes a short coat from the backpack and wraps it around himself. He can only wear it like a shawl, as his arms are too long for the sleeves.

"Is everyone all right?" Stag's Blood asks.

Brattle rolls his shoulder and winces, cupping his hand over a spot on his jacket where fresh blood is blooming. "I caught a rock," he says. "Hurts a treat, but it's nothing I can't handle."

Stag's Blood glides over to nose at Brattle's arm. He nudges the little coat aside with his snout, revealing a weeping tear on the ball of Brattle's shoulder.

"It's a nick," Brattle says. "And I heal good. Don't worry about me."

Stag's Blood paces for a moment, his tail twitching. Then he sits again, apparently fine with Brattle's display of machismo – or at least too tired to challenge it. Brattle uses his soiled mortcloth to wrap the wound.

"Sister Sophia?" Stag's Blood continues. "Your presence here is an unexpected pleasure. Are you whole? No nicks on you?"

"By the Framer's will and King Toven's lucky ignorance, I am happily intact," says Sophia, moving her hands down the curves of her lustrous frame. "Thank you."

Stag's Blood bobs a scholarly nod. Alan wonders how religious he is.

"I'm as well as I was this morning," Stag's Blood says. "I have you to thank for that, Alan. Partly, anyway. You and your remarkable new robe. I saw many stones hitting you. Are you hurt at all?"

Alan pushes his hood back and rubs his fingertips into a hot ache at the base of his neck. "Physically, I'm fine," he says. "Shaken, but with no bruises. I wanted to stop the shadow. I wanted more mercy, but I didn't get any. I don't like feeling powerless."

"Mercy's eminently human," Brattle says. "At least in excess. That's something I'm learnin'.

Alan looks at Brattle. There are white sparks dancing across his brow. His eyes are wide and bright. He is on the wild edge of exhaustion.

"I'm not angry," Alan says.

"Me neither," Brattle says, "but let's clear the air."

"My sister killed herself six months ago because she felt responsible for the accident that killed our parents when we were kids," Alan begins. "She always blamed herself, but I was in that car when the accident happened. They died, and I have never been able to say beyond any doubt that it shouldn't have been me instead. My sister was already falling apart, and then she had to raise me. I turned her guilt into a reason to be angry with myself. I've lived my whole stupid life with death on my conscience, and I feel broken down. I can't carry it anymore.

"Life is rich with pain. Love and hope just spill out of it. Sometimes, I feel cursed to see the beauty in it. Being such, I can't end life. I don't have it in me; I'm absolutely certain of that. I can only stand in awe of it. Does that make sense?"

Brattle nods and mulls this over. Outside, the storm has gone quiet. Rain pats the weather decks like little drumming fingers. The wind soughs at the boards of the hull. There is a tailwind pushing them now. Alan can feel the Mercy Gale's legs working to compensate. Sophia sits back on her heels and props her chin in her hand to hang on every word.

"You got your limits," Brattle finally says. "I can respect that. But they ain't mine, like I said, and you ain't my leader. I ain't deep, but I got thoughts about death, too. I got just as much hurt as you do. I won't philosophize with you about it. All our differences gone from the question, me, you, and Stags, we're equals. You do as you do, and I do as me, and that's the nature of this arrangement."

With this, Brattle crosses his arms and sits back against the table, implacable. The frown on his face is effortless and kingly – as if he was born certain. He kicks his shin up across his knee and bounces his foot. His sole is leathered over with calluses. Alan stands and extends his hand, and Brattle rocks forward to accept it.

"Fair enough," Alan says.

Brattle grins. "Knew you'd see it my way."

"And now all is well," says Stag's Blood with a yawn. "Thank the Framer for small favors. Though Alan does make a good case."

"Yeah, well, you do you, Stags," Brattle says.

"If I may," Sophia chimes, "mercy will either calm a storm or prolong it. Without discretion, mercy may as well be cowardice."

Alan sits down again, content that he has said his piece even if he achieved nothing else. If he is a coward, then he will be an honest one.

"Sister Sophie, right?" Brattle says. "How'd you end up on the Mercy?"

"King Toven was unhappy with my presence at Gimcrack," Sophia explains. "He demanded that I leave, and he would not answer my questions. Then he locked me in his round room with his Framer Gem. He doesn't know much about the Sisters of M."

"Me and him both," Brattle says.

"We're glad you are safe," Stag's Blood adds. "But I wish we could have saved more from the shadow. Clearly, we had friends among the servants."

The four fall silent for a moment. Alan realizes the wraiths on the weather decks are singing. The sound is low and cheerless, a ghost song, and other voices rise to answer it from deep in the holds.

"Why'd he do it?" Brattle asks. "And whadda ya think happened to him?"

"I don't suspect we'll ever know the answer to either of those questions," Stag's Blood says. "He had some kind of life of his own. Some kind of guilt."

Sophia sits down on the edge of the table and chimes in. Alan is growing to love the musical tinkle of her voice. "Whom do you mean?" she says, "if I may ask. I do not mean to pry."

"Mawn," says Alan. "He turned on the other soldiers to give us time to escape."

"He was one of Toven's golems?"

"Yes. And I think Toven must have protected him at some point before he was what we saw. Toven helped him somehow, and what he did must have been so important that Mawn felt indebted to Toven with his life, but he couldn't buy Mawn completely. That's what I was thinking, anyway. It's a feeling I get, you know? The same thing might've happened with Toven and Winter White."

"I had the same suspicion," Stag's Blood says. "But I get the feeling that you've taken it further than I have. Are you worried that this might be what's happening to you?"

"Not just me," Alan says. "If someone really is looking out for us, what's going to happen if whoever it is decides it's time to collect on our debt?"

"I been going back and forth on this, Al," Brattle says. "I never been able to get a good hold on destiny. Sometimes, I can't believe in it, and, sometimes, I can't not. What I think you got here is a purpose more than anything else, but what you do is your call. And you been making good calls, you been stickin' to the purpose, and that's why luck's been in your favor. So you're guidin' this. It ain't guidin' you. You're on the right side of it 'cause you're a right-side kinda guy, as we were just sayin. You got your morals. Even if there was some mastermind behind all this, you ain't Mawn, and you ain't Toven. You're better, and that's why fortune favors you – why it's your destiny and not either of theirs to do somethin' great."

"I couldn't have said it better myself," Stag's Blood laughs.

"We cannot help what we want," Sophia says. "And if what you want is to do good, then you will. You will not be able to help it. That is what the Mothers say."

"Your Mothers are wise," Stag's Blood says. "And you are wise to listen to them."

Sophia bows. "Thank you," she says. Her hands clink together at her chin. She makes a glassy creak when she bends her knees. "Along those lines, Alan, did I hear correctly that you are human, like Winter White?"

The ship shakes suddenly, and a bang reverberates deep in her belly. Everyone sits quiet for a minute, listening to the wraiths above howling to each other. Their voices are thin and brittle, and they seep through the hull like slow trickles of water.

"Do we need to go up?" Stag's Blood asks. He stands and starts to pace again.

Brattle fidgets, too, feeding Stag's Blood's worry back to him. "It's amazing how tight this space gets real quick," he says.

The wraith voices sink back into song. The Mercy Gale continues across the storming moors at speed, apparently untroubled by anything more than minor adjustments to her repairs, but the middle deck doesn't become any taller. Alan hunches reflexively.

"Yes," he says. "You heard right, Sister. I know I don't look it. I've lost a bit since I arrived here alive."

"That is the nature of the exchange," Sophia replies. "Nothing slips the veil whole and stays that way. They say that Winter White has been the only exception."

"They do?" Alan says. "But you don't."

"They say a lot of things about Winter White that I do not say," Sophia says. "When I was a shardling, I had a dream. I was living in the wild then, in the long grass at the mouth of the river Ash. It was terrible, but not because it was frightening or sad. It was just terribly urgent. I went to the Sisters of the Necropolis with it, and they took me in, though I was full of black. They made me pure and clear, as you see me now, and, when I was old enough, one of the Mothers took me to Gimcrack.

"The Sisters of M renounce prophecy, you see. I had to give my dream away to someone who had appeared in it, and the only person I could describe was Toven. He was a clockwork king of the north with a crooked face, and he had a boat that could go over mountains. I did not know him, but the Sisters at Welkinbright did, through his wife. When they realized who he was based on my description, they sent me to him. I gave him my dream – my prophecy – and, perhaps seeing some opportunity for fame, he took it as his own."

"His own prophecy," Alan says. "Winter White."

"Her arrival here brought him notoriety, and I imagine that is what brought her to him. I remember him in his youth as implacable, but his will to power threatens to consume him now. I wonder if he can be saved anymore."

"The prophecy has to be about Al," Brattle says, patting his palms on the bench in excitement.

"I hope not,' Alan says. "Fulfilling prophecy seems like a lot of responsibility. They offered me a manager's job at Ray's, and I turned it down. I didn't even want to do *that*."

Brattle chuckles. "You're all skull and little spine, lumpy, but you could stand to give yourself a tad bit more credit than that."

"What happened in the dream?" Stag's Blood asks. He has stopped pacing and is now sitting upright, his eyes wide. "What did you prophecy? Will you tell us? Do you remember?"

Sophia shakes her tiny head. Light dances through her hair to sparkle on the ceiling. "I am sorry. I purged it, as was my duty. I do not remember. I gave it all to Toven, but now, it pains me to admit, I wish I had not."

"I know how you feel," Alan says. "I gave everything to Toven, too." The others stare. "I showed him the notes from Pwysh, and I showed him my phone, and I think he stole it."

"No, no," Brattle says, plunging into the knapsack to find Pwysh's books and papers. "I have all that right here. He ain't got it. Wait."

Brattle stops and looks at the notes in his hand. He reads aloud from the leaf of yellowed paper that is protruding from between the pages of Pwysh's grimoire.

"Bell, star, and spirit?" he asks. "This ain't in wizard writing. What the hell is this?"

"Another part of the puzzle," Alan replies. "I didn't show it to you when I found it, and then I just kept not showing you. I'm sorry, but I still don't know what it means, and I think Toven does. We still have all that, but he's seen it. And he stole my phone from my room, so he has the coordinates on it, too. I guess he's probably worked out what's going on. Do you think you could find him, Sophia? How far can you go through the Framer Gems?"

"As far as I wish," Sophia says, her wings chiming. "And right away. He blinded the Framer Gems when he moved the Necropolis. The Framer provides, but we should act now. It may be that he has not provided us much time. Such is his mysterious way sometimes."

With this, Sophia makes a sign in the air and bows her head for a moment.

"Let's get, then," Brattle says, pushing himself hard to his feet and knuckling for the stairs toward the weather decks.

The others follow suit, and Alan offers Sophia his hand. She stops him with a ringing call, and leaps into the air with her arms outstretched.

"Please wait," she says. "I would prefer to use the Framer Gem further below, if it is all right with you. We have at least that much time, and it might still be raining."

Alan leads the way to the orlop deck. The ship's primary eyestone is humming there, warm and purple, with banners of gold light spinning around it. Sophia circles it once, pulling a trail of shimmers that fall across its surface as she settles atop it. The orb responds to her touch with a bright pulse, causing the Mercy Gale to creak a restless sigh.

"This gem is unique," Sophia says. "It has a twin somewhere in this sphere."

"Yeah," Brattle replies. "Up top."

"Not that one," Sophia explains, looking deep into the eyestone. Alan sees only her reflection there. "That one is false. It was not born. It was made. This gem does not like it, but it works with it easily enough. It makes me feel sad." She puts her hand on her hip and hmms, a sea green light growing in her breast. "Oh well. Not all things are whole. I am going now. Framer, may I find something."

"How long do you expect this to take, Sister?" Stag's Blood asks.

Sophia looks over her shoulder at him. Her green light blazes to red with touches of purple-black. "As long as necessary," she says.

With this, she falls into the eyestone in a crackle of sparks. For a moment, the orb looks like it could dribble from its column. Then Alan puts his hands on it, and it is hard as glass again. A pulse beats under his palms, wet and hot, like the heart of the sea.

"I'm sorry I didn't show you Pwysh's other note," Alan says to Brattle. "Pwysh's ghost gave it to me, and we were misfiring a little, then. But now you know about it, and I don't understand 'bell, star, and, spirit' any more now than I did before, so we're basically even. That's what I'm saying, anyway. What do you think?"

"You trust too much in capricious spirits," Brattle answers. "And *even* is eating our dust, but you ain't got us killed yet, so consider your apology accepted."

"It's not like you don't have secrets," Alan says. "Sister Sophia called you Conservator before. What's that all about?"

Brattle folds his arms up over his chest, elbows jutting out like dares, and draws his lips thin as he squares his jaw.

"Everybody knows the M nuns are crazy," says the ghoul. "They cling to old tales like gospel, but look how they treat genuine augury! They give perfectly good dreams away, an' they keep the ones that are broke in half and wrong. 'Conservator' don't mean nothing."

"Not to you, perhaps," Stag's Blood says, "but maybe you could indulge us. What does Sophia think she means?"

Brattle gives Stag's Blood a complex frown. Alan remembers how difficult some of his facial expressions seemed before. Now they are old; Alan barely thinks about interpreting them at all. He knows them too well.

"She thinks it means that ghouls were somethin' like umans once," Brattle says. "We guarded something, but we fell. Now we're dead-eaters, muck-crawlers, mud worms reduced to living

274

in our own filth." He spits on the floor. "Everybody's got their own reason to look down on us. Some are prettier than others, but they're all the same ugly in the middle."

"Maybe," Alan says. "But maybe there's something to it. Why did Winter White need Nettle? What did Pwysh want us to find that she's also looking for? It's something to think about."

Brattle only sighs in response. A weight falls on him, slumping his shoulders and pressing his head down toward his sunken chest. He swallows it, hurting himself. Alan can see the pain in his eyes. Brattle stands, straightening himself up, and walks over to splay his fingers over the surface of the eyestone.

"She's walking into danger, isn't she?" Alan asks. "For us?"

"For the Sisters of M," Stag's Bloods says, "and their old, broken stories."

Presently, the orb begins to hum. Alan looks down at his own reflection in its surface. The Seal of Aiwass is glowing on his forehead. Light fills the hood of his robe and the hollows of his orbits, making him look like something holy. Alan's reflection sinks into the heart of the orb and disappears, and a new image replaces it. He sees blood and dancing fire. The orb heats up, and Brattle has to pull his hands away. It begins to smoke, and Alan worries that it will crack. Stag's Blood pads over to watch, his whiskers twitching and his ears turning back to lie flat against his head.

"What's happening?" he asks. "Do you see her in there?"

"Don't see nothin'," Brattle says. "Not even myself."

Banderoles of gold and flame-orange light unfurl above the eyestone to race around it. They make a soft shushing sound as they spin, like winter pines waving their branches free of snow. Alan can see the light-dance reflected in Stag's Blood eyes. Brattle puts the blade of his hand to his forehead and squints.

"Can we pull her out if she needs help?" Stag's Blood says. "What's that light?"

"It's what I see every day," Alan replies, "everywhere, swirling in the sky. It's beautiful."

275

Stag's Blood shakes his head. "Faint is the line between beauty and peril."

The lightshow continues, accompanied by a rising sound. The ribbons fold in on themselves and become orbs. The orbs swell and pale to gilded bubbles, settling one after the over on the sides of the eyestone. Eventually, the whole pulsing gem is covered with them. They quiver and flow, reaching for each other, and they amass in the center of the eyestone as its surface begins to ripple again. The sound becomes piercing. When Sophia's beating wings appear under the bubble cluster, Alan realizes it's a scream.

Sophia tumbles from the eyestone backward. The bubbles of light burst apart around her, leaving flashes lingering in the curve of the gem. For an instant, gold light clings to her like dust, and she is an aureate wonder screaming in mortal fear as she falls toward the floor. Then, Brattle catches her, and the light-dust scatters away. The eyestone goes back to glowing dimly, as if it had never been penetrated. Alan's reflection moves across it as he kneels.

"Sister," he says. "What happened? It's all right; you made it out!"

Sophia cowers in Brattle's rough hands. He stands, lifting her up to let Alan take her.

"What did you see?" Brattle asks. "It didn't sound good."

Sophia glows bright yellow for a minute. Then the fire inside her ebbs, and she goes perfectly clear again. Her wings slow, and she steps carefully onto Alan's palm.

"Fire," she says. "Mother, I am safe! Toven is burning his catharsium. He'll blind the Framer Gem beneath wood and ash; I was nearly buried myself."

"He's giving up," Alan says. "He's a Bleeding thing now – or he soon will be."

"A monstrous shame," Sophia says. "Toven was so full of hope when we first met. But hope can make monsters of us." She turns to Brattle, her hands together under her chin, and cobalt light spreads through her belly. "Thank you for protecting me, Conservator. I owe you my continuity."

"No debts," Brattle says. "You were falling. There's no need to thank me. Don't those wings work?"

"If you do not mind, I will decide for myself whether or not to shoulder the obligation of gratitude," Sophia says. "But I appreciate your modesty. And yes, they work just as the Framer intended. It happens that he did not intend them to work very well to lift all my weight for very long – especially when I am staring down the gullet of mortal peril. Regarding Toven's whereabouts, I am sorry I could not learn anything helpful."

"We know for sure whose side he is on," Stag's Blood offers. "It's good to know your enemies. But where will we go now that we've secured *our* continuity as well as yours, Sister? We will need safe haven for a while."

"That can wait," Alan says. "I know I'm not the leader here, and I don't want to step on anyone's toes, but we've been through some interesting shit tonight. A rest can only help."

Brattle croaks his agreement. "We'll be better equipped to plan after a good curl up, much as I hate to choke our momentum now. But if you want to pull an all-nighter, Stags, I think I can manage."

Stag's Blood arches his back and stiffens his tail. He opens his mouth and heaves a huge yawn from deep in his chest. His broad tongue curls into a cloverleaf behind his silvery canines.

"No," he says, grinning. "You're right, Conservator. There is no more midnight oil left to burn. Do you know what this boat has in the way of beds, Alan?"

"I have no idea," Alan replies. "But let's head up for a quick search. I imagine we'll find some hammocks somewhere."

The crew deck is empty and half-finished. Part of it is new pine, while the rest is worm-bored and sagging over the next deck's ceiling beams. Where there should be hammocks, there are only bare anchors. Stag's Blood returns to the orlop to sleep in the

277

heat of the eyestone, and Brattle joins him after a brief moment's nosing around the deck for dead rats. He finds a small heap of them in a wet corner and stuffs them into one of the knapsack's many pockets for later.

"The Framer provides," he laughs as he disappears down the companionway. Sophia sits in the crook of a joist and says nothing.

In the morning, Alan pulls on his basteta robe and goes topside to watch the sunrise. The storm is blowing away over the mountains, leaving dawn quivering behind it. Light slinks up the dome of the sky like a wary dog until the thunderheads disappear. Then, emboldened in eggplant pink, it swells to its full glory, and the suns arrive crowned with little cloudlets.

The Mercy Gale has stopped. She sits lightly on her keel, leaning a little, her legs shifting beneath her to keep her stable. Her starboard side is turned east toward the little wood where the Gimcrack Mountains hook into high, colorful country. The trees are blooming there, their branches nodding low, untouched by Toven's shadow. The dolmens and the empty heather are far away. The space where Gimcrack Castle used to be is just a dot on the mountainside at this distance. Nothing remains of the hill with the secret door.

Alan walks from the forecastle to the bridge in a cloud of busy wraiths. They move over him, unconcerned with his presence. Some of them are insubstantial enough to pass through him. Those of these he can feel hit him like freezing winds, tugging every tissue in his body. He avoids this experience whenever he can after the first time. Reaching the quarterdeck, he finds Sophia sitting on the eyestone, swinging her legs, waiting for him.

"You are up early," she says.

Alan props himself up on the railing. "I always am," he replies.

Sophia nods. "You do not sleep."

"Not anymore. I don't know why."

"You have been asleep too long, maybe," she says. "Too much catching up to do."

Alan nods and leans over the bulwark. "That might be one way to look at it."

Sophia flits from the eyestone and makes a few slow circles around Alan's head before settling down on the railing beside him. She sits down, propped on the small pillars of her arms with her wrists turned backward, and swings her feet in the air. A red light warms inside her.

"Far away from here," she says, "there is a forest. It stretches for miles between an inland sea and a mountain of ice, and all around it are fields of white flowers. The trees are high and old, their leaves gold beneath, and their bark star-silver. Dreamers come there from many spheres – it is one of the dim places, where only they can go. I have seen human children walking there, hand in hand with daemons and white spirits from the Coma. It is a refuge from the fear and the cruelty of their lives. We call it Fetchwood, and I miss it."

"You've been there?" Alan asks.

"I was born there," Sophia replies. "I am a Fetchlight. I still have the glow of Fetchwood dawns within me." She straightens her back and shines pimpernel red.

"Death and sleep grew side by side in the same womb," Sophia continues, "but they had different fathers."

"I think I'd like to trade one brother for the other," Alan says.

"Alan," Sophia chimes, looking east across the blackened field, "I would like to ask you about your family. May I? I understand if it is too difficult."

"Ask away," Alan says. "If it's too difficult now, I might as well just quit."

"They are all passed? They have all made the exchange?"

"They're all dead now, yes. I'm the last one left. I come from a long line of limited-timers."

Sophia puts her tiny hand on his. She can only really hold his knuckle. "They may be here then – in Midion," she says.

279

Alan nods. "I've thought about that. I haven't seen the Plutonian Shores. I don't know if I'm ready for that yet. It sounds unpleasant."

"Have you considered that it might have been they who brought you here?" Sophia asks.

Alan thinks about this for a long time. He isn't sure how it makes him feel. He isn't any more ready for this thought than he is for the Plutonian Shores right now.

"No," he finally says. "I hadn't. But it's something to think about."

Sophia pats his knuckle and glows a calming green for him. Then she stands and looks athwartships. Alan turns around, puts his back against the rail, and stuffs his hands into the pockets of his sleeves. He tries to follow Sophia's gaze, but he can't tell where she's looking.

"What do you know about Watchers?" he asks.

"Not much," says Sophia. "They dream beautiful dreams. Why?"

"We were attacked by two of them," Alan explains. "Brattle, Stag's Blood, and me. In the dust city. I can't remember its name – Elrafa. I was just wondering why and what they wanted."

Sophia puts her chin in her hand. "They do not act on what they want," she says. "They are almost always slaves. If they attacked you, it is because someone directed them to."

"Winter White?" Alan asks.

"That is a stretch. I doubt they would answer to her. What makes you think she was involved?"

"When we found this ship, there was a daemon guarding her," Alan says. "It was in the form of a dragon. How likely is it to come across two Watchers and a daemon in the span of a few days?"

"I have never asked that," Sophia says, "but 'not very likely at all' seems right. They only come here to fight each other, and that has not happened for a long time. It is dangerous."

"Something Toven said got me thinking about how long the daemon we saw had been here," Alan says. "It was huge, and, if it'd been living here for a long time, it probably would have broken the Mercy Gale to pieces. The mast wasn't even cracked when we got her, though. And she still ran fine. I'm just trying to make sense of all this, that's all.

"Winter White is looking for something. I think that's why Toven contacted her after he saw the notes from Pwysh, and that's why he stole my phone. It's probably even why he moved the Necropolis. He's helping her, and Pwysh must have been helping her, too. But what if she's got Coma and Avernus working with her as well? Is that even possible?"

"Anything is possible," Sophia says. "And if what you suspect is the case I think I know what she is looking for."

"I'm accustomed to longer naps," Stag's Blood says, blinking in the growing light.

"Sun'll do ya good after what we been through," Brattle replies. "And who's to say what darkness ain't still ahead, waitin'?"

The four are gathered on the bridge of the Mercy Gale. Sophia is pacing the top of the eyestone, stiff as a deacon priest preparing to give a sermon. Her wings droop down her back like the broad ends of an orarion. An uncertain light burns in her.

"What's this announcement you've got for us, Soph?" Brattle asks. "And what's *that* sittin' in on it for?"

He points to the thin wisp of the chief mate on the starboard side of the bridge.

"I think it just wants to know what we're doing next," Alan says.

The wraith does not attempt to reply. It only shivers in place, heat rolling off it, the starry clusters of its eyes twinkling.

"I'm curious about that myself," Stag's Blood says. "You woke me from a dream of storms and hundred-foot shadows. I'm ready to be quit of this blasted heath."

"All right," Sophia begins. "I know as much as Alan has told me about the way you three have come, and I believe I see a ghost of the path that lies before you. Before I elucidate, I want to know how far you plan on following that path – how much of what I will say you have patience to hear – and if you are comfortable with my accompanying you on any further journeys you plan to undertake."

Stag's Blood speaks up immediately. "I am on the road for the walking," he says, "and I want to see the last horizon."

"I come too far from home and Da to quit now," Brattle adds.

"I have nothing to turn back to," Alan says. "And I want to know why. We're in this for the long haul, Sister, and you're welcome to come along. There's no such thing as too much help."

Sophia nods and crosses her arms under the featureless curves of her breasts. "It is a quest then," she says. "And this is the beginning, wherein I will tell you the stakes, as I see them. And I hope I'm wrong.

"The Mothers tell all of us this story. It is our most important one, and encapsulates all our hopes in the Sisterhood of M. Life flows from every sphere. Even the Bleeding has its font. But this sphere, Midion, is dead. It is wasting away because the source of its life was cursed long ago, in the land of Nudd. It is in me to preach, but I will try to keep this brief.

"Midion was green and beautiful once, and Nudd was at its heart. It was a garden, and there was a well in the middle of it. Life flowed from the well into the exchange – the blind storm of energy between all the spheres. Conservators guarded the well and kept it pure at all times. But something came in from outside, hating the well and all of Midion, and tried to burn the garden of Nudd to the ground. The Conservators prevented this, and they killed the Outsider, but its blood was poison. It got into the well, and life stopped flowing from it. Now, all it produces is a gray wasting; you see it all around you, tearing things down, driving Midion insane. It disgusts us." She jerks her head back and makes a motion as if she's spitting. "The curse affected the Conservators, too. They became small and slithered away to live in the swamps, disgraced. Their children are called ghouls."

"I heard that bit," Brattle says. "Folk stories they tell to make it OK to keep on hating us. It makes me more than a little uncomfortable to hear you preachin' it, Soph."

"Whether or not any of this is true is not important," Sophia says. "All that matters is that Winter White believes it, and I suspect that she does. Nudd is lost, and only a Conservator can find it again. We know that she has been involved with ghouls; she may be trying to find Nudd. If Avernus and the Coma are helping her, then she is playing them against each other; they would never willingly work together."

"The mystery of the Watchers at Elrafa," Stag's Blood says, "and the daemon dragon. It's troubled me, but this answer is no comfort. She can only be lying to them. And what has she offered? It's not the sturdiest of stories, but it's worth a search."

"If this is really what is happening, we would be fools now to dismiss it out of hand," Sophia says. "We should at least look into it."

Brattle sits back on his haunches. "OK," he says. "So where does that leave us? How do we know where to look?"

"I think Pwysh told us," Alan replies. He presents the map that Toven marked and lays it out on the deck, kneeling on one end to keep it from blowing away. "And Toven did, too, before he knew what he was doing. See these?" He points at Toven's circles. "This is where we go, and we do the things on Pwysh's list."

Something flutters in Alan's breast. He feels the Seal of Aiwass glowing on his forehead. This is his cataclysm. In the teeth of this new peril, he will finally become himself. How could he not, with the fate of Midion bearing down on him? Death will breathe hard on him, and he'll be forced to develop into the kind of person who can endure it.

The quest that will make me, he thinks, and then he feels a little sad.

Brattle is nodding. His eyes are dark. The shadow of the mast falls across him, and Alan sees his old hunger lined across his face. "All right," he says. "OK. But how are we gonna stand against Toven and Winter White with the Coma and all of Avernus warring? We got nothin' but the search. When it comes to steppin' up, we might have a bit of Al's weird luck, but we ain't equipped to save anyone's day – not as we are."

"The Framer provides," Sophia says.

Alan watches Brattle fight to keep from rolling his eyes.

"How is that enough for you, Soph?" Brattle asks. "If we're jumping off a cliff here, don't you wanna know that your wings work?"

"We shall descend into the chasm taking every precaution," Stag's Blood purrs, "and, when bridges appear, we shall cross them. I'm content with what we have."

Brattle snorts. "A few more friends would be nice."

Alan looks up at the chief mate, which is billowing where it was, almost invisible in the direct light of the sun.

"Will your wraiths fight for us?" he asks it.

It shimmers for a second before answering in its well-deep voice: "Your wraiths."

"That's a few more friends than we had before," Brattle says. "What about the hymies?"

Stag's Blood grumbles and tosses his mane. "The dradtails and their generosity," he says. "They've closed their borders. They stand where they are."

"We're not marching off to war just yet," Alan says. "There are things to do first. I'm sure we'll make some friends along the way. This is what Pwysh planned; it has to be something we can accomplish without raising an army."

"Assumin' he got his plan finished before Winter White's hobs killed him," Brattle says.

Alan nods. "And trashed his catharsium," he replies, "looking for the notes that *we* found. Toven said they were working together, but he must have turned on her when he realized what she wanted."

Sophia descends from the eyestone to land on the map, soft as dandelion seed. She walks the yellowed paper, tracing the toeless tips of her feet over the dark lines of rivers and mountain ranges. She turns to Alan with the map magnified behind her.

"You showed these notes to Toven?" she asks.

"Yes," Alan says. "We went to him looking for help. I thought he was going to help us."

"And your phony-thing, too," Brattle says. "You said he stole that."

Sophia strokes her chin, her fingers making the faintest clinking sound. "What does he have on the phony-thing?"

"Coordinates," Alan replies. "An intersection of ley lines. He couldn't find it on this map; he said he'd have to look for an older one."

"Nudd," Sophia says. The bell of her voice is low and quiet. Alan wonders what the violet light in her chest signifies. Perhaps pensiveness?

"Maybe," Alan says. "That was the one part of the puzzle that never made sense, and it still doesn't. Pwysh didn't have anything to do with what happened to my phone. It was like that when I found it."

"Essentially, he knows where we're going to be," Stag's Blood says. "We might as well assume that Winter White does, too. So where do we go from here, knowing that? How do we proceed?"

Brattle reaches for the map and puts his thick finger in the circle around Cheel Gar.

"White's got him whipped," he says. "She'll take your phone-thing and go looking for Nudd, and she'll send him and his golems after us. You know that's the way it's gonna go down. This is the closest place to here, so that's where we don't go."

Sophia walks the distance between Gimcrack and Cheel Gar, counting her steps carefully. Her wings tremble.

"There's a Framer Gem there," she says. "And an Abbey of my sisterhood. Here, too." She counts her steps to Welkinbright and then to Sepulchra. "There are abbeys in all these places. Mother Nerina's Abbey in Sepulchra is empty, and the Framer Gem there is blind, but it remains. There are Sisters who still keep the abbey clean."

"Wait," Alan says. He pats himself down, looking for something to write with, though he knows he has nothing. "Here. Look. Watch my finger."

Starting from Sepulchra, he traces a shape between the three points Toven has marked.

"Do you see it?" he asks.

Stag's Blood nods. "The triskelion. Toven's seal. It was all over Gimcrack Castle – on every available doorplate and bare wall. He was in love with it."

"Why?" Brattle asks. Then he stands for a moment, his mouth working, confused. "Why'd he mark these places for you if he knew they were in that shape? The shape of his seal?"

"Because it's not his seal," Alan says.

Stag's Blood finishes his thought. "It's Pwysh's."

"He orchestrated all of this," Alan says. "Maybe he *did* give me the coordinates on the phone; I can't know for sure. He knew what was going to happen to him, and he knew that Toven was going to inherit his servitude to Winter White. He gave us a way to fight back. That's the message. We can do this."

"All right," Brattle says again. "I'm convinced. But there's still the question of where we start. We can't go to Cheel Gar."

"The farthest point is Welkinbright," Stag's Blood says. "I've never even heard of it."

"He married a princess of the Sky City," Sophia says. "He took her away from them. They are hostile to him now, but they are sympathetic to my Sisterhood. Welkinbright is the best place to start our search."

Alan looks up at the chief mate, but it is already gone. The Mercy Gale heaves forward, creakingly tremendously. Her legs unfold to lift her up and point her east toward Welkinbright. Alan rolls the map and stands, holding it in both hands like a weapon. The suns have burned every cloud from the sky, leaving it gem-blue and clear as far as he can see. The wind whispers over him, tugging his hood back.

"Welkinbright it is," Brattle says. He knuckles up to the gunwale and stands up to rest his elbows on it. It's the first time Alan has seen him at his full height. His spine is bent, his shoulders are bowed, but there is definitely something there that Alan has seen before – a secret strength that could well be the remnants of an old purity cursed sour.

"We are equals, Alan," Stag's Blood says, standing tall at the aft end of the bridge, the wind tousling his mane, "but you do make a fine leader."

Brattle turns to put his back to the headwind. He drops back into his ghoulish crouch and watches ground passing under the Mercy Gale from beneath the gunwale railing.

"Last horizon," he says, "here we come."

www.ingramcontent.com/pod-product-compliance
Lightning Source LLC
Chambersburg PA
CBHW020047180626
46812CB00006B/2215